Love is on the Air

KILTIE JACKSON

ISBN-13: 978 – 1999866686

DEDICATION

For Pam Howes, who led me towards the path of this writing malarky and John Hudspith, who continues to guide me along it.

My thanks and eternal gratitude to you both.

xxx

.

Also by Kiltie Jackson

A Rock 'n' Roll Lovestyle
An Artisan Lovestyle
An Incidental Lovestyle
A Timeless Lovestyle

Waiting Since Forever

The Bay of Lost Souls

The Prosecco Pact

A Snowflake in December

ACKNOWLEDGEMENTS

There are always so many people to thank when a new book baby hits the shelves and the list only seems to grow longer with each one that is released. I will do my best to keep it short without missing anyone out.

The first thank you has to be for Dave Berry and his team on The Dave Berry Breakfast Show on Absolute Radio for providing the inspiration behind this tale of love on the airwaves. The first part of a gentleman contacting the station for assistance in finding a date for a Couples Only party is all true. The rest grew from my overly-fertile imagination.

My support network, which every author needs – I couldn't do this without the following cheering me on: The Fiction Café Book Club – thank you Wendy, and all the admins, for always bigging me up and for all the Authors Live events. Chick Lit & Prosecco – Anita Faulkner is a generous soul who thrives on embracing all the authors in her group and their victories, no matter how big or small. TBC – Helen Boyce, thank you for the work you put into getting my books out for review and chasing up afterwards. These wonderful clubs are all on Facebook and are definitely worth joining. To the members of my own little FB group – Kiltie Jackson's Books, Bits & Bobs - thank you for joining in with the day-to-day fun and frolics and who continue to read everything I churn out. You're so awesome. I also need to give an extra-special thank you to my wonderful administrator, Sue Baker, who organises and posts so much of the great interactive games and gives me the time out I need to get on with writing these books.

To Zoe-Lee O'Farrell who organises the amazing book tours through ZooLoo's Book Tours and all the generous book bloggers who freely, and willingly, give their time to read my missives and offer up wonderful reviews on how much they enjoy them. Thank you, thank you & thank you again.

John Hudspith is my awesome editor and Berni Stevens is the outstanding designer who creates these fabulous covers. I thank you both, from the bottom of my heart, for everything.

Mark Fearn, is my beta reader extraordinaire and I love him dearly for his truthful support.

Kym Wood – My best friend ever. Thank you for reading, the feedback and just being so amazing.

Stuart Dunne – The BFF who keeps on giving. Always a star and forever special.

My family who read my books, tell me they love them, read them again and tell me they love them even more. Thank you.

The Moggy Posse who provides the material I post on social media. Without you fluff-balls, the only thing I'd be sharing is tumbleweed as this author's life is not an exciting one.

My Mr Mogs. I still love you… to the end of eternity… and a day.

Finally, to all my readers – thank you for giving your time to my stories and for enjoying them enough to keep asking for more. You thrill my withered old heart more than you could possibly know.

Till the next time…

Kiltie

Xxx

ONE

BARP! BARP! BARP! BARP!

A skinny arm, with a bony hand balled into a fist, flew out from the duvet-covered mound on the bed and landed on the goose-honking alarm clock with a thump. Silence filled the room as the stick-like limb was reeled back into its little den of warmth. A small snuffle escaped from the miniscule opening before the duvet was grabbed tight and all escape routes were closed off.

For a time, nothing moved and then, gradually, the mound began to stir. The tortoiseshell shape began to unfold and two long, narrow feet made a break for freedom, thrusting themselves out bravely from the warm confines of the bed. Two puny legs slowly followed until finally the duvet slipped down as the semi-comatose body sat up. A small pot belly rested upon its owner's lap, partially obscuring the saggy, grey boxer shorts underneath, but drawing emphasis to the meat-free ribs above it. Jagged elbows landed on knobbly knees and a headful of super-shaggy, blond threaded with gunmetal grey, shoulder-length hair landed in the waiting hands for a good scratch to be administered. The head raised itself and the same hands rubbed the stubble-riddled face as one eye-lid used all its available strength to lift itself up, allowing the vivid blue iris underneath a brief moment in which to read the red neon numbers on the bedside clock.

3.45 AM

A low groan forced its way out of dry lips as the right hand slid down towards the floor and felt around blindly until it landed on the thermal cup placed there the night before. It grasped the silver container in the same manner as a grabber machine at the fairground and raised it up slowly. The left hand, not wishing to be left out, reached across to pop open the drinking spout before dashing south to support the bottom of the container as it was lifted towards the downturned mouth. Warm, extra-strong, Java coffee flowed down the dry, raspy throat, with the kick of Jack Daniels hot on its heels. By the time the cup was empty, both blue eyes were open and alert and the previously sagging body was sitting to attention. A moment later, it stood and with a large stretch and an even larger yawn, began to make its way towards the en suite shower.

Marky Sparks, 80s DJ extraordinaire, was back in the land of the living!

TWO

Mats Davidson looked up as her mobile phone rang out. Her eyes felt dry and scratchy but as she'd barely slept and had been up since four-thirty am, that was hardly a surprise.

She swiped the screen and putting the call on loudspeaker, placed the phone on the work top.

'What?' she barked.

'Hey, babes, I'm sorry...' Whining toffee-tones floated in the air towards her.

'Oh yeah? For what?'

She lifted the scissors she'd been holding when the phone rang and carried on snipping the buttons off the charcoal-grey suit jacket in front of her. She was about to drop them in the black bin bag by her feet but stopped to take a closer look. Hmmm, they were actually rather nice – almost pearl-like. Figuring she could use them at a later date, she pushed them to one side and began cutting the bespoke, Richard James of Savile Row suit – well, that's what it said on the label – into small, one-inch sized squares.

The whining noise came out of her phone again. 'What do you mean, "for what"? For not being able to make our anniversary dinner last night. I know you went to great lengths to cook a special celebratory meal—'

'Not as great a length as your tongue did!'

'Excuse me?'

'Victor, how far down the blonde's neck did your tongue make it? Because, from what I saw, she was getting the full colonic irrigation treatment!'

'Err… err… what are you talking about?'

'I'm talking about you, a ditsy-looking blonde and our favourite window seat at Luigi's last night.'

'I told you I had to work late. I was at the office until after eleven.'

'Of course, you were. So how come Penny saw you doing your take on "The Lady and the Tramp" at eight-thirty, huh?'

There was a miniscule pause, barely noticeable, but notice it she did. 'She didn't see me, honey, like I said I was in the office.'

'Victor, "Mats" is short for Matilda, not Doormat! Penny sent me the video. I watched you with my own eyes, doing all your little moves – the same ones you use on me – and it is you.'

'But—'

'Victor, you're not in court now and I'm not one of your clients – don't play me for a fool.'

Mats took her fingers out of the scissors, gathered up the grey squares in front of her and dropped them slowly, like wayward confetti, into the black plastic bag.

'Victor, I need to go now. I've put your belongings, including that grey suit you like so much, into a black bin bag and it's going outside the front door. You have approximately…,' she looked up at the clock on the wall, '…two hours to rescue it before the bin men arrive.

Goodbye!'

She ended the call and blocked the number – she couldn't be bothered listening to his ranting when he saw what she'd done to his clothing. She picked up the bin bag and heard a tinkling sound as the broken bits of an electric toothbrush, after-shave bottle and a pair of designer glasses fell to the bottom. In fact, the only item belonging to Victor which had not been carved up into a thousand pieces was the C J Sansom novel he'd been reading. Mats loved books and loved to read, so it was the only thing to escape her wrath. She picked it up from the kitchen work-top, pulled out the credit card receipt she'd forced Victor to use as a bookmark, and walked through to the lounge to place it gently and carefully on the already bulging downstairs bookcase.

'There, there, my pretty,' she said softly, stroking the cover of the book, 'time for you to have a new home where no one bends your spine or turns over your corners. I'll look after you.'

Her eye caught the mantelpiece clock as she turned around and the actual time registered in her brain.

'Oh bugger!'

She scurried off up the stairs to her bedroom. The way she was feeling after her sleepless night, she was going to need a strong cold shower to revive her and it was not a prospect she was looking forward to.

THREE

Steven Byrne slowly came to as the alarm on his mobile phone buzzed on the bedside table and he fumbled about, trying to tap the snooze button. No way was he hitting the gym this morning – not after last night. His body felt as though it had been tripping the light fantastic until the not so early hours of the morning. The truth was he'd been home just after midnight but with a greater quantity of beer under his belt than would be the norm mid-week although there was no doubt it was the tequila slammers which had done the damage he was now feeling. His mate, Paul, from work had landed a major account yesterday and he'd begged a few of the marketing team to go out and celebrate. A celebration that went on longer than anyone had planned. Steven knew he wouldn't be the only one feeling fragile this morning.

He dozed lightly for a while longer, snoozing his phone twice more, before finally throwing the quilt back with a groan. He staggered into the bathroom and after relieving himself, gritted his teeth, stepped into the shower, and turned it on, letting the freezing cold blast of water bring him back from what felt like the brink of death. By the time he'd shampooed, lathered, and scrubbed, he felt almost human again and was even humming tunelessly while he shaved.

Once dressed, he walked down the stairs to the kitchen and turned on the coffee machine. An extra-strong, double espresso would see him ready to face the day.

'Miaow.'

'Good day, young Percival, how are you this morning? May I interest you in some,' Steven paused to look at the label on the tin he'd taken from the cupboard, 'pulled pork with cranberry for breakfast, sir?'

His purring flatmate, a white Maine Coon, wound himself around his legs, and as the machine spluttered and coughed, while the strong, tantalising smell of fresh coffee began flowing around him, he spooned a portion of the cat food into the bowl on the floor. He put the rest of the tin in the fridge and then fixed his tie using his reflection in the window as a mirror and smoothed down his damp, blond hair. When he turned back to pour his coffee, his eye was caught by the party invitation propped up on the shelf. His twin brother's engagement party. The engagement party he couldn't, at this time, attend because it was for couples only and since last month, he was no longer a "couple". He let out a sigh and walked into the lounge with his drink. Maybe, he thought, he could ask Jo from the marketing team if she would come along with him as a friendly favour. They'd gotten along okay last night and she was nice enough. It might be a bit short notice though, given that today was Thursday and the party was on Saturday. He just had to hope that she didn't already have plans.

It was after he'd opened the curtains in the lounge, and was gathering up some bits he needed for work, that Steven noticed his laptop was ajar.

'Huh?' he muttered aloud, while walking over to open

it fully. He hit the keyboard, bringing it back to life, entered his password and waited for it to boot up. Why had it been open? He never left it like that. Had he used it last night when he got home? He sure couldn't remember. Finally, after what felt like forever, the screen lit up in front of him and he saw he had logged into his email account.

'Phew! That's a relief!' he said to the empty room. 'No drunken purchases made.'

He noticed that he'd read a few emails, including one from his brother, Stuart, asking if he'd found anyone to bring on Saturday. Steven was about to reply when he decided to check his outbox, just in case he'd already done so last night. He was pleased to see he hadn't, having been concerned he may have sent an alcohol-fuelled rant about Candice's refusal to allow him to attend on his own, and was about to reply when he noticed an email he *had* sent. What the f—? He opened it up and began reading. By the time he reached the end, his heart was racing and a cold sweat was breaking out on his forehead.

'Noooooo!'

'No! No! No! No! Noooooooo!

Steven's head dropped into his hands as his eyes stared through his fingers at the words on the screen in front of him.

What the *hell* had he done?

FOUR

Ninety minutes after falling out of bed, Marky Sparks scanned his lanyard and walked through the quiet reception area of the Smile-A-While Radio building. He gave a brief nod to Bill, the security guard manning the desk, while making his way towards the lift which would whisk him up to his studio on the seventh floor. The old tower block was in dire need of a lick of paint and some other decorative TLC but Smile-A-While Radio didn't have the money right now to spare on such frivolities. Trying to hold its own in a world where more and more digital stations were coming on board, thinning out the already depleted listeners, was becoming a bigger battle every day. Marky knew he was their biggest star and he also knew he needed them as much as they needed him. He'd revelled in great success back in the 80s when he'd been among the first handful of DJs who'd introduced the likes of The Pet Shop Boys, The Housemartins, and INXS to the nation. They'd gone on to become pop royalty and he'd been feted as the disc jockey with his ear to the ground. It hadn't taken long for the record companies to begin sending their white-label discs in his direction, anxious for him to pick out their new up-and-coming acts and send them soaring up the charts. TV producers had also come knocking on his door, declaring that his popularity with the teenagers, coupled with his blond-haired mullet, deep-blue eyes, and razor-sharp cheekbones, would make him the perfect frontman to present the plethora of music shows they were lining up. His career had taken off like a rocket and for the next few decades, he'd soared high above everyone else in his field only to spectacularly crash-land when the Noughties came to an end. The increasing ease with which people could use new digital technology changed everything, including the music business. Up-coming new musos no longer had to sell their souls to the record execs – they could load videos onto websites like Myspace and were there for the whole world to see within a matter of moments. Myspace, much like his career, hadn't been able to hold its own in the rapidly expanding web-sphere and was soon overtaken by Facebook, YouTube, and Twitter. It, just like him, had sunk into relative obscurity and now here he was, the flagship breakfast show on a barely heard of radio station.

He pushed open the door of his small studio, shrugged off his leather jacket and dropped it onto the back of the chair which he then sat upon. He gave a grin and grimace combination to Dave, his producer, on the other side of the glass as he twisted round to pull his notebook from his jacket pocket.

'Morning! You okay?'

Dave walked in and slid a large filter coffee towards him. One of the few, and they *were* few, perks of working the breakfast show was that the coffee was still fresh and hadn't turned into stewed, percolated sludge which the poor woman after him had to endure.

'As I'll ever be,' Marky replied, trying not to shudder at the taste of the alcohol-free beverage. He'd sort that out when Dave returned to his cubby hole.

'Any grand ideas for today, or even the rest of the week? We need to do something to get those listener numbers up or else we're done for!'

Marky flipped open the notebook in front of him, praying that something he'd scribbled in there last night might A - make sense and B - be worth using.

'Urm...,' he quickly tried to decipher his inebriated scrawl. 'How about folks getting in touch sharing the naughtiest things they did as children? Or...,' he squinted at the page. What the hell did *that* say? 'Err... people sharing the antics of their pets? Folks seem to love a good animal story.'

'Hmm, they're not really going to cover the show in glory though, are they?'

'S'pose not.'

'Oh well, I suppose we'd better get set-up, kick-off is only thirty minutes away.' Dave walked towards the door but stopped before he reached it. 'Oh, by the way, this dropped in on the email last night.' He pulled a folded piece of paper from his back pocket and threw it over to Marky. 'I dunno if you want to go with it – it might be something different. Read it and see what you think. I'll leave it with you to decide.'

Marky looked at the paper lying on the desk where it had landed in front of him. He opened it up and began to read:

Dear Marky Sparks,

I hope this email finds you well.

I'm very sorry to bother you but you are my last hope. Last month, my twin brother, who is also my best friend, became engaged. His new fiancée has organised their engagement party on a Thames Riverboat which is for couples only. Unfortunately, my girlfriend and I recently split up and I have no one to take with me. My, soon-to-be, sister-in-law refuses to budge on her "Couples Only" stance which leaves me in the precarious position of not being able to attend my brother's special night.

Would you mind, if it's not too much trouble, doing a shoutout on the radio to see if a nice young lady in London would like to join me on Saturday evening for this event.

Thank you for your time and assistance,

Steven Byrne.

Underneath was a return email address and a mobile phone number.

Marky read the email a second time before muttering, "Loser!" under his breath, scrunching it up and chucking it in the bin.

'Who does he think I am, bloody Cilla Black!'

He took another slug of coffee, pulled a face again as he did so, and after adding a few tots of additional flavouring from the hip-flask in his pocket, began doing his own pre-show checks.

'And now it's over to Cindy Arthur for the seven o'clock news bulletin. Take it away, Cindy…' Marky drawled into the mike before switching it off. The dulcet tones of the newsreader came through the speakers in the studio.

Marky swivelled in his chair, hooked his foot around the bin at the side of the desk and pulled it towards him. The email he'd so unceremoniously binned earlier had been playing on his mind and a tiny germ of an idea had begun to sprout. He flattened the paper out and read the typed words again before looking up and beckoning Dave into the studio.

'What?' The producer stuck his head around the door.

'Dave, get this bloke on the phone. I've had an idea… I think we can do this.'

FIVE

'So, have you spoken with Vic the Prick yet?'

'Yes, Penny, I have.'

'And?'

'He tried to deny it, as we knew he would.'

'Good thing I had the sense to video his sorry cheating ass then, huh! I guessed he'd try to deny everything. Isn't that what he tells his clients to do?'

'Pretty much.'

Mats smiled at the lady who'd just joined her at the bus-stop. She didn't know her name, and they never spoke but every morning, without fail, she arrived to stand behind Mats as they waited for the number twelve bus to come and carry them towards the centre of London.

'Let that be a lesson to you, my friend, never trust a defence barrister or a lawyer. They lie for a living!'

Mats couldn't help the little giggle that popped out – Penny had been saying this from the first time she'd met Victor. She hadn't liked him on sight and nothing he'd done in the following twelve months had changed her mind.

14

'Anyway, how are you feeling? Are you okay? I'm sorry I had to be the one to drop that on you – you know I hate that you've been hurt.' Penny's voice softened.

'I'll be okay, Pen. I'm angry right now but that's good. It'll see me through the day.' She went on to tell her life-long best-friend what she'd done to his belongings and felt so much better when Penny let out a roar of laughter.

'That's my girl! Well done you. Now, you need to get back on that horse and get out there. No point in letting the grass grow under your feet.'

'Give me a break, Pen, I've only been single for…,' she looked at her watch, '…an hour and thirty-five minutes.'

'Which is an hour and thirty minutes too long! Do you remember that DJ, Marky Sparks, who used to be on the TV when we were kids?'

'How could I forget him given that you *still* have a crush on him to this day?'

'Well, you could possibly be getting a phone call from him—'

'I *what*?'

'—do me a favour and go with it okay? Just play along…'

'Play along with what? Penny, what are you talking about? What have you done?'

'Hey, gotta go. Keep smiling, beautiful lady, I luvs ya!'

'Penny! Don't you dare hang up… Penny? PENNY?' Mats looked at the call ended screen on her phone. Damn that woman. What on earth had she done now?

The question was still bothering Mats as she alighted from the bus at the Elephant and Castle. She'd tried to call Penny back but the bitch was now ignoring her calls. She crossed

15

the road and followed the throng of people ahead of her down into the bowels of the London Underground. She loved living in East Dulwich but she really wished they could get an Underground station – it would make life easier on so many levels.

A train arrived on the platform just as she reached the bottom of the stairs and with a quick skip and a jump, she managed to squeeze herself on before the doors slid closed behind her. Her nose was pressed up hard against the blue jacket of the man in front and she had to twist her head to one side in order to breathe. Thank goodness she only had to endure this daily torture for two stops – some of these poor folks had been squished in like this all the way from Tooting!

A collective sigh of relief could almost be heard, both inside and outside the tube, when the first batch of commuters spewed out onto the platform at London Bridge and once upstairs, they dispersed like ants, all rushing off to their respective place of work. Mats walked over the concourse of the funky, newly-modernised station, still awe-struck after all this time at how different it was from the dingy, dirty, 1970's station it had been when she'd first set up shop in the area. Now it was bright, clean, airy and had a fabulous selection of shops and outlets. She was heading to one now, where they knew her so well her morning coffee was always sitting ready for her by the time she reached the counter. She was nothing until she'd had her Grande Mocha with an espresso shot and topped with whipped cream. They even knew to add two sugars before the cream went on. The combination of caffeine, carbs and protein set her up for the day, rendering her capable of dealing with even the stroppiest of musicians.

She pushed her purse down inside the canvas bag slung across her torso like a school-bag, smoothed down the sharp, easy-to-keep, shoulder-length bob and picked up her drink while throwing a grateful thank-you smile to the young barista – a smile which reached all the way up to her eyes and created a fan of tiny wrinkles at each outside edge.

Mats didn't care about frown lines, crow's feet, or any of that kind of nonsense. She was a no-nonsense, inside and out, kind of woman. She wore flat shoes because she could walk quicker in them and she favoured trousers over skirts for the same reason. Many of her clothes were bought from charity shops and second-hand market stalls – not because she couldn't afford top-of-the range designer gear, for she most certainly could, but simply because she couldn't "be arsed with the palaver". Mats Davidson had spent most of her life surrounded by glitz, glamour and "all that jazz" and had met enough asshole pop stars, arrogant supermodels and drama-queen actors to know that no amount of fancy wrapping could make a shit gift any better.

She'd just hip-bumped open her office door when her mobile began to ring. She dropped her bag and coffee onto the desk and pulled it out, checking the screen – "Unknown Number" – before answering.

'Hello, Mats Davidson speaking.'

'Hi there, Mats, this is Dave Maim, the producer of "The Marky Sparks Morning Show" on Smile-A-While Radio. I'm responding to the message you left for us…'

SIX

Steven moved his mobile over to his other ear and wiped his hand on his trouser leg. How on earth could this be happening to him? When his phone had rung forty minutes earlier, he didn't think for a moment it would be the producer for the Marky Sparks Breakfast Show.

After the initial shock from reading the email he'd sent when he'd arrived home last night, clearly in direct response to the one from Stuart, he'd calmed down by telling himself that the radio show must receive thousands of emails from their listeners and there was no way they would pay any attention to his. Unfortunately, he'd only just sat down at his desk when he was proved wrong. They *had* paid attention and he was live on the air, talking to Marky Sparks, before he'd had a chance to say it had been a drunken mistake and he didn't want them to do anything. He'd tried to play it down and hint to Marky Sparks that there was no need to go to all this bother, but the DJ was having none of it – he was determined to find Steven a date and get him to the party. So now, here he was, hanging on the line waiting to talk to three women who had responded to the earlier radio shout-out. Somehow, he had to choose one to "take to the ball"!

'Okay, Steve, here we go… lady number one, Fiona from Acton. Take it away, Fiona, tell Steve three things about yourself that you think he'll find interesting.'

'Hi Steve, I'm Fiona. Lovely to meet you.'

'Hi Fiona,' Steven replied politely, while the hairs on the back of his neck crawled at her breathy girly tones. There was no way he'd be able to sustain an evening of conversation with someone who sounded twelve-years-old. He'd already binned her by the time she got around to telling him she collected dolls and had over a thousand in the spare room of her flat. Somehow, this was not a surprise.

'Okay, Steve, time for lovely lady number two, Linda from Loughton…'

'Hey, Steve, me old mucker, how ya doing?'

Oh, dear Lord, Linda was even worse. He didn't mind an East London accent but this one was rougher than a three-hundred-year-old ship covered in barnacles! And the hacking cough in the middle of her spiel did nothing to enhance her chances in any way. By the time she'd finished off with telling him she worked with her father down the local fish market, he was already out of there! Not a chance!

'And, finally, Steve, lovely little lady number three. It's Matilda from East Dulwich…'

As soon as she began talking, Steven sat up a little straighter. He'd made his decision.

'Hi, Steve, the first thing I would like to tell you is that no-one calls me "Matilda." I prefer "Mats" although it would seem that Marky Sparks doesn't like to listen as I've already told him this three times.'

'Hi, Mats, I hate being called Steve. My name is Steven.'

'Okay, Steven it is. Secondly, I didn't apply to participate in these shenanigans, it was someone who used to be my best friend although she was fired from the position approximately ten minutes ago. I am, however, sorry to hear about your predicament. It's rather unfair, in my opinion. It shows how much love you have for your brother if you're prepared to do this just to be there.'

'What if I said there had been a little bit of alcohol involved...'

Mats burst out laughing at the sheepish voice in her ear.

'Oh, blimey! Drunk texting just got a whole lot more serious!'

'Can we move it along please, Matilda, Steve here needs to make a decision, the other ladies are waiting on the line.'

Mats rolled her eyes at Marky Sparks interjection – really, that man could do with listening more carefully.

'Okay, third and final piece of information – I love music and I *really* love reading. If you were to interrupt me while I was curled up with a book, I would very likely punch your lights out!'

There, she thought to herself, that should put him off. No one's gonna pick a woman who admits to having violent tendencies.

'Right then, Steve, it's make your mind up time! Do you like Fiona, who would love to add you to her collection of dolls? Or maybe you prefer Linda who could gut you like a fish and smoke you like a kipper? Or perhaps having your lights punched out by Matilda is more up your street. The choice is yours!'

Mats was already forming her loser's speech in her

head when she heard, *'I'd like to take Mats from East Dulwich, please, if she's up for it. Even though she didn't actually choose to be my date.'*

Aw, shit! She hadn't seen that coming.

'So, Matilda from East Dulwich, will you be Steve's date on Saturday night at his twin brother's engagement party?'

Every part of Mats' was screaming, "NOOOOOO". She absolutely did not want to be this bloke's date on Saturday night... or any other night for that matter.

'Errmmm...'

'Come now, Matilda, are you going to leave poor Steve hanging here?'

Shit, bollocking shit! Marky Sparks was right. She couldn't knock the poor bugger back on live radio. He'd already suffered enough by sending his drunken email, she couldn't add to his misery. And anyway, it was only for one night. She could manage that.

She cleared her throat, took a deep breath and replied in the breeziest voice she could muster, 'Of course not, Marky Sparks. I would *love* to be Steven's date on Saturday night. Send me the details and I'll be sure to be there!'

SEVEN

'This one would look good.'

Penny held up another strappy dress from the back of the wardrobe.

'Penny, I'm going to be on a boat, on the Thames, in the middle of sodding February! A strappy, almost-nothing-there dress is the last thing I want to be wearing.'

'What do you suggest, then?'

'I already know what I'm wearing—'

'So, why am I here?' Penny gave a small humph of annoyance.

'You are here to grovel profusely, lady! YOU put me in this position and right now I'm rather pissed off with you.'

'Yeah, yeah, whatever!' Penny gave a small toss of her head. 'What are you thinking of wearing then since none of my suggestions are floating your boat?' She laughed like a drain at her pun.

'Oh, you're so not funny,' Mats rolled her eyes before continuing, 'I'm thinking my red culottes, the black jumper with the sparkly beads, my leather biker jacket and the black boots with the stiletto heels.'

'You can't wear trousers. You were told this was a dressy affair.'

Mats rolled off her bed and walked over to the wardrobe.

'I can wear these.' She pulled out the culottes.

'Oh, I thought that was a skirt.'

'Exactly!' Mats smiled as she held the trousers in front of her. They did indeed look like a flowing ankle-length skirt but when you pulled the material to the side, the subtle trouser legs became apparent. She'd found them in a vintage shop in Camden Market a few months ago and now finally had an occasion to wear them.

'Are you really going to wear your leather jacket? Again, I repeat the words, "dressy affair".'

'Penny, this "sister-in-law-to-be" sounds like a bitch to me! She wasn't prepared to bend her "Couples Only" rule to allow her fiancé's twin brother to join the party. She's clearly a high-maintenance little bitch madam and while I have no intention of spoiling her night or showing Steven up, I am going to be the little flea in her ointment by not bending to her pettiness.'

'Oh, so she's a "high-maintenance little bitch madam" is she?'

'Penny, she's having a party on a boat, on the Thames, in bloody February! What do you think? Most folks would be sensible and hire a hall or a function suite. And she clearly doesn't understand the meaning of compromise otherwise I'd be sitting on the sofa with a book in one hand and a pizza in the other right now instead of faffing about in here!'

'If you didn't want to do this, you could have said no.'

'Penny, I wasn't about to humiliate the poor chap on the radio. His life would have been utter hell if I'd done that to him. No, if me spending one night of torture helps

23

this man to save face, then so be it. I can say afterwards that I've done all my good deeds for the year with this one act.'

'Fair enough. Where are you meeting and how will you know it's him? Will he be wearing a daffodil in his lapel?' Penny waggled her eyebrows like Groucho Marx causing Mats to burst out laughing.

'No, he's not, you daft mare! We're meeting by the Boudica statue at Westminster and he'll be wearing a dark navy suit. He's also five-foot-eleven and has spiky blond hair. That should be enough to find him.'

'Blond, eh? You like blonds…'

'Wink like that again, missus, and you will be permanently fired as my best friend.'

'I thought I already was!'

'Temporarily suspended for the moment, position under review, so you'd better watch out.'

'Oh, see me trembling with fear…'

Mats laughed again. She could never stay angry with Penny for long, no matter how much trouble she'd dragged her into over the years.

'Oh, come on you, I'm in the mood for pizza now. Fancy sharing one while drooling over a bit of Tom Hardy?'

'That sounds perfect. No pineapple though! Pineapple does not belong on pizza.'

'Yes, it does and yes, there will be. You're still in my bad books – you owe me!'

'Cowbag!'

'You had better believe it! Now shift yourself! Go and sort out the film while I order the grub.' Mats picked up her phone and smiled to herself at Penny's chuntering as she left the room. Putting pineapple on the pizza was a good enough punishment for now.

EIGHT

Steven looked at his watch again. Damn his fear of being late. It was only ten minutes to seven. He had another twenty-five minutes to wait before Mats was due to meet him. He'd been so paranoid about the trains being late or the buses being on strike, he'd left home far too early. Herne Hill wasn't the back of beyond but he lived equidistant from the Brixton tube station to the Herne Hill over-ground train line and owing to the greater regularity of buses and tube trains, he normally opted for the bus and tube option when it came to travelling into central London.

It was a chilly night and he was wearing his heavy overcoat although he would have to unbutton it soon to show off his suit otherwise Mats may not realise it was him. He stamped his feet to warm them up and wondered what his blind date would be like. Her self-description of "brunette, shoulder-length hair, medium height" hadn't given much away. He hoped they would get along for the few hours they'd be in each other's company. She liked music and reading, as did he, so with a bit of luck, they might have an author or two in common. He felt the small package in his pocket bump against his hip as he walked back and forth. He'd been down to Brixton Market earlier in the day and had come across a small leather-bound copy of the novel "To Kill a Mockingbird" by Harper Lee. It was one of his favourite novels and he hoped Mats liked it too for he'd bought it as a thank-you gift for helping him out this evening.

He looked up at the clock tower across the road. Five past seven. He'd better unbutton his coat—

'Hi, are you Steven?'

He looked at the woman standing in front of him. Like him, she was bundled up in a warm-looking coat although hers was bright red with black lapels and went all the way to her ankles. His was a rather staid black number which stopped just below his knee.

'Er, yes, I am. Hi. I'm guessing you must be Mats.'

'Are you expecting several women to meet you here this evening? Did you go for safety in numbers in case I didn't turn up?'

'Urm, err… no. No, I didn't.'

'Well, I must be Mats then!' She stuck out her hand for him to shake while a big grin sat on her face beneath her twinkling eyes.

'Hi, Mats, I'm Steven.'

'With a "P H" or a "V"?'

'A "V".'

'Nice. I like that spelling. Looks good.'

'Thank you.'

'Are we too early to step aboard ship only it's a bit nippy out here?'

'Not at all. They allow boarding from seven so we're good to go. It's this way.' He pointed her along the Embankment and they walked towards the pier where the party boats were moored up waiting.

Steven tried not to be too obvious as he took in Mats'

appearance from the corner of his eye. She'd been quite truthful in her description but she'd omitted to mention the high cheekbones, the cat-like shape of her eyes and the fullness of her lips. Her smile had revealed lovely white teeth although the two front ones had a slight overlap going on. It worked well though for this slight imperfection took away the severity of her facial features and instead gave her a certain cuteness. Although given the few sentences they'd exchanged thus far, he wasn't all that sure she would thank him for saying so.

'Here we are. After you.' He waved her onto the pier ahead of him and hoped the rest of the evening would go as well as these first few minutes. After all, once the boat set off, they were trapped in each other's company for the duration of the sail. Unless Mats was an exceptionally good swimmer that is, but he prayed his company would be enjoyable enough to prevent her going to such extremes.

Mats walked across the gangway and followed the steward's directions to the cloakroom to hand in her coat, glad she'd had a last-minute change of mind when the sharp breeze off the river had blown around her legs as they'd made their way towards the boat. She hoped Steven hadn't noticed her surreptitious glances while they'd been walking but there was something very familiar about him. She was quite sure they hadn't met before and yet… she couldn't shake off the feeling of knowing him.

'Champagne?' Steven broke into her thoughts. They were walking in the direction of the main room, following the other party-goers in front of them. Waiters were standing by bearing trays of drinks – both alcoholic and non-alcoholic.

'Thank you, that would be nice.'

Mats noticed that Steven took a rather large gulp of his. Oh blimey, she thought, I hope he's not planning to get legless – I'm not in the mood for babysitting some drunk I barely know.

It didn't escape her attention either, that he was gripping the wine glass with some force. His knuckles were quite pale.

They walked past the buffet and headed over towards the tables set up around the dance floor which was primed and ready to accommodate the boogying and twerking bodies that would fill it before too long. Steven checked one of the seating plans and led her to a table set for six. Another couple were already seated there and he introduced her to Mike and Alison – old friends from when they were children.

They sat making small talk until the music faded away and the DJ announced the arrival of the happy couple.

Everyone stood up to applaud but Mats' view was blocked by Mike and Alison. It wasn't until they all sat down again that she got her first glimpse of the guests of honour.

'Oh, my goodness, isn't that Stuart Byrne, the computer bloke?'

Before Steven could answer, the "computer bloke" bounced over to their table, pulled Steven from his chair and into a massive bear hug.

'Baby Bro, you made it! Drastic measures to get here for sure, but you're here!'

He allowed Steven to extricate himself from his embrace before leaning across the table to shake her hand.

'I'm guessing you must be Mats! Nice of you to help my little brother out of his predicament. I couldn't believe it when I was told how he'd found a date for tonight - ingenuity has never been his strong point.'

Mats now realised why Steven had seemed familiar;

Stuart Byrne was his – rather more famous – twin brother. Stuart Byrne who was the UK's answer to Bill Gates and Steve Jobs. Stuart Byrne whose company, Easy PC's, was challenging Microsoft and Apple for dominance in the computer industry. Stuart Byrne, who was just a little bit more blond than Steven, whose eyes were just a little bit more green, and whose cheekbones were just a little bit more chiselled.

Stuart Byrne who was also just a *big* bit more of an asshole!

Now Mats understood the gulp of Champagne – it had been Dutch courage. Steven appeared to have shrunk as he stood in the shadow of his brother and Mats wondered if it had always been thus. Stuart had twice referenced his brother as being the younger of the two and this made her suspect that he did so to remind Steven of his superiority. He was first and always would be. Stuart hadn't even cared to wait for her reply; he was already off mixing with his other guests. He'd belittled his brother in front of his date and had put him in his place for the evening.

Mats thought he was an arrogant twat!

'Hey, Steven, is it a free bar tonight?' She gave him a large smile.

'Erm, yes, it is.'

'Then how about we try to put a nice big dent in your brother's credit card? Why don't we go and grab some more glasses of Champers and a few cocktails? I've got a feeling they'll help to make this evening more palatable!'

A look of gratitude swept over Steven's face and Mats cursed as her protective instincts for the underdog rose to the fore!

Shit, she thought, I didn't come here to be someone's knight in shining armour. I knew I should have stayed at home.

She caught sight of Stuart working the room – all

smiles and more genuine with his greetings to others than the one he'd given his brother. Mats swallowed down her disgust and her desire to "go and have a word". She didn't think it would go down very well to call Stuart out on his behaviour at his own party but she could damn well go the extra mile to ensure Steven had a good night.

NINE

Mats pulled the long, thermal, fur-lined wrap around her a little tighter.

'Is it all clear?' she asked Steven.

'It looks like it,' he replied, after looking discreetly over both shoulders.

Mats leant forward and carefully lowered the bottle of Champagne she'd hidden up the leg of her culottes onto the wooden decking.

'Here's the glasses.'

Mats gave Steven a cheeky grin when he produced two glasses from beneath the wrap which he'd casually thrown over his arm. He held them out as she poured the fizzy wine in.

Wedging the bottle between her feet, she raised her glass in a toast. 'To blind dates and breaking the rules!'

She sat back in her seat, tilting her head up to look at the ink-black, star-filled sky above her. She and Steven were the only two guests up on the open deck of the boat and she was quite happy about that. They'd been in the party room for about an hour and a half, watching Stuart talking and laughing with those around them. He'd come over to their table twice to talk to Alison and Mike but on both occasions, he'd completely ignored his brother. The second time he did this, Mats had really had to bite her tongue and when he'd wandered off onto the dance floor, in a display of bonhomie with some mates, she'd turned to Steven and said, 'I need to get out of here! NOW!'

She'd gone to the bar for another bottle of Champagne and nodded to Steven to bring the glasses. Unfortunately, the rather diligent steward at the bottom of the steps up to the open deck had advised them that no alcohol was allowed up there. Never one to be deterred, Mats had smiled apologetically and headed back in the direction of the bar while asking Steven to grab them some thermal wraps. She gave him a wink as she detoured into the Ladies loos and when she came out a few minutes later, her hand was nonchalantly in her pocket and the bottle of wine was nowhere to be seen. Steven had carefully placed one of the long fur-lined cloaks around her shoulders and this time, the only thing the steward said was, 'Enjoy the view,' as they walked past.

'Do you remember those funny tin aliens they had on the Smash adverts all those years ago?'

'Err, yes…'

Mats pointed her glass in the direction of the O2 arena which was lit up against the sky. 'That always makes me think of them. The dome is the head and the spikey bits are the antennae on the top.'

'Yeah, I can see that!' A small chuckle followed Steven's comment.

'Steven, I need to ask… why did you refer to Stuart as your "best friend" in the email you sent to the radio station when he quite clearly isn't?'

Steven let out a sigh. 'To be honest, Mats, I really don't know. I was drunk when I sent it and I suppose somewhere in my rather sozzled brain, I must have thought it would come across better if I said that.'

'Would you have sent the email if you'd been sober?'

'Hell, no! I couldn't believe it when I saw what I'd done! And I was mortified when the radio station got in touch to say they were going to run with it! I tried to talk them out of it, saying I had changed my mind but they wouldn't listen.'

'Oh dear! That's a bummer!'

'Tell me about it! I don't know how Stuart found out but I suppose he has fingers in many pies and ears against many walls – no doubt some stringy little cohort thought they could curry favour by bringing it to his attention.'

'So, what's the story with you two? There doesn't appear to be much love lost between you. I'm deducing he was pushed out first and has spent most of his life lording that over you?'

'You deduce correctly. He's always managed to be the golden child. He'd break something and blame me. He'd take money from mum's purse and blame me. He'd cause trouble at school and blame me. My parents always believed him. In their eyes, he could do no wrong. The truth is, Stuart has always hated having to share with me. He would have revelled in being an only child and getting all the attention. Making me out to be the trouble maker ensured he was always bathed in glory.'

'But surely your teachers and parents knew who was really being naughty?'

'As you may have noticed this evening, we do look very alike. When we were kids, it was virtually impossible to tell us apart and our few differences have only become noticeable as we've grown older. It was all too easy for Stuart to pretend to be me when he was caught out and then I would be accused of lying when I denied the charges against me.'

'Wow! That's pretty shitty! Why, then, were you so determined to attend tonight if feelings between you are that bad?'

'I wasn't going to give him the satisfaction of being able to hold another failure over my head. Even if I'd had to bring Fiona or Linda, there was no way I wasn't going to be here tonight!'

'Ah, now they were interesting ladies… I can't think why you didn't choose either of them.'

'Well, I have to be honest and say it was a rather tough decision…' Steven let out a small chortle as he drained his glass. 'Got any more Bolly down there, Edina?'

'Of course, dahhhh-ling. Would I ever let you run dry, Patsy?'

Their laughter floated across the water as Mats refilled the glasses.

'Are you an "Absolutely Fabulous" fan then?' she asked.

'It had its moments and their passion for a glass of Bolly is quite legendary. Plus, sneaking a bottle of booze around, hidden up her trousers, is *exactly* the kind of thing Eddy would do!' They both giggled again as they recalled some of the antics the ditsy pair had come up with.

'Anyway, Mats,' Steven said, 'how about telling me something about you? I know next to nothing other than you don't like to be called Matilda and all this was somehow set up by a mate.'

'There's not much to tell. I'm an only child so no siblings to detest, I'm newly single having dumped my cheating arse of a boyfriend approximately two hours before agreeing to go on this date and I own a recording studio near London Bridge.'

'Oh wow! Really?'

'Yup, really.'

'How on earth did that come about?'

34

'I enrolled on a music business management course when I left school. I love music and wanted to become a part of it. I loved going to gigs and seeing new bands perform. Whenever I chatted with those bands though, the one thing that always came up was the cost of recording studios when they wanted to put together a demo to send out to the record companies and agents. That's when the idea was born to set up a small studio where unknown bands and artists could record their demos and not have to sell a kidney to do so.'

'Have you had any go on to make the big time?'

'Yes, quite a few.' Mats named a handful of her success stories.

'No way! For real?'

'Yup, for real.' She smiled at the astonishment on Steven's face. She rarely dropped the names of the artists she worked with but whenever she did, the outcome was always the same – astonishment and surprise.

'Does that mean you know Tinker Taylor?'

In that instant, Mats got an insight into how Steven must feel whenever people found out who he was related to. He would suddenly become less noticeable when compared to his better-known brother. For Mats, the same thing happened when people found out she knew the world-renowned record producer, Tinker Taylor. In a heartbeat, she became less important against his fame. Few people knew the name of EmmDee Studios but everyone knew Tinker Taylor.

'Yes, I know Tinker. He's my in-house producer.'

'Amazing! That must have been quite a coup getting him. He could work for anyone.'

'He could but as he's my business partner, I think it might be difficult for him to do so.'

'Oh, right! So how did you end up working together?'

'We met on our first day at Uni and quickly became

bezzy mates. We had the same taste in music, shared many views on the business and went to all our gigs together. By the end of our course, he'd decided producing was where his talents lay and was trying to get into a studio. A couple of years passed and I found myself in the position of being able to open my own studio. I asked Tinks if he wanted to be a part of my venture and he came on board. To begin with, the whole shebang belonged solely to me but after a time, I began to notice Tinks was being requested more and more frequently. Not only that, a couple of our first customers were breaking through into the music charts and they were giving a lot of credit to Tinks for helping them to perfect "their sound". It didn't take long for his name to spread, the studios became better known in the industry and after five years, we had to move premises because we'd taken over all the available space around us and it still wasn't enough. We sat down, had a long talk about everything and agreed to become partners. He acknowledged that I ran a good tight ship on the business side of things and I accepted that his name and talent brought in the customers. We've been partners for several years now and the studios have gone from strength to strength.'

'Is it as glamorous on the inside as it looks on the outside?'

'Let's just say there's been more than one interview in the media where I've almost choked on my coffee at the bare-faced lies being told…' She gave him a wink.

'No way!'

'Yes, way!'

Mats filled their glasses again, this time emptying the bottle.

'Anyway, Steven, your turn now. What do you do to pay the rent?'

She was surprised to see his shoulders droop as he

muttered, 'You don't want to hear about my job – it's incredibly boring. Especially given the circles you move in.'

Mats turned sideways to face him and in what Penny called her "pep-talk voice", she said, 'Steven, do you enjoy your job?'

A little smile turned up the corner of his lips. 'Yes, Mats, I do. Very much.'

'Then don't demean what you do by calling it boring. The world would be a right rum joint if everyone only worked in the high-flying positions. Just think, no binmen, no waiters or waitresses, no people to serve us in shops or mend our boilers when they break… These may not be considered "glamorous" positions but by golly, they're damn well essential for the rest of our industries and nation to tick along. My job title might be CEO but I'm really nothing more than a glorified office manager. So, I'm asking again, "What do you do to pay the rent?" and this time, I'd like a more positive response, please.'

'Very well, I'm the Assistant Sales and Marketing Director for a financial software company in the City.'

'That's better.' The pride in his voice this time could not be missed. 'Please, tell me more. Financial software? What is that?'

Steven drew in a breath, about to speak, when Mats said, 'Actually, hold that thought. I need to "go to the loo".' She gave him a wink, leant forward, and hid the empty bottle of Champagne back up inside her culottes. 'I'll be back in a few minutes.'

TEN

'Thank you again, Mats, for coming along this evening. I really appreciate it. I hope it wasn't too painful for you.'

'Actually, it was more fun than I expected. I hope your brother doesn't give you too much grief over how I came to be with you.'

'I'll just avoid him for a few weeks. He's so shallow and self-centred, it should eventually slip his mind.'

Mats smiled at him as he gently closed the taxi door. He stuck his head through the driver's window and passed over a handful of notes as he said, 'East Dulwich, please. The lady will give you the exact address.'

He stepped back and waved until the cab had disappeared around the corner. Once it was out of sight, he climbed the steps to the front door of the converted semi-detached house. He opened and closed it quietly then made his way stealthily up the stairs, taking care not to disturb Florrie who lived on the ground floor. She claimed to be a light sleeper but having heard her snoring louder than an elephant on more than one occasion, Steven had his doubts about that.

He closed the flat door behind him and wandered into the lounge. Percival lay sprawled across the expanse of the sofa. He opened one eye, pierced Steven with his dark amber glare, and then closed it again while emitting a snuffle which told Steven in no uncertain terms, that he was not for budging.

'Fine, Perc, you stay there. That's why I bought myself this nice, funky La-Z-Boy chair – so I don't have to wrestle your eight-kilogram weight whenever I want to put my feet up.'

He checked the time and was surprised to see it was only half-past midnight. It felt later than that. However, despite the three bottles of Bollinger he and Mats had managed to charge to Stuart's credit card, plus a decent number of cocktails, he didn't feel at all drunk. Maybe the fresh air of the river had helped to keep him sober. He was starving hungry though. The buffet had consisted of silly finger food which wouldn't satisfy a mouse! He headed upstairs to his bedroom to change out of his suit but not before making a quick detour to the kitchen to open a tin of chilli con carne and stick a packet of steamed rice in the microwave.

A few minutes later he was ensconced in his La-Z-Boy with his feet up, a bottle of beer keeping cool in the chiller on the side, a bowl of chilli and rice in his hand and his laptop resting on his thighs. With one finger, he tapped Mats' name into the search engine and took a mouthful of food as his screen filled with images of her at various music ceremonies and gigs and in the company of several well-known celebrities within the music industry. He clicked on the website for EmmDee Recording Studios and scrolled through to her bio but it didn't contain anything more than what she'd divulged to him earlier in the evening. He clicked on a few other links but the information there was just as sparse. It seemed that while her image was all over the internet, her personal life was not.

Steven leant back in his chair, took a swig of beer, and gazed out of the large picture window as he finished his chilli. The park opposite was in darkness but he could make out the odd light still on in the houses beyond it. He reflected on the evening and concluded that all things considered, it hadn't been too bad at all. Mats had been entertaining company and given the manner in which she'd come to be his date for the night, there hadn't been any awkwardness or stilted conversation. He wouldn't have minded seeing her again but she hadn't given any indication of that being a possible option and he hadn't wanted to end the night on a sour note so he'd let the taxi whisk her home and out of his life.

Although…

He tapped the keyboard and his laptop sprang back to life. The webpage for the studios was still open… The webpage which had the address of the studios…

A thought wedged itself in his head.

He closed the computer down, finished his beer and stood up. It was time for bed. Percy thumped off the sofa and followed him up the short flight of stairs, jumping up onto the bed and settling himself in his corner while Steven cleaned his teeth. By the time he got into bed, the thought had manifested itself into a certainty. A bouquet of flowers would be sent to the studios on Monday accompanied by a thank you note and his phone number. The onus would then be on Mats over whether or not she chose to call it.

The less-than-dulcet tones of The Proclaimers declaring they would walk five-hundred miles sledgehammered their way into Mats' ears and around her head. At that moment, as she let out a groan and a very unladylike burp, she wished they really *were* five-hundred miles away. She pulled the duvet up over her head in an attempt to drown them out and after a minute, they stopped. The silence around her was bliss and she could feel herself slipping back into the land of slumber when, all of a sudden, those Scottish boys were at it again! Muttering a string of expletives, Mats grabbed her mobile and answered the call.

'What?'

'My, my, listen to you, little miss ray of sunshine. Is someone feeling a little bit the worse for wear this morning?'

'Fuck off, Penny!'

'I'm on my way round and I'm bringing gifts of coffee and fresh Danish pastries. I just need to know if I'm catering for two or for three…?'

'To repeat my earlier comment, fuck off, Penny!'

'Right, catering for two. See you in ten.'

The phone went dead leaving Mats to scream into her pillow. Or rather she would have done if a pneumatic drill wasn't already going off in her brain. A scream at this point would have been a step too far. In fact, even a weedy little whimper would be pushing its luck. As she lay still, hoping the room would have stopped spinning the next time she tried to open her eyes, she heard the front door opening downstairs and Penny's chirpy greeting flew up the stairs. A few minutes later, it was followed by the lady herself who barrelled into the bedroom and bounced down upon the bed. The sudden motion was too much for Mats and she felt her stomach lurch. Before she could move, however, the duvet was pulled back from her face and a bottle of Lucozade was thrust in front of her.

'Come on, sit up and get this down your neck.'

'Urgh! I can't!'

'Yes, you can! Come on.'

Mats, her eyes closed once more, let Penny pull her forward and prop a couple of pillows behind her, effectively pushing her into an upright position. She felt the damp fizz of the Lucozade under her nose as Penny held it out to her again.

'Come on, drink it. The sooner you do, the sooner you get this lovely Grande mocha with a *double* espresso shot to help ease you back into human form.'

Mats knew she was not going to win against the force that was Penny so she took the bottle, held it to her lips, and tried not to gag as she forced half of it down her throat. She held out her hand and Penny dropped the four extra-strong vitamin C tablets into it. Mats stuck them in her mouth and glugged down the remainder of the glucose-infused drink. She knew this was their tried and tested hangover cure which would begin to work its magic very quickly but until it did, it was a case of mind over matter as the contents now in her stomach tried to make a reappearance.

Still unable to open her eyes, she lay against the pillows, listening as Penny moved about the room picking clothes off the floor and either hanging them up or putting them in the laundry basket. Mats was not a slob by any length of chalk but compared to Penny's obsessive tidiness, she often felt like one. The bed dipped again and this time the smell of warm, strong coffee beans wrapped in rich soothing chocolate, made her nose twitch. She prised her eyes open a fraction of a millimetre and gathered the extra-large mug into both hands. The warmth, along with the Lucozade, slowly began to ease her sozzled state and the pneumatic drill began to downgrade itself until it reached the level of a muted hammering.

'Where's the Mars bar?'

'Honey, you don't need the Mars bar.'

'Always need the Mars bar.' Vitamin C, Lucozade

and a Mars bar – that was their set-in-stone hangover cure.

'Not when we have cinnamon buns.'

Mats' eyes sprung open. 'Cinnamon buns?'

'Yup!'

'Made by Carl?'

'Yup!'

'Cinnamon buns with two inches of thick, gooey icing on top?'

'You got it, girlfriend.'

'Why didn't you say so sooner?'

'I like to see you suffer!'

'You do know you're still on suspension pending review?' She peered at Penny through slit eyes, trying to give the appearance of being fierce and unforgiving.

'Yeah, sure, whatever you say.'

Penny laughed as she walked out of the room and Mats felt a little grin lift the corners of her mouth, knowing it was pointless trying to be mad.

'Here you go, get that down you.'

Mats placed her coffee on the bedside table and took the fork and plate Penny was holding out to her. The iced-smothered delight filled the side-plate and Mats wasted no time in tucking in. Carl was a baker who lived across the landing from Penny and he regularly sent over delicious baked goods for the girls to share. When his shifts allowed it, he would join them on nights down the pub or at the cinema. Mats was convinced he had a thing for Penny although he'd denied it vigorously when she'd asked. A little *too* vigorously she felt but she didn't push him any further. It wasn't for her to interfere although clearly her so-called chum didn't hold the same scruples.

'So, come on then, spill the beans – how was it? Was he hot and gorgeous?'

Mats pointed to her rather full mouth. She took her time chewing and swallowing to work out how best to reply.

Finally, she said, 'It was alright and so was Steven.'

'Whoa! Back up your truck on the hot steamy romance there, girl, I'm gonna need a cold shower if you carry on like that!'

'What? You asked a question, well, two questions and I answered them.'

'Yeah, with probably the most bland, insignificant response I think I've ever heard. Surely you can do better than that?'

'Okay! He was already waiting for me when I arrived. He is blond, green-eyed and of medium build. Looks-wise, I'd say pleasing to the eye but not over-the-top.' An image of Steven's brother popped into her head and she gave a small shudder which did not go unnoticed by Penny.

'So, what's with the grimace then? What happened to make you look like that?'

'Oh, nothing untoward. I met his brother and while he was the full brass band in the looks department, he was also up his own butthole and made no effort to hide the fact that he looked down on us both. They might be siblings but they definitely *don't* get along.'

Penny wrinkled her brow. 'But… I'm sure his email to Marky Sparks said his brother was his best friend and that was why he was desperate to go to the party.'

'Erm, yes, well… apparently, he was rather the worse for wear on tequila slammers and the email was sent in a drunken haze. He thinks he over-egged the brotherly-love sentiment in the hope it would add some poignancy to the request.'

'Fair enough. So, was he interesting? Boring? Funny? What? Honestly, Mats, it's like pulling teeth here!'

'He was…nice! Pleasant. I found his company pleasing. I wasn't bored and the night passed without incident. What more do you want me to say? Did I ravish him in the loos? No, I didn't. Did I engage in tonsil tickling with him? Again, no, I didn't. Did I sit up on the open deck of the boat and share three bottles of Bollinger with him before going back inside to work our way through the cocktail menu... Well, yes, that one I did!'

'And that explains the beautiful, blood-shot eyes which currently match the lovely red culottes you wore last night.'

'Thanks for that, Pen! You sure know how to make a girl feel so much better.'

'My pleasure. Always happy to big you up. Anytime! Now, stop trying to change the subject... Are you seeing him again?'

'No.'

'No?'

'No!'

'Why not?'

'He didn't ask.'

'Didn't you?'

Mats gave a small sigh. She was now full up on delicious cinnamon goodness and rich, chocolate coffee – all she wanted was to burrow back down into her quilt and enjoy a few more hours of sleep.

'Well, clearly I didn't ask, otherwise my answer to your question would have been yes.'

'Why not?'

'Why not what?'

'Why didn't you ask to see him again?'

'Because I'm just out of a crappy relationship, because he's not my type and because he didn't give any sign of being interested in me. That's why I'm not seeing him again. Now, can I please go back to sleep, I'm shattered.'

Penny got off the bed and gathered up the cups and plates.

'Fine! I'll wash these up and get out of your hair. I'm sorry it didn't work out, Mats. After Vic-the-Prick, I was hoping you'd get right back out there again.'

'I know you were, Penny, but I'm quite happy to take some time out for now. I'll call you later. Maybe we can do a takeaway and a movie again tonight?'

'Sounds like a plan – as long as I get to choose the film.'

Mats was almost asleep as she muttered, 'Sure, whatever,' knowing she'd just subjected herself to some loud, explosion-filled, bullet-ridden, action movie which were always Penny's first choice. Her last thought, before heading off to the land of nod, was that as long as it starred Ryan Reynolds, she could cope.

ELEVEN

Marky Sparks pushed open the studio door. How on earth could it be Monday again already? He wouldn't feel so bad if he'd had a fun-filled weekend with a hot babe but necking a couple of bottles of Jack Daniels and watching some boxing wasn't going to feature too highly on the "Trip Advisor" list of things to do in London on a Saturday night.

He slung his leather jacket over the back of his chair and sat down. Dave had left some notes on the desk for him to read through in preparation for the show. He pulled on the headphones and Dave's voice immediately filled his ears.

'Alright, Sparky? You ready for today? Listening figures have dropped again – we really need to get some buzz on our airwaves, think you can manage that?'

'Don't you mean "some Sparks on the airwaves", Dave?'

'Ha! Nice one! Yeah, some of the old Marky Sparks magic wouldn't go amiss, that's for damn sure.'

'I'll see what I can do.'

'By the way, are you planning to get in touch with that bloke you set up the date for, to see how it went?'

'Of course. With a bit of luck, they got on really well, shagged each other's brains out and I'll get an invite to the wedding. After all, it worked for Cilla Black didn't it!'

'Yeah, right! Good luck with that pipe-dream, mate. More likely that she stood him up.'

'Well, we'll find out in a couple of hours. Now it's time to get to work.'

He listened to Cindy winding up her news bulletin, waited for the sponsor's jingle to end and then stepped up to the plate.

'Good morning, my little sparklers, and welcome to a fresh week on the Marky Sparks Breakfast Show…'

Just after eight-thirty, Marky nodded to Dave. It was time to get the love-birds (hopefully) on the blower and find out how their hot date went.

A few minutes later, Dave gave him the thumbs-up through the window as he patched the calls through.

'Hey there, Steve, how you doing, my man? Y'alright?'

'Erm… yes, thank you, Marky.'

'And Matilda, you okay, babes?'

'I was until five seconds ago.'

Cheeky bitch, thought Marky but he didn't let her sarcasm break his stride.

'So, I'm calling to find out how the big night went on Saturday. Was it love at first sight?'

'Err, NO!'

'No, Marky, it wasn't.'

Well at least Steve had some manners. Marky was beginning to think this Matilda one was a right stroppy cow.

'How about "like" at first sight? Was there even a hint of a *spark* between you?' He chuckled at his little joke, not noticing that no one else did.

'Mats was lovely and I enjoyed her company. It meant a lot to me to be able to attend my brother's shindig and I'm very grateful to Mats for agreeing to be my guest on the night.'

'And the magic?'

'I'm afraid not, Marky.'

'Matilda, you're not saying much…'

'Steven has explained perfectly well. We shared an enjoyable evening and I'm happy to have been of assistance in his hour of requirement. There's nothing more to add.'

'Any plans to meet up again?'

The replies came back in unison. 'No!'

'Why not? You're both single…'

'I'm not looking for a relationship right now.'

'But, Matilda, sometimes it's when we're not looking that we find exactly what, or who, we need.'

Dave gave him a thumbs-up through the window, clearly impressed with his rather profound comment. Marky sent up a silent thanks to his local Chinese take-away who'd chucked a few fortune cookies in his bag last night.

When there was no reply, Marky tried to chivvy Steve along.

'Steve, what do you think, man? Would you like to see Matilda again?'

'I think the lady has made her feelings clear on the matter, Marky, so I suggest we leave it there. I would like to thank you again for your hand in sorting out my problem, I really appreciate it.'

'Well, thank you both for coming on the show this morning and letting us, and our listeners, know how it all went.'

Marky cut the lines and hit the button for the next song to come on.

'Jeez, those two were hard work! I'm beginning to wish I hadn't bothered now.'

'Well, we're a radio show, Marky, not a dating agency,' Dave said in his ear. 'Just be glad the woman turned up – it would've been a lot worse if the poor bloke had been stood up.'

'But it would have been great on the radio!'

'Sparks, you can be a right shit sometimes!'

Marky grinned at Dave as he took a slug of coffee and got on with the show.

'You're quiet, what gives?'

Marky had wrapped up the show and handed over to Olwyn Evans, the soft-spoken Welsh lass who came on after him. He'd then normally have some daft banter with Dave as they did a quick post-mortem on the show and discuss if there had been any material which they may be able to use the following day.

'Sorry, mate. I just can't stop thinking about that Steve-bloke. I think he liked Matilda more than he was letting on.'

'He didn't say anything to that effect when you asked.'

'But he never say he didn't either. Think back to his answer, he was diplomatic and used the opportunity to thank her for being his date. At no point did he give any indication that he wouldn't like to see her again.'

'Well, I think *she* made it perfectly clear that the buck stopped at Saturday night. You can't force her to go out with the bloke.'

'No, I can't "force" her but I can persuade her.'

'You? You have all the subtlety of a wrecking ball!'

'I'll have you know that back in my younger days, I was quite persuasive when I needed to be. I could have charmed the proverbial knickers off a nun!'

'Yeah, well these days, mate, you'd be lucky to pull the knickers off a washing line!'

'Ha-bloody-ha! Anyway, I have an idea…'

'Which is?'

'Alphabet Dating.'

'Excuse me?'

'You heard me! Where do we keep the file on all the freebie offers that come into the station? I'm thinking we can use a few of those to send our lucky couple off on some dates. Nothing too heavy but it'll give them the chance to get to know each other better. The small twist is that we do their dates alphabetically.'

'Why?'

'Why what?'

'Why alphabetically?'

'Just to be different. To mix it up a bit.'

'I think you're off your trolley, Marky.'

'Look, you wanted me to find something to give the show more oomph and get the listening figures up – well, this is as good a suggestion as any. Have you got a better idea to put forward?'

Dave sat back with a sigh. 'No, I haven't.'

'Well then! What do we have to lose? We might as well give it a try.'

'Fair enough! I think you're mental and I think Mats will tell you exactly where to get off but if you're feeling lucky, then go for it.'

'I am and I will. So, where's that file?'

TWELVE

'Okay, upon checking my records, I can see The Crazy Horses overran their studio time by two days when they were last here. Have they factored that into their latest booking request or should we take the precaution of adding it ourselves?'

Mats and Tinks were in their weekly Wednesday morning meeting, going over the recording schedules for the following month and discussing the booking requests which had come in since their previous meeting. Running a successful, in-demand studio meant the requests for rooms far outstripped the availability and it had become almost an art form when it came to juggling the bookings. They now employed several excellent sound engineers but it was Tinks who was always in demand and the fun lay in making sure he wasn't double booked.

Tinks had barely opened his mouth to reply when Mats' mobile rang. She glanced at the screen but not recognising the number, declined the call.

'Sorry, Tinks, you were about to say…'

'I think it would—'

Mats' mobile cut him off when it began ringing again. She let out a humph as she picked it up. It was the same number as before and for the second time, she cancelled the call.

'Persistent!' Tinks nodded at the now silent device.

'Yeah, well, that's what voicemail is for. They can leave a message. You were about to give me your thoughts on the Horses—'

Before Tinks could speak, the mobile rang for a third time.

'Oh, for the love of—'

'Maybe it would be better just to answer it, Mats. Clearly whoever it is, doesn't plan on going away.'

She snatched the poor offending phone, gave it a quick swipe and all but growled into it.

'Hello, Mats Davidson speaking.'

'Hi Mats, it's Dave Maim from Smile-A-While Radio, how are you today?'

'I'm very well, thank you, how can I help you?'

'Would you be available for a meeting this afternoon? There's something I'd like to discuss with you?'

'And what would that be?'

'I'd rather fill you in when we meet.'

'Well, I'm extremely busy so *I'd* rather you just told me now over the phone.'

'I appreciate you're a busy lady but I really would prefer to speak with you face-to-face, if you don't mind.'

'One moment, please.'

She put the call on mute and turned to Tinks.

'It's the producer from that radio show – he wants to meet me to discuss something.'

'What?'

'I don't know, he won't say. Said he'd rather we discussed it in person.'

'When?'

'This afternoon.'

'And?'

'And I don't know if I should go. I don't like the fact he's being so secretive. What do you think?'

'Well, I dunno… I'm not the one he's asking to meet up with.' Tinks gave a small shrug.

'Honestly, Tinks, sometimes you're as useful as a chocolate teapot!'

'It's for you to decide, Mats. You can either say no and spend goodness knows how long wondering what it was about – which we both know you'll do! – or for the sake of an hour or two, you can go along, find out what it's all about and sleep easy for the rest of your days. It's your call.'

'Damn you! Why do you have to know me so well?' Mats replied crossly, knowing that Tinks was absolutely spot on with his statement. She unmuted the phone,

'Very well, what time and where?'

'Do you know the Old Thameside Inn in Clink Street?'

'Yes, I do.' Very well as it happened but she wasn't telling Mr Radio Man that.

'Can you meet me there at about two-thirty?'

'Hang on…' Mats hit her tablet and brought up her diary. Damn! Her lunchtime meeting was scheduled to finish at two – she had no excuse. 'Yes, I can do that.'

'Great! I'll see you then.'

Without even a goodbye, Dave hung up, leaving Mats with a dead line against her ear.

'Going then?'

'It would seem so! Now, let's see if we can get through the rest of *this* meeting without any further interruption!'

Steven looked at his watch before taking a sip of his drink. Yet again he was early. As he enjoyed the slight burn of the ginger beer slipping down his throat, he wondered for the umpteenth time since receiving the call from Dave at the radio station, what this was all about. Dave had been tight-lipped, refusing to give anything away over the phone. Steven still wasn't sure if it had been luck or not that he'd had a twelve pm meeting over this side of the river and therefore making it easy to stop by the pub on his way back to the office.

He was about to take another drink when he saw Mats walk in the door. He stood up and waved when he saw her stop to look around. He instinctively knew her being here was something to do with Dave and his phone call.

'Hey, how are you? Can I get you a drink?'

'Hi! Erm... yes please. Thank you.'

'What would you like?' Steven felt his pulse speed up at being in her presence again. She was dressed in a business-like, dark purple trouser suit. The long, thigh-length jacket was nipped in at the waist making her look both feminine and assured. With her hair styled in the same sleek bob as Saturday night, she oozed power and confidence. What had really gotten his blood pumping, however, were her eyes. She had purple eyes. They were absolutely mesmerising. He hadn't noticed on Saturday night because the lighting on the boat had been muted.

'What are you drinking?' She glanced at him curiously before nodding at his glass. Suddenly, realising he was staring at her, he dragged his eyes down to his glass.

'Ginger beer.'

'Oh my, I haven't had ginger beer for years. I'll have a glass of that please.'

As he placed the glass in front of her a few minutes later, the first thing she said was, 'I'm guessing you're here to meet the bloke from the radio station too?'

'Yup! He called me this morning and said there was something he wanted to discuss. Refused to say what though.'

'Yeah, same here. He was rather evasive when questioned. Didn't even tell me you'd be here.'

'Likewise. Any thoughts on what it's all about?'

'Hopefully he's after suggestions on how to take out that slimy little weasel, Marky Sparks. I'm sure I could come up with a few.'

'Well, we won't have to wait any longer, he's just walked in the door.'

'Excuse me, did I just hear you right? You want to put together some kind of "Blind Date" thing on the radio and you want Steven and I to be a part of it?'

Mats stared at Dave in disbelief. She couldn't think of anything more abhorrent – having her love life on show for everyone to hear.

'I suppose that's a more succinct way of putting it although you would both be the main players. As I said, we'd arrange for you to go on a number of dates—'

'Whoa! Just stop right there, mister!' Mats held up her hand and stopped Dave mid-speech. 'There is no way, on this planet, that I am having the details of our dates broadcast across the airwaves to the whole nation! No siree! It's not happening!'

'I think you overestimate the size of our listenership, Mats. We're a small radio station and we're just about lucky to reach any listeners north of Watford Gap, never mind the other side of the M25. In fact, that's our biggest problem. We're losing listeners hand over fist and unless we come up with something new and different very soon, we're going out of business. We rely heavily on our advertising revenue but if the ears keep moving elsewhere... well, companies ain't gonna pay to advertise to fresh air.'

Unknown to Dave, his little speech had just hit all the right notes with Mats. She knew all too well how it felt to try and grow a small business when it was surrounded on all sides by bigger, better-known and often revered, companies. Nearly every artist in the music business wants to record their sound at the famous Abbey Road studios – fortunately for her, not everyone could. She also knew her business would be nothing without Tinks. He'd been her lucky break and she never forgot that. It stood to reason that Marky Sparks was the "big money" on Smile-A-While and if his show sank, it took the whole station down with it.

'Steven, what are your thoughts on this?' Dave looked at Steven.

'I just want to clarify things, if you don't mind. You, or rather the radio station, want to send Mats and I on twenty-six dates, *together*, with each date representing a letter of the alphabet and they would be in alphabetical order.'

'That's right.' Dave nodded.

'How often would these dates be? Are we looking at twenty-six weeks which is six months of our lives?'

Dave put his pint back down on the table before speaking. 'The idea is to mix the dates up. Some of the dates would be suitable for an evening, some for an afternoon, some will be all-day events – just the way it would be if you were dating each other for real.'

'How would the radio station gain anything from this?'

'Erm, ideally, you'd both actually fall in love with each other and we'd benefit from that because... well...

who doesn't like a good old love story?'

'So, there'll be some kind of publicity?'

Dave turned back to Mats. 'Yeah, if it takes off. We'll keep it low key to start with – you know, try to let the interest of the listeners grow naturally – but then we'll slowly begin ramping up the hype with the hope it garners some interest over social media. Ideally, if we could get trending on Twitter, or X, as they're trying to call it these days, that would be a massive boost. Do you both have Twitter or X accounts?'

'Yes.'

'No.'

Steven and Dave turned as one to Mats.

'You don't have a Twitter account?' Mats felt Dave couldn't have looked more shocked if she'd told him her great-grandmother was a Martian.

'No, I don't. Never felt the need for one. Like I said, I keep things private. I'm not one for airing my life to the world at large.'

'We'll need to sort that out if we go ahead with this. *Are* we going ahead with this?' Dave looked at Mats with hope in his eyes.

'What happens if we end up not getting along? I don't want to be forced into the company of someone I don't like. And I'm sure the same can be said for Steven – it's not just about me.'

'We'd draw up a contract. You would both have to commit to fourteen dates. After that, if you're still friends, we'd continue through to the end.'

'And when would you be looking for this to start?' Mats was hoping he'd say next month so she'd have time to get her head around what she was letting herself into.

'You'll come back on the radio this Friday morning. There will be two sealed envelopes numbered 1 and 2 for you to choose from and whatever number you select will be your date which will take place on Saturday. We'll call you on Monday morning for an update on how it went and then you choose the next date. That will take place mid-week and on Friday, we'll speak to you again, get your feedback, you choose the next date and so on, and so on.'

'So soon?' Mats felt a bit faint.

'Gotta strike while the iron's hot!'

'Steven?' She looked at him in the hope he'd veto the whole thing.

'What kind of dates will we be sent on?'

'Oh, all sorts. We want them to be fun and unusual. Nothing too ordinary if we can help it.'

'I seem to remember you saying you liked a bit of adventure, Mats. Shall we do it? Shall we live life a little bit dangerously?'

Mats looked at Steven, trying to hide her dismay. So much for him putting a halt to this. She hadn't wanted to come across as being the wet dishcloth by refusing outright to get caught up in all this nonsense. It would seem, however, that by trying to be the nice guy, she'd only gone and got herself well and truly lassoed!

'Oh, okay then. But I want to see the contract BEFORE we go on air on Friday. Have it with me by noon tomorrow or I'm out.' She passed Dave her business card with her email address on it. Steven did likewise.

'You'll both have the paperwork by ten in the morning.' Dave sunk the rest of his pint, put the two cards in his wallet and stood up to leave.

'Oh, Dave,' Mats stopped him in his tracks. 'Just so you know, I'll be adding a clause to the contract. The first time that weasel, Sparks, calls me Matilda, babes, darlin' or some other patronising put-down, the deal is off! The same again if he says "Steve" instead of Steven, Got that? He can begin to treat us with respect since we'll be helping to keep him in a job. Capisce?'

'Understood.'

Dave nodded, turned and scurried out of the pub.

There was silence for a moment until Mats said, 'I'm going to the bar for a real drink. Care to join me?'

'Hell, yes! And can we make them doubles?'

'That, Steven, was already a given!'

THIRTEEN

'And then the big bad wolf huffed and puffed but he couldn't blow the house down because the three little pigs had built a bunker underground and the only thing the wolf could see was a strange funnel which began pelting tennis balls at him...'

'Uncle Steven, that's not in the story!'

Letting out a giggle, six-year-old Lucy slipped off his knee and went running through to the lounge, no doubt to tell her father that Uncle Steven was making up stories again. Lily, her older sister by eighteen months, was only a few steps behind.

Steven was sitting at the table in the kitchen where Emma placed a glass of cider in front of him.

'You really are incorrigible, you know.' She gave him a grin.

'Only bringing these fairy tales into the twenty-first century, Ems.'

He took a drink and placed the glass down as he sat back and gave a little inward sign of contentment. He'd been best friends with Neil since senior school and Emma had joined them at university. She and Neil had made their joining permanent eleven years ago and to ensure Steven would always be a part of their family, he was godparent to both of their girls. Their house, purposely purchased only two streets away from him, was his second home. Emma had vetted his various girlfriends over the years and more recently, interrogated them after Stuart's rising star had begun to dazzle. She'd very successfully wormed out the couple of "girlfriends" who were, in fact, only using Steven as a stepping stone to his brother.

'Did you send the flowers to Mats on Monday as you intended?'

'No.'

'Why not?'

'Didn't you hear her on the radio? She wasn't keen for any further contact.'

'You could still have sent the flowers as a thank you. I'm sure she'd have appreciated the gesture.'

'I could have but I didn't want to appear pushy. Anyway, before you start nagging me, there's been a development which I'll tell you about when we eat.'

'Oh, tell me now!' Emma pulled out the chair opposite him and sat down, giving him an imploring look as she did so.

'No, because I'll only have to repeat myself when Neil comes in.'

'Oh, you're no fun!' She flicked the tea towel lightly at him.

'And your spaghetti is about to boil over!'

'Ah, shoot…!'

She rushed over to turn down the heat, grabbed the cutlery basket and placed it on the table.

'Give the sauce a couple of stirs, hon, while I go up and say goodnight.' Emma briefly touched her husband's arm as they passed in the doorway. Steven looked away.

Even after all these years together, they were still very much in love and it often brought a little lump to his throat when he witnessed these small, unconscious moments of tenderness. He would be lying if he said he didn't want what they had. With his own upbringing being somewhat love-deprived – he'd always felt he got Stuart's leftovers – he really wanted to meet someone he could settle down with. Which probably went some way to explaining some of his more unusual choices of girlfriend in the past. He still had the occasional nightmare about the tree-hugging hippy who'd made a big thing about everything being cool, how the paths of life were already pre-ordained and how karma was all around them but had in fact turned out to be a psycho stalker whom, in the end, he'd had to take out a restraining order against. Petunia was another blast in his past which also made him shudder. In the beginning he'd admired, and slightly envied, the close relationship she had with her parents, especially her mother, but when said mother began to come along on their dates, he'd quickly become less enamoured with it. The day Petunia was supposed to stay over at his place for the first time and she arrived with her mother in tow, both carrying overnight bags, was the day he'd put an end to the relationship. You didn't need to be a rocket scientist to see how that would work if they'd ended up tying the knot. A pushy, overbearing mother-in-law was the last thing he needed!

'So, how you doing, mate? How's work?'

Neil sat in the same seat Emma had occupied a few minutes earlier, placing his own drink in front of him.

'Not too bad, thanks. The markets are a bit challenging right now but, ironically, that helps us because everyone is clamouring for our software. How about you?'

'About the same. Brexit caused a small hiccup in that some of the parts we used to get from Europe went up in price but we managed to find a company in, of all places,

Iceland, who were able to fill that gap so we're getting back on track.'

'Good. And is the slowdown in car sales affecting you at all?' Neil worked for a company who supplied car parts to both large and small garage repair shops around the UK.

'Not at all. Like you, it's working in our favour. Instead of trading in their old bangers, folks are holding on to them and having them repaired.'

'Are you boys talking shop again?'

Emma walked back into the kitchen and stopped to take a quick drink of Neil's cider before going over to stir the pasta sauce again.

'Did they go down okay?' Neil asked.

'No problems at all despite the dodgy bedtime story Steven decided to tell them! I'm sure Lucy was asleep by the time I got to the bedroom door and Lily wasn't far behind.'

A few minutes later, three large steaming bowls of spaghetti Bolognese were placed on the table and there was silence as they tucked in. Emma was a great cook and they never spoke while eating out of respect for her efforts.

Once the bowls were empty, and the last of the sauce had been scooped up by the accompanying garlic bread, Emma wasted no time in pinning Steven down with a no-nonsense stare.

'Right, Steven, time to spill the beans. What's this "development" you mentioned?'

'What's this?' Neil looked at them both.

'*Someone* told me earlier that there had been a development further to his mystery date on Saturday but *someone* refused to go into details until you were here. So, now you're here, it's time for him to 'fess up!'

'I saw Mats yesterday.' Steven went in with the blunt force comment, knowing it would wind up Emma. And he was right.

'You WHAT? How? Tell me more!'

He filled them in on the phone call from Dave Maim, the request for a meeting and Mats also turning up.

'You didn't know she was going to be there?'

'No, Ems, the first I knew was when she walked through the door.'

'And how did you feel when you saw her? Did your pulse race a little?' Emma grinned as she asked the question.

'Actually, yes it did. And it raced a bit faster again when she got closer and I saw her amazing eyes.'

'Her eyes?'

'Yes, she has purple eyes.'

'No one has purple eyes – are you sure they weren't contact lenses?'

'Definitely not contacts, they were the real deal.'

'I'm quite sure no one has purple eyes, Steven.'

'I looked it up on the internet when I got back to the office. Without getting too technical, it's all to do with mutation and lack of melanin etc. It would seem her eyes are actually an unusual shade of blue which can appear violet or purple depending on the light being reflected on colours and stuff around the subject. Yesterday, Mats was wearing a purple suit so I expect that enhanced their shade. It did not, however, detract from them being so distinctive and hypnotising. I actually caught myself staring at her.'

'Did she notice?'

'I hope not.'

'So, why were you both there? Did this Dave bloke show up or did he just organise a meeting for the two of you to bump into each other again?' Emma got up to refill the glasses as she spoke.

'Oh, Dave turned up all right and wait till you hear this…'

Steven repeated everything that had happened the day

before to his friends and tried not to laugh at the looks of identical incredulity on their faces. When he finally finished, he picked up his glass and took a long drink as he waited for them to digest what he'd just told them.

'But... I don't understand...,' Emma looked confused. 'If Mats wasn't keen on seeing you again when asked on Monday, what on earth changed her mind to make her agree to this?'

'She was completely against it until Dave played the sob story card. The radio station is sitting in the last-chance saloon and unless they can increase their listener numbers, it's going to go under. Apparently, this struck a chord with Mats – something to do with remembering her own struggles when setting up her business and always trying to compete with the big fish in the pond.'

'And that was enough to make her change her mind?'

'No, Neil. She said she'd "agreed" to do it so that she wouldn't come over as being negative and mardy but had expected me to decline as she didn't think I would be keen to do it either. She said she just about passed out when she heard me say yes.'

'Why did you say yes, Steven? You usually avoid anything that puts you in the spotlight because you don't like people making the connection between you and Stuart.'

'I like Mats and it was clearly the only chance I was going to have of spending more time with her.'

'What makes her so special, Steven? I thought you disliked all those power-seeking, promotion-hungry type females?'

'The ones I usually meet in my line of work are exactly like that, Ems. They're so focused on the "top jobs", they leave much of their humanity behind but Mats isn't like that. She was kind to me on Saturday. We all know she didn't want to be there but she came along anyway, prepared to help out a total stranger. She was also decidedly less than impressed with Stuart so that immediately shot her up in my estimation.'

'You didn't tell us this when you came round on Sunday, why not?'

Steven gave Emma a small smile. She was now giving him the interrogation treatment.

'I did mention that she didn't like Stuart…'

'Yeah, but you omitted the bit where her response impressed you.'

'Ems, it was all still fresh on Sunday and I was more than a bit knackered too so I maybe didn't realise myself. Seeing her today, watching her talking to Dave and being in her company again… well… I enjoyed it. Something about her relaxes me. I don't feel I need to go out of my way to try and impress her. In fact, I suspect if I did do that, I'd get short-shrift. I have the feeling she's big on honesty and has no time for fools. Well, I know she has no time for fools given the way she speaks about Marky Sparks. She's certainly not his biggest fan.'

'And what do you expect to happen with all these "dates"? Do you think it'll end up being some big love affair with a happy ending?'

'Who knows, Emma, but I've got nothing to lose by trying. I like Mats and this gives me the chance to get to know her better. Hopefully, I'll like what I find. And more to the point, she gets to know me and will, with a bit of luck, like what she finds too.'

Emma leant over the table and placed her hand over his.

'Then, Steven, I wish you all the luck in the world. I hope it works out for you and we'll be rooting for you on the side-lines.'

'For sure we will, mate. I think it's a bit of a drastic way to find love but we're here for you regardless. Now I think we need some more cider to help us get our heads around this!'

FOURTEEN

Mats held the phone to her ear, listening as Marky Sparks
filled his listeners in on the developments since Monday.
He'd named the venture "Love is on the Air" – a play on
words from the old 70s song, "Love is in the Air" by John
Paul Young. With reluctance, she had to agree it was a
touch clever. He was now expanding on what this entailed
and her stomach began to tumble and flutter as it finally
sank in exactly what she had agreed to.

The contracts had been received yesterday morning,
exactly as Dave had promised, and they'd been identical
for she'd been on the phone to Steven while they'd gone
through them together. In fairness to Dave, what he'd put
together had been more than reasonable and he'd even
included her specified clause on Marky Sparks using their
preferred names and being respectful. And listening to the
show thus far, the DJ had been exactly that whenever he'd
been putting out teasers in the build-up to the big
announcement. She couldn't help but wonder exactly what
Dave had had to do to achieve that!

'And now, without any further ado, let's welcome

back to the Marky Sparks Breakfast Show, Mats and Steven.'

'Good morning, Marky.'

Steven repeated her greeting.

'How are you both today? Are you ready to choose your adventure for tomorrow? As you will have heard me explain to our listeners, I have two envelopes here marked 1 and 2. Now I know one contains something which some listeners may call an extreme adventure and the other contains a rather less hair-raising event. Both, as you know, begin with the letter A. So, who's going to choose?'

Mats heard Steven put her forward to go first reasoning that, since this is an Alphabet Dating game, they may as well make the choice in alphabetical order. Jeez, what a cop out, she thought.

'Hi Marky, in that case, I would like you to open envelope number 1, please.'

The sound of rustling and ripping paper came down the phone.

'Ooooo, Mats, now this is interesting. Nice one. Tomorrow, you and Steven will be…' There was a dramatic pause.

'You'll find out after this word from our sponsors!'

Mats laughed as Steven cursed while trying to line up his bow and arrow. She was quickly finding out that coordination was not up there as one of his main skills.

'You're not helping, Mats,' he grumbled, as another arrow landed far beyond the target.

'Would you rather have gone abseiling?'

'Blimey, no! I prefer to keep my feet firmly on the ground, thank you very much.'

'Well, stop moaning then and be grateful. Especially

as you've said you'd have chosen the other envelope.'

'I do tend to go for even numbers. I think I prefer the symmetry.'

'Now I know what you'll be picking on Monday.'

'Don't be so sure, lady, I could just as easily break the habit of a lifetime and choose number one.'

'Yeah, you could. But will you, that is the question?'

'You'll just need to wait and see. Now hush, I need to concentrate here.'

'You do know you're supposed to be aiming for that big round multi-coloured thing over there, don't you?' Mats was bent double with laughter as yet another arrow went astray. 'That poor pigeon – its life must have flashed before its eyes when your arrow flew past!'

'Well, that was my last arrow for this round. Your turn next, let's see how *you* do.'

Mats stepped forward, picked up the bow she'd been given and allowed the instructor to show her how to hold it and how she should load her arrow. She fumbled a bit with placing the arrow as her fingers were cold but then what would you expect standing outdoors in North London at midday on the first Saturday in March. Although she'd most certainly rather be doing this than an abseil down a cliff somewhere – the option she'd managed to avoid. Steven wasn't the only one who was relieved to see that one rejected.

Mats settled the bow into position, pulled the bow string back with her three fingers as instructed and let go. She couldn't contain her whoop of joy when the arrow landed in the circle of the red zone on the target.

'Get in!' she hollered. Behind her, she heard Steven let out a groan.

The instructor advised her to aim a little bit more to the right but she went too far and the second arrow landed in the blue zone. She pulled back a bit and the third came in above her first. She got it right after that and her remaining three arrows all landed in the golden centre although none managed to find their way into the bullseye. The instructor expressed his delight at her natural ability before going off to retrieve the arrows for Steven's second attempt.

'Okay, own up, you've done this before, haven't you?'

'Nope! I absolutely haven't, honest.'

'Then how are you so good? That was quite amazing.'

'I think I just have good eye to hand coordination, Steven. I always manage to hit the target whenever I try my hand at those sideshows at the fairground.'

'Have you ever played darts? I bet you'd be good at that.'

'Now you mention it, I recall having a few games with Tinks back at Uni. Can't remember if I was any good though – think I was pissed most of the time!'

Steven laughed as he picked up his bow and stepped up for his second attempt. This time he was better and managed to get all six arrows on the board although not all landed inside the target. Mats gave him encouraging feedback from the side-lines.

'Now you're cooking with gas! Well done, Steven, you're doing great.'

Steven grinned with delight as they swapped places.

'I think I'm getting it now.'

'I would say so. You did good!'

It didn't take Mats long to disperse her six arrows. They all landed in the golden circle this time but still no bullseye. She didn't mind, she'd get it with her next attempt – she was sure of that. When Steven walked past her to take up his third, and final, stint she butted him with her shoulder as she said, 'C'mon, Byrne! Show me what you've got.'

She watched Steven pick up his bow again but this time his stance was more confident and his aim was steadier. She could see him taking in deep breaths before letting the first arrow go.

With a "ferlump" it landed in the golden circle. As did the second arrow and the third.

'Oh, my, there's a bloke up in Sherwood Forest beginning to get a bit worried now, Steven. You're doing brilliantly!'

He gave her a quick smile as the instructor handed him the fourth arrow and whispered a small bit of advice. Mats gave a small gasp for it was the first truly happy smile she'd seen from him. His face had lit up in that brief second and he'd looked utterly carefree and relaxed. In fact, he must have been very relaxed for the fourth arrow landed in the bullseye.

Mats whooped with joy. 'Awesome! That is wonderful. You're rocking this, dude!'

She waited until he'd shot his last arrows, which also landed in the golden circle although there were no more bullseyes, and then ran forward to take a picture on her phone.

'This is going straight onto my Twitter page.'

'Don't you mean X and I thought you weren't on it?'

'Can we just stick to calling it Twitter – it's easier – and Penny set me up and showed me what to do when she came over on Thursday. I'm a bit slow but Pen said I'll get quicker with practise. I just need to remember that any tweets I make which relate to us and our dates are followed by the hashtags "Loveisontheair" and "SmileAwhileRadio". There, all done!'

She turned her phone to let him see. "Practise makes Perfect!" was written above the photograph of the target and followed by several smiley faces.

'Now it's my final moment of glory. Let's see if I can

get a bullseye too!'

Five minutes later, Mats handed her bow back to their instructor and thanked him for his time. Unfortunately, she hadn't managed the elusive bullseye although she'd come mighty close to it on two occasions. A couple of millimetres was all she'd needed.

When she picked up her phone, she let out a little squeal! 'Look, I've already got two likes on my picture.'

'I think one is Penny and the other is me!'

'How did you do that?'

Steven gave a little grin, walked to her side and pointed out the search facility. 'I saw your twitter name when you showed me the picture, searched for you, and now follow you. If you click there…' he pointed to an icon on her screen, 'you can see who likes your tweets and you also have the option to follow that person back.'

Mats clicked the "Follow" button next to Steven's name. 'Does this mean I'm following you and can see your posts?'

'That's right. So now I'm going to retweet your picture to my feed, tagging you within it and my friends will be able to see it. That should get a few more likes and you may get a few more followers. Did Penny not explain that to you?'

'I think she was going with the "one step at a time" approach – just getting me onto Twitter was a big deal but as it was part of the conditions of this thing we're doing, it had to be done.'

They talked as they walked and were soon back at the archery clubhouse. They thanked the instructor one last time and left to walk back to the tube station.

'Going back to the Twitter thing, Mats, I'm a little confused because I noticed that EmmDee Studios has a twitter account and posts to it regularly. You're named on there often so how come you know so little?'

'Because I have a marketing chap who is responsible for all our social media and PR. Anything you see on Facebook, Twitter, Instagram etc regarding the studios is all Gavin's doing.'

'Ah! Fair enough.'

They scanned their Oyster cards and made their way to the southbound platform. The sun had broken through the clouds and it was a pleasant day despite the nip in the air.

'What are you up to now?'

She looked at the clock hanging over the platform – it was just after one o'clock.

'Not much really. By the time I get home it's going to be after three so I'll probably just grab a sandwich and curl up with a book.'

'Would you like to go for a bite to eat?'

Mats took a moment to think over Steven's offer. Penny was working today so she wouldn't be seeing her until tomorrow and while the idea of curling up with her book was very tempting, she was enjoying Steven's company and if they were going to be stuck together for another thirteen dates, at least, it would be worth getting to know him better. With her mind made up, she turned and gave him a big smile.'

'Sure, why not.'

FIFTEEN

Steven hoped his surprise at Mats' answer wasn't too obvious. He really hadn't been expecting her to agree and had asked out of politeness although he was delighted she'd accepted his invite. The only problem now was where to go.

'Is there anywhere in particular you fancy eating?' he asked, hopefully.

'No, I'm flexible.'

Damn! That didn't help him at all so he decided to go with a methodical approach.

'Well, we're heading back into the city centre so do you fancy going into the West End?'

'On a Saturday afternoon? It'll be heaving. Probably not a good move.'

'Fair enough! The next tube is going via Bank, maybe we could head into the City and see what's doing there?'

'Now that sounds like a plan.'

He was rewarded with one of Mats full-on smiles, the one which reached all the way up to her eyes and made them crinkle at the edges. He'd caught himself being mesmerised by her eyes more than once today and he'd had to make a real effort to not just stare into them like some kind of love-struck fool. Today in the brilliant sunlight, he could clearly see they were a deep shade of blue and not the violet he'd initially thought although they did seem to change colour frequently, depending on the light around them.

'Err... Steven, you're staring at me!'

'Oh, shit! I'm sorry.' He could feel himself turning red and so decided to come clean. 'Look, I apologise but... it's your eyes. They're stunning and every time I look at you, I feel I'm being hypnotised.'

Mats let out a small laugh and he felt his embarrassment slip away.

'If it makes you feel any better, you're not the first person to have said pretty much the same thing. I've kind of become used to it over the years.'

'I'm sorry. It's so rude to stare and I find myself doing it to you rather often.'

'No, honestly, you're fine. You've been a lot more subtle than some people are!'

Just then, the train arrived on the platform. They entered the carriage in front of them and sat down. Mats carried on talking as though there had been no interruption.

'My eye colour comes from my mother's side of the family although it does seem to jump about. My mum had rather ordinary blue eyes, as did my grandmother, but apparently my great-grandmother had the same shade as mine. I looked it up once on the internet and it's a genetic mutation which means you're about to have lunch with a mutant! How does that make you feel?'

The peal of laughter which accompanied her comment was light and infectious and Steven couldn't help but join in.

'Now *that* would be something to tell Marky Sparks

on the radio on Monday morning.'

'Don't you dare!'

'No worries, your secret's safe with me… X-woman!'

'Cheeky sod!' She elbowed him in the ribs and he laughed again.

The journey passed quickly as Mats shared a few childhood stories of mischief she'd gotten into but the trouble she'd also managed to get out of by fluttering her eyelashes and flashing her baby blues.

They were just approaching Moorgate station when Steven suddenly said, 'Do you fancy a walk? There's something I'd like to show you.'

Mats gave him a small surprised look but followed his lead as he stood up to get off the train.

'Where are we going?'

'Have you heard of Postman's Park?'

'No, I can't say I have. What is it?'

'It's easier to show you than to explain. You see, the good thing about working in the City is that it has many little nooks and crannies for people to discover if they take the time to look for them. Have you ever noticed how many churches there are in the City of London?'

'No, I've never really thought about it. I don't come over this side of the bridge very often. My life tends to hang out on the south bank unless I'm going up to the West End for a gig.'

'Then please allow me to be your guide for a few hours and show you some of the delightful treasures that don't normally appear on your usual, run-of-the-mill, tourist guides.'

They walked out of the tube station onto the deserted pavement outside.

'Wow! Where is everyone? It's like a ghost town. Has there been a zombie apocalypse in the last twenty minutes?'

Steven laughed. 'Nope! Welcome to the City on a Saturday. The weekend is the best time to walk around it if you're in the mood for exploring. When the weekday hustle and bustle slumbers, the City opens her arms and lays out her beauty to be seen by those who care to look. Come...'

Without thinking, he took Mats' hand and led her down the main road.

'It's roughly a ten-minute walk.'

'So, how did you discover this Postman's place we're going to?'

'My grandfather loved London and its history and he often brought me here when I was a child. He would point out things to me that most people walk by without seeing every day. He especially loved the churches. He called them "little pockets of peace" and told me that, whenever my soul was troubled, sitting in a church garden would always ease it.'

'Was he a religious man?'

'No, not really, but he did have a point. Church gardens are incredibly peaceful. This garden I'm taking you to see has a couple of churches in its grounds.'

'How many churches are there in London?'

'In the City alone, there are – give or take – about fifty. Before the Great Fire in sixteen sixty-six, there were almost a hundred.'

'Wow! Why so many?'

'I can't really say. I suppose people were more fearful of God back then and the demographic of the area was different too. Now it's all towering office blocks and workers who commute in and out every day. In days of yore, people lived here and went about their day to day lives. It was a densely populated area so I expect more churches were required to accommodate them all.'

'Yeah, I can see that. It's something I've never given

much thought to.'

'Here we are. That didn't take long.'

Steven walked through a gate and led Mats along the path until they were standing in front of a structure which resembled a long, old-fashioned, brick-built bus shelter.

'It's called "The Memorial to Heroic Self-Sacrifice" and it commemorates people who died while saving others. If you read the plaques, some of them are quite amazing.'

He watched Mats as she walked along reading the glazed Doulton tablets and taking in the feats of people long forgotten but who had died as heroes. As he watched, he questioned why he'd felt the need to bring her here to see this. He'd certainly never shown it to any of his previous girlfriends.

'Oh my, some of these are so touching. *"Elizabeth Boxal, aged 17 of Bethnal Green, who died of injuries received in trying to save a child from a runaway horse. June 20 1888"*', Mats read aloud. 'How incredibly moving. And this one, *"Thomas Simpson who died of exhaustion after saving many lives from the breaking ice at Highgate Ponds. Jan 25 1885"* – this is so beautiful, to know these ordinary people will always be remembered for the moments when they became extraordinary.'

'I know. In some ways, the acts of bravery were small but they saved a life while losing a life. It always makes me feel something deep down inside. My grandfather said it was a nice, gentle reminder of how much better our lives are today even though we often don't appreciate that.'

'Your grandfather was a wise man. I take it you were close to him.'

'I adored him. He seemed to be the only member of my family who didn't think the sun shone out of Stuart's backside. He always gave me his undivided attention and Saturday visits into the City were a regular thing. He brought Stuart along once but all he did was whine and

80

whinge that he didn't want to see boring old buildings and memorials to dead people. He rather spoiled the day and never came out with us again.'

Mats moved over to sit on one of the benches and Steven sat beside her. For several minutes there was silence and then she said, 'Your grandfather was right. It is very soothing. I can almost feel all my stress just oozing away.'

Steven sneaked a look to see if she was taking the mickey but her closed eyes and face tilted up towards the sky told him she meant every word.

Following her lead, he closed his own eyes, lifted his face upwards and allowed the quiet solitude to seep into his soul, just as his grandfather had advised.

SIXTEEN

'*Good morning, Mats and Steven, and welcome back to the Marky Sparks Breakfast Show on Smile-A-While Radio. Tell me, how did date number one go?*'

Mats grimaced as she listened to Marky's introduction. How long was it going to take for her to find him less annoying?

'Hi Marky, I can't speak for Mats, but I had a great time. I've never tried archery before but I found it really enjoyable.'

'*That's cool, Steven, we saw the picture on Twitter – hashtag "LoveisontheAir" listeners, if you want to follow along – and it looked like you did well. Mats, what did you think?*'

'Well, Marky, as the picture said, "practise makes perfect" – Steven's first few attempts had the local wildlife flying for cover.'

'*Really? Care to elaborate Steven?*'

'I confess, my first six arrows seemed to have a life of their own and went every which way except where I wanted them to go. One poor pigeon almost met its maker but I soon got the hang of it.'

'*And did you enjoy yourself, Mats?*'

'Yes, Marky, surprisingly, I did. Archery's something I've never considered trying but I rather enjoyed it.'

'*What about the company? Did you enjoy that?*'

'Yes, the instructor was rather tasty!'

'*WHAT?*'

'Only messing with you, Marky! I enjoyed being out with Steven.'

'*And, Steven, did you enjoy being out with Mats?*'

'Yes, she's great company.'

'*So, I have to ask, is there "Love on the Air" for you both? Did Cupid's arrow fly and hit the spot?*'

'It's early days for that yet, Marky, but we didn't part ways full of intense dislike for each other so it's a good start.'

'*That's good to hear, Mats. So, are you both ready for your next date? I have the envelopes ready and waiting. Who's making the decision today?*'

'It's Steven's turn, Marky.'

'*Right then, Steven, what's it going to be – envelope 1 or envelope 2?*'

Mats waited for Steven to give his answer. She sincerely hoped envelope 2 didn't hold a nasty surprise. This would be their mid-week "date" and she wasn't up for anything too outrageous – not on a "school" night.

'I'll have envelope number 1 please, Marky.'

Mats sat up straighter. Why the cheeky little sod... She had to smother the laughter which rose up. So much for being predictable. Steven had just slipped up another little notch in her estimation.

'*Thank you, Steven. And the details for your next date are... You've got it... You'll find out after the break!*'

83

'I don't believe it! A bakery lesson… I chose a bakery lesson!'

'That'll teach you to go off-piste! Now get creaming that butter and sugar while I sieve this flour.'

Mats thrust the wooden spoon at Steven as she picked up the mixing bowl and placed it on the scales. Personally, this wouldn't have been her first choice of the two options which had been contained within the envelopes and it would have been fun explaining away any black eyes or bruises which may have come about from their boxing session, but it was what it was. Steven, on the other hand, was gutted with his selection. The boxing session had been at one of the premier clubs in London and their trainer would have been the current, middle-weight world champion. His name had meant nothing to Mats but apparently everything to Steven.

She looked over at him as he half-heartedly mixed the butter and sugar together.

'Hey, you need to put a bit more effort into it than that, Steven. It must be light and fluffy otherwise your sponges will come out looking like pitta breads!'

'Hmph! Why can't we use a mixer like they do on that TV show? Why do we have to do it by hand?'

'Because, young man, you need to feel the change in the texture to know you have got it right. Machinery is for those who know what they are doing, you do not. Now move your wrist like so… and it will be easier.'

The grey-haired teacher watched Steven for a moment before walking off to the next workstation.

Mats was chewing the inside of her cheeks, trying desperately not to laugh. Steven had managed to beat the mixture too hard and now had a small globule of sticky, buttery mixture perched on top of his gelled hair spikes. Given his less than cheery mood, she didn't think it was the best time to share this with him.

'How's that mixture coming along, Steven? Is it ready for the eggs yet?'

'I don't know, what do you think?' The bowl was thrust under her nose.

'I think it needs another minute or two – shall I do it?'

'If you don't mind.'

'Fine, but you'll need to separate the eggs.'

'Do what?'

Mats gave a little humph of annoyance. She got that this date was not what Steven wanted to do but as he damn well chose it, she'd have more respect for him if he just got on with joining in.

'Separate the eggs... you know, split the egg white from the yolk...'

'How do I do that?'

'Were you not paying attention during the demonstration?'

'Obviously not!'

Mats pressed her lips tightly together to prevent her next comment from escaping, for it contained several words she'd never say in front of her father and didn't think this was quite the place for them either.

'Get a saucer, crack the egg onto it. Take an egg cup and gently place over the yolk. Holding the egg cup firmly, tilt the saucer vertically and shake the egg white into a bowl. Et voila, you have separated the yolk from the white.'

Mats turned her back on Steven and vented her frustration on the unsuspecting butter and sugar mixture. She got that he was disappointed but if he'd bothered to ask her, she'd have told him she was a bit too. Okay, she may not have been aware of the importance of who was teaching them the moves but she'd have loved the chance to try out a bit of ducking and diving, bobbing and weaving. Baking was something she'd done once at school, had hated it enough to change her class and was not high on her must-try-this-again list.

'Have I done enough eggs or do we need more?' Steven's voice was quiet behind her. She turned around and saw he'd split out the six eggs in the box. She ran her eyes over the recipe.

'No, six is perfect.'

'I'm sorry, Mats, for being a stupid, sulky kid tonight. I'm disappointed but I shouldn't be taking it out on you.'

'No, you shouldn't. And, for the record, I would have quite enjoyed trying out boxing.'

'You would?'

'Sure! It would have been fun but here we are, playing at being Mary Berry and Paul Hollywood. That's just the way the envelope opened.'

Steven grinned at her then, the first smile she'd seen all night.

'Well, you're much scarier than I am so you can be Hollywood!'

'Cheeky sod!'

'Am I forgiven for being a brat?'

'I suppose so! Now, come on, let's get this mixture finished and into the tins or the sponges won't cool in time to be decorated.'

'How come you know all this stuff? Did you do girlie cookery lessons at school?'

'Don't be so sexist! I simply listened to the demonstration earlier. And just for the record, I did do a baking lesson at school but detested it so much I changed over to woodwork instead. So there!'

'Well, well, well! Check you out, Leonardo da Vinci!'

'I wouldn't go that far!'

'You've done a better job than me, Steven. My icing was all over the place. You've done a cracking job there'

Steven could feel the heat rising in his cheeks. He wasn't used to compliments although it was nice to hear this one from Mats. He'd behaved badly earlier this evening and he was lucky she'd been so understanding.

They'd been told to decorate their three-tiered creations however they wished and Mats had tried to do some free-hand iced scrolls but they'd been a disaster. He'd stepped up, moved her gently to one side while saying, 'Let me have a go.'

He'd quickly rolled out a slab of white fondant icing, placed it over the sponges and gave Mats the job of smoothing out the creases while he got to work with the food dye and a second lump of icing. By the time Mats had finished, Steven had worked up some dark blue icing which he rolled out, made a few cuts into, and then laid across the top of the cake. He'd grabbed some more icing, cut it into several smaller pieces and, ten minutes later, he'd fashioned them into a small rowing boat, with two occupants, a couple of oars and a champagne-shaped bottle in between them. He found a wooden skewer which he wrapped in the left-over blue icing and then stuck a little crescent shaped moon on the top. He gently pressed the skewer into the cake and stepped back.

'There you go. Our first date immortalised in a cake!'

Mats was shaking her head.

'It's fantastic! I am so impressed. I love it.'

'As do I! That is very good, young man. Simple, cute but most effective. Now I must have a taste to see how good you have baked.'

The class teacher took a sharp knife and cut out a small wedge.

'It is baked well, nice and springy and...,' she placed

a forkful in her mouth, 'it is deliciously moist. Your ganache filling is tasty and not too sweet. I like the hint of lemon you have added, it gives a lovely tang and compliments the fillings perfectly. Well done. I am most impressed. You make an excellent team.'

As she walked over to the next workbench, Steven looked at Mats in delight.

'Did you hear that? We baked a bloody good cake!'

He cut another slice and placed it on a plate between them.

'After you,' he said, handing Mats a fork.

He watched her take a mouthful and close her eyes as she savoured the delicate combination of sponge, ganache, and icing.

'Oh, Steven, it's wonderful. Here, you must try some.'

She scooped more cake onto her fork and held it out for him to try. Steven hesitated for a fraction of a second as he realised the intimacy of the moment although Mats appeared oblivious to it. He leant forward and took the proffered cake.

'Hmm, it's lush. Well done us, I say.'

He looked at Mats grinning away in front of him. She had a little blob of cream on the side of her cheek and she looked decidedly cute.

'Erm, you've got some cake on your face...' He pointed to his own cheek.

'Oh!' She tried to brush it away but only succeeded in smudging it across her chin.

'Here. Let me...' Steven picked up a piece of paper towel, moved in closer and with great gentleness, wiped the sticky smear away.

He was about to step back when their eyes met and for several seconds, the air went still around them. Steven felt his breath catch in his throat as he breathed in the cakey-sweetness of hers. He felt himself being pulled towards her and his eyes took in her soft, parted lips…

'Okay, everybody! Make sure your workstations are clear and all utensils have been washed and put away. Cake tins have been provided for you to transport your creations home. I suggest you place the cake on the lid and put the tin over the top. This will make it easier for you to remove it later. Thank you all for being my guests tonight.'

Steven stepped sharply away and disguised his flustering by clapping enthusiastically along with the rest of the class. He sensed Mats by his side, clapping just as vigorously but he daren't look at her. He was feeling slightly lightheaded and right now, he just wanted to get home and examine the sensations running through him.

'I'm just going to ask if we can buy a second tin, be back in a moment…' Mats' voice broke into his thoughts.

'What for?'

'So that you can take home your half of the cake.'

'No, it's fine, you can have all of it.'

'Well, that's not fair. Besides, I can't eat all of that. What are you trying to do? Turn me into a Weeble?'

Her light jest made him laugh and he felt the tension ease out of him.

'I think it'll take more than a piece of cake to do that, Mats! Take it into the office tomorrow and feed it to whatever cash-strapped band you are giving loft-space to.'

'Ha! We don't have any bands tomorrow, just one solo artist who is also vegan so I don't think it'll be up his street. I'll take some in for Tinks though, he's never said no to food in his life although he's never had a cake that I've baked before so there might be a first time.' She grinned up at him and set about placing the cake in the tin. They caught the bus just around the corner from the baking school and speculated on what the next challenge could be. When it was his stop, Steven asked Mats to text him once she was home and stood waving goodbye when the bus pulled away. As he made the short walk home, he pondered on the fact that Mats had given no indication that she too had sensed the change between them and he began to wonder if the magic of the moment had been his and his alone.

SEVENTEEN

'Oh, blimey! This is bloody gorgeous!'

Penny shoved another piece of cake into her mouth.

'I can't believe you baked this. You've kept that skill quiet.'

'I'll be honest, Pen, it's a skill I didn't know I had. Nice to know I've got something I can fall back on if the studios ever fail!'

'Ah, but you'll need to hook up with Steven to do the decorating.' She slid a sly look in Mats' direction. 'How is love's young dream? Are you both feeling the romance yet?'

'Hardly, Penny. We've only been out four times and two of those weren't really dates.'

'You think? I'd have called the first one a date. Getting pissed on cocktails and bubbles with some bloke you barely know sounds like half the dates I've been on!'

'Well, it does not sound like any of the dates *I've* been on!'

'Then you need to loosen up, babe. You don't know what you're missing.'

'I'd say evil hangovers and beard-rash – both of which I can live without.'

'Talking of beard-rash—'

'Were we?'

'We are now! Have you snogged him yet?'

'PENNY!'

'What? After four dates, it's a pretty obvious question to ask. So, have you?'

'No, I have not! And how many times, it's only been two dates!'

'Why not? I've seen the pictures on Twitter – he's a bit of alright. If he'd fallen out of the ugly tree and hit every branch on the way down, then I would understand your reluctance…'

'Penny! You can't say things like that. Looks aren't everything.'

'I know they're not, honey, but they do make a difference when you want to get jiggy-jiggy with someone!'

'Right, that's it! No more cake for you. Clearly too much sugar is bad for your potty mouth.'

Mats went to lift Penny's plate away.

'Nooooo! Give it back. I'm starving. I've been so busy today I haven't had time to eat.' Penny grabbed the plate and pulled it back towards her.

Mats released her grip and let Penny take possession once more.

'Why didn't you say, I'd have rustled you up some pasta. I've got spuds in – I could pop a couple to bake in the microwave.'

'No, you're fine. This cake is hitting all the right spots.'

'And some of the wrong ones…'

'Okay, I will ask politely, why has this thing not moved along yet?'

'I don't know. I guess it is kind of nice just getting to know each other slowly. We've got another twenty-four "proper" dates to get through so there's not exactly a need to rush.'

'But even so, I'd have expected a kiss to have occurred by now. Not even one on the cheek?'

'Nope!'

'On the hand?'

'Nope!'

'On the—'

'Penny…'

'Okay! Okay! Has there even been a hint of one in the brewing stages?'

Mats remembered back to the night before when Steven had stepped closer to wipe her face. She thought there had been a moment where a spark had passed between them but she wasn't sure. Maybe she was the only one who'd felt the little thrill of that pause in time which occurs just before a first kiss is exchanged. It had felt like everything around them had faded away and they were in a small bubble all on their own.

'Ha! There has been, hasn't there? I can tell from your face!'

Damn! By hesitating before answering, Mats had just given the game away and Penny was no fool – she'd pounced immediately.

'Oh, alright. There was a sort of a moment last night.'

'What kind of moment?'

Mats went over what had occurred the night before and by the time she was finished, Penny was bouncing up and down in her chair.

'Yes! Yes! Yes!'

'Look, don't get excited, it was probably nothing. Most likely all in my imagination.'

'Imagination my ass! I'll bet Steven felt it every bit as

much as you did.'

'Well, he gave no indication of it.'

'Did you?'

'Of course not! I wasn't going to make a fool of myself.'

'Honey, that kinda thinking works both ways. I'm a-guessing that you two will be giving it tongue sandwiches by the end of the weekend.'

'Oh, shut up and eat your cake!'

EIGHTEEN

BARP! BARP! BARP! BARP!

Once again, a skinny arm, with a bony hand balled into a fist, flew out from the duvet-covered mound on the bed and landed on the goose-honking alarm clock with a thump. Silence filled the room and the reed-thin limb was reeled back into its little den of warmth. It was Saturday morning and unlike each weekday morning, the alarm had sounded its rousing alert at a more acceptable eight a.m. The duvet was thrown back and Marky Sparks bounded out of bed. Okay, he concurred that his quality of "bounding" would probably be classed as a "woeful slither" by most other early risers but for him, being vertical within two minutes of the alarm sounding was a damn near miracle!

He instructed his WI-FI speaker to turn on the radio as he made his way into the bathroom and surprised himself by singing along to a few golden oldies while having his shower. When he looked in the mirror to shave, he was even more surprised to find his eyes actually sparkling and the bags underneath were half their usual size.

'Marky, if this is what waking up without a hangover feels like, maybe you should try it more often!' he told himself sternly as he lathered up.

He'd just finished his coffee when the doorbell rang. He popped his mug in the dishwasher, grabbed his jacket, and smiled at the waiting taxi-driver as he locked up. He wouldn't say he was looking forward to today but it was going to be rather interesting.

Forty minutes later, the driver parped his horn and within a few minutes, Mats was locking her own front door, a gym-bag holdall in her hand. The driver stepped out to take the bag from her and opened the back door of the taxi. Mats slipped in and seeing Marky sitting there, gave him a look of thinly disguised disgust.

'Oh! What are you doing here?'

When Dave had suggested they accompany Mats and Steven on this particular outing, Marky hadn't been keen.

'Why do we need to go?' he'd whined, like a petulant teenager.

'Because you need to mend bridges with these guys and get them on your side if you're to have any chance of saving both our skins and the station.'

'But I've been really careful to call them by their preferred names and I've avoided calling Mats' "sweetie" or "babe" because you told me she hates it.'

'I know, Marky, but it's not enough. You need these two to become your new BFF's. You can sense the underlying air of animosity during the on-air conversations – that needs to be sorted otherwise there's no chance of winning any new listeners. Would you want to listen to your morning DJ being snarled at by one of his contestants three times a week?'

'I suppose not...' and with a sigh any self-respecting teenager would've been proud of, Marky had agreed to Dave's proposal and so now, here he was, cocooned in the back of a taxi with a woman who gave every indication of disliking him intensely.

'Morning, Mats, are you well today?' He dug down deep and mustered up his charm offensive – he could do this. He'd win her over if it killed him. He then thought ahead to the forthcoming surprise and realised there was every possibility the day's event might just kill him first.

'I'm fine, thank you. You didn't answer me – what are you doing here?'

'Dave and I thought it would be a good bit of team bonding if all four of us did today's event together.'

'So, is this the surprise part of the day?'

'No, Mats, the surprise is yet to come.'

When they'd been putting the dates together, Dave had mentioned that it might be worth throwing in a few curve balls to keep everything fresh for the listeners. This had been one of them. Neither Steven, Mats or the listeners knew what was on the agenda for today. All that had been revealed was that they would be going on a course and to bring a change of clothing for the evening.

'I see.' Mats turned away and looked out of the window.

For several minutes there was silence until Marky decided he was going to take this bull by the horns.

'Mats, I can't help but get the feeling you don't like me – may I ask why?'

Mats turned her unsettling blue gaze upon him and Marky felt a slight stir in his nether regions. Blimey, this woman had it all going on! That Steven must be made of stone if he wasn't already feeling something for her by now. Finally, she answered him.

'I think you're rude and patronising. Two qualities

97

which I have no time for.'

'When was I rude and patronising to you?' He'd barely spoken to her, for goodness' sake! How could she think that?

'The first two occasions when we were on the air, you spoke over us and the other ladies, you completely ignored Steven and I when we told you we didn't like the names you were using and since we embarked on this farce, your whole demeanour is like you're the one doing us a favour!'

'Oh! I see! But I make a point of using your preferred names now.'

'Yeah, but you've never apologised for how you spoke to us before. At no point have you got your sagging, skinny arse down off your pedestal to try and connect with Steven and I on the same level. Dave gave us the impression that we were all in this venture together but it would appear someone forgot to send you the memo.'

When he failed to reply, she turned her head and went back to looking out at the passing scenery.

Marky mulled her words over in his head. His first reaction had been to make a sharp retort but he clamped his tongue between his teeth and held it back. On any other day, when Mr Jack Daniels was flowing through his veins, he probably would have done but in his refreshingly sober state, Mats words had cut deep.

'I'm sorry,' he said quietly. 'I'm sorry for the lack of respect I've shown to you both and I'm sorry for not realising my bad behaviour sooner.'

Mats looked his way.

'Accepted.'

'Do I really come across as patronising?'

'Hell, yeah! If I may be blunt – you seem to think you're still the great superstar you were back in the nineties and don't seem to realise the world has moved on and didn't take you with it.'

'It's all an act, you know. People expect you to be a certain way and if you don't step up to the plate, they turn against you.'

'Then perhaps you need to consider the type of people you're trying to impress. If they're so shallow they can't accept you're no longer the same man you were thirty years ago, then they shouldn't be in your life.'

He noticed that Mats' voice had lost its hard edge and had softened.

'Although, it might well be that if *you* haven't changed in that time, how can you expect these people to accept a new you?'

'I'm not quite sure what you mean.'

'Well, look at you, Marky – you're still sporting the same hideous hair-do you had when I was a kid. It wasn't the best look back then and it sure ain't doing it for anyone now.'

'But it's my trademark! My hairstyle is my signature.' His hand went up to caress his lanky, blond-grey locks.

'Pat Sharp had the worst mullet on the planet, Marky, and even though that was his trademark, he still had the sense to get rid of it when we hit the twenty-first century. Not only does he now look waaaay sexier but it was also his way of telling people that that was then and this is him now, so deal with it! And people did. What's that expression? "If you want change, then be the change...", something like that?'

'So, you think I should get a haircut?'

'If you really do want to move on from your past, Marky, then it might be the best place to start.' Her voice was gentle now and Marky felt he may just have mended part of the bridge he needed to rebuild.

'Unless of course, all of this is just a bit of flannel to get me onside...' The gentle tone had disappeared and Mats eyes were glaring at him once again.

'No, it's not. Yes, we do need to get along better – I acknowledge that – but this was not how I intended it to happen. Note to self – stick to being drunk, less likely to overshare.' He gave a small grin as he spoke.

Mats grinned back. 'Second note to self – sober self considerably easier for others to tolerate.'

'Thank you for your honesty, Mats, I appreciate it.'

Just then the taxi-driver indicated and pulled into a lay-by.

'First stop, Mr Sparks.'

Marky leant forward, removed an item from the seat pocket in front of him and turned to Mats.

'Right, Mats, I need you to work on the trust aspect of this new budding friendship by putting on this blindfold.'

'What? Why?'

'Because we're close to our destination and I don't want you to spot any signage which would ruin the surprise. See the car parked in front of us,' he pointed through the windscreen, 'Steven is in there being asked to do the same thing.'

Mats looked at him for a full ten seconds before letting out a sigh!

'Oh, I suppose so! Give it here!'

NINETEEN

'You have *GOT* to be pigging well joking me!'

Mats looked at the scene in front of her in dismay! No bloody wonder they'd kept this one a surprise for she would have told them, in no uncertain terms, exactly where to stick it.

'Come now, Mats, where's your sense of adventure?'

Mats looked at Marky standing beside her and was giving serious reconsideration to the friendship path they'd been about to embark upon.

'There is a sense of adventure and there is blind stupidity! This is the latter!'

'D'you know, I've always fancied having a bash on an army assault course. I think it must have something to do with all the episodes of "The Krypton Factor" my grandfather liked to watch.'

'Thanks for the support here, Steven, means a lot!'

'Oh, come on, Mats, it'll be fun. Are you both joining in?' Steven looked at Marky and Dave.

'That's the plan,' replied Dave, 'and to be specific, this is a commando training assault course. Hence the 'C' part of the deal!'

Mats turned to Marky.

'Are you seriously telling me you're up for doing this? That you really think this is a good idea?'

'In all honesty, Mats, I was very NOT up for it when Dave first broached the idea but then he reminded me of how much I used to enjoy doing the assault courses on that daft tv show I hosted and I gave in.'

'Ahem! Not actually true that, is it, Marky?'

'Oh, alright! He said it was probably a good thing I was bailing out as I'm too old and decrepit these days and would never manage to get around one now!'

'Aye, that's more like it! I'll tell you now, guys, he changed his mind faster than Michael Schumacher off the start line!'

'Am I the only one who can see the dangers here? I'll break my neck – I know I will.' Mats looked at the zip wire which brought them into the finishing post where they were currently standing. She wasn't scared of heights or anything, she just knew her upper body strength left a lot to be desired and she had visions of falling off and landing in the thick, black, mud underneath.

'Well, Mats, you've disappointed me! I never had you down as scaredy-cat. I thought you would face up to anything but instead, you're just a big bit of a wuss. Aren't you?' Steven gave her a small dig in the ribs as he spoke.

The same glare which had earlier been focused on Marky Sparks now focused itself on Steven.

'I am not a wuss! How dare you! Right, that does it!' She bent down and grabbed her holdall. 'I'm going to beat all of you when we hit that thing. See you at the starting point!'

As she stomped towards the nearby pavilion and changing rooms, she heard Steven laugh as he said to Dave, 'See, you're not the only one who can use reverse psychology!'

Mats adjusted the helmet on her head, making it sit more comfortably. The legs on her boiler suit were too long so had been rolled up before being tucked into the green socks and sturdy boots. Thankfully, the venue had supplied all the kit they required for she hadn't fancied doing this in her own clothes.

She listened to the course commander as he ran through a few safety instructions and advised them that assistance would be on hand should they run into any difficulties. She looked over to the starting line of the assault course in front of her although there wasn't much to see – some low, stepping-style parallel bars and a brick wall. Beyond the wall was a mystery to them all. The last of the commander's words registered in her brain – the first person over the line was the winner but to also remember they were, first and foremost, a team.

As he raised his arm with the starter's pistol in the air, Mats looked forward and focused on what lay ahead. She recalled seeing a programme on the television some time back and the repeated theme had been that being focused and mentally determined was half the battle in these things.

BANG!

Mats was off the line before the smoke had even cleared above the commander's head.

THUMP! THUMP! THUMP!

Jump!

She was over the parallel bars and flying towards the wall. With a strong push of her knees, she managed to get a good enough purchase with which to pull herself up. She'd always been quite "springy" and this served her in good stead now given her wimpy arm strength.

She hauled herself over the wall in the horizontal

manner she'd seen in various movies, ran a few feet and then threw herself onto her stomach to crawl under the low-lying net. As she pulled herself to her feet, she allowed herself a second to glance over her shoulder to see where the others were and saw them all clearing the wall and heading to the net. They were close but she was ahead, albeit by a small margin. She quickly sprinted to the next obstacle – a vertical wooden wall with ropes hanging down. Once again, she made a leap and managed to grab the rope half-way up. Somewhere, in the deepest recesses of her brain, a memory pulled itself out and pushed its way to the front – use the strength in your legs to push yourself up rather than trying to pull yourself up with your arms.

Mats put this thought into action and found herself at the top of the wall in mere seconds. While going over the top, she caught sight of her team members right below her, working on pulling themselves up the ropes. She was still in the lead but they were gaining on her. She dropped to the ground on the other side, turned and was over the monkey-bars before the others had cleared the crest of the wall. Up the angled rope-net wall she went, down the other side and back on to her stomach again to crawl through the pipe-tunnel in front of her.

When she came back out into daylight, she ran to the metal climbing frame and pulled herself up. Her breath was now coming in short bursts, her sides were beginning to ache but she was determined to keep going. Steven's comment about being a wuss had rankled and she was not going to give anyone the satisfaction of thinking she wasn't up to this.

She got to the top of the frame and with her arms out by her side, walked over the single plank of wood. She had taken her last step and was turning to climb down the other side when she looked up to see both Steven and Dave running along the same wooden planks towards her. There was, however, no sign of Marky. She began descending the frame when she spotted him. He was half-way up the angled rope-net wall but had stopped moving. His arms were thrust through the ropes and his head was leaning against them. He was still in this position when her feet touched the ground. She stopped to see if he was making any effort to get over the obstacle but it didn't look like he was.

Steven landed beside her and called out as he rushed by, 'Hey, Mats, this isn't the finish line – have you given up already?'

Dave was right behind him but he was too puffed to say anything. She looked again at Marky but he still hadn't moved. A quick turn showed her the other two men were already over the next two parts of the course. She turned to give chase but stopped again after only a couple of steps.

'Oh, bloody hell! Every sodding time… What is it with me and damned waifs and strays?'

With these words, she turned on her heel and stepping off the course, ran along the path at the side until she was back at the rope wall. Marky was still hanging where she'd first seen him. She climbed up. His eyes had been closed but now they opened as she drew level with him.

'Hey, Marky, I don't think this is the best place in the world to stop for a snooze.' She gave him a small smile.

'I can't do it, Mats. I'm knackered. I'm too old and too past it for this.'

'Nonsense! Of course, you can do it.'

'No, I can't! Just you go on. I'll see you back at the pavilion afterwards.'

'Marky Sparks, if you think for a minute I'm going to just walk off and leave you behind, you've got another think coming! Remember what the commander said – we're a team! I am not leaving one of my team behind. So, move yourself. We'll do this together. Okay?'

'But—'

'I said, "Okay"?'

Mats wasn't sure if it was a grin or a grimace which hovered around Marky's lips but he slowly pulled his arms in and began to climb the ropes towards the top. Mats followed behind, ready to give words of encouragement if she thought they were required.

The unscheduled pit-stop seemed to have helped Marky regain some energy for he kept pace with her through the tunnel and they cleared the climbing frame at a reasonable pace. Another brick wall loomed ahead.

'I'll jump up first and then help to pull you up,' she called across to Marky as his step wavered.

She sprang up again but didn't make the same clearance she had on the first wall and landed with most of her body still hanging down. She was tired now and found herself struggling to pull herself up. As she began to slip down, she felt two hands beneath her feet, pushing her upwards. Marky was pushing her from below. With his assistance, she soon found herself lying across the top. Marky then made a run for it, jumped up and she helped him over. They both landed on the ground together, ran side-by-side along the uphill path until they came to a high-rise metal frame which had swinging ropes over water pools, more rope climbing, a rope bridge to traverse and what appeared to be the zip-wire to take them to the finish line.

Marky let out a groan when he saw it all.

Mats put her hand on his arm. 'You've got this, Marky, we're on the home stretch now. You can do it – you know you can.'

She gave him a little shove and watched him place his hand on the first metal rung. With words of encouragement constantly falling from her lips, they both finally arrived at the top of the frame. Two instructors were there, ready to help them onto the zip-wire.

'You go first, Mats, you shouldn't be last because you came back to help me.'

'Marky, being first or last no longer matters. It's being part of a team that's more important. We'll do this together. On the count of three, we'll both go.'

She smiled again and Marky smiled back.

'Okay,' she said, 'One… two… three…'

TWENTY

'To Mats!'

Steven, Dave and Marky raised their cocktail glasses in Mats' direction. She tried not to blush but she could feel her cheeks warming up.

'Oh, you guys! Give over!'

She picked up her own cocktail glass and tried to hide behind it. They were now on the second surprise event of the day – cocktail tasting in a small bar just off Piccadilly. Marky and Dave had added this as they felt the assault course was so challenging, a nice reward was merited. That had been the reason for the change of evening wear they'd been instructed to bring.

Mats glanced again at her little trophy sitting on the table in front of them. Steven had won first place but she had won the "Team Player" award. No one had disagreed with the decision.

She caught Sparks' eye and he gave her a small wink. This evening was supposed to have been just for her and Steven but she'd shared the taxi back with Sparks and her mind swung back to the conversation they'd had…

'Thank you again, Mats, for what you did today. It means a lot.'

'It's okay, Marky, you don't have to keep thanking me.'

As this was about the twentieth time he'd done so, Mats was beginning to find it a bit awkward. She hadn't stopped to help him for glory or thanks but just because it was the right thing to do.

'I'm looking forward to these cocktails though, I think I've earned them!'

She made a point of changing the subject and hoped he'd follow her lead.

'It should be a good night although I would give a word of caution because you can get drunk rather quickly on them and the hangovers tend to be absolute killers!'

'Oh, I know that!' She thought back to the morning after her first night out with Steven. 'So, what are you up to tonight, Marky? Got a hot date?'

'Ah, no! It'll be me, a ready-meal and the television.'

'Are you seeing anyone? Do you have a partner?'

When he took his time replying, Mats began to regret asking. She was just about to apologise when he spoke.

'No, I don't have a partner or a girlfriend. I'm not very good on the dating front. I don't stick around for long.'

'I see. May I ask why? Are you one of these blokes who doesn't do commitment?'

'I wanted to do commitment once, very much so, but now it scares me.'

'Why?'

'Because the woman I loved more than anything else in this world was taken from me three weeks before we were due to be married.'

He turned to her and she had to suppress her gasp of shock when she saw the anguish on his face.

'Oh, Marky, I'm so sorry. What happened? If you don't mind me asking?'

'I met Eloise when I began working on my first television show. She was one of the lighting technicians. We didn't get on to begin with – I thought she was a hard-faced, mouthy broad but then, one day, we were having a massive argument...' He stopped and gave a wry, little smile. 'D'you know, I can't even remember what it was about... Anyway, all of a sudden, something just clicked. We became a couple soon afterwards. She was my soulmate. We were so in tune and there wasn't much we disagreed on. I asked her to marry me, she said yes and we began to plan the big day. Everything was going well – Eloise was delighted because her diet had been successful and she'd lost the weight she'd hoped to lose to fit into the dress she'd chosen. Personally, I thought she'd lost too much but you know what you women are like – there's no such thing as losing too much. Anyway, one day she mentioned feeling a bit bleugh but didn't do anything about it. She reckoned she was simply tired from rushing around trying to fit work and wedding stuff into too little time. A few days later, she collapsed at work and was rushed to hospital. That's when we found out she had cancer. Riddled with it, she was. The doctors gave her three months, the cancer took her in two. If we'd known she wouldn't see our wedding day, we'd have brought it forward but we went with what the doctors said and thought we had time.'

'Oh, my goodness, Marky, I had no idea. I'm so sorry.' Mats could see that, even now, he was struggling with his grief.

'Since then, I've found relationships difficult. I always leave before I get too close. I just have this deep fear of being hurt all over again.'

'But you can't go through life always worrying like that. It's not good for you. And it must be so lonely too.'

'I confess that I do spend most weekends alone. I rarely date anymore because I can no longer face the part where I break things off.'

'Well, in that case, I think you and Dave should join us this evening. Don't go home to an empty house or flat tonight. Hang out with us and have a laugh.'

'I can't do that – this is supposed to be your date night. How are you going to get it on if you've got a couple of old fogeys hanging out with you?'

'I won't tell Dave you called him an old fogey – I don't think he'd thank you for it. Besides, when dating, it's normal to occasionally go out with friends.'

'Steven might object...'

'I doubt it. He's actually quite laid-back. And besides, we've all had such a good time together today, it seems only right to carry it on into the evening. Call Dave and tell him there's been a change of plan.'

When Marky came off the phone, Mats pulled him up on one thing that had been bugging her for a couple of weeks.

'Marky, I need to ask... what gives with the name, huh? Further to what we were chatting about earlier, don't you think "Marky" is a bit too... well... young for a middle-aged man?'

'I only get called "Marky" in showbiz circles. My mum and sister call me Mark, the few friends I've known since I was a kid call me Sparks. "Marky Sparks" came about it because it sounded good back when I was first starting out.'

'But Dave's your friend and he calls you "Marky"?'

'It's a work thing. We feel it's better if he sticks with the stage-name so there's less chance of slipping up whenever we do public gigs.'

'I see. So, Mark Sparks, did you do something to upset your parents that they named you this way?'

'It was my dad's idea of a joke. I was a difficult birth and mum was housebound for a while after she had me. This meant dad had to register my birth. I should have been called Joseph after my grandfather. On the way to the registry office, my dad thought it would be funny to change that to Mark, just to wind my mother up. What he didn't realise, the daft prat, was that you couldn't go back and change it afterwards! My mother, apparently, went through the roof and I've had to live with being Mark Sparks ever since. Or, when I was at school, Marks and Sparks! Such fun!'

'Oh dear!' Mats tried to contain her laughter but failed. 'I'm sorry but that is rather funny.'

'It's okay. I've grown used to it over the years.' Marky grinned back.

'Look, I have to be truthful here, I feel silly calling you "Marky" – it doesn't sit right with me so I'm gonna call you Sparks, if that's alright with you? Obviously when we're on air, I'll stick with Marky but whenever we're in situations like this and away from public occasions, I'd be much happier with Sparks.'

'As I said, Mats, it's friends who call me Sparks…'

'Then, I suppose we'll need to be friends.' She stuck out her hand and after a brief second of hesitation, Sparks took a hold and they shook on it.

'Friends,' he said, with a happy smile.

When the next tray of cocktails arrived at their table, Mats picked up her glass.

'Right, it's my turn to make a toast.'

She looked at the three men in front of her, raised her glass and said, 'To friendship.'

TWENTY-ONE

Steven looked at his reflection in the mirror and gave his bow-tie a slight tweak.

'Never straight, always slightly crooked,' he muttered to himself, as he recalled his grandfather's words the first time he'd had to dress in black-tie attire. When he'd asked why, he'd been told it was supposed to suggest the bow was a proper hand-tie rather than a clip on. He gave his shoulders a quick brush with his hand, tugged the jacket a little straighter along the bottom and then smiled with satisfaction. It was nice to wear the suit for something other than the office Christmas Ball and the occasional industry awards ceremony. He checked his watch… oops, better get a move on – the car would be arriving soon.

He made his way down to the lounge and stood by the window to look out for the car turning into his street. Mats had already been picked up for she'd sent him a text to let him know she was on her way. A shiver of excitement ran through Steven. This was the first time he'd been to a film premier and he couldn't wait to walk along the famous red carpet which came with these events.

He was looking forward to tonight in more ways than one – the idea of just sitting down and relaxing was more than a little appealing. As fun as these "dates" were turning out to be, they were also just a little exhausting. The darts night last week had been a laugh and being an elephant keeper at Whipsnade Zoo, along with meeting some of their other residents, had been out of this world. It had, however, also been a long day by the time their travel to and from Bedfordshire was added in. He was more than ready to kick back and chill while sipping posh bubbles in a nice dark cinema.

More than that, however, he couldn't wait to spend more time with Mats. He'd found himself beginning to count the days and hours until they were together again and suspected she might be on the cusp of feeling the same for on the days they were apart, they spent a considerable amount of time texting and phoning each other. Whenever he sent her a text or messaged her on Facebook, he found himself holding his breath until she replied. Sometimes, the speed of her replies made him wonder if she was doing the same. He saw a pair of headlights swing into his road and at the same time, his phone pinged. It was Mats' texting to let him know she was here.

'Hey, you,' he said in greeting, as the uniformed driver closed the door at his side. He leant over to give her a small kiss on the cheek before looking around him. 'This is a bit swanky! Very nice!'

'I confess I was rather amused to see a big, black limo pull up outside the door. It's pretty groovy though. Would you like a glass of Champagne, Patsy?'

'Is it Bolly, dahling?'

''Fraid not, Pats, it's the cheap stuff.'

'Oh, well, it'll do. Fill me up, Eddy!'

Steven took a large sip of the chilled wine and as it slipped down his throat, he felt himself relaxing. He took a hold of Mats hand and gave it a gentle squeeze.

'Are you looking forward to this evening?'

'I am, as it happens. I do like Tom Cruise so I'm thrilled to be attending this premier. I've never been to one of his before.'

'So, you've been to other film premiers?'

'I have. Only a handful though. Sometimes, if one of the bands who've recorded at the studio appears on a soundtrack or has performed the theme tune, we'll receive courtesy invites. I only go, however, if it's a film I would like to see. I don't attend them all.'

'Well, that makes you quite the old hand at this. I will be following your lead to ensure I don't make a fool of myself.'

'Oh, there's not much to it. We just get out of the car and walk up to the entrance while smiling and waving at the crowd. We won't get any press interest or have to pose for photographs like the big celebs do – we're not newsworthy, or famous enough, for them.'

'Ah, I wouldn't be too sure about that, Mats.'

'What do you mean?'

Steven pulled out his phone and looked at the text he'd received from Dave an hour earlier. He passed it to Mats for her to read.

'*The video has gone viral and you need to break the news to Mats gently...* What exactly does he mean?' She looked at him in confusion as she handed his phone back to him.

'As you know, the video, which we didn't realise was being filmed at the commando course, was put up online for the listeners to view last week.'

'Yeah, I know about that. Permission to release photographs and videos online was within the contract. I don't have a problem with it.'

'You might, however, have a problem with the fact it has now been viewed over six-hundred-thousand times and the number is increasing by the hour. The radio station's followers on both Facebook and Twitter are almost hitting half a million.'

'But surely that's a good thing? Isn't that one of the aims of all this – to increase exposure for the station and grow their audience share of the market? What I don't understand is why you "need to break the news to me gently"!'

'It is and no one is complaining about that. The bit I need to tell you is that someone has doctored the video. It now focuses primarily on you... and the fact you gave up a possible win to go back and help Marky finish. It's YOU everyone is talking about. Here, look at your Twitter page – *you* now have nearly three-hundred-thousand followers.'

'How many?' She took the phone from him again and stared at her Twitter page on the screen. 'Flaming shitballs!' She looked up at him again and Steven could see the panic on her face.

'Hey, it's alright, there's nothing to worry about. Well, unless you have dead bodies buried in your cellar at home of course...'

'No, there are no dead bodies—'

'Well, that's a good start!'

'—They've all decomposed by now!'

'WHAT?

'Ha! Gotcha!' Mats giggled as she took another drink of Champagne. Steven let out a small sigh of relief. Her panic had been temporary. It had been surprising to see it though as she was always so calm and level-headed. Even when faced with the assault course, she hadn't panicked, she'd simply been horrified!

'Are you okay now?'

'Yeah! The great thing about the internet is that something else always comes along quickly and we'll be forgotten within a day or two. As my old granny used to say, "Today's news is tomorrow's chip paper!" I doubt anyone will remember my name by this time next week, Steven. Now, how do you fancy a quick top up of bubbles? We're not far from Leicester Square and it'll soon be time for you to strut your funky stuff up the red carpet.'

Steven let her refill his glass and sat back in the plush leather seat. He could see through the windscreen that they had joined the cavalcade of cars waiting in line to drop off their V.I.P guests. While the line ahead was slow moving, it didn't take long for them to reach the crowd-control barriers. He watched the myriad faces pass by, straining to see beyond the smoked glass windows which protected him from their view. He looked at Mats and found her watching him.

'It's a bit weird, huh? You feel like an exhibit in the zoo.'

'Yes, it is strange, watching people trying to scrutinise you.'

'If it helps, and not meaning to undermine you in any way, they're actually trying to see if it's some big celebrity in the car. Or someone from Love Island which, in their minds, equates to the same thing.'

Steven gave a small laugh. 'Actually, it does help. While I also have no bodies – dead or decomposing – in my cellar, or loft as the case may be, I still wouldn't want that level of scrutiny directed at me. I'm happy to be a nobody.'

'You're the brother of a pretty famous I.T developer…'

'A brother who likes to keep his limelight to himself and not share it with anyone else!'

Steven heard the bitterness in his voice and gave a

laugh to try and cover it up. Mats, however, was not fooled.

'Why do I get the feeling there's more to your story with Stuart than just mere sibling rivalry? What have you not told me?'

He looked away and saw the car in front had dispelled its guests. They were next. He turned to Mats and gave her his widest grin.

'It's us next, you ready to go?'

When she didn't reply, he said, 'I promise I'll tell you. Just… not tonight. I want to enjoy this moment.'

She reached across and took his hand.

'Then let's get to it!'

The driver pulled the car up to the stopping point, stepped out to open the door and Mats slipped gracefully out. Steven slid across the seat and followed her. In the bright lights beaming down onto the red carpet, he saw her outfit for the first time. Her dark scarlet, ankle-length dress clung to her figure in all the right places. It wasn't so tight as to be a second skin but tight enough to show she was a lady. His mother would have approved. When she turned, she revealed the dress had a deep V at the back and a split which ran to above the knee. Her hair was pinned up on her head in loose curls and her feet were shod in black patent shoes with red soles. Steven wasn't that up on ladies' fashion but even he knew a pair of Christian Louboutin's when he saw them. In her hand was a small black patent clutch and a fine, silk throw which she allowed to casually fall and drape on the floor. Steven couldn't help but be impressed. Mats may have only walked the red carpet a "handful of times" but she certainly had the moves down to a fine art. She could have been as much of a celebrity as the movie stars the crowd had gathered to see.

Once he was standing beside her, an assistant wearing a headset and a promo T-shirt of the film, came over and said they were clear to go. He held his arm out to Mats and she slipped her hand into the crook of his elbow. She flashed a smile at him and they turned to walk towards the door.

For the first couple of seconds, everything seemed normal but then he became aware of a change in the crowd. It started as a small ripple of voices whispering but quickly grew into a roar of shouting. Suddenly, the cameras around them went crazy.

'MATS! LOOK OVER HERE!'

'HERE, MATS, SMILE FOR THE CAMERAS.'

'MATS, WHERE DID YOU GET YOUR DRESS?'

'MATS…'

'MATS…'

'MATS…'

All around them, people were screaming at her while cameras and phones were being thrust across the barriers as people tried to get close. She looked up at him and while she was maintaining the wide smile on her face, her eyes told him a different story.

As subtly as he could, Steven quickened his pace as he aimed to get her through the big double doors ahead. All he could hear, coming at them from every direction, were people screaming and shouting her name.

It felt like an eternity but eventually they were inside the cinema and the noise outside subsided.

'What the hell was that, Steven?' She stared at him in bewilderment.

'I think, Mats, that you've probably gone even more viral than we'd anticipated. I sort of suspect you may not be chip paper any time soon.'

'But… why? I don't get it. I'm nothing special. I'm *no one* special. There are far better people out there who deserve recognition.'

'People don't see it that way. Doctors who cure cancer

and firemen who save lives are not considered newsworthy but go viral on Twitter, and everyone wants a piece of you. The priorities of the world are arse-about-tit and there's nothing you, nor I, can do about it.'

'Hmm! I never thought I'd see the day when I'd be the focus of all that shit and I don't think I really like it that much.'

He felt her slip her hand into his and hold it tightly. A steward came forward, presented them both with glasses of Champagne and offered to show them to their seats as the movie was due to start shortly.

Once seated, Mats turned to him.

'Thank you,' she said.

'What for?'

'For staying by my side out there. It was rather scary.'

'Mats, I'll be right by your side for as long as you need me to be.'

She didn't reply to that but instead smiled, took his hand again and turned back to face the screen.

As the lights went down, and the vast red and gold curtains began to slowly glide open, Steven realised he'd meant every word.

TWENTY-TWO

"C FOR COMPASSION" screamed the Entertainment & Arts headline in the on-line newspaper which Dave had printed off.

"C-ING KINDNESS" yelled another.

"MATERNAL MATS" hollered a third.

"CAT PAW PRINTS FOUND ON THE MOON!" bellowed the fourth.

'Seriously?' Marky pointed at the latter.

'Printed out for the sake of context.'

'Dave, there are times when I wonder about you.'

Dave grinned at him. They were sitting in a small pub down a side street in Covent Garden. All the pubs in the vicinity of the radio station had suddenly become rather busy and one of the secretaries had informed him that people were waiting there in the hope of seeing either Steven or Mats. Suddenly, everyone wanted to see them and know them. By default, their celebrity status had also pulled Marky back into the spotlight as he was the one who'd brought them together.

'I think we can say our plan has worked, Dave.'

'I would say we can – with bells on, mate!'

'So, where do we go from here?'

'What do you mean?'

'Do we continue with their alpha-dating?'

'Too right we do! If those Twitter numbers are translating into listeners, then we'd be off our trollies not to.'

'We'll need to check that both Mats and Steven are up for it first. I have a feeling Mats won't be too chuffed with this level of exposure.'

'Tough! She signed a contract. She's ours for another eight dates – or four weeks. Whichever you prefer.'

'I know that, Dave, but I don't think anyone foresaw this outcome. It's gone more than a little bit mental you know.'

Marky knew Mats would not be happy about this. Over the last ten days, there had been text messages where she'd asked him how he was, what was he up to and had generally shown an interest in him. It had been a long time since anyone had done that and he didn't want to jeopardise this new budding friendship.

'If I didn't know you as well as I do, Marky, I'd say you had a soft-spot for the woman?'

'Then it's a good thing you do know me well for I can assure you I don't. I like her and I respect her. We're becoming friends, nothing more, and I don't want to see her upset.'

'Look, we'll try to protect her as much as possible. Although, there's bound to be fringe benefits for her too.'

'Meaning what, exactly?'

'She has her own business, that recording studio. Any media attention Mats gets will reflect onto her business. You know as well as I do there's no such thing as bad publicity.'

'Actually, Dave, I think you'll find there is – just ask

Gerald Ratner!'

'Who?'

'Google him!'

Marky picked up his mug of tea and was unamused to find it empty. He stood up to get another. Nodding at Dave's glass he asked him if he wanted another beer.

While waiting at the bar, Marky caught sight of his reflection in the mirror behind the spirit bottles. A sad-looking old man stared back at him with hair too long for his age and a shirt that belonged in a museum. Mats was right, he mused, the time had more than come for him to grow up. There was a good hairdresser a few streets away from the pub, he'd pop in when they left here and see if they could fit him in. Now that he'd made the decision, he didn't want too much time to dwell on it as he knew he'd only change his mind if he did.

'What gives with the cups of tea, Marky? You'd normally be on your third or fourth pint by now.'

'I woke up and smelt the coffee! The day after the assault course, and those cocktails, I woke up with the mother of all hangovers. I thought about how I used to be able to run those things with one arm tied behind my back and yet that day, I barely managed to get a third of the way round before collapsing. It made me realise how much I've let myself go. So, I decided to sort things out.'

What Marky wasn't sharing was that he had, quite literally, smelt the coffee. Or rather, the Jack Daniels he liked to spike it with! The smell of the booze, on top of the hangover he'd been nursing, had been too much and had sent him running to the bathroom where he'd thrown up like it was an Olympic sport. Lying against the cool wall tiles afterwards, he'd vowed to give up the drink and get his act together. The patience Mats had shown him the day before and the support she'd given, had touched something deep down inside him and he felt a slightly better person for it. He'd decided it was time to build on that so here he was, ten days later and still booze free. It hadn't been as easy as he'd thought it would be and more than once he'd really craved a few tots – especially in his first morning coffee when he got up – but he'd struggled through and had to admit he was beginning to feel better for it. He was even sleeping more soundly and had woken up that day totally refreshed and raring to go – even at silly o'clock in the morning.

'Well, good on you, dude. I must say, you're not looking quite as pasty-faced either so there must be something in it. Keep it up for who knows, with all this new-found glory, you may be asked to do some interviews. You want to be looking your best for those.'

'Good point. I think it might be worth speaking with the PR department tomorrow. They'll need to get a handle on the situation if this wave of interest continues.'

'Do we have a PR department, Marky?'

'I think you'll find Janice looks after that side of things.'

'But… I thought Janice was HR?'

'Welcome to working for a small, two-bob-bit, radio station, Dave!'

TWENTY-THREE

Swatterhouse put down his fork, picked up the remote control and paused the large, sixty-inch, television in front of him. He leant forward and took a good look at the couple frozen on the screen. So, this is who all the chatter in the office today had been about.

He wound back the news segment for another listen, picking up his fork to continue eating while the broadcaster gave him the information he'd so far missed out on – basically a couple who'd been introduced via a blind date on the radio and who were now being sent on a number of alphabet-themed dates to see if they could fall in love. He gave a small dismissive shrug as he shovelled his lamb bhuna and pilau rice into his mouth. He was about to fast forward to the second half of the film he'd been watching when the scene on the television changed and a video clip popped up showing the woman running back from her lead position on what looked like an assault course to chivvy up a team-mate who'd fallen behind. The lens zoomed in, providing a close-up of a considerably older, but still recognisable, Marky Sparks looking almost half-dead as he held onto the ropes for dear life. What everyone was talking about, however, was the look of compassion on the woman's face. There was no audio to the video but the reporter was doing a voice over and advised a lip reader had provided what she believed was a reasonable interpretation of the dialogue which, in short, was the woman encouraging the DJ to keep moving forward.

The segment closed with the reporter talking once again to the camera and informing whoever was watching that the video had gone viral and had now had over one and a half million views with no sign of that slowing down.

Swatterhouse paused the television again and stared at it for some time, his brain mulling over what he'd just watched and heard.

While he was pondering, his gaze slowly swung around the room. On the wall to the right of the television was a framed front page of "The Weekday News". The headline announced, **"Grooving Guy Garry is Gay!"** Ah, it had been one hell of a shock to the nation that day. Millions of teenage girls had sobbed into the knickers they'd been planning to throw at the handsome, young heart-throb when he'd gone out on tour to promote his second, record-busting, album. Swatterhouse was still more than a little bit proud of that story.

His eyes moved over to the frame on the other side of the television – his second favourite coup. **"Samantha's Sexy Substance Snorting"** was the bold headline above the photograph of a once-famous soap actress shoving cocaine up her nose. She'd been booted off the soap and he'd been booted out of the marital home by his wife who'd said she'd had enough of him ruining people's lives. She hadn't been so quick to release her hold on his wage packet though and still lived in the swanky house his lifetime of dirt-digging had paid for.

Swatterhouse placed the now empty plate on the floor,

took a swig of his beer and pulling his lap-top off the table, booted it up. Every one of his senses was screaming there was a story here to be found. And if anyone was going to find it, it would be him. After all, he'd been turning the screws on the rich and famous for the best part of thirty years – he knew when to trust his instincts.

TWENTY-FOUR

Mats pushed her front door closed and leant against it, kicking off her shoes with a sigh of relief and letting the shopping bags in her hands drop to the floor. She was home at last and for the first time in what felt like an eternity, she had a Saturday night in. It had been necessary to take a break from her dating adventures this week due to work commitments in the office. Sid, her weekend manager, was on holiday and she'd had to cover today. Saturday was the busiest day of the week for that was when the new kids on the block came in, having worked Monday to Friday to earn the bucks to pay for their studio time. It was rare for them to have an empty studio on a Saturday and today had been no exception. She never worked on a Sunday though. From the early days when she and Tinks had worked six days solid, Sunday had always been their golden day off. She used to spend it with her dad but since he'd moved to Devon, she would either be home alone or hanging out with Penny.

The chimes from the old grandfather clock in the dining room made her move swiftly through to the kitchen although the warm, beefy smell which permeated the house told her she had nothing to worry about.

She plonked the shopping bags on the table, lifted the lid on the slow cooker and gave the stew inside a stir. The fragrant steam assaulted her senses and Mats hoped the taste was equal to the smell. She went to the fridge, took out the dumplings she'd made the night before and carefully dropped them into the pot, replacing the lid before bending down to check the heat on the oven. Thank goodness for timers, she thought, as it was perfectly hot and ready for the baked potatoes she just had to wash.

A few minutes later, everything was as prepped as it could be. The bottle of wine was breathing, another was chilling in the fridge along with a few bottles of beer and cans of cider. The custard on the sherry trifle had set and once she'd grabbed a shower and changed into her comfies, she would whip up the cream to smooth across the top.

Mats jogged up the stairs and wondered what Dave and Sparks would say if they knew she was spending the evening with Steven. There had been nothing in the contract to say they *couldn't* spend time together outside of the radio's organised events but they both felt it wouldn't go down too well if it was known. So, tonight was a secret just between the two of them. Even Penny didn't know.

It wasn't that their "dates" weren't enough but the requirement to share photographs and then talk about the experience on live radio afterwards kind of took the intimacy out of them. When they'd been bobbing happily down the canal on Wednesday night, enjoying the unusual experience of their HotTug, people had been lined up along the towpaths shouting and waving to them. All that attention would cool even the hottest ardour never mind one which was still trying to come to the boil.

On the way home afterwards, Mats had suggested that, "off-the-record", Steven came round for dinner and a movie on Saturday night. Two conditions were attached to the offer. The first being that they told no one of their plans and the second that they had to wear their comfiest clothes. NO dressing up was allowed. Steven had agreed immediately.

Mats paused in pulling on her fluffy, slouchy socks to ponder on how she felt. When Penny had asked her earlier in the week if she liked Steven, she hadn't hesitated in replying yes, she did. When Penny had followed up with how much, she'd come unstuck because she simply didn't know. There had been hand holding and pecked kisses on cheeks but nothing more than that. The moment from their baking class hadn't been repeated and Mats had now put it down to her own imagination. After nine dates, she honestly couldn't say where she was on the emotional scale where Steven was concerned. While it hadn't been her plan when she'd made the suggestion, she kind of hoped to have a better idea of where this "thing" was going after tonight.

Steven pulled into the parking space he'd been lucky to find just four doors away. He had dithered all day over whether to drive to Mats this evening or take a taxi. He didn't know what kind of message either one would give. In the end, he'd popped round to Neil and Emma's to get their opinion, safe in the knowledge they would keep his secret. Neil had all been for him getting a taxi – 'You can use it as an excuse for stopping over, mate,' he'd leered – but Emma, after giving her husband a sharp dig in the ribs, came up with a better suggestion. 'Drive over and if things aren't going too well, you have an excuse for not drinking and getting out of there at a reasonable time. If things *are*

going well, and you're both all relaxed, you can get a taxi home and we'll take you back in the morning to collect your wheels.' Steven had kissed her on both cheeks and told her how wonderful she was. Naturally, she'd agreed.

Carefully moving the bunch of tulips he'd brought to his left-hand, Steven pushed the doorbell. He was surprised to see only one nameplate and doorbell for he knew that most of these large, three-storey houses had been made-over into flats. He'd looked at a few in this area before he'd settled on Herne Hill.

'Hey, come on in. Did you find it okay?'

Steven walked in and found himself in a nice, bright hallway. He handed the flowers and bottle of wine he'd brought to Mats and shrugged off his jacket. She pointed towards the coat stand in the corner and he hung it on a spare hook.

'Wow!' he said, as he looked around. 'This is still a house?'

'Yup, one of the few non-conversions in the street. You've got no idea how many letters I find behind the door every week from developers wanting to buy it and split it all up.'

They walked down a small flight of stairs into the kitchen which was modern and airy. A wall of bi-fold doors was directly opposite him and the garden lights lit up a decking area which preceded the lawn.

'I see you stuck to the remit, nice one!'

Steven looked down at his loose, jogging pants. 'Well, you did say it had to be comfies and these are what I chill-out in at home.'

'Hey, I'm not knocking them. I'm delighted you took me at my word. The purpose of tonight is to kick back, relax and not be on show or standing on occasion – tonight is our chance to be real with each other.'

'Real works for me. And something smells absolutely

delicious.'

'Beef stew with dumplings and baked potatoes. Is that alright for you?'

'More than alright, thank you.'

'Would you like a beer, wine or cider? Or if you would rather have a soft drink, I have Coke or orange juice?'

'I've driven over but as we're about to eat, I'll have a beer for now. Thank you.'

Mats handed him a bottle and then moved over to the stew. She lifted the lid before turning to say, 'Everything is ready whenever you are. Do you want to relax in the lounge for a few minutes first or would you like to eat now?'

'I'm flexible, whatever you prefer.'

'Then I suggest we eat first as that will allow us to relax properly afterwards'

She placed some heat mats on the table, carried over the stew pot and put it on top of them. A bowl of baked potatoes landed next to it along with a plate laden with big, thick, slices of crusty bread.

His eyes must have given him away because Mats said, as she sat down, 'You need to have crusty bread to soak up the gravy.'

'Good point.'

'Well, tuck in.'

Steven put a few ladles of stew on his plate and added a baked potato next to it. He watched with amusement as Mats took a potato, sliced it open and then ladled the stew over the top.

'I wish I'd thought of that…'

'There's plenty of spuds, you can do it on the next one.'

For a short time, there was silence as they ate. The stew was as delicious as it looked and the big meaty chunks simply melted in his mouth. When Mats said he was welcome to seconds, Steven didn't need to be told twice.

'This really is tasty, Mats, thank you.'

'You're welcome. It's my grandmother's recipe. She enjoyed being in the kitchen and was always scribbling notes in the margins of recipe books. When I'm feeling brave, I have a delve and try some out. This is one of the easier options and it's never let me down yet.'

'Were you close to your grandmother?' Apart from her unusual eye colour, this was the first time Mats had shared anything further about her family and Steven was keen to learn more.

'Yes, quite close but then, we did live under the same roof for several years so it would have been difficult not to be.'

'I see. Was she unwell and that's why she came to live with you?'

Mats smiled at him. 'As it happens, we came to live with her. Here. In this house.'

'Oh!'

'She came to "keep house" for a "professional gentleman" – her words, not mine – not long after the war. He was a single gentleman who never married. Somewhere along the line, Granny fell pregnant and gave birth to my mother. It was only when she was dying that she revealed the professional gentleman had been the father. Turns out, they'd been having relations for many years but neither was inclined to make a big deal about it or get married. When he died, Granny inherited the house and she, in turn, left it to my mum.'

'When did you move in? Can you remember?'

'I think I was about five or six. Granny's suite was up in the loft when she was the housekeeper. Before we moved in, she had some alterations done and turned it into a nice little studio flat. She said the house was too large for her on her own and it made no sense for my parents to be struggling with two jobs, a mortgage and childcare when there was more than enough space here for everyone. She would keep out of the way in her little flat and we could have the rest.'

'What did your parents do for a living?'

'My mother was a West End actress; my father was a musical producer and director. He also worked in the West End and that was how he and my mother met.'

'Blimey! That must have been exciting for you.'

'Not really. Showbiz stuff kind of loses its sparkle when you grow up surrounded by it. My mum loved what she did and achieved a moderate degree of fame and success. The same with my dad. His name might mean something to theatre-going aficionados but I doubt the man in the street would know who he was.'

'Did they want stardom and glory?' Steven was fascinated by Mats' story. His own parents were so suburban, they made beige paint look like it should be centre stage at the Rio Mardi Gras!

'I believe my mum always wanted more although my dad seemed happy with how his career panned out. Mum, however, absolutely doted on me – I never had any doubts over how much my parents loved me – and I believe that was the biggest reason behind us moving in with Granny; mum wasn't happy leaving me with babysitters every night. She told me it was okay before I started school because I could go to the theatre with them and we'd all sleep late the day after but that wasn't practical once formal education came along. Granny became my night-time babysitter.'

'She didn't mind?'

Mats shrugged. 'She never seemed to. All my childhood memories are happy ones, being surrounded by three adults who only ever seemed to have my best interests at heart.'

'But you never got any brothers or sisters?'

'No, I'm an only child, as you already know. Granny was an only child, as was my mum and I am too. To be honest, I suspect it was a career choice on my mum's part. I was enough to appease my father but she wasn't going to jeopardise her career by falling pregnant a second time.'

'You don't still live with your parents, do you?' Steven took a quick glance around the kitchen but could see nothing to suggest other people also inhabited the space.

'No!' Mats gave a little giggle. 'We are quite alone.'

'Oh… I didn't mean…' he felt his face flush at Mats interpretation of his words.

'I'm teasing you!' She gave his arm a gentle swipe before standing up to clear away their plates. 'No, you stay where you are,' she said, as he stood to help. 'These will be going straight into the dishwasher. I've made sherry trifle for dessert – shall I load up a couple of bowls and we can take it into the lounge to eat while we choose a movie?'

'That sounds like a good plan to me. How about I refill our glasses?' With the booze in the pudding and the couple of bottles of beer he'd had over dinner, the taxi versus driving decision had been made.

It was only as the opening credits of "Deadpool" were rolling that Steven realised how adeptly Mats had changed the subject when he'd touched on her living arrangements. The next obvious question would have been where were her parents now but she'd somehow managed to body swerve it rather neatly. He couldn't help but wonder why.

TWENTY-FIVE

Mats made a point of sitting next to Steven on the sofa when she brought their trifle through. She hoped he hadn't noticed her moving the conversation away from her parents – it hadn't, after all, been particularly subtle.

It wasn't that she didn't want to share more with him, if anything, it was quite the opposite – she felt incredibly relaxed with him and had been happy telling him about her childhood and Granny. She just wasn't ready to share the next part of her story – not yet anyway. Maybe one day… But then, she'd been with Vic the Prick for a year and she'd never told him so maybe she wouldn't. Time would tell.

She focused her attention on the screen in front of her. "Deadpool" might not be the kind of film to enhance what should have been a romantic date but when they'd exclaimed in unison that it was a brilliant film as they'd scrolled through the on-screen options, the decision was made to watch it. Besides, she mused, it's a sort of romance movie – Ryan Reynolds only turns into a mutant because he wants to live longer to be with the woman he loves. In its own way, that is rather romantic.

She leant forward to place her empty bowl on the coffee table and as she sat back, Steven lifted his arm and said, 'Fancy a snuggle? I can protect you when it's the scary bits.'

Mats let out a laugh as she closed the gap between them and nestled into his embrace. 'Steven, let's be honest here – I'm more likely to be protecting YOU at the scary bits!'

'Okay, okay! Couldn't you just pander to my fragile male ego this once?'

'Oh, go on then, be my protector.'

'My lady, I will always be your champion and guardian.'

He placed a small kiss upon her head and squeezed her shoulder gently. Mats felt the grin on her face grow wider and was glad Steven couldn't see it as she wasn't yet sure she was ready for him to know just how much "in like" with him she was falling. When she'd opened the door this evening and he'd heeded her request to dress in comfies, she had felt her heart give a little jump. Whenever she'd asked Victor to dress down, he'd still always looked as though he was about to head out to some posh, Chelsea wine bar. He'd been so intent on always looking good that he'd never understood what it was to have a night off. Steven, on the other hand... he'd nailed it the first time around. He got it and he also got her. As they sat chatting over dinner, she came to realise that the more time she was spending with him, the more he was growing on her. Her instincts were telling her that that was a good foundation upon which to build this brewing relationship. She placed her arm over his midriff and snuggled in a little bit closer as a happy and content feeling washed over her.

Three hours and one dose of Ryan Reynolds and then Julia

Roberts later, Mats switched off the television. The grandfather clock had just begun his midnight chimes and they resonated in the silence.

'I think it's time, Cinderella, for this ugly sister to go home.'

'You're not my sister…'

'Hey! You're supposed to say I'm not ugly! Just for that, I'm going to have to tickle you…'

'NO! Don't you dare!'

Mats tried to escape but Steven had been too quick and his fingers were running around her stomach, just under her ribcage.

'Stop it,' she squealed through her laughter. 'I'm sorry, I'm sorry, I didn't mean to suggest you were ugly!'

'Ah, it's too late now! I am the tickle monster and you are at my mercy!'

Mats squealed again as he waggled his fingers in front of her. She didn't have many penetrable defences but fingers under her rib cage would lay her out every time. People said it was mind over matter but she'd never been able to manage it.

Steven went for her ribs again and she squirmed about on the sofa, trying to get away from the fingers that seemed to hone straight in on the sweet spots which rendered her incapable of moving. She gasped for air in between her fits of giggles.

'Please, no more…' she begged. 'I'm going to wet myself if you carry on!'

'Ewww! You're gross!'

'Yeah, you had better believe it, matey!'

They were now lying side by side on the sofa with Mats pinned against the back. Steven turned on his side and propped his head up on his hand. He gave her an intense look and the giggle which had been brewing died in her throat. She knew he was about to kiss her and she held her breath, waiting for the feel of his lips against hers. He lowered his head until their lips were mere millimetres apart…

And then he stopped.

Mats paused for a few seconds before moving to close the gap between them. She stopped when he whispered, 'No… wait!'

He pulled back a fraction and said, ever so quietly, 'The first kiss is so special, so unique, so wonderful and totally unrepeatable. You can never have it again. I want to savour every last second beforehand so I can always remember how it made me feel. I just know my first kiss with you will be like no other kiss I've ever had. You're a truly amazing woman, Mats Davidson, and I like you a lot!'

With those words, he finally placed his lips softly upon hers. Mats felt a warmth grow inside her and she slipped her arms around him, pulling him closer to her. The pressure on her mouth increased and a small moan escaped from her. She couldn't recall any kiss ever feeling like this before. Kisses, up till now, had been nice and sometimes even rather pleasant. But this, this kiss was none of those. This kiss was fizziness in her tummy, shooting stars in the sky and even the old cliché of the earth moving beneath her feet. Now she knew what all the fuss was about. Finally, it all made sense.

She turned slightly, her spine pushing into the back of the sofa, and tightened her embrace. She felt light-headed and breathless as Steven's lips slipped round to her ear and then moved down the side of her neck. His touch was so light, so delicate, that her skin tingled where his kisses landed. She slipped her fingers through his blond hair and pulled him back to face her, lifting her own lips up to meet his again. She felt a tremor flow through him as her tongue teased the tip of his.

Mats didn't know how long they lay together, just kissing and whispering endearments but when Steven gave her one last, lingering kiss before sitting up and turning away, she suddenly felt cold and bereft.

'Where are you going?' she whispered.

'Home.' His reply was as quiet as her question.

She pulled herself off the sofa and followed him to the hallway, watching his fingers fly across his phone – fingers which, only seconds before, had been dancing up and down her arm and running through her hair.

'There, an Uber is on its way.'

'You could stay the night… if you wanted to…'

He pulled on his jacket then walked back to where she was standing by the lounge door and gathered her up in his arms again.

'Mats, you have got no idea how much I would love to accept your offer but I am really liking the slow road our relationship is taking. I adore thinking about you and wondering what you're doing. I sit and imagine what you might be up to. I love missing you. People are always so quick to take their relationships to the next level and don't take the time to absorb the beautiful moments along the way. I don't want to miss a single beautiful moment of being with you and so for that reason, I am dragging myself away from you tonight. And trust me when I say "dragging" because every part of me wants to stay.'

He lowered his head and Mats was glad he was holding her so tightly because, for the first time in her life, her knees actually gave way. She felt his kiss absorb her as much as she was absorbing him.

The toot of the taxi outside broke the moment and Steven let her go with a sigh.

'Goodnight, my beautiful lady. Thank you for the most amazing evening. I have enjoyed every moment.'

He took her hand, bent down low, placed the softest

kiss upon the back of it and then was gone, the door clicking quietly shut behind him.

Mats stood for a moment, watching his receding back through the frosted glass of the door, while she gathered her thoughts together before making her way into the kitchen to tidy up with a smile as wide as the Thames dancing over her face.

TWENTY-SIX

Beep! Beep! Beep, beep, beep, beep, beep!

'What on earth?'

Steven looked on as Mats rummaged in her handbag and pulled out the mobile phone she'd put in there a mere moment ago, having just turned it back on after their flight.

'Everything okay?' he asked, as she thumbed through the texts which were still arriving, if the continual beeping was anything to go by.

'They're all from Penny. She needs me to call her urgently.'

He looked around and saw what looked like a quiet corner, away from the passengers who were waiting for their luggage to come out onto the carousel. 'Why don't you go over there,' he pointed, 'and call her. I'll wait for you here.'

Mats had already dialled Penny's number and started walking as she waited for her to reply. She turned around and beckoned to Steven to follow her. He arrived by her side just as Penny answered and he could hear her screeching down the phone.

'Hey, Pen, calm down, calm down! Take a deep breath... hold it... now let it out and tell me what's wrong?'

Mats' soothing voice worked and the screeching stopped.

'We've just landed, I only put my phone on a few minutes ago. All your messages are still coming through and what looks like several missed calls. What's going on? Is my dad okay?'

She looked at him as Penny spoke and he saw the relief on her face as Penny assured her the panic was nothing to do with her dad.

'Right, so why the twenty million calls and texts when you knew we were flying to Dublin first thing this morning?' Mats rolled her eyes as she repeated Penny's reply. 'You forgot, did you? My first overnight stop with this hot bloke and you forgot about it? What kind of a best mate are you?'

Steven felt the blush rise up his cheeks at Mats words although she seemed to find it amusing judging from the way she was grinning at him. He grinned back and went to move away to award her some privacy for her call but she grabbed his arm and pulled him back to her side.

'Oh, shit! That is a bit of a bugger...' She moved the phone and whispered to him, 'The DJ for today's wedding fell off the stage while they were setting up and has broken his leg... Needs an operation to pin it... Totally out of commission for the wedding gig this afternoon...'

'Yeah, I'm listening, Penny... ah... I don't know... give me a moment to think...' She whispered to him again, 'She's asking if I know of any bands who might be able to step in and help out,'

'Do you?'

'Not off the top of my head, no.'

'No, Penny, I'm still here – just filling Steven in on

the problem. No, you won't be able to get a hold of Tinker, I had a text from him when I woke up this morning. He was at the studio until three-thirty a.m. and so has gone off radar for the rest of the weekend. Yes, that is a bollox because he would, most likely, have been able to help you.'

Steven heard Penny's voice rise again in panic and Mats held the phone away from her ear as the screeching escalated. Suddenly, Mats eyes lit up, the frown left her face and she flashed a bright smile at him.

'Penny, Penny, stop! I've had an idea. I *might* be able to get you a DJ. Did your chap take his gear away when he left? No! Cool! Do you think he'd mind someone else using it?' She held the phone towards him so he could also hear Penny's flowery reply as she stated he wasn't going to get a choice in that one if he ever wanted any decent bookings again in the future.

'Okay. Well, let me see what I can do. I'm not promising, mind, so don't get your hopes up. Text me the address of where you are. Now bugger off, I've got a phone call to make.'

Mats ended the call, looked at him and grinning widely, said, 'Now this is where it gets interesting...'

'What are you up to?'

'You'll see!' was the reply he got as Mats fingers flew through her contacts list. She hit her screen and put the phone to her ear.

'Who are you calling?' he whispered.

She put her finger up as the call was answered.

'Yo, Sparks, are you still in yer fleapit? It's almost ten o'clock, ya lazy git.'

Steven knew his eyebrows had just flown upwards at a rate of knots – she wasn't seriously going to ask Marky Sparks to stand in, was she? As he listened, he realised that that was exactly what she was planning to do.

'Look, sunshine, if you're going to send Steven and I

over to Ireland at the crack of dawn, then don't think for a minute I'm letting you get a long lie. Anyway, enough of your bellyaching, I need to ask you a massive favour – how do you fancy being the knight in shining armour to my best mate's damsel in distress?'

Mats filled Marky in with all the details and Steven waited to see what the answer would be. She'd already told him about Penny's life-long crush on the DJ and he knew that without her interference, the two of them wouldn't be standing here in Dublin, on the "I for Ireland" part of their alphabet dating. He hadn't yet met Penny but the stories Mats had shared thus far had led him to believe she was a force to be reckoned with. He tuned back into the conversation that was still going on.

'Look, Sparks, what are you going to be doing this weekend, huh? Sitting on your backside, eating junk food, drinking more than you should and watching dodgy box-sets. No, I haven't been spying on you – it's what you've done almost every weekend since I met you! Look, this will get you out of the house for the day, you'll feel good because you've done someone a good turn and who knows, you might even enjoy yourself. It won't do you any harm to remember how you started out.'

Steven worked on containing his smirk – it always tickled him the way Mats spoke to Marky. His fame held no sway with her.

'Nice one! I knew you'd come round to my way of thinking. Penny will be over the moon and the happy couple will have a lovely wedding surprise. You're doing a good thing, thank you. I'll text you the details. What's that? What's Penny like? Let's just say that when it comes to taking no crap, she makes me look like a beginner! Have fun!' and with that, Mats ended the call.

'Game on, Steven! Penny's about to find out that she's not the only one who can meddle in other people's love lives!'

'Do you think it'll work out?'

'We'll find out in due course. Now, I believe we have a driver waiting to pick us up and a glorious city out there waiting for us to explore, so let's go.'

Mats took a hold of her small suitcase, put her arm through his, and guided them both towards the exit.

TWENTY-SEVEN

'Are you alright, Mats? You've gone a bit quiet.'

Mats turned to look at Steven and saw the concern on his face. She took his hand and squeezed it.

'Yes, I'm fine, thank you. Sorry, I'm still thinking about that poor man from the Easter Risings that they tied to a chair and shot. He was mere hours away from death as it was, why did they still have to execute him?'

They were standing outside Kilmainham Gaol – the first stop on their little whirlwind, sightseeing tour. Their driver had dropped them off there before taking the luggage to their hotel while they visited the famous museum. Mats had been excited to see it – one of her father's favourite films was "The Italian Job" with Sir Michael Caine and some of it had been filmed here. It had been interesting to visit the museum but Ireland's dark past was strongly tied up within it and seeing how the people of the country had been so badly treated by the English governments of the previous centuries had left a bad taste in her mouth.

'I guess they were making an example of him –

showing the local population that no mercy would be shown to anyone who rebelled against the tyranny.'

'I know, I understand why, I just don't *like* why.'

'Good! I think it speaks volumes of how society has evolved in the last one-hundred years. We should be appalled by the atrocities carried out by our ancestors. Folks still harp on about the poor behaviour of the Germans in World War II but turn a blind eye to all the cruelty the English bestowed upon many nations over the centuries.'

Mats smiled as she listened to Steven getting quite het up on the subject. He must have noticed, even though she'd tried to hide it, because he stopped talking.'

'What?'

'You do love your history, don't you?'

His face turned a pale shade of pink. 'Oh, I'm sorry. I went off on one there, didn't I?'

'It's alright. I like that you're so passionate about it and have the knowledge to match the passion.'

'My grandfather has a lot to answer for.'

'Your grandfather has a lot to be proud of. Don't be ashamed or shy to share what he passed on to you. My historical knowledge is not as hot as I'd like it to be so I love hearing about it.'

'Just don't let me lecture you, okay. I'd really hate to become a bore!'

Mats squeezed his hand again and reached up to place a soft kiss on his cheek.

'I promise that there is no way you could bore me but if it's looking likely, I'll be sure to let you know.'

Steven bent down and brushed his lips across her mouth which sent little tingles of joy through her and she felt her earlier melancholy slip away. She was about to return his kiss when a toot of a car horn grabbed her attention.

'I think our chauffeur has arrived to take us on to our next port of call which is,' she looked at the agenda in her hand, 'Dublin Castle.'

'Fantastic! More history for me to bore you with!'

'I can't wait!'

They'd barely been in the car ten minutes when it was time to get out again. As they exited the back seats, their driver handed Mats a small business card while explaining, 'When you've finished your tour of the Castle, it's only a short walk into the centre of the city. If, however, you would rather I collected you, that's not a problem. I'm available to you for the duration of your visit. A map was included within your welcome pack along with some other sightseeing suggestions, most of which are within walking distance of each other. If you do need me, you have my number.'

Mats looked down and saw "Paddy Lennon" and a mobile number printed on the card.

'Thank you, Paddy, for looking after us this morning. We don't mind a bit of walking so hopefully we won't need to call on your services.'

'In which case, I will see you at six o'clock tomorrow evening, outside your hotel, to take you back to the airport. But if you *do* need me, please don't hesitate to call.'

'We will, Paddy. Thank you again.'

As the car pulled away, out into the traffic, Mats put her arm through Steven's and said, 'Well, come on then, history buff, let's go and get educated some more before we hit the shops.'

'Shops? Seriously?'

'Ha! Gotcha again!' Steven had a strong dislike of shopping and Mats smiled teasingly at him as they walked under the brick archway which led into the courtyard of the castle.

'Are you enjoying the trip so far?'

Mats glanced up at Steven before answering. 'Very much so! The last time I was here it was with a hen party so taking in the local culture wasn't on the agenda. I think the only thing I saw that weekend was our hotel room and Temple Bar. Both are a vague and hazy memory. What about you?'

'Pretty much the same although it was a rugby bash, not a hen party—'

'Shame! I think you'd look good in a pretty pink tutu and a pair of fairy wings.'

'Is that what you had to wear?'

'Yup! It was fun though. I even had a wand with a star on it.'

'Hmph! The way England played on that rugby trip, we could have done with a magic wand or two!'

'Oh, I think that's our tour guide over there. Let's do this.'

For the next hour, they followed their guide and spent a good chunk of it oohing and aahing over the décor, the stories and the legends. Mats was particularly impressed with the hedge garden which the guide informed them was planted to depict the snakes being driven out of Ireland by St Patrick. She also shared the story of St Stephen while discussing the number of saints revered by the Irish people.

'St Stephen, eh? Don't you be getting any ideas, matey,' Mats whispered, as she dug an elbow into Steven's side.

'No chance of that with you around to keep my feet firmly planted on the ground,' he replied in a droll tone.

This caused them both to have a fit of the giggles which earned them a few snooty looks from their fellow tourists and just made them laugh even more.

'Right, so now we've done that, what's next on your list?'

They were once again back in the castle courtyard and Steven looked at Mats as she perused the map.

'If you really want to hit the shops, we can. I don't mind – whatever you fancy.'

Mats felt her heart give a little tumble at Steven's words. Even though he abhorred main street shopping, she was touched that he was prepared to suffer it if it was what she wanted to do. Lucky for him though, it was the last thing on her mind.

'Shopping? When Trinity College Library is just a short walk from here? Not a chance! I want to see the books! Show me the books!'

As they set off, Mats voiced the thought that had been hovering around the back of her head all morning, 'I wonder how Sparks and Penny are getting on...'

TWENTY-EIGHT

Marky stood in the hotel reception and waited for Mats' friend to come and collect him. It had been a long time since he'd DJ'd at this level and he was nervous as to how it would go. Technology had changed the way disc jockeys worked now to how it had been when he'd started out all those years ago. Back then, it had involved carting about case upon case upon case full of vinyl records and hoping you had that one elusive track which someone always requested. These days, everything was on computer and there was no longer such thing as an elusive track because a few taps on the keyboard was all it took to add even the obscurest of songs to your playlist.

He looked around and safe in the knowledge that no one was watching, rubbed his clammy palms on the thighs of his jeans. He could really have done with a quick nip of Jack D right now but he'd been doing so well with cutting back his alcohol intake of late and he didn't want to undo his progress. Hopefully, a nice strong coffee or two would take the edge off although maybe not as efficiently.

He heard footsteps approaching behind him and

taking a deep breath to steady himself, he turned around to greet the wedding coordinator and Mats best friend.

'Hi, I'm Penny. Thank you so much for coming today— Oh my goodness? Marky Sparks? Oh... Oh!'

Out of nowhere, Marky found himself trying to cope with a sudden weakness that had hit both of his knees. The woman standing in front of him was breath-taking and she had completely taken *his* breath away. Eloise had been the last woman to make him feel like this and that had been far too long ago. While trying to slow the dance beat of his heart, Marky took in the visual explosion that was Penny. Individually, her features were all fairly ordinary but together they created a vision of pure loveliness. Her ash blonde hair was pulled back in a professional chignon and framed an oval face with high cheekbones, a strong chin and a straight, ordinary nose. Her eyes were an unusual shade of pale brown and a combination of her height and high-heels, put them on a level with his own. He felt himself being pulled into them and he had to give himself a mental shake to clear the dizzy sensation in his stomach. Marky had met more than his fair share of beautiful women – they were ten-a-penny in his line of work – but he'd never met one who not only looked this stunning but who also exuded a magnetic energy that drew you towards her. He didn't know that Mats often used the description, "There's charisma... and then there's Penny!" but if he had, he would not have disagreed with it.

'You've cut your hair.'

'Er, what? I'm sorry?' The vision was speaking and he needed to get his act together pronto or she'd be writing him off as a total loser.

'I said, you've cut your hair. It really suits you. It makes you look younger. Oh, I'm so sorry! That was rude.' Penny's hand came up to her mouth and a look of consternation flew into her eyes.

Come on Mark, get your shit together here! Bloody breathe, you moron! Marky took heed of his inner voice, took another deep breath and replied, 'Rude? I don't think so! Being told I look younger can only be a compliment. Thank you.'

'When did you have it done?'

'Erm, a few weeks back now. Mats hinted that my trademark mullet may not be doing me any favours now that I'm older.'

'Mats *hinted*? Are you sure about that?'

'Okaaaay… Maybe not hinted as such but with you being her best friend, I didn't want to be undiplomatic.'

To his delight, Penny let out a squeal of laughter.

'Marky, you don't need to worry about that. I've known Mats long enough to know she wouldn't hesitate to be "undiplomatic" if the roles were reversed. Now, please forgive me for my initial surprise earlier – Mats only said she'd sorted out a DJ, she clearly didn't think it was worth telling me she was roping in the services of my favourite DJ ever.' Penny gave a light giggle. 'Oops! That wasn't very cool or sophisticated of me, was it? Can you forgive me for my fangirl moment?'

'I think I could manage that, Penny. Now, do you want to take me through to the function suite and let me see what I'm going to be working with?'

As Penny led him down the plushily carpeted corridor, Mark knew that he was already lost. He would forgive this goddess anything and what's more, she'd been fangirling over *him*… Talk about a result! Sending a silent prayer of thanks across the sea to Mats, he resolved that he'd pluck up the courage to ask Penny out for dinner before this day was over.

TWENTY-NINE

Mats slipped the key card into their hotel room door and pushed it open when the green light flickered on. Steven followed behind. They walked into a small hallway with an even smaller hanging space to their right.

'Blimey, that's a bit pokey. It's only big enough for a couple of coats.'

Steven didn't reply but he agreed with her. He hoped this wasn't a portent of what was to come. Their day had been good so far and he didn't want a shoddy bedroom to take the shine off it. Although, the receptionist had said something about a suite when he'd handed over the key cards.

'Oh wow! I take it back! This more than makes up for pokey hanging space.' Mats moved to the side of the door she'd opened and Steven got his first view of the room in front of them. Or rather, their sitting space for the only furniture was a beautiful cream, three-piece suite, a shabby-chic coffee table bearing an ice-bucket with a bottle of wine chilling inside and a small dining table with four chairs placed discreetly in the corner. He glanced across to look out of the full-length floor-to-ceiling windows and could see the far side of the River Liffey flowing past below. The sitting room had three doors off it and after a quick bit of exploring, they found a small kitchen area with a door that led out onto a wrought-iron balcony with a table and chairs. On the marble worktop was a basket of fruit and a box of pastries which had been placed alongside a card of welcome.

'I'm guessing the other two doors must lead to the bedrooms,' said Mats, as they made their way across the room.

She opened the door to her right and they stepped into a large bedroom with another floor-length window. The sunlight streaming in gave the room a light, airy feel. The king-size bed was a four-poster in the same shabby-chic style as the furniture in the sitting area. Their suitcases had been placed by the mirror and glass wardrobes and a doorway next to them led into a cream and black tiled bathroom with a large walk-in shower, a free-standing claw footed bath and a counter with two sinks set into it. Steven couldn't help but be amused at Mats excitement when she saw these.

'Is having two sinks that much of a luxury?' he asked.

'Oh yes! It means I don't have to wipe off the toothpaste stains that you will leave splattered all over the place.'

'I don't splatter toothpaste all over the sink!'

'Humph! We'll see. If you don't, you'll be the first bloke I've met who doesn't. I'm beginning to think it's one of those secret blokey rituals where you see how far back you can stand from the sink yet still reach to spit into it!'

'You do have some lowly opinions of my fellow men, don't you?' he smirked.

'All gained from previous experience, dear chap! Now where does this door go?' She opened it up and walked into the second bedroom.

'Oh, this one's a little disappointing. That skylight is a poor excuse for a window and it only has a double bed.'

Steven looked around him and had to agree with her. It was still designed in the shabby-chic style and wasn't unpleasant but it lacked the plush, luxurious feel of the master bedroom.

'Maybe this is the servant's quarters,' he joked.

'It would have been better if the rooms had been equally nice because we'll now have to toss a coin to see who has which room.'

'No, we don't, Mats. I'll take this one. You have the big room.'

'Oh, I can't just take it. That's not fair on you.'

Steven turned, took Mats in his arms and kissed her protest away. 'Yes, I can. It's only for one night and I'm only going to be sleeping in here. You should have the other room – after all, don't you ladies require a million mirrors to check out your dresses before you go out?'

'Oi! No, we do not! Well, this one certainly doesn't.'

'Well, that's the opinion I have gained from previous experience, dear lady.'

Mats burst out laughing as he threw her own words back at her.

'Touché, dude! Touché!'

They went back into the lounge and Steven picked the wine bottle out of the ice bucket. 'Wow, Champagne. And not a cheap one either.' He held the bottle up for Mats to see. Her eyebrows went up when she saw the expensive label but then she grinned.

'Nice, but it's not Bolly though, is it Pats?'

'No, Eddy, what cheap-skates! Do you want a glass?'

'Hmm, no. Let's save it for later. I'd rather have a coffee right now and then we need to get ready for dinner. I believe our restaurant reservation is for seven-thirtyish.'

She picked up their itinerary from where she'd dropped it on the sofa to check.

'Ahh, seven-forty-five. And as it's Hughie O'Grady's flagship restaurant, I don't think it would go down too well if we arrived late.'

'Oh yes, Hughie O'Grady! Ireland's answer to Gordon Ramsay. Do you think his profanities match the levels of Ramsay's?'

'From what I've seen, he makes Ramsay look like a boy scout.'

Steven laughed at her pithy reply. 'One thing I don't get though, Mats, is how is the radio station able to pay for all this? Marky and Dave made it clear from the start that it was close to going under and we were their last chance to save it yet here we are in Ireland, about to have a meal at the most exclusive restaurant in town.'

'I asked Sparks the same question and I can tell you the station isn't paying for any of this. Companies donate freebies to them in the hope they will garner some free advertising. Our first batch of dates were all old ones they had on file but as the popularity of our "Love is on the Air" spot has grown and our social media pages are gaining more attention, the station is now receiving higher-end freebies. All of this,' she waved her arm around, 'has been given by a certain High Street travel agent and all we have to do is tweet about the great time we're having. Which we would be doing anyway as that was part of the deal with the station. So, it's a win-win for everyone.'

'Well, I have to say, Ms Mats, you chose well this time around for as much as I like ice-cream, and a day of ice-cream tasting would have been rather nice, this is a far superior date.'

'I aim to please, young sir! Now, I'm going to chuck the kettle on and after I've had a cuppa, I'm going to drown myself in that waterfall of a shower. What you having – tea or coffee?'

Steven sneaked a glance at Mats again as they walked to the restaurant. She was wearing a stunning beaded purple, 1920s, flapper-style dress which, she'd informed him, was a genuine vintage piece. With her hair blow-dried and straightened into her usual smooth bob, she looked the genuine article and he was sure his eyes must have popped out of his head when she'd walked out of her bedroom. The long shift design of the dress really suited her and the colour only served to emphasise her unusual eyes. She looked absolutely amazing and he felt truly honoured to be walking beside her.

They'd discussed calling Paddy to drive them to their dinner date but upon looking at the map and seeing it was no distance at all to the restaurant, they decided to walk there. It was a glorious sunny evening and they'd deemed it a shame not to enjoy it fully. Mats was carrying a silver shawl over her arm just in case it should get chilly later.

They chatted as they walked up the street and soon arrived outside the restaurant. There was a small queue and they smiled at the couple in front of them as they took their place to wait behind the red-rope barrier. It only took a few moments for the queue to move along and soon they were second in line. At first, they paid no attention to the older couple ahead of them until the raised voice of the gentleman made Steven's ears prick up.

'You must have a reservation! I booked it over three months ago…'

'I assure you, Mr O'Shaunessey, we do not have a booking for you this evening. You can look for yourself.' The door hostess turned her booking ledger around to back up her claim.

'I don't need to "look for myself", young lady, I know

I made the booking and it was confirmed. It's our thirtieth wedding anniversary today and my wife has wanted to visit your establishment since it opened. I made the booking to ensure our day was even more special.' He took his wife's hand and the look of love he bestowed upon her brought a small lump to Steven's throat. He was touched to see how much this man still cared for the lady in his life even after all these years.

'Once again, Mr O'Shaunessey, I can only advise you that we do not have a booking for you this evening. Please, look for yourself.' She pointed again to the ledger in front of her.

'Oh, for goodness' sake...' Mr O'Shaunessey leant forward, looked at the book in front of him and then gave a 'Hah!' of satisfaction. He turned the ledger back around and pointed to the page. 'Well, if we don't have a reservation, what is that there?'

The hostess looked and then turned a pale shade of pink. 'Oh, Mr O'Shaunessey, that booking was for last night. The red line through it is because you didn't show up.'

'Didn't show up! Of course, I didn't show up – the booking was for tonight!'

'Perhaps you booked the wrong date—'

'Are you telling me I don't know the exact date this beautiful woman became my wife?'

'Erm, um... no, but that perhaps you gave the wrong date in error...'

'I can assure you I didn't give the wrong date.' Mr O'Shaunessey fumbled with the pocket inside his jacket and pulled out a piece of paper which he unfolded and passed to the hostess. 'This is the email confirmation you sent to me and you can see that it states today's date, not yesterday's date. So as the error is clearly yours, I suggest you find us a table tonight.'

'But we're fully booked—'

'I don't care—'

'Michael, just leave it be. Don't get worked up, think of your heart…' Mrs O'Shaunessey tugged on the sleeve of her husband's jacket. Steven saw the tears in her eyes and came to a decision. He turned to Mats and whispered in her ear, 'Please forgive me for what I'm about to do…'

Not giving her a chance to respond, he let go of her hand and stepped forward to stand beside the O'Shaunessey's.

'Excuse me,' he smiled politely to the couple before facing the hostess, 'I believe you have a booking for Davidson and Byrne at seven-forty-five.'

'Oh, yes, Sir, we do. The best table in the house awaits you,' she gushed. 'Please let me take you through.'

'I'm sorry but we won't be dining here this evening.'

'You what?' The flush on the hostess's face drained away and she went quite pale. 'But, you're our VIP guests tonight. Your meal is compliments of the house…'

'I'm aware of that but I'm afraid we're unable to make it. Instead, I would like you to give our table, and the complimentary meal, to this lovely couple. I would also suggest you throw in a nice bottle of expensive Champagne to compensate them for the upset your error has caused them this evening.'

'But—'

Mats came to stand by his side. 'Look, Marie,' she said, looking at the name tag on the girl's waistcoat, 'we have to leave a review on social media telling our followers of our experience at your establishment tonight. Now, we can leave a review saying the staff were unhelpful, unfriendly and we chose not to eat here because of it or we can leave a review saying that we gifted our table to a lovely couple who were at risk of missing out on their anniversary dinner but that we fully intend to visit on

162

another occasion because the staff were friendly, helpful and delightfully understanding. Now, which of those two options do you think Hughie O'Grady would prefer millions of people to see?'

Steven took Mats' hand and gave it a little squeeze. This woman by his side was bloody awesome!

'Erm... the second one...'

'Exactly! So that's all sorted then.'

'But... we can't let you miss out on your meal.'

Steven gave Mrs O'Shaunessey his biggest smile. 'Please, it's not as important as your evening. Thirty years of a loving marriage should be celebrated in style and I'm sure Marie here,' he flashed the same smile at the hostess, 'will ensure your evening is everything you hoped for and more. Happy Anniversary to you both,' and with those words, he and Mats stepped out of the queue, gave the O'Shaunessey's a wave and then moved away. When they'd crossed over to the other side of the street, he threw a glance over his shoulder and saw the couple being escorted to a table in the window and a waiter arriving with an ice bucket and two Champagne flutes.

'You, Mr Steven Byrne, are a very, very, *very* nice man.'

'I'm sorry, Mats. I know you were looking forward to your meal.'

'Don't be so daft. I was actually about to do the same thing myself. You beat me to it by a matter of seconds.'

'We now have the small problem of finding somewhere to eat. Everywhere is going to be full with it being a Saturday night.'

'Actually, I have an idea – do you trust me?'

'Mats, you know I do.'

'Then follow me...'

THIRTY

Mats felt the skin on her face tighten across her cheekbones as she slurped up the dregs of her thick, creamy, banana milkshake.

'Oh, but that was good! I enjoyed it far more than some poncy designer plate with half a lettuce leaf and a teaspoon of tuna on it.'

'Not a fan of high cuisine, then?'

'Not particularly. Whenever I have to attend industry award ceremonies, they often drag in some famous TV chef to provide the nosh and I'm always starving by the time I get home! I like a plate of food to have food on it, not some tiny little thing in the middle of it which looks more like a plate design than a meal.'

'So, this was more to your taste, was it?'

Mats looked at the fast-food bags in front of them and smiled. 'It sure was.'

When Steven had said he trusted her, she'd dragged him off to a well-known, fast-food, burger joint they'd passed on their way to the restaurant. Once the bags of goodies were in their hands, Mats had walked quickly up

Grafton Street and into St Stephen's Green where they'd found a small grassy area overlooking the lake and had sat down to eat their impromptu picnic. Steven had offered her his jacket to sit on so she wouldn't get stains on her dress but she'd declined saying she could sit on her shawl.

The park was now quiet and the trees were reflected in the lake as the sun began to slowly set. Mats shook her cardboard drinks container to ensure there was nothing left. Disappointed to find it really was empty, she squashed it carefully and placed it inside the paper bags which now contained the left-over wrappers from their meal.

'I wished I'd bought the large drink now – I really enjoyed that.'

'Why didn't you?'

'I was trying to be good.'

'With the amount of walking we've done today, and will probably do tomorrow, I'm sure you could have treated yourself.'

'I realise that now.'

'Would you like me to go and get you another one? It'll only take me ten minutes there and back.'

Mats looked at Steven and smiled. This man had kindness oozing out of every pore. She hadn't been lying earlier when she'd said she had been about to offer their table to the O'Shaunessey's but it thrilled her to the core that he'd made the offer first. Kind men like him were a rarity and she was coming to realise that this one would be worth holding onto.

She rolled onto her side and looked up at him. The sun was shining down onto his face and made his blond hair sparkle like golden threads.

'Have you seen your family recently? Have they said anything about all of "this"?'

'Oh, I've had my mother on the phone several times saying I'm trying to steal my brother's thunder and that I should know my place. He's the star in our family and I'm showing my jealousy by trying to push him aside.'

'Wow! That's harsh! Doesn't she realise that you can both be stars' that shine?'

'Like I said before, my mother only ever sees Stuart's success and I'm not permitted to have anything which might detract from it.'

'But you've been successful in your own career, does she not give you credit for that?'

'Absolutely not! In her eyes, I walked away and left Stuart high and dry. I wasn't prepared to let him take all the credit for my hard work and to her, that was unforgivable. She fully believes my only role in life is to support my brother.'

'Please don't take this the wrong way, Steven, but don't feel the need to introduce me to the rest of your family any time soon. I'm not known for my diplomacy and I would hate to say something out of turn.'

'Aw! Are you sure? I was kinda hoping you might join me at my parents for Sunday lunch next week.'

Mats looked at Steven in horror. 'Please tell me you're kidding!'

'Why? Would it be so terrible?'

'After what you've just told me… it would be carving knives at dawn! The temptation to shove your mother's face into her crystal-cut trifle bowl would be too difficult to refuse.'

'Now, you see, I already know you'd get on well. You know she has a crystal-cut trifle bowl – you were both made to be best friends!'

Mats sat up and glared at him. Just then, the sun slipped behind a cloud and she could see humour in his eyes as he bit the inside of his cheeks to prevent himself from laughing.

'You!' She gave him a light punch on the arm. 'You

really had me going there. I thought you were being serious.'

'Mats,' he took her face in his hands and looked into her eyes, 'I want you to fall in love with me as I am falling in love with you. Introducing you to my mother is a sure-fire way of preventing that from happening so you can rest easy that you will not be meeting her any time soon.'

With those words, he leant forward and kissed her. Mats felt her toes curl once again and knew she was also falling in love with Steven. It was going to take more than one harridan of a mother to get her off this slippery, but welcome, slope.

'I think we need to get moving,' Steven whispered in her ear, 'it'll soon be time for the park gates to be locked. You don't want to be stuck here all night, do you?'

Mats snuggled up closer to his chest, which she'd been happily lying against for the last half hour, and thought there were much worse places she could think of to be right now.

'Oh, I don't know, it would be another adventure to add to our growing list.'

Steven's reply was a long and lingering kiss before he stood up and holding out his hand, helped her to her feet.

'We've got a beautiful hotel suite, a bottle of Champagne chilling in the fridge and a balcony with a glorious view – why don't we go back and enjoy it all?'

'Or,' Mats replied, hiding her grin as she bent down to pick up her shawl, 'we could hit up Temple Bar and do a pub crawl – a shot of some dodgy, sweet liqueur in every bar then onto the next one.'

'Oh, well… if that's what you would prefer, we can do that too. I don't mind.'

'I'm teasing you, Steven, but I adore that you were

prepared to go along with me if I had been serious. You do know you're allowed to say "No" sometimes, don't you? You don't always have to be agreeable.'

'Yes, I know and when you come out with a suggestion that I find intensely disagreeable, I will say. So, while sipping Champagne on a balcony with you would be delightful, I'm sure seeing you get shit-faced on fruity vodka shots would be fun too.'

'I shall keep that in mind for the future, then.'

'Seriously, Mats, if you'd rather go to Temple Bar, I really don't mind.'

Taking his hand, she began walking towards the park gates. 'Not in this dress, sweetie, not in this dress!'

They had just exited the park and were standing waiting to cross the road when Mats' mobile phone buzzed. She took it out from her bag and looked at the display.

'Ooh, it's from Penny. This could be interesting!'

She opened the text and held it out so they could both read it at the same time.

I hate you!

'Erm, that's not so good…'

'Give it a minute,' Mats smiled.

Sure enough, barely thirty seconds had passed when another message landed on the screen.

But I also bloody love you!
Thank you. xxxxxxx

'Would I be right to assume that she's not annoyed with you sending Marky to assist today?'

'Nope! She's good with that. She just hates me because I gave her no prior warning which meant she didn't have time to check her hair, put on some lippy and ensure she was the ultimate picture of ice-cool gorgeousness when she came face-to-face with her childhood idol for the first time.'

'Wasn't that a little mean of you? I didn't realise sending Marky would be *such* a big deal to her.'

'Look, Mr Nice Guy, this is the woman who set me up on a blind date on a radio station with half of London listening in! This was small fry compared to that.'

'Maybe so, but,' Steven squeezed her hand, 'that didn't turn out too badly, did it?'

'Hmmm, I'll get back to you on that one but I have to say, it's looking good so far!'

She treated him to her biggest smile and plonked a quick kiss by the side of his mouth. 'Now come on, let's get a move on. I can hear that bottle of Champers shouting from here.'

Within a few minutes, they were back at their hotel. They'd barely walked through the suite door when Mats was pulling off her shoes and enjoying the coolness of the parquet floor.

'Ahhhh, that's better.'

'You should have said your feet were sore, Mats, we could have grabbed a taxi back.'

'Not so much sore as hot and swollen. Stockings plus walking in the warm night is not a great combo. They'll be fine in a couple of minutes. Now, get that bottle open and let's see what Dublin looks like from up here at this time of night.'

She threw her shawl over the sofa, picked up the Champagne flutes from the coffee table and headed towards the small kitchen area. She stopped to pick up a couple of napkins and after wiping down the table and chairs on the balcony, placed the glasses down before returning to pick up the box of pastries.

'Champagne and cinnamon rolls?'

'Yeah, I'm a classy bird, me!'

Steven came out to sit beside her and poured the fizzing, golden, liquid into her glass.

'Aw, you opened it inside?'

'I thought it might be safer. I didn't want an errant Champagne cork hitting some poor sod on the head while he's on his stag do or whatever.'

'You're always so thoughtful. It's one of the things I love about you—'

Mats stopped talking when she realised what she'd just said. Shit, shit, shit! That wasn't supposed to pop out. She felt her face grow warm and unable to look at him, she stood up, walked the few steps to the balcony railing and stood looking over the lights of the city below.

There was silence behind her.

Her heart pounded while she waited to see what Steven would say. The pause lengthened and just as she was about to try and find something with which to fill it, she heard him get off his chair and step over to stand behind her. His hand came around the front of her and in it was her glass of wine. She took it from him and his arm came to rest upon her waist, pulling her ever so gently against him. His other hand appeared in front of her, also holding a wine-filled glass which he chinked against hers.

'Here's to finding out lots of things we love about each other,' he whispered in her ear before placing a kiss just behind it.

When Mats heard his softly spoken words, she felt the last line in her resistance crumble and slip away. She wasn't *falling* in love any more, she was already in love with Steven and she was now finally ready to admit it to herself.

They stood looking out over Dublin for a few more minutes until Mats twisted around to face him and said, 'I think it's time we took this inside.'

THIRTY-ONE

Steven lay on his side, his head propped up on one arm while the other held Mats close to his chest. The morning sun had found a small gap in the floor-length curtains and a golden ray had squeezed through to shine on Mats' face, totally relaxed as she slept. Her hair had fallen behind her ear, giving Steven a clear view of her strong chin, slightly pointed nose, full lips and smooth neckline – all of which he had kissed many times over the night before and again in the early hours of the morning. When he'd tried to do the gentlemanly thing of leaving to sleep in his own bedroom, Mats had clung tightly to him, telling him in no uncertain terms that he was staying put. She'd let him leave once – he didn't get to do it a second time. In truth, he had been happy for her to call the shots because he'd doubted his resolve would have been as strong as it had been before.

When they'd finally worn themselves out from exploring each other, Mats had spooned into him and they'd drifted off to sleep. Steven had been surprised to find himself still in the same position when he'd woken up. He liked his own space to sleep in and wasn't good at sharing it meaning previous girlfriends had often woken up to find him either clinging onto the furthest away edge of the mattress or on more than one occasion, in the spare bed next door. He couldn't ever recall finding himself still physically entangled when sleep had departed. Even more surprising was finding that he was most reluctant to move. The warmth from Mats body was flowing into him and he wasn't yet ready to put any space between them.

He watched her for a few minutes more, making the most of this opportunity for seeing Mats in an unanimated pose was rare. She looked so peaceful and he felt his chest swell with love. She was slowly consuming him and he would happily serve himself up to her on a silver platter if it would keep her by his side. He'd never felt this deeply about a woman before and he didn't want the feeling to end.

Finally, unable to hold back any longer, he bent his head down and began placing light, butterfly kisses along her neck and jawline. It didn't take long for her to stir.

'Don't,' she moaned, 'tickles…' She rubbed her hand on her face before turning around to lie on her back and look up at him.

'Then allow me to kiss you fully awake.'

Not giving her a chance to speak, Steven bent his head and kissed her into full consciousness. Her arms found their way around his neck and she pulled him closer to her.

'Now that's how a girl should be woken every morning,' she murmured against his neck before slipping down to place her own featherlight kisses upon his chest while gently scratching the inside of his thighs with her fingernails.

Steven drew in a sharp breath under her touch and knew then that he wanted to kiss this gorgeous woman awake every day for the rest of his life.

'What time are we due at the Guinness factory?'

'Ten o'clock.'

Steven picked his phone up off the bedside table and saw it was just after eight.

'Shall we get dressed and head downstairs for breakfast or would you prefer room service?'

Mats looked up at him, a small wicked smile on her lips.

'I very much doubt anything could match the room service I've just had!'

Steven felt the heat rush up his face as Mats laughed in his arms.

'You,' he said, as he placed a kiss on her nose, 'are absolutely incorrigible!'

'Yes, I know. It's great!'

He laughed along with her, rejoicing in her happiness. The sunlight was still dancing on her face and her eyes were their natural deep blue. It continued to fascinate him how they appeared to change colour depending on her moods. It was difficult not to notice for you couldn't look at Mats and not feel yourself being pulled into their deep, bluey-purple depths. Even now, he'd find himself so lost in them that he'd miss parts of their conversations. Luckily Mats would simply smile or laugh and repeat what she'd said.

'Well, for being so lewd, young lady, I think it would be best if we hit up the breakfast buffet. I'm starving and the horse I feel like eating won't fit on a tray!'

'That sounds like a good plan to me. I'm starving too!'

'Well, you can find your own horse, I'm not sharing mine.'

'Fine! In that case, we'd better share our shower to save time... Come on!'

Mats got out of the bed and skipped over to the en suite,

throwing a wanton look in his direction. Steven let out a small growl of desire while ignoring the growl of hunger from his stomach. He wasn't going to be seeing a plate of bacon and eggs any time soon but oh boy, what a way to work up an appetite!

THIRTY-TWO

'Oh, wow! Wow! Wow! Wow!'

Mats' head was moving round in delight as she took in the stupendous views from the Gravity Bar above the Guinness factory. They'd just completed the factory tour and were now about to finish off with the free drink that came at the end. She walked around, enjoying the 360-degree vista, before joining Steven at the bar to redeem their drinks vouchers.

'I'll have a Guinness please. Mats? A pint of the good stuff for you?'

'Urgh! No, thank you – I can't stand the stuff. I'll just have a Coke please.'

'Okay. Why don't you go and find a table and I'll bring these over?'

Mats wandered away and sat down at a table with a view over the distant Wicklow mountains. It was another glorious day and the countryside all around was shining in the brilliant sunlight. They'd been on the first tour of the day and the Gravity Bar was still quiet and peaceful. Mats suspected it wouldn't be like this for long and closed her eyes to soak up the relaxing ambiance.

'Hey, sleepyhead!'

Steven placed her drink in front of her and took a large sip of his own. She smiled at the white, foamy, moustache left behind on his lip.

'I've got beer on my face, haven't I? That's what you're smiling at...'

He ran his tongue along his lip to lick it away and Mats felt a tingle that made her squirm slightly in her seat. She was remembering where that tongue had been earlier this morning. She raised her own glass and took a long drink, hoping the icy-coldness would bring her bodily sensations under control. She could now say, with her hand on her heart, that last night was the first time she'd ever made love. All previous encounters had just been going through the motions. With hindsight, it had just been sex. Being with Steven, however, and finally acknowledging how she felt about him, had raised her emotions to a whole new level. Every kiss had been deeper and more meaningful than she'd ever known. Every touch had carried an intensity that left her craving more. In the past, once the act of love had ceased, she'd been quite happy to turn over and sleep. Last night had been quite different for she hadn't wanted it to ever end. It was exhaustion which finally closed their eyes and it hadn't taken long for them to pick up where they'd left off this morning. Mats admitted to herself that, right now, she'd happily swap this stunning view for that of their bedroom interior.

'You okay over there? You're rather quiet.'

'Oh! Yes, I am, thank you. Just revelling in this view and the quiet of the bar. It's very relaxing.'

'It is quite something. Are you sure you don't want a sip of this Guinness, it's lush? Much nicer than the stuff we get back home.'

'I can assure you I don't, thank you. My mum drank

177

enough of the stuff to put me off for a lifetime!'

'Oh! I'm sorry…'

Mats caught the look on Steven's face and gave a small smile.

'No, she wasn't a raving alcoholic, it's nothing like that, I can assure you.'

'I wasn't thinking that…'

'My mum died of breast cancer. She used to drink Guinness because it's full of iron and antioxidants. In the later stages, it was often the only thing that didn't make her feel sick so we always had a ton of it in the house.'

'I'm sorry to hear that. Was it long ago?'

Mats looked at Steven and decided it was time to share her story with him. It felt right to do so.

'Mum was diagnosed just over thirteen years ago. She knew for three months before she told me. I was at Uni and she swore my father to secrecy that I wasn't to be informed until after I'd graduated. Despite going through some very intense treatment, she still managed to dress up to the nines and attend my graduation. Four days after throwing my mortarboard in the air, my parents sat me down in the kitchen and shared their news. From that day on, I barely left my mother's side. I cared for her through the day, my father took over at night.'

'That must have been difficult. You were only young yourself.'

'I was in my twenties so not that young. Besides, my mum had many friends so we often had visitors dropping in to see her. Dulwich is rather popular among the artistic sorts and they'd stop by on their way to work in the afternoon. It worked well because it meant I could go to the shops to get in dinner etc and be safe in the knowledge that she wasn't alone.'

'Even so, seeing your mum so ill must have been hard to cope with.'

Mats looked up as her vision blurred with tears.

'It was difficult but I'd do it all again in a heartbeat if it would give me some extra hours by her side.'

'Were you with her at the end?'

'I was. Both my father and I were sitting on each side of the bed, holding her hands.'

'I'm sorry.'

'No, it was a relief in a way. Mum fought as hard as she could, right up to the end, but she was in so much pain – the morphine could only do so much. I was glad she was no longer suffering but also felt guilty for thinking that way. It was the guilt which skewed my emotions and made the grief twice as hard to cope with. It's also why my marriage failed.'

'Marriage?' Steven had been about to take another drink but his arm stopped in mid-air and the shock was evident in his voice.

'Yes, marriage.' Mats stopped to take a sip of her own drink. She hadn't intended to share this part of her life but somehow it was all tied in together and now that she'd started, she didn't want to stop. Only her father, Penny and Tinks knew the whole story. Until now...

'I'd met a bloke – Jim – at Uni in my final year. He was nice and we got along well. I suspect that, had it not been for mum's illness, the relationship would have petered out after graduation, we'd have split up and gone our own way. As it was, the knowledge that I was possibly going to lose my mum made me cling to everything else far more tightly. And that included Jim. Anything familiar was safe in a time of uncertainty. The more my mum began to slide downhill, the closer I pulled Jim to me. He was my rock and let me take all my pain and frustrations out on him. I couldn't go to my dad as he had his own pain to deal with. Three weeks after mum died, Jim and I were engaged. Dad tried to talk me out of it, tried to explain that it was the wrong time to be making such life-changing decisions but I refused to listen. Within three months we were married.'

'Wow! That was quick.'

'Yup! I pushed it through. Mum was only in her mid-forties when she died and my thinking was that life was too short to waste time on a long engagement.'

'I can see how you would think that. How long were you married for?'

'I was back home with dad before we'd even had our first anniversary. Not long after our six-month celebration had passed, I woke up one morning and realised I'd made a big mistake. Mum had been dead almost ten months at that point and I'd finally taken dad's advice to visit a grief counsellor. It only took a few sessions for me to see how I'd let my grief and my guilt dictate my decisions, including getting married.'

'How did your husband, Jim, take the news?'

'Not well. Not well at all. To paraphrase his own comments, he'd never expected us to last beyond graduation and had always known I was out of his league. He'd rejoiced in the news of my mum's illness for he knew he could use it to keep me. He was always so accommodating, so helpful, so understanding – I never realised he was actually manipulating me by making himself indispensable. When mum died, he used my grief to step in and propose marriage, knowing that it was unlikely I would say no. And he was right.'

'He actually told you this?'

'Not in so many words but I was able to piece together what he was saying to work it out. When I challenged him, he broke down and told me the full story which confirmed what I had ascertained. The next day I moved back home with dad and began the divorce proceedings. I never saw him again.'

'Sounds like he took it all quite well in the end.'

'Oh, I wouldn't say that. The house was in my mum and dad's names and she'd inserted a specific clause in her will stating that my name was to replace hers on the deeds. Apparently, it was to prevent my father ever selling the house and also because it was to be passed down through the women of the family.'

'Why was your father's name on the deeds, if that was the case?'

'They had to take out a small mortgage a few years prior to do some work on the house. It's old – things wear out and need to be replaced.'

'Fair enough!'

'Anyway, Jim thought he could go after a share of my half of the property – he turned out to be really unpleasant in the end – but the name change hadn't yet gone through as probate hadn't been completed. He didn't get a penny.'

'Quite right too! So, did you use that as collateral to get your business up and running.'

'No. What neither my dad or I knew was that mum had set up a fund for me when I was born. Both she and my grandmother had been paying into it over the years and it came to me on my twenty-fifth birthday. I received a phone call from her solicitor, asking me to visit, and he handed over a letter which explained that she wanted me to be strong and independent of any man. She hoped the money from the fund would be used wisely as an investment in my future but if I wanted to squander it all on a trip around the world, that was my prerogative for I had earned the right to do that when I had given up so many hours to look after her. That's when I checked and found the letter had been written two weeks before she'd died.'

'How did that make you feel? Knowing she was still looking out for you?'

'Sad, happy, ecstatic, sad again… When the doors of

the studio opened that first day, I cried because she should have been there with me, to see it all happen. It was Tinks who said there was a damn good chance she was there, even though we couldn't see her, because my mum had never been one to miss out on a party and he doubted even death would be able to prevent her being around on my special day.'

She smiled at Steven as she heard Tink's words so clearly in her head.

'So, does your dad still live with you in the house?'

'No. Five years ago, he met a lovely lady called Susan and two years later, they moved to Devon. Sue's parents were retiring from their own little business so Sue and Dad moved down to take over. They run a small B&B with a bakery attached. Sue's in charge of the shop and the baking, my dad has full control of the B&B. They love it and dad is in his element.

'And you, Mats, would you say you're happy?'

Mats looked at Steven, the kind concern for her clearly expressed on his face. She thought of the kindness and respect he'd shown her since they'd met and the laughter which they'd shared. She thought of how her body was still singing after their night together and how she wanted many more nights with him. She thought of how she loved him and it made his question very easy to answer.

'Yes, Steven, now I am happy.'

When they stepped back onto the street outside the Guinness factory, Mats looked at Steven and asked, 'Where do you want to go now?'

He took her hand, gave her a long kiss and whispered, 'I believe we have a late check-out on our suite. Why don't we pick up some cream cakes from that gorgeous delicatessen we passed and take them back to eat in our room?'

'You want to sit indoors and eat cream cakes?' Mats looked at Steven as though he'd lost all his marbles.

'Yes, I do!'

'We've still got a load of Dublin to explore and you want to eat cream cakes?'

'Ah, but Mats, I haven't told you *how* I plan to eat the cakes…' He whispered in her ear and as he spoke, the tingle she'd suppressed a short time earlier made a reappearance.

When Steven pulled back and looked at her, Mats had only one thought on her mind.

'I'll race you to the deli!

THIRTY-THREE

'So, are you two a "couple" now?' Emma paused in her stirring of the Thai Green curry she was cooking to put her annoying air quotes around the word couple.

'What's she's really asking you, mate, is did the two of you get down and dirty in Ireland?'

'NEIL!' Steven and Emma exclaimed in unison.

'What?' Neil looked at them both. 'I'm only saying it as it is.'

'Well, to answer *Emma's* question, while we haven't actually stated we're a couple, I suppose we kind of are.'

Emma had been at Steven's flat on Sunday night feeding Percival when he'd arrived home from the airport. Naturally, she'd asked how the weekend had gone but he'd kept his answer deliberately vague. He wasn't ready to share anything at that time. It wasn't that he was being secretive, he just wanted some alone-time to go over the weekend again in his head, re-live the special moments and fully digest all that Mats had shared with him. Not just about her mother but also how she felt about him. He still couldn't get his head, or his heart, around the fact that his feelings were reciprocated. He knew his lack of self-belief came from his upbringing – having a mother who consistently told him his brother was so much better meant it had taken a long time for him to realise he was worthy in his own right. However, knowing this didn't stop him from having to fight the self-doubt which still reared its ugly head on a regular basis and he'd been having a major self-doubt crisis. One of Emma's special gifts, however, was her intuition. She'd quickly gathered up her bag, kissed him on the cheek and told him to come round for dinner on Tuesday when he could tell them everything about Dublin once he'd pulled his head together.

Steven had been grateful for her understanding and the large bouquet of flowers he'd brought with him this evening was both a thank you for feeding his four-legged flatmate and for her understanding. Now, both her and Neil were standing looking expectantly at him, waiting for him to impart more information.

Neil waved a bottle at him. 'Steven, if you want this beer, then you need to spill just a little bit more than that.'

He sighed. 'Okay! All I am saying is this – the suite had two bedrooms but we only used one!'

He tried to hold back his grin as Emma and Neil high-fived each other.

'Nice one, Steven.' Neil passed over his beer and chinked his own bottle against it.

A few minutes later, bowls of curry and rice were placed on the table and along with instructions to "Dive on in", Emma also demanded that he share everything which he did whilst he ate. When he got to the bit about giving up their table at the restaurant, Emma was gobsmacked that Mats hadn't been annoyed about it.

'You're honestly telling me that she was happy about substituting an evening of fine dining at Hughie O'Grady's for a take-away Happy Meal in the park?'

'Yup!' Steven smiled at the memory and for a moment, he was back lying on the grass with Mats in his arms as they chattered about nothing important.

'Uh oh! Look at the mushy expression there, Emma. I think our boy has caught the love-bug.'

'I suspect you could be right there, Neil! It had to happen one day I suppose. Our little man is growing up…'

'Oh, piss off you two!'

Laughter filled the kitchen and Steven felt the warm glow wash over him that being with his best friends always brought. He knew they cared about him and their teasing came from a place of love. Still smiling, he finished sharing his weekend with them although there were a few moments he chose to keep to himself – such as the look on Mats' face when they'd first made love and how it had felt for him. He also didn't think there was a need to expand on how the cream cakes had been consumed on Sunday afternoon. Saying they had shared a Cream Tea was all they needed to know.

'So, what now? What will you be telling Marky Sparks tomorrow morning? Are you prepared to share all this with the whole of London?'

Emma's questions brought with them a feeling of horror. He and Mats hadn't discussed what they were going to say – they'd been so wrapped up in each other, they'd pretty much forgotten what had brought them to that point.

'Damn! Good point, Ems. We haven't talked about that and we really should. I don't know if we're ready to share this yet.'

'If I might make a suggestion – keep it under your hats for a little while longer. You're already starting to gain media attention. Once they find out you've moved up to the next level, you won't get any peace.'

'I agree with Emma, mate. I know neither of you

anticipated the level of interest you're now facing but you've hit a sweet spot in a time when there was nothing of importance going on. People were bored of politics and bad news – you guys are something positive at the right time and now everyone wants to know everything about you. Look at these…'

Neil walked over to the cupboard and came back with a couple of newspapers. 'Yesterday's morning papers, Steven.'

He opened them up before passing them across and Steven saw photographs of him and Mats on the gossip pages, taken as they'd left the airport on Sunday night. He looked at them in horror.

'Please tell me there aren't any from Dublin?'

'We haven't seen anything. I'm guessing the radio station kept your location quiet in order to protect you both to some degree.'

'Yes, you might be right there. I did wonder why Marky told us not to post anything about where we were and what we were doing until after the show tomorrow morning.'

'He's been dealing with the fame monster for many years,' Emma answered, 'you'd do well to follow his guidance.'

'Anyway, to lighten the mood and change the subject, when do we get to meet the lovely lady who has stolen your heart? Emma here wants to check her out and make sure she's good enough for you.'

'Oi, you! Don't be making out I'm the nosy one when it's you who's been chuntering about it all weekend. Although,' she turned back to Steven, 'I am desperate to meet her. She must be rather special for you to be in this state.'

'I'm not in a state and you can meet her whenever you wish.'

'Tell you what, it's Lily's birthday on Sunday. We were going to have a roast dinner but why don't I do a barbeque instead and you can both come round for that? It'll be low-key, only our parents will be here, so no need to worry about strangers.'

'Are you sure? I'd hate to intrude…'

'Steven! You would never be intruding – we were going to invite you anyway as you are a part of our family. A barbeque is less formal than a sit-down meal and if Mats comes along, it'll be more relaxing for her.'

'I would love for you guys to meet her. She is rather amazing.'

'Ahhhh, young love, such a precious thing…'

'Sod off, Neil!'

Steven stood and helped Emma to clear the plates off the table and into the dishwasher.

'I'll need to speak to Mats tonight to go over what we're saying tomorrow morning, I'll ask her about Sunday and let you know.'

'No problem.' Emma smiled at him. 'Now, let me just pop on the kettle for coffee and then you can describe Mats' purple dress to me in more detail. I'm hoping you took photographs because it sounds divine.'

'You're such a girly at times, Emma.'

'Oh, honey, you had better believe it and I'm really praying that this time you get your happy ever after – you deserve one. Now take these cups through to the lounge while I sort out the coffee.'

THIRTY-FOUR

Marky glanced at the internet print-outs of the various gossip columns Dave had passed to him on Monday. The media love for Mats and Steven wasn't abating. Instead, it was growing greater each day and the station's marketing department was now hounding him for guidance on how he wanted to move it on. The problem was, he didn't know. He hadn't expected this level of interest but it had been a slow news month and their "Love is on the Air" spot had captured London's heart. There had even been talk of syndicating it to a few other stations around the country. On top of this, the phones were ringing off the hook as various magazines and newspapers rang frequently to request interviews. They all seemed to be of the same mind – calling often enough will wear down the resistance against them.

Marky sighed. He was going to have to sit down with Mats and Steven and bring them up to speed on the latest developments and discuss what came next. The station owner was rubbing his hands with glee at the attention and Marky knew he'd want to exploit it as much as he possibly could and he couldn't blame him. After all, the bloke was in the business to make money and the advertising revenue had gone stratospheric. The newly hired advertising director had whispered to him yesterday that they were now having bidding wars with companies desperate to buy the advert spaces around the "Love" slot. The only thing surprising Marky was that neither Steven or Mats had made any mention of being door-stepped by the paparazzi. Having experienced it in his heyday, he knew it was only a matter of time. If the papers didn't get their interviews one way, they would get them another and that would be more difficult to control.

He glanced at the clock and sighed again. It was almost time for todays' catch-up. Just one more – very highly priced – advert to go and then Mats and Steven would be on the air. They'd cancelled the Monday morning catch-up for two reasons – the first one to allow Mats and Steven some time to get over their trip and the second, considered to be far more important, to let the listener tension and expectation build up.

Dave waved to catch his eye.

'Mats and Steven are on the line.'

'Patch them through for their warm up before we go live after the ad…'

A second later, using his most jovial tone of voice, Marky enquired quickly on their wellbeing before hitting the button that would open up the conversation to their growing army of listeners.

Swatterhouse listened to the interview in his home office before thumping his fist down on the "Off" button. His secretary had been calling Smile-A-While radio for the last ten days, trying to get an interview with the couple, but kept coming up against a brick wall. The only thing which gave his miserable little soul any pleasure was knowing that none of the competition was getting close either. He didn't know why the station was being so protective with their new stars but he suspected it was down to timing. Alphabet dating meant there should be twenty-six dates to get through – it wouldn't bode well if everything fell apart after ten!

Swatterhouse was itching to run his own style of investigating but Barbara Coulsen, or "Big Cheese" as most people called the executive editor, had requested a honeyed piece rather than a hatchet job. She said she was sick of her newspaper's continued reputation for destroying people's lives and right now, it would not do them any favours if they were to print anything adverse about the current "Golden Couple". She'd looked straight at him when the directive was given. He'd had to use every ounce of his will-power not to make a sarcastic retort. Dishing the dirt on folks was their stock in trade – why the hell should they be giving this couple the cotton wool treatment.

'Yeah! Why indeed?' he muttered aloud. 'Well, to hell with that!'

He fired up his laptop and as he waited for the internet to load, he came to a decision. Dishing dirt was what he did best and he wasn't about to change that for a woman who was having some kind of hormonal crisis. Everyone has buried secrets – it's just a case of digging until you find them.

THIRTY-FIVE

'Hi, Mats, it's lovely to meet you. Steven has spoken a lot about you.'

'Hey, you're not supposed to say that.'

'Oops!' Neil grinned. 'Then maybe you should have told us to keep it a secret.'

Mats laughed as Steven laid a punch on Neil's arm. Beside her, Emma giggled at their antics.

'Come on, lover boy, help me with the barbie and leave the ladies to gossip about us.'

'Gossip about you? The day you do anything worth gossiping about, there'll be a full-page spread in the Daily Bugle!' Emma placed a kiss on her husband's cheek before slipping her arm through Mats. 'Come, Mats, let's go and find a nicely chilled glass of wine before I introduce you to our folks. We'll leave the Neanderthals to play with the hot, burny, thing!'

Mats laughed again as Emma led her out of the garden and into the cool shade of the kitchen. The terraced house wasn't too dissimilar in lay-out from her own. Many of the terraced houses in South-East London had been built to pretty much the same floor plan and the variance between them was often minimal. Like so many had now done, Emma and Neil had redesigned the ground floor to create a large open-plan kitchen-diner with folding doors which opened right up onto a paved patio. On warm days like today, it created a lovely, happy, ambience.

'I've got rosé or white wine here in the chiller or there's red over there on the counter-top. What do you fancy?'

'White would be good, thank you.' Mats tried not to ogle too much when she was handed a glass large enough to contain half of the bottle. Emma had emptied the other half into her own glass.

'Cheers!' Emma chinked their glasses before taking a big slug from hers. 'Ah, I needed that. I've been rushing around all morning getting things prepared. I love Neil but like many men, he lives under the illusion that barbecues are quick and easy. He is oblivious to everything else that needs to be done.'

Mats smiled at her comment. Other friends had often said the same.

'Maybe, the next time he suggests it, you try not doing anything additional and see how he likes eating a cheeseburger or his hot dog without a roll to put it in or any salad to accompany his chicken drumstick.'

'A tempting idea!'

'I know someone who did exactly that. Her husband suggested a barbie for her birthday and she figured that, as it was her special day, she wouldn't have to do anything so didn't. Twenty people turned up and had a protein-fest because her hubs had given no thought to all the extras.'

'Goodness! What happened?'

'I don't believe they've had a barbecue since and that was two years ago!'

Emma's laughter burst out of her and Mats found

herself laughing too. Emma had a good jolly laugh on her and it was difficult not to join in.

'Then it is definitely worth a try. Now come, let me introduce you to the parents then we can grab a couple of sun-loungers and chill for a bit. I reckon we're looking at about an hour before Laurel and Hardy over there will be ready to feed us.'

Once they were reclining under a large, leafy, oak tree, Mats turned to Emma and asked, 'How long have you all been friends?'

'Steven and Neil hooked up when they were about fourteen, I came along at Uni. We met at a fancy-dress party. I was dressed as Princess Leia from Star Wars and for reasons unknown, so were they.'

'What? Both of them?'

'Yup!'

'And you don't know why?'

'Nope! To this day, they've never told me and I gave up asking a long time ago.'

Mats looked over at Steven's slim build standing next to Neil's solid rugby-player body. 'I'm guessing they looked more comical than comely?'

'Neil did! Steven, however, and more worryingly, looked really quite appealing. He had a few offers that night – I think he still has nightmares about it!'

Their laughter rang out again which earned them a look from the chefs on the other side of the garden. Mats raised her glass in a salute to them and Emma followed suit.

'I have photographs somewhere, from that night. I'll dig them out for you.'

'Oh, please do, I would love to see them.'

They chit-chatted for a while longer until the call came out that grub was up and everyone should grab their plates.

With Lucy and Lily insisting on sitting beside their grandparents as they ate, Mats found herself at a separate table with Emma, Neil and Steven.

'Are we allowed to know how yesterday went,' Emma asked, 'or do we have to wait until it airs on the radio?'

Mats swallowed her mouthful of cheeseburger before replying. 'I don't see any harm in sharing the details of our afternoon with you, do you Steven.'

Before Steven could answer, Neil chipped in. 'Hey, I need to ask – why are your dates so secretive now? Before, when this first started, we knew all the details but now we're being given the briefest of information. This week, all we got told was "it's J for Jumping" and last week, we weren't even told it was "I for Ireland" until you returned. What's that all about?'

'Well, when we did the HotTugs, lots of people came out to see us and it caused some safety concerns. Not just for us but also for the crowds along the river bank and on the bridges. There was a meeting – we weren't included – and it was agreed that going forward, it was in everyone's interest to keep an air of secrecy around the dates until they were complete.'

'I can see the sense in that.' Emma nodded her head.

'So, what did "J for Jumping" entail? Were you sent off to Epsom for a nice day at the races or something?'

'Oh, I wish! Unfortunately, the event was not quite as genteel as that.'

Mats looked at Steven. 'Would you like me to explain?'

'Be my guest!'

Mats looked at Emma and Neil. 'We went…' she deliberately paused for a few seconds, 'Bungee jumping!'

'WHAT? No way!'

Emma looked at them both in amazement while Neil hollered with laughter.

'But…,' he spluttered, 'Steven can't do heights. He hates them. We've been trying to get him to do the London Eye for years but with no joy!'

'I kind of found that out yesterday. Let me tell you, it was a bit of a surprise.'

'Oh, come on, you two, I'm not *that* bad!'

'Did you tell Mats that you declined a nice corner office at work because it had floor to ceiling windows and it made you dizzy?'

'Err, no, he didn't!' Mats looked at him.

'As always, only half the story.' He looked at Mats. 'The office is on the thirty-eighth floor so it's just a bit on the high side to feel comfortable with such large windows.'

'Never mind that,' Neil waved his hand at Steven, 'I want the full low-down on yesterday afternoon, Mats, and don't you dare leave anything out. Did Steven actually wet his pants?'

'No, he did not, Neil. He was very brave and I am so proud of him.'

'You're not telling us he did a bungee jump?

'That's exactly what I'm telling you.'

'Hang on!' Emma jumped up, went into the kitchen and returned a moment later with two beers and another bottle of wine. 'Right! Now we're ready.'

Mats took Steven's hand in hers and squeezed it as she began recounting the previous afternoon…

THIRTY-SIX

'Are you okay?' Mats glanced at Steven. He'd been very quiet on the tube and he now appeared to be growing paler by the minute.

'Yes, I'm fine.'

'Okay, if you say so.' She looked back at the instructions she'd been given to follow. They still didn't know what the actual gig was for today – only that it somehow involved jumping. They'd received an email the night before directing them to the vicinity of the O2 Arena on the east side of London. The information was rather sparse and the last sentence simply stated, *"You'll know what to do when you see it!"*

They followed the small, coarsely drawn map and found themselves in one of the many car parks which surrounded the area. The only thing in sight was a large crane a short distance away. Beneath it there appeared to be a huge air-bed, just like the ones you see on the television when people are threatening to jump off high buildings.

Mats looked around but there was nothing else close-by which could be their final destination. It would seem the crane was where they should be heading.

'Oh, shit! I feel sick!'

She turned to Steven in concern. He did look really quite ill now.

'What's wrong?'

He nodded at the crane. 'It's what I suspected, it's the bloody bungee jump...'

'What? You're kidding?'

Mats spun round in time to see a small body launch itself from the cage at the top. It flew down before coming to a sudden halt and bouncing back up again. The body bounced a few more times and then, when it stopped, it was slowly lowered to the ground as it swayed back and forth in the wind like a pendulum on a grand-father clock.

'Oh, wow! Awesome! I've always fancied doing one of those. Come on, let's go!' She grabbed Steven's arm and tried to pull him along. The last thing she was expecting was his resistance.

'I can't do that!' He looked at her and then back at the crane. 'I can't go on that thing!'

'Hey, it's okay! They really strap you in tight. You'll be fine.'

'No, Mats, I won't. It's not the bungee that I'm afraid of... it's the height! I can't do heights.'

'But... we went on an aeroplane to Dublin and you said nothing. We did the climbs on the assault course and they didn't bother you. I'm confused.'

'Planes are okay because there's only a tiny window and you don't see much. I wasn't being a gentleman by letting you have the window seat – I just can't bear to look out. The assault course climbs were only about ten feet or so which doesn't bother me. It's when we get higher that I begin to have a problem.'

'But, The Gravity Bar at the Guinness factory—'

'Where I didn't once look out of the window, didn't admire the view and kept my eyes focused only on you the whole time we were sitting there…'

'You should have said something.'

'We were having such a lovely time and I didn't want to spoil it.'

Mats turned to face him. 'You sat out on the balcony of the hotel with me!'

'AFTER I'd had a big slug of Champagne to give me Dutch courage. *That's* why I opened the bottle inside.'

Mats stared at him for a few seconds before turning back to look at the crane. 'Well, that's a bit of a bugger,' she said, as she saw the small cage ascending to the top where another jumper prepared themselves for their adrenaline fix. 'Look, how about we go over and see what the deal is? No one is going to force you to do anything you don't want to do.'

'But—'

'Steven, we need to at least show our faces. They'll be expecting us. Now, come on.'

Mats took his hand and all but dragged him over to the area where the bungee was set up. It hadn't looked that high from a distance but as they approached, she began to realise that the distance had been deceptive. It was bloody huge!

They gave the air mattress a wide berth and found a small gang of workers on the other side. They all wore T-shirts with the company logo on and a gorgeous, blonde-haired girl, carrying a clipboard, walked towards them.

'Hi, how ya doing? Have you made a booking?'

Mats smiled at the broad Australian accent. She'd known many Aussies over the years and they'd all been into their high-octane sports. She explained who they were and immediately, the welcome level bounced up higher than their bungees did!

'Hey, great to meet ya. I'm Verity and I'll be looking after you this afternoon. Jono and Greg over there will be in charge of your jumps. They've been doing this for years and they'll take great care of you. You have nothing to be worried about. Now, if you would like to step over here, we'll need to weigh you to ensure we use the correct bungee ropes.'

They followed Verity over towards a small, pop-up gazebo. Steven's hand now felt clammy and there was a distinctly pale-green tinge around his gills.

'Are you going to throw up?' Mats whispered.

'Trying really hard not to…'

'Look, I'll tell them you're not jumping and it's just going to be me. They should be alright with that.'

'But then I'll look like a complete wimp when we tell Marky I didn't do it.'

'Steven, you can't help your phobia. It's a pretty common one and I'm sure there'll be plenty of listeners who'll sympathise with you. Don't worry about it.'

'Well, if you're sure you don't mind.'

'Of course, I don't mind. Don't be so daft. Now, you can just stand back, relax and be convinced that I really am off my trolley when I throw myself out of the cage!'

'You're still going ahead with a jump?'

Mats found herself having to hold back a sharp retort. She got that Steven wasn't for doing this but she wasn't about to pass up the chance to do something she'd had a fancy to do for years. Just because she'd never gotten around to actually sorting something out didn't mean she was about to let this opportunity go to waste. She drew in a breath before answering.

'Yes, Steven, I'm still doing a jump and I'm expecting you to be supportive. It might not be your thing but that doesn't mean I should miss out.'

'You want me to watch the woman I love throw

herself off the top of a crane, a million miles up in the air?'

'A million miles? Get real! It's probably not even a hundred feet!'

'It's five-hundred and twenty-five feet actually,' said Verity, as she returned with their harnesses in her hand.

'Oh! A bit higher than I realised…' Mats felt herself go a little lightheaded at the thought.

'You can still pull out, you know,' Steven spoke quietly at her shoulder.

'No, I can't! I am doing this.'

'Why?'

'So, I can say that I did it, Steven, that's why! In years to come, if I ever have grandchildren, I want them to think I had an exciting life and this is right up there in the excitement stakes.'

'So, who's first on the scales?' Verity smiled at them both.

'That'll be me, please.'

Mats stepped forward and Verity made a note of her weight. She stepped off, waited a moment and then stepped back on again as Verity explained they weighed people twice for precautionary purposes as it was imperative the correct bungee rope was used.

They quickly explained that Steven wouldn't be doing a jump after which it wasn't long before Mats was ready to go. She hopped over to Steven and placed a big kiss on his rather worried face.

'Look, I'm going to be fine. Smile! It'll all be over in a few minutes.'

'Just be safe, Mats. I love you.'

'I love you too, you worry-wart. It will be okay.'

As the cage began its ascent up to the top of the crane, however, Mats did begin to doubt her show of bravado. She looked over the London skyline as she found out that five-hundred and twenty-five feet afforded her one hell of a view.

'Okay, Mats, are you ready to go?'

She didn't know if it was Jono or Greg who was talking to her and at this point, it didn't really make much difference.

'Is it something anyone is ever ready to do?'

'Not the first time but after that? You'd be surprised! Now, you can just step out whenever you're ready or if you prefer, I can give you a push. Most folks take the push option, if it helps.'

'Yeah, okay. Do that one.'

She stood perched on the edge of the cage, hands crossed over in front of her chest to prevent them hitting the rails by her side, and waited. Just as she thought nothing was going to happen, there was some light pressure between her shoulder blades and she was falling through the air! The wind rushed against her face and a scream charged forth from her lips. The bouncy mattress below grew closer and closer and just as Mats thought she was about to hit it, there was a tight sensation around her ankles and she was being pulled back up into the air. This time, she was uttering squeals of delight and joy as she bounced up and down a further four or five times before she was lowered to the ground and onto a smaller airbed. She felt the adrenaline speeding through her bones as Verity came over to help her to her feet. Once upright, she threw her head back and let out the loudest of screams.

'Oops! Sorry, Verity, are your ears alright?'

Verity looked up from where she was kneeling at Mats ankle, undoing the straps around them, and smiled. 'No worries, Mats, I'm used to it. It happens a lot after a first jump.'

Once she was released from her harness and bonds, Mats all but skipped over to Steven, threw her arms around him and squeezed him tight, her euphoria flowing from every pore. Steven clutched her close to his chest and it was then she realised he was trembling.

'Hey!' She pulled back and looked at the pallor on his face and the fear in his eyes.

'I'm sorry, Mats, I was just so scared for you. I was fighting between not wanting to look but unable to take my eyes off you. I'm such a wuss, I know, I'm sorry, I'm sorry…'

His voice tailed off as his chin dropped and he stared down at the ground.

'Oi, you!' Mats whispered softly as she grabbed both his hands in hers and bent her knees so he could see her face.

'You're not a wuss, Steven, and don't ever think otherwise. You have a phobia about heights – big deal! It's not something to get hung up over. I've already said this to you. It doesn't change how I feel about you or what I think of you. Everyone has a vulnerable point, heights are yours. I'm sorry that I scared you – I wouldn't have done it if I'd realised it would make you feel *this* bad.'

'No, Mats, no! You must *not* apologise for being brave. I saw how pale you were when you hopped onto the crane. I watched you mustering up the courage to do the jump as the crane ascended and took you away from me. I admire every single part of you for being so brave and it's that admiration which makes me feel so ashamed of myself. I wish I had your bravery.'

'You are brave in other ways, Steven. It would be rather dull if the whole world was brave against the same fears – I think we'd live in a rather unbalanced society if it worked like that, don't you think?'

'I suppose! Like… if everyone was scared of bees, we wouldn't have honey!'

'Exactly! And if everyone was scared of heights, we wouldn't have bridges or aeroplanes.'

'And if everyone was scared of water, I suppose we'd all be rather smelly!'

'For sure! Can you imagine? The expression, "The great unwashed" would have a whole new meaning to it. Quite literally!'

Mats caught Steven's eye as she said this and suddenly, they were both rocking with laughter. The tension broke and she could see his shoulders drop as he began to relax. She put her arm through his, called out a goodbye to Verity and turned towards the car park exit.

'Come on you,' she grinned, 'I think we could both do with a very large drink after that!'

THIRTY-SEVEN

Steven listened to Mats gently humming under her breath as they traversed the large expanse of concrete, heading back to the exit from the car park and leaving the scene of his humiliation behind with each footstep. Unfortunately, the sense of shame had insisted on accompanying them and was making itself quite comfortable across his shoulders. How could he have allowed Mats to take such a risk while he'd just stood by and watched? Why had he been unable to find the courage to join her? Sometimes, he felt his phobia was more of an excuse than a reason when it came to avoiding things he didn't have the courage to try. There had been a sponsored parachute jump arranged by a number of his work colleagues but he'd thrown his phobia around like it was some kind of trump card because he'd lacked the courage to try. Even little Suzy, the eighteen-year-old office junior, had jumped and she was scared of *everything*! Spiders, heights, the dark, cracks on the pavement... He'd admired her spirit along with the rest of the office which now made him wonder what their impression had been of him. No one had said anything but the thought must have crossed their minds – Suzy, the baby of the office, had more balls than him.

The further away they walked from the bungee crew, the more his self-respect shrunk. As they walked out of the car park gates, a long-forgotten conversation with his grandfather surfaced in his mind.

They'd been sitting on their favourite bench in Postman's Park, eating a picnic lunch his grandfather had brought. Steven reckoned he must have been about eight or nine-years-old. They'd been discussing the plaques on the wall and the bravery of those commemorated. Steven had commented on how scared they must have been and his grandfather had replied, 'Steven, there will always come a day when each man must face his fear and conquer it. When I fought in the war, my comrades and I had to face our fear of dying every day. For too many, it became a reality. On the day of the Normandy landings, my unit, along with many others, were squashed onto boats and false bravado joined us. There was much banter and raucous joking on the journey until the last few final minutes when our fear became too much and silence fell over us. We were terrified of what we were about to face but we also knew that, by facing our fear, we would be helping our nation to maintain its freedom. Yes, many lives were lost that day but they were not lost in vain. Their courage saved so many more. I hope that one day, if you ever need face up to something which frightens you, it is not the freedom of your country that you gain but a personal freedom from whatever caused the fear in the first place. Never hesitate to be brave, Steven, for it will bring you more happiness than living in fear ever will.'

He'd looked up at his grandfather and replied, 'I will always be brave, Grandfather, just for you.' Steven smiled as he heard his childhood voice in his head.

'Steven,' his grandfather had said kindly, 'Be brave

for yourself but, if it helps, then you can be brave for me too.' He'd then ruffled his hair, put an arm around his shoulder and had held him tightly by his side. Steven had never felt more loved than he had in those few moments.

'Mats…' He stopped, took his arm from hers and stood still.

She turned to look at him.

'Are you okay, Steven? What's wrong?'

'I have to do the jump!'

'No, you don't. I told you – no one will think any less of you for not doing it.'

'*I* will think less of me. And I matter more to me than other people. Will you come back with me? Will you help me? Please?'

'Of course, I'll help. What do you want me to do?'

'I don't think I've got what it takes to do this alone but if you were with me…' He looked at her beseechingly.

'A tandem jump?'

He nodded, unable to get the words out of his mouth which was now drier than he'd ever known.

Mats smiled at him with such radiance. 'Steven, it would be my pleasure to share this with you. Let's see if Verity can accommodate us.'

She took his hand and they quickly retraced their steps. Mats clearly wasn't giving him the chance to change his mind a second time.

'Oh! Hi again.' Verity looked surprised to see them. Mats filled her in on their discussion and when she looked at him, he merely nodded. It seemed that this courage thing brought with it the inability to speak. 'Give me a couple of minutes, let me see if I can shuffle some bookings.'

When she returned, Verity was smiling widely. 'Your luck is in… or out, depending on how you want to view it. We've just had a text from a couple who are on their way but have been delayed on the tube. By pushing their slot back, it enables us to fit you in. We'll do all the weighing now, get you into your harnesses and you'll go up in about twenty minutes.'

'Okay. Thank you.' Steven managed to croak out some words but he felt like he was about to pass out.

Verity pointed them towards the weighing-in area and as Mats took his hand, she whispered, 'You can do this and I'm going to be right by your side, every single step of the way.'

'I think you mean every single step over the edge…'

'Gallows humour, Steven, I like it.'

'Well, if I'm going to die, I might as well go out smiling.'

'You gotta die of something, right?'

'Yeah, and at least I'll go with you in my arms.'

Mats stopped, turned to face him and stretched up to place a kiss on his lips.

'I can't think of a better way to go,' she said quietly in his ear.

In what felt like the fastest twenty minutes ever, Steven found himself on the crane, being hooked on to Mats harness, his ankles bound tightly together and their arms wrapped around each other. When they'd hopped onto the cage down below, Mats had smiled at Jono and Greg and had said, 'Same again, please.' Steven didn't know what she meant but they did for they just nodded and said, 'Okay'.

'Steven, if you go over backwards, that might be better… Steven, open your eyes!'

'Nope! If I can't see, I can pretend this is not happening.'

He really wished it wasn't. Oh, dear goodness! What on earth had possessed him to think he could do this? His stomach was churning beyond belief! His bowels felt like they were about to give way any moment and if it wasn't for Mats holding him tightly, he would be a quivering heap on the floor of the cage.

'Steven, open your eyes and look at me. Don't look at anything else, just me.'

Feeling like he was facing the jaws of Cerberus, he managed to force his eyelids to perform an upwards manoeuvre. Mats' dark blue gaze seared into his.

'Now breathe with me. In… out. In…out. In—'

Suddenly, and without warning, he saw a hand land between Mats' shoulder blades and they were falling through the air. He'd barely registered the light fluffy clouds above him when they twisted in the air and the white lines of the concrete car park were flying up to greet him. A scream flew from his lips and his heart, which had already been pounding faster than he'd ever thought possible, felt like it was about to rip through his rib cage.

In the fraction of a nano-second, when he'd decided it was game over and they were about to crash onto the ground, he felt the tension in his ankles and they were being pulled back up into the air.

That was when he began to laugh!

THIRTY-EIGHT

'YOU DID A BUNGEE JUMP?'

Emma looked at Steven, her mouth opening and closing like the proverbial goldfish.

'I sure did!'

She looked at Mats. 'You got him to do a bungee jump? The man who can't look out of his own office window?'

Mats took his hand, gave it a gentle squeeze, and replied, 'The only thing I did, Emma, was be by Steven's side in his moment of bravery. It was his decision to do the jump, I was merely his wing-man.'

Neil took his hand and shook it. 'Fair credit to you, Steven, you've got bigger balls than me! I'm not scared of heights but even I wouldn't do one of those. That really took some guts. I'm proud of you, man, really proud.'

Steven felt himself choke up at Neil's words; words he'd so rarely heard in his life and not since his grandfather had passed away. In the last twenty-four hours, however, he'd heard them several times over. From every member of the bungee crew and from Mats all the way home. She'd even stopped to buy a couple of bottles of Bolly on the way – 'After all, Patsy, we've definitely got something to celebrate tonight!'

After they'd hoovered up a large Indian takeaway – it seemed adrenaline rushes were soon followed by the urge to eat several horses, scabby or otherwise – and were making good inroads on the second bottle of fizz, Mats had asked him why he'd changed his mind. He'd shared the memory with her and her reply, 'Your grandfather would be so very, very proud of you for doing it,' would stay with him until he drew his last breath.

'I like her! A lot!'

'I'm sorry, what?' Steven jumped when Emma came to stand beside him in the kitchen. The parents had said their goodbyes and left, Neil and Mats were tidying the garden and Emma had been putting the girls to bed while he'd loaded the dishwasher and cleared up in the kitchen. He'd been lost in his thoughts from the day before, staring out of the window at Mats and hadn't heard Emma come into the room.

'Mats! I like her. She's a keeper, my friend. Don't let her go.'

'Crikey! That's quite the compliment coming from you, Ems. I'll ask her to marry me now, shall I?'

She grinned and tapped the top of his arm gently. 'Ya daft eejit! You know what I mean! But yes, marriage would be good although it might be a bit soon. You do like her a lot though, I can tell.'

'As do you, by the sound of things.'

'I like the fact she supports you, Steven. Many women would have taken the opportunity earlier to have poked fun at you and belittle you but she didn't. She stood proudly beside you and delighted in telling us of your triumph.

That's the kind of partner we all should have – someone who always has our back and rejoices with us through the good times and stands with us through the bad times.'

Steven didn't have an answer to that so he just smiled and then chuckled with Emma as they watched Mats ordering Neil about in his own garden.

'As I said, Steven, I like her a lot!'

Later that night, when they were curled up in bed, Steven shared Emma's comments with Mats.

'That's nice, I really liked them too. I liked how they were so informal and welcomed me as though they'd know me for years. I felt really comfortable in their company.'

'So, you wouldn't mind seeing them again?'

'Not at all.'

'Emma also said I've to keep you. I suspect she's hoping there'll be wedding bells sometime in the future…' Steven didn't know what Mats' views were on marriage now, it wasn't a topic they'd gotten around to talking about yet so he figured this was the perfect excuse to open up that discussion. Might as well know the lie of the land before he did something really stupid further down the line.

'Is she now? Interesting to know.'

'So, is it something you think you might do some day? Get married again?'

'Is that an offer?'

Steven felt his cheeks flame up and was glad of the darkness which hid them.

'Err, no! Gosh no! Just a general enquiry. These days, people have so many different views on the subject, I just thought I'd ask.'

'Well, I'm not averse to the idea of marrying again and I suppose, when I was younger, I probably thought it would be a given. But here I am now, mid-thirties, still single, no kids and it's made me see that nothing is guaranteed. I'm quite happy with my life, I don't feel unfulfilled or that I've failed and I detest how, even now, society in general still makes women feel that marriage and childbirth is all they're good for.'

'So, you don't have some deep, dark desire to walk down the aisle in a big white meringue dress while half-a-dozen golden horses wait outside to pull the carriage with you and your Prince Charming off into the sunset?'

'Blimey! Absolutely not! Nothing could be more abhorrent to me! That is one thing that is guaranteed if I do ever remarry – there will be no bells and whistles, no big ceremony, no pomp and circumstance. The Arrival of the Queen of Sheba will not be played on my wedding day. I never want to walk down the aisle again – the best I will manage is a fast sprint through the registry office.'

'Does Penny, the supremo wedding coordinator, know this?'

'It's Penny that has put me off ever wanting the traditional big day. These days it's all bridezillas and hysterics and her talk of them fills me with horror. There's no way I'd put myself under that kind of stress. No siree! I'm sure she thinks she'll be organising my big day for me but the only "big" she'll be getting is a disappointment!'

Mats turned around and spooned her back against his chest.

'What about you, Steven, does marriage feature in your future?'

'It would be nice, I think, to know that someone whom you love enough to marry also loves you enough to agree to spending the rest of their lives with you.'

'Would you want the big bash?'

'I'd just go with whatever made my wife-to-be happy. I don't have a preference either way.'

'Hmmmm…'

There was silence after that and it wasn't long before Mats' breathing deepened and Steven knew she was asleep. He wriggled closer to her and held her tightly to him.

'I'd happily sprint through a registry office with you, Mats. Anytime!' he whispered. He lay, breathing in her sweet smell until he too, drifted off to sleep.

THIRTY-NINE

'Marky, you can't protect them forever! The whole deal with this dating thing was to raise the profile of the station. They need to begin doing interviews and putting themselves out there.'

Marky raised his eyes up from the black coffee in front of him and looked into the frustrated gaze of the P.R. executive – another recent hiring by the station. He knew Paul was right. But he hadn't expected to become so attached to Steven and Mats and he sure as hell hadn't anticipated falling in love with Mats' best friend!

Marky had never believed in love at first sight. He'd always pooh-poohed the idea as lovey-dovey nonsense but he'd soon changed his mind when he met Penelope Laidlaw. Something had fallen into place that day – like the piece of a jigsaw which never seems to fit anywhere until, suddenly, it does! – and despite it only being a couple of weeks, Marky knew he would be spending the rest of his life with this amazing woman. He adored everything about her – her feisty personality, her off-beat sense of humour, her ability to turn every crisis into a raging success… although, he supposed, in her line of work, the latter was an everyday occurrence—

'Marky, are you listening?'

'Yes, yes! I am! Sorry. I was just thinking about the best way to move this forward as you wish but without exposing Mats and Steven to the harsher side of the media.'

'Have either of them made any mention about being door-stepped yet?'

Marky shook his head. 'Surprisingly, no. Dave? Have they said anything to you?'

Dave also shook his head.

'Well, we'd better get them in and prepare them because ten other radio stations have agreed to air the spot live on their breakfast shows. They need to go on television and announce themselves to the nation so that, when the syndication rolls out, the new listeners will know who they are and what it's all about.'

Paul cleared his throat, stared at Marky and carried on. 'We also need to know if there is anything in their past which could take us by surprise. You can guarantee there will be some tacky little journo somewhere trying to find a skeleton or two in their closets.'

'Swatterhouse has been sniffing about. He's put in several requests for an interview, along with a few of his colleagues.' Paul's secretary reeled off a few names from The Weekday News along with those of other big, nationwide, media outlets.

'Marky, this interview has to be done soon. It really should have gone out weeks ago after the assault course although I do agree that letting everyone stew hasn't done us any harm. I suppose allowing the mystery and mystique to build has kept the public interest bubbling along.'

'Exactly!' Marky slammed his hand on the table. 'If you give the public what they want straight away, they don't appreciate it. Forcing them to wait will make them hungry for more. No matter how much we give them, it'll never be enough. Mats and Steven's celebrity status will be cemented and the station will be riding high right beside them.' He looked at the nodding heads around the meeting room table.

'Look, I suggest we hold off just one more week. Let's get dates 'K' and 'L' done and then roll out the carpet when they get to 'M'. That's the midway point of the alphabet and I think, the perfect time to let them become public property. Get them on that evening show on the BBC.'

'On the Sofa?'

'Yeah, Dave, that one. It's a magazine show so not exactly fierce or hard-hitting – it'll be a gentle breaking-in for them both. They're not celebrity seekers so their introduction to TV interviews will need to be handled carefully.'

Once again, the rest of the table nodded their agreement.

'Yeah, good call, Marky. We'll get on to that straightaway. You,' the P.R exec pointed at him, 'need to get your little ducks lined up and prepped for what's coming next. They've had the fun stuff, now they need to give some payback.'

Marky smiled until everyone had left the room and it was only him and Dave left.

'Dave, do you get the feeling Paul hasn't fully read the contract?'

'What do you mean? I'm sure he has.'

'Then why was there no mention of the fact that Mats and Steven can walk away from all this in less than two weeks' time. They're only contracted to do fourteen dates. After that, they can "leave" at any time, no questions asked.'

'Oh, shit!'

'Yeah, Dave, "Oh shit" indeed!'

'Do you think they will?'

'I'm hoping not. They seem quite happy with how things are but as that's all about to change…'

'Hmm! I agree although, right now, I have to say I'm more concerned to hear that Swatterhouse has been sniffing about. You know what he's like – he could dig up dirt on the angel Gabriel if he put his mind to it. No matter how clean Steven and Mats are, everyone has at least one secret and he's the expert in finding them.'

Marky chewed on his thumbnail. The problem with Swatterhouse was that you were damned either way. Don't give him the interview – he'll print something sensationalist but if you do give him the interview, he'll STILL put out something sensationalist! It was what he did best and it was also why he was one of the most detested men in the industry.

'There's not a lot we can do there, Dave. We just have to hope that, for once, there really is nothing to find. Now, let's see what options we've got for the next two dates and then we can arrange to meet Mats and Steven to discuss what's coming next.'

FORTY

Mats took a sip of water and sat back to let Karen, the make-up lady, do her worst. She hated wearing heavy make-up but knew it was a necessity for television if you didn't want to look half-dead under the bright studio lights. She hadn't lived in a theatrical family all her life without picking up a thing or two along the way.

She thought of her mother as Karen got to work and wished she was around now. She could have done with some advice on how to deal with the media when all their attention was focused on you. It was easy to answer questions on artists and bands who'd become successful once they passed through her music studio – it was much less fun when it was *you* they wanted to know more about.

'Close your eyes for me, please, Mats,' Karen said and Mats felt the gentle pressure of thick foundation being wiped over her eyelids and forehead. In some ways it was quite soothing and she felt herself relaxing. Oh, how her mother would have loved this, having her performance face put on by someone else. One of Mats earliest memories of her mum was when she was about five and

219

her grandmother had taken her to see a performance one night at the theatre. They'd arrived early and had gone in via the stage door. All around her the actors were bustling about – some in various stages of dress, some were pacing while practising lines and others were just standing about in small groups chatting. One thing they all shared though, was a nervous energy in anticipation of the evening's show. Even at such a young age, Mats had been able to feel the fizz in the air.

When they'd been shown into her mum's dressing room – she was the understudy for the leading lady who didn't perform on Wednesdays – her mum had been sitting in front of a big showbiz mirror surrounded by lights, putting on her stage face. Mats had dragged a small stool over and clambered up to watch her mother work. She'd been fascinated at how the make-up changed her mother's face and how she'd become "older" right in front of her eyes. She couldn't remember a single thing about the actual show itself but that memory of her mother was one which had stayed with her.

'Okay, nearly done, Mats, I just need you to open your eyes so I can put on the mascara.'

Mats blinked as Karen's voice brought her back into the present and she realised the same buzz of anticipation was in the air of the television studio now and it felt exactly as it had that special night. Trips to the theatre to see her mum perform had become rare treats as she grew older and none of them had stuck with her in quite the same way.

'Finished. What do you think?' Karen stepped out of the way to allow Mats to look in the mirror.

'Wow! That's good!' Mats was impressed. She could feel the make-up on her face was considerably heavier than what she was used to but at the same time, it all looked so natural. Karen had done wonders with her eyes which made them look more purple than blue. Mats leaned closer into the mirror to see how they had been done and tried to memorise it to try in the future.

'You have Elizabeth Taylor eyes. I rarely get the chance to work on such a versatile palette so I took the opportunity to enhance the purple hues. I hope you like it.'

'Karen, I love it. Thank you. I'm just taking note of some of your little tricks for future reference.' Mats smiled at Karen in the mirror.

'Right, we'd better get you into your outfit and out to the studio. We'll be going on air very soon.'

Ten minutes later, Mats was gingerly stepping over cables and around cameras as the floor manager guided her over to Sparks and Dave. They were talking quite heatedly but stopped mid-flow when she approached them.

'Oh wow! Don't you look something else. I'd give you a hug but I'm scared I might smudge ya!' Sparks smiled at her.

''Thank you.' She smiled back. 'What's wrong?'

'Nothing. What makes you think there is?'

'Sparks, your hands were flying about and I could hear the tension in your voice as I walked over. What's going on?'

Dave let out a sigh. 'One of the usual presenters is on holiday – which we didn't know – and her stand-in is a bit of a journalistic shark. She cut her teeth amidst the old Fleet Street hacks and doesn't hold back on her interviewing techniques. What should have been a gentle walk into the media circus might turn out to be a baptism of fire. "Gentle" is a word which has never appeared in this woman's vocabulary.

'So, who is it we're going to be facing?'

'Katherine Adamson.'

'Oh, shit!' Mats felt her mouth dry up. Dave's description of "shark" was bang on the money. In fact, Mats would go as far as to say it was an insult to the generally feared occupants of the sea. She'd seen a few Adamson interviews in the past and the woman was brutal.

'Why on earth have they brought her on? I wouldn't have thought this was her kind of show.'

'Goodness only knows. You just need to be ready for anything she throws at you. Now, remember the trick I told you – if you need a few seconds to think of an answer, take a sip of water to kill a bit of time. You never want to look like you're thinking about your answers so that's how to hide it.'

'I'll remember, Sparks, thank you for all your tutoring – we both really appreciate it. Well, I say both… where's Steven?'

'Just coming up behind you now.'

Mats turned as Steven arrived beside her.

'Oh, you are kidding me! Seriously?'

She looked at the charcoal suit he was wearing which was beautifully cut and fitted perfectly. The lilac shirt and purple tie, which was almost an exact match for her dress, is what had brought about her dismay.

'We look like posh shell suits! Could they have made us any more "coupley"?'

'But you are a couple now!'

Mats looked at Sparks in surprise as they hadn't yet shared this news with him or Dave.

'Excuse me?'

'Look, Mats, we're not stupid. We can see the glow surrounding you both and the small unconscious touches you make.'

'You didn't say anything?'

'It was a future discussion for when we felt it was the right time to make it public. So, for now, keep schtum out there and let everyone believe love is still waiting to happen.'

'Okay, fair enough, we're a couple but back to the

subject of what we're wearing – we can still dress independently of each other. I've never dressed to match my other half in my life and I don't appreciate having to do so now.'

'Well, it's too late to do anything about it, they're calling you over to get into position so stop scowling and start smiling. Good luck. We'll be here rooting for you.'

FORTY-ONE

'So, Steven, you've been very quiet about your relationship with Stuart Byrne – the founder and CEO of Easy PC's. Is there a reason why?'

Katherine Adamson looked sternly at him and her fake smile didn't reach her dead, dark, eyes. Mats watched and listened to her verbally circling Steven and longed to touch his hand in a show of support but daren't do so for she knew Adamson would notice and use it against them.

'No reason at all, Katherine,' Steven smiled as he replied.

'Then why keep it so quiet?'

'I haven't kept it quiet, Katherine, I simply didn't feel it was something that needed to be discussed.'

'But he's your twin brother.'

'That's correct, Katherine, he's my *twin* brother, not my *Siamese* twin brother – we're not joined at the hip and we lead our own lives. He's busy with his career and I'm busy with mine.'

Oh, you didn't like that, did you lady, Mats thought as she watched the small shark eyes narrow at Steven's answer. Since they'd sat down on the famous yellow sofa, Adamson had oozed animosity. Mats could feel it flowing in waves around them. Apart from a brief introduction, she'd ignored them until they were on air. Her co-host, and regular presenter, Tim Branson had been friendly enough but Adamson had taken over the interview and wasn't letting him get a word in.

'Talking of your careers, though, didn't you begin yours by working for your brother in Easy PC's early days?'

'I didn't work *for* Stuart, I worked *with* Stuart.'

'You created the company together?'

'When Stuart came up with the idea for his first product, I offered to help him market it. I'd recently qualified and was full of beginners' enthusiasm.'

Mats risked a swift glance at Steven and noted the tightness in his jaw. She knew he wasn't happy with the turn the interview had taken. For goodness sake, he hadn't gotten around to sharing his deepest, darkest secrets with her yet and now Adamson was trying to air them on live television.

'But,' Katherine Adamson looked at her clipboard before pinning her steely gaze upon Steven again, 'there's no mention of you in the official company biography. There's nothing to suggest you had any actual input in the company's development. Why is that?'

'Stuart is the face of Easy PC's – everyone knows who he is. He is the brand and that's how it should be. The backroom staff are exactly that – backroom. Their role is to ensure the brand stays on track and in this case, ahead of the competition. Clever marketing means nothing detracts from the brand, which is a risk if there appears to be more than one figurehead at the top of the tree.'

'Did you dislike working for your brother?'

Mats tried not to squirm at the hard line of questioning

Adamson was throwing at Steven. Why wasn't she being reined in? This style of interview was not the remit for this show. It was supposed to be a gentle, after-tea, slot, not something from the Spanish Inquisition. So far, with the exception of when they were introduced at the top of the show, there hadn't been a single comment as to the reason why they were there.

'It was an interesting time, Katherine, and I enjoyed what I was doing very much. Why would you think I disliked it?'

Nice one, son! Steven kept using Adamson's name deliberately to defuse the tension and prevent her manipulating him. Mats wondered if he'd ever considered a career in politics – he had the diversion tactics down to a T! Mind you, she looked at his white knuckles as he gripped the water glass and knew the calm exterior was a mere façade. Inside, he was clearly furious.

'Well, you don't work for him any more – why not?'

'Oh, there's nothing sinister in that, Katherine. As the company grew, I realised I lacked the experience to take it to the next level. It was my first job after all. Someone with more knowledge in the field was brought in and I moved on to allow them the freedom to openly express their own ideas.'

'I see.'

Mats wasn't sure but she suspected Adamson was more than a little disappointed that Steven hadn't crumbled under her interrogation.

Without warning, the dead-eyed gaze swung round, landing on herself and she felt as if she'd just been impaled against a brick wall.

'Mats,' the sudden silky-smooth tone put her on her guard, 'please tell the audience at home about your last two dates. I believe it was the letters 'K' and 'L' – is that correct?'

'Err, yes, it was. For 'K' we joined a karaoke night at a pub near St Paul's. Marky Sparks and his show producer, Dave, came along and we had a fun night.'

'Did you get up to sing?' The cold smile accompanied the question and Mats couldn't help the feeling of trepidation which was beginning to form in her stomach. After what Steven had been subjected to, this was too easy.

'I did, although I can tell you it wasn't pretty. I could give a cat's choir a good run for its money.'

'So, no recording contract for you in the future?'

'Absolutely not. The world of music is all the better for me being behind the scenes.'

'And what did you do for the letter 'L'?'

'We visited a llama farm and spent the day learning about them and alpacas – their history, how to care for them, and how their wool is used in the world today. It was really interesting and we enjoyed it very much. They're gorgeous creatures.'

'Which means then, if I know my alphabet correctly,' a dead-eyed smile was given to the cameras, 'the next letter will be 'M'.

'It is indeed.'

'Do you know what you'll be doing for that one?'

'No, we won't find out until tomorrow morning when we choose an envelope live on The Marky Sparks Breakfast Show.'

'Well, I think I might just have a small clue for you...'

Mats, along with the whole of the nation, watched as Katherine Adamson took a piece of paper from the back of her clipboard, unfolded it and then held it up to the cameras before turning it round towards Mats and Steven.

As Mats read the front page of "The Weekday News" she felt her blood run cold and a buzzing sound began growing in her head.

No... this wasn't true... it couldn't be... why... why

would they print that?

She looked at Steven but he was staring at the blown-up cover. She looked at it again and felt herself begin to slip off the sofa. The headline was the last thing she saw before everything turned black…

"M for Mats Mother Murdered!"

FORTY-TWO

Swatterhouse kicked his heels with glee against the sofa. The story was out there now and he'd get all the credit for breaking it! Okay, so Katherine Adamson had been the one to reveal it on live television but it was his name on the by-line. Everyone would take notice of him again – it had been a while since he'd had such a juicy morsel to serve up to the great British public.

His mobile phone began ringing at his side. He glanced at the screen and saw Barbara Coulsen's name flashing on it.

'Hmm, I don't think so,' he murmured as he pushed himself up from the sofa and went into the kitchen to treat himself to a celebratory beer from the fridge. The phone had stopped ringing by the time he returned to the lounge but he'd barely plonked his ass back down when it started again.

'Look, Barbara darling, you can call as much as you like, I'm not picking up. Not tonight.'

He waited for the call to trip over to his voicemail then turned the phone to silent. He suspected there might be a few more calls before the evening was over – after all, what had just been revealed on the television wasn't *actually* the front page of tomorrow's paper. Well, it hadn't been at the time of the reveal but it would be now!

Barbara Coulsen would be livid at the trick he'd pulled but it was a dog-eat-dog world out there and sometimes you had to play a bit dirty to stay on top. It hadn't been all that difficult to knock up a mock front-page with the fake headline and email it to Adamson. He'd overheard her talking in the pub the night before and that was when he'd learnt of tonight's interview with the Alphabet Daters. Being cut from the same piece of dirty cloth, Swatterhouse and Adamson had scratched each other's backs many times over the years so it had been easy to email the fake page to her and let her do the rest.

Swatterhouse knew Barbara Coulsen would now be running about like a blue-arsed fly, halting the current print-run and changing the newspaper to accommodate the story. No way was she going to let it be known that a staff member had gotten the better of her.

He thought back to when he'd started digging into the so-called "Golden Couple". Steven had been as boring as he'd expected. Apart from his brother being the main dude behind that I.T company, there had been very little dirt to find. Mats, however, had proved to be a different story. When he realised who her parents were – Alicia and Alexander Davidson had been a golden couple in their own right – his detective work began to pay off.

Luckily for him, a good number of actors are gossipy little attention-seekers and it hadn't been too difficult to find people who'd worked with the Davidsons in the past and were happy to spill the beans. The majority of those he'd spoken with had had nothing but good to say about Alexander. Alicia, on the other hand, had been quite another story. He'd heard everything from her trying to upstage the leading ladies when on stage, throwing histrionics if any of her lines were cut to having a string of lovers all the way through her twenty-year-plus marriage to Alexander. The first two were nothing unusual within the cut-throat world of the dramatic arts but the latter – the string of lovers – had been more interesting. This had led to him tracking down Alicia's last lover before she died and he had provided the juicy morsel Swatterhouse had been searching for – Alexander Davidson had killed his wife!

FORTY-THREE

'Mats, wake up, can you hear me? Mats…'

Mats heard the voice calling her through the darkness. She tried to call back but her lips couldn't quite form the words. Her head felt heavy and her eyelids didn't want to open no matter how hard she tried.

'Mats, sweetie, please wake up…'

It was Steven's voice in her ear. She felt herself smiling – his voice did that to her now. She liked it when he whispered to her, the sensation of his breath against her neck always made her want to grab hold of him and kiss him into eternity.

'Sh-teven-sh…' Was she drunk? She didn't think so. She couldn't recall them being out on the tiles. In fact, the last thing she remembered was—

Her eyes sprang open as it all came back to her. Finding herself lying down on the small chaise longue in the dressing room, she grabbed the back of it and pulled herself upright.

Her eyes whirled around the room, taking in Sparks, Dave and Steven grouped around the chaise, Tim Branson standing near the door and Katherine Adamson perched on the table by the wall.

'YOU FUCKING BITCH!'

Mats stood up, crossed the room and punched the journalist square in the mouth before anyone realised her intention.

'YOU EVIL FUCKING COW! HOW DARE YOU DO SUCH A THING! I'M GOING TO FUCKING KILL YOU!'

'Mats, calm down, please. Come and sit here with me.'

Mats felt Steven grab her arm as it came up to wallop Katherine a second time.

'Did you shee that? I'm going to shue you for ashault! How DARE you hit me. I have witneshes – you are shooo going to regret what you have jusht done.' Katherine wiped the blood from her mouth and let out a scream as one of her front teeth fell into her hand.

'I didn't see anything... Dave?' Sparks looked round as Dave gave a shrug.

'Nope, I don't know what she's talking about, mate.'

'Steven?'

'No, Marky, I haven't seen anything untoward.'

Katherine glared at them before turning to Tim.

'I saw you tripping over one of the camera cables – there's a lot around and they can be a hazard if you're not paying attention—'

'Argh! You've not heard the lasht of thish!'

'Oh, I think we have,' replied Dave, as the dressing room door slammed closed behind the journalist as she left.

Tim Branson walked over to Mats, who was sitting again on the chaise, and knelt in front of her.

'Mats, I am so very sorry this has happened tonight. No one knew she was going to hi-jack the show in this way. I could hear the director screaming at her through our earpieces to stick to the script but she ignored him. She actually removed it when the cameras were off her for a few seconds.' He looked up at Dave and Marky in distress. 'I swear, this is not how we do things on our show. This is going to cause a shitstorm of trouble on so many levels.'

He stood up.

'I'm going to leave you alone now as I'm sure you all need to talk. Take as much time as you need – this room is not required for the rest of the night and I'll ask security to make sure you're not disturbed.'

There was silence once he'd left the room until Mats let out a moan.

'Owwwwwwwww!'

She looked down at her hand and saw the bruising already beginning to form. There was also a small cut on her middle knuckle where it had connected with Katherine's tooth.

'Here, hang on, let me get you some ice.'

She watched Steven go over to the small buffet in the corner, take a cotton handkerchief from his pocket and put some ice from the ice-bucket in it. He came back and held it gently against her hand as he sat down beside her. Sparks sat on her other side and Dave pulled over a chair to sit in front of her.

'Mats,' she looked at Sparks, 'you need to tell us what's going on.'

'I don't know. I really don't.'

'But you must. Is it true?'

'No, it's not, Sparks, I promise you.'

She felt herself sway and leaned into Steven. He placed his arm around her shoulder and held her tight.

'How can you be sure, Mats?'

Mats drew in a breath and forced herself to face the memory she still found so hard to cope with. Looking at Dave, she answered simply, 'Because I was there when she died!'

'Here, Mum, let me help you with that. Do you want another pillow?'

'No, Darling, I'm fine like this, thank you.'

'Would you like me to brush your hair?'

'If you don't mind, that would be lovely.'

Mats picked up the small baby hair brush, with its extra soft bristles, and began to gently brush the faded golden wisps that were left on her mother's head. Barely eight months ago, her mother had sported the most fabulous strawberry-blonde mane that had swung gloriously down her back. Unfortunately, the highly aggressive chemotherapy treatment had put paid to that. The wig that sat in the corner of the room had seen a few outings but her mum had soon begun to complain about the weight of it. A shorter length option had been made by one of the make-up artists in her mother's circle of theatrical friends but Alicia hated it. She'd never been one for short hair and she wasn't about to start now.

'Over my dead body,' had been her response but while Mats hadn't appreciated her gallows humour, her mother had laughed loudly, not realising the pain her words had caused. The short wig was disposed of and the long one only came out for visitors and special occasions because Alicia Davidson was adamant no one outside of her family would see her looking anything less than her best.

As Mats brushed, she recalled the day her parents had sat her down and broken the news to her. She'd graduated a few days before and had just returned home after clearing out the digs she, Penny and Tinks had occupied for two years. When her dad had asked her to take a seat at the kitchen table, she'd been expecting ground rules to be laid down now that she was living at home again. Being told her mother had been diagnosed three months earlier with a particularly virulent form of breast cancer had left her speechless. Being told her mother had refused to tell Mats until she'd graduated, because she was scared that Mats would leave Uni early, had left her incandescent with rage.

There had been some shouting, some slamming of doors and a lot of tears but eventually, Mats began to understand her mother's reasoning. Alicia already knew in her heart that the cancer was going to beat her, not the other way around, and she'd wanted to give her daughter as many good memories as possible before the cancer shattered their happy little world forever.

'Hmmm, that's nice.' Alicia let out a small purr of pleasure and tried to hide a grimace of pain but Mats had spent so much time at her mother's side, she'd become attuned to her every expression and knew when she was hurting.

'What time is it, darling?'

'Almost two o'clock.'

'Oh, good! Freddie will be here soon and you can take some time out.'

Freddie Haycock was her mother and father's best friend and had been a part of her life since forever. He came to visit three afternoons a week which gave Mats' time to go out and do shopping or any other chores which needed to be done. Her father was contracted to the theatre and had tried to take time out but his wife wouldn't hear of it. She was determined that Alex's career should not suffer because her health had "had a small set-back"! Instead, he'd managed to cut back his hours but like so many people, neither of them had invested in health insurance and so they were now living off their savings. Alex had to keep working to bring home a wage. Between the three of them, however, they managed to ensure that caring for Alicia wasn't all left to Mats, no matter how often Mats objected that she didn't mind.

'Pass me my hair, darling, and I think a little spot of blusher might be required today.'

Mats forced herself not to smile. Her mother may have known Freddie for more years than she could remember but she still insisted on being "tidy" when he visited.

When she'd helped Alicia to sit up a bit further in the bed, plumped a few more pillows behind her and made her presentable for her intended audience of one, Mats said, 'I need to go to the chemist to pick up your new morphine prescription which means I'll be going past Nettie's. Would you like me to bring you back a big, fat, chocolate éclair?'

'Oh, I shouldn't really, I need to watch my figure but… go on! Just one won't hurt.'

It took all of Mat's will-power not to retort that a hundred and one chocolate eclairs wouldn't hurt right now. To say her mum had lost weight was an understatement. She was positively skeletal. Her once peachy-soft skin was now a dull yellow and stretched tightly over her face. When she smiled, her teeth looked huge and out of place – almost as though she had accidently put in someone else's dentures. The beautiful, periwinkle-blue eyes were now pale, washed out and looked insipid against the yellow-tinged whites. The plump, shapely lips which had kissed so many sore knees and had bid her sweet dreams as a child, were now so thin and brittle they caused pain when her mother smiled. The hands that had once brushed Mats' hair, pushed her on the swings and held her close had become claw-like; fragile bones held together beneath tissue-thin skin and nails like unkempt talons because cutting or filing them caused too much pain.

The woman in the bed, whose body had been ravaged by the disease, bore absolutely no resemblance to the wedding day photograph on the table at the side.

'You look tired, darling. Why don't you take a book with you and treat yourself to a nice leisurely coffee when you go to Nettie's? I'll have Freddie to keep an eye on me – take some time for yourself.'

'That's a good idea, I might just do that.' She smiled at her mum, hiding the fact that she was exhausted and what she really wanted to do was go to her bed and sleep for a few hours. There had been no mention of the doctor's visit in the early hours of the morning when Alicia had, without any warning, taken a turn for the worse. Dr Charles had increased her morphine dose and explained it was, sadly, par for the course with this illness.

The doorbell rang.

'That'll be Freddie.'

'Just send him up, dear, he knows where to find me. You go off and get that coffee.'

'And your chocolate eclairs?'

'Oh, yes! Don't forget those.'

As Mats was walking out the bedroom door, her mother called her back.

'Darling, don't say anything to Freddie about the incident during the night, it'll only bring the mood down and I can't be doing with trying to cheer him up.'

'Okay, no problem.'

Mats opened the door to Freddie, gave him a hug and told him to go straight up the stairs. As she was putting on her coat, she heard her mother greet her visitor.

'Freddie, darling, aren't you a sight for sore eyes. Come, sit here and tell me *all* the latest gossip? Did Fat Fran manage to lose the half stone or did she burst the seams of her costume on stage...'

Mats smiled as she listened. No matter how ill her

mother was, there was no stopping her inner actress and she was giving Freddie everything she had.

'That's it, Mum,' she whispered, 'you keep on fighting. Don't give up.'

'Here, Dad, you might as well have these, they're only going to go to waste.' Mats put the two cream cakes on a plate and passed them to her father.

'You couldn't persuade your mum to eat them?'

'I barely managed to get two spoons of soup inside her, I didn't stand a chance with these.'

'At least you tried, love. That's all we can keep doing. Put them in the fridge – your mum might be more inclined to have one tomorrow.'

'Hmmm... maybe!'

'What time are you meeting Jim at? Are you doing anything special this evening?'

'I've cancelled tonight. I'm tired and I wouldn't be good company.'

'Oh, Mats, I'm sorry about that. This is really taking its toll on you. It's not fair.'

'Hey, Dad, it's not fair on any of us, least of all mum. It's taking its toll on us all – we just need to keep muddling through the best we can.' She put her arms around her father and hugged him close. He rubbed her back and held her just as tightly.

'I know, love, I know. So, want to join me for this evening's reading session. Alicia wants me to read "The Secret Garden" again. I know you like that one too.'

'That sounds lovely. You go on up and I'll finish tidying down here. I'll be with you in a few minutes.'

'I'll wait until you join us.'

'Dad,' Mats gave him a smile, 'I think I know how the story goes by now. There's no need to wait.'

Her father dropped a kiss on her head, picked up the tray with the teapot and cups on, and made his way up to the bedroom.

The smile left Mats face as soon as his back was turned. They still maintained the little ritual of a proper pot of tea on a tray, with the sugar bowl, milk jug and tea cups with matching saucers because her mum enjoyed it so much. Lately though, her mum's cup of tea had been untouched when the tray came back down the stairs. If Mats had needed any indicator of how ill her mother was, this was it. Her mum had never let a cuppa go cold on her – she loved her tea. Letting out a sigh, she placed the tea-towel on the hook, switched the light off and walked slowly up the stairs.

The bedroom door was open and her father's melodious tones floated along the corridor towards her. With his good looks and rich, smooth voice, Alex could easily have joined her mother on the stage. She'd asked him once why he hadn't become an actor and he'd said, quite simply, that he preferred life behind the scenes, not in front of them.

Mats stopped at the door for a moment, letting her father's words wrap themselves around her and comfort her. The story was her mother's favourite as a child and Mats had grown up loving it too. The familiar tale briefly eased the constant ache in her heart. Her chin dropped down to her chest and she leant against the doorframe as she listened, all the while wishing she could turn back the clock to the days when she'd snuggle up in her mother's arms and listen as she read the story aloud.

Suppressing a small sigh, Mats straightened up, forced herself to smile and walked into the bedroom.

Alicia was lying down, a single pillow under her head. Her eyes were closed and her hands lay on top of the lightweight blanket which covered her. Alex was sitting on one side of the bed, holding one hand gently while he read. Mats walked round to sit opposite him, pulled her chair closer and took her mother's other hand between both of hers. She bent forward, placing her head in the crook of her arm on the bed, and gave her mum's fingers a light kiss. She lay there quietly and tried not to let the sound of her mother's shallow breathing upset her.

She didn't remember falling asleep but the next thing she knew, her father was by her side, gently shaking her awake. She sat upright and shook her head to clear away the grogginess. It was as she was rubbing her eye's she became aware of the change within the room. She stopped, trying to figure out what was different. She looked at her father and saw the tears running down his face. That was when she realised what was wrong. She couldn't hear her mother breathing.

Her father wrapped his arms around her as he cried, 'She's gone, Mats. She's gone.'

Mats took the tissue Steven had passed to her and wiped the tears on her face. She looked at Sparks and Dave – Sparks looked like he was about to cry too.

'I was there, I was with her when she died. She wasn't murdered. Who would say such a thing?'

'So, you *do* know someone called Fredrick Haycock?'

'Freddie? Yes, he was best friends with my parents before my mother died.'

'Well, reading this, I don't think he'll be a best friend any more…' Dave looked up from his phone as he spoke.

'I… I haven't seen him in years. In fact, come to think about it, I haven't seen him since the funeral. I've just realised. Why? Why would he do this?'

'None of us know, Mats, and – right now – we're not

going to find out anything further while sitting here. Let's go home and we'll talk in the morning.'

'Yeah, I'll be suing this paper and Freddie Haycock for every penny they have. How dare they print this slanderous trash!' Mats felt her upset turn to anger as she stood up. 'I'll be speaking to the police about this. It's preposterous for allegations like this to be made.'

'Mats,' Steven laid his hand gently on her arm. 'Be careful. You don't want to make matters worse—'

Mats looked at him in surprise.

'Worse? How could I possibly make matters worse?'

'Because…' Steven hesitated before he answered her question. 'Because… you were asleep when she died.'

'Wha— Oh!'

She sat back down heavily on the chaise. Steven was right – by her own admission, she hadn't witnessed anything because her father had woken her after her mother had died. She looked up to see a look of concern pass between Sparks and Steven. She knew what they were thinking and she couldn't contradict their thoughts because, the truth was, by being asleep, she knew nothing of how her mother had breathed her last.

FORTY-FOUR

Steven turned to look at Mats but she was staring straight ahead. She hadn't spoken a word since they'd entered the taxi after leaving the television studio and her tight, rigid, posture was screaming "Stay away". He'd tried to take her hand, after giving the driver his address, but she'd moved further away from him until she was hard up against the door on the opposite side of the seat.

'Look, why don't you stay with me tonight, I don't like the thought of you being alone.'

'No! I want to go home.'

'Then I'll come with you'

'No! I want to be on my own.' The words were clipped and her tone was short.

'But—'

'Steven, for fucks sake, shut up! I'm going home, on my own! Just leave it!'

He recoiled in the face of her angry retort but did as she asked. He looked out of the window but was oblivious to the world on the other side. Mats had just received one of the biggest shocks of her life and she was shutting him out. He wanted to help but she wasn't letting him. Okay, there wasn't much he could do but surely his support and being by her side had to give her some kind of comfort. He didn't want to crowd her, he wanted to give her whatever space she needed to resolve this but he didn't want her to think he didn't care. He leant back and watched the street lights as they flashed by above his head while the atmosphere in the cab grew heavier. Mats was so wound up he could feel the waves of anger flowing from her. He wanted to speak but didn't know what to say. He suspected he'd have his head bitten off regardless of what words he chose so he decided to stay quiet as she'd asked.

Finally, the cab pulled into his road and he told the driver where to stop.

'Mats, please stay with me tonight, please don't go home on your own. You shouldn't be alone with this. Not tonight anyway…'

He waited for her to reply but she continued to stare out of the taxi window, wrapping her silence around her like an impenetrable shield. He let out a small sigh and was stepping out of the cab when her words hit him like a round of bullets.

'This is all your fault!'

'I'm sorry? What?' He swivelled round to look down at her.

'This is all your fault. If you hadn't sent that damned email, none of this would have happened.'

'Mats, there's no way we could have known this would happen…'

She slid across the seat and grabbed the door handle. 'I blame you. This is your fault. I never want to see you again.'

The door of the cab slammed closed and it pulled away, driving around the square before disappearing into the night. Steven stood on the pavement, unable to comprehend what Mats had just said, unable to take in that she was blaming him. He looked up to the sky above him while his mind whirled. It came to him that the last time he'd stood like this, he'd felt so alive and full of hope that something wonderful was growing between him and Mats. Now he felt as though his whole world had imploded. The woman he loved more than he had words to describe now hated him. He told himself that Mats was in shock and would feel differently once this had all been resolved but as he turned to walk up the path to his front door, a little voice in his head was telling him that this was it, it was over.

He was never going to see Mats again.

FORTY-FIVE

Mats groaned and threw her arm over her eyes as she rolled onto her back. Her head was thumping and she lay there wondering if she was coming down with something. Her eyes felt sore and puffy as she struggled to open them.

'Shit! No!'

The memories flooding back from the night before soon had her moving into an upright position.

When the taxi had arrived at her house, there had been a couple of blokes standing on the pavement opposite. Other than a cautious glance to see if they looked shifty, she hadn't given them much thought until, as she walked towards her gate, one began taking photographs while the other came to stand in front of her while throwing questions.

'Mats, did you know your mother was murdered? Did you help to do it? What was it like watching your mother die? Have the police spoken to you yet? Have you been to the police station?'

For a brief second, she'd stopped in her tracks and was about to answer when her brain caught up and she'd realised they were journalists. She'd barged them out of the way and ran down the path into the small porch in front of the main door. She'd dropped her handbag, swung round and probably for the first time in her lifetime, closed the two big, heavy, wooden storm doors, throwing home the bolts along the top and bottom. The two journalists had hammered against them and shouted at her through the old cast iron letterbox which had caused her to fumble with her keys and drop them. The tears had started again at that point and it had felt like an eternity before she'd managed to open her front door. Slamming it shut behind her, she'd locked it, bolted it, put on the chain and then pulled over the large, heavy, velvet curtain which was only ever used in the winter. She'd leant against the wall, trembling from the shock, when a noise had come from the front room – the journalists were banging on her lounge windows! A roar of anger had escaped from her lips and she'd run in to close the old-fashioned wooden shutters before also pulling the curtains together. This managed to dull the noise of the men outside but they'd persisted with their banging, their voices muffled as she'd curled up on the sofa, her hands over her ears, trying to block out the noise.

She didn't know how long she'd lain like that but after a time it went quiet. She hadn't dared to look outside and had gone into the kitchen to put on the kettle when the security light in the garden had flashed on. Not taking any chances, Mats had flipped the switch which turned the clear glass of the patio doors to opaque. It had probably just been a cat or a fox but she knew journalists would do anything to get their story and she wouldn't put it past them to be climbing over garden fences to get to her. She'd switched the overhead light off and propped the fridge door slightly ajar to give her just enough light to see by. With a cup of tea in her hand, she'd walked up the stairs to the attic and had curled up on the big cuddle chair in her reading room. She'd pulled a throw over her shoulders and had sat there, nursing the mug of hot liquid in her hands, while her mind tried to make sense of what had happened just a few hours earlier. She'd been lightheaded and everything had felt wrong. It was like she was standing outside of her body, seeing someone else but all the time knowing it was her.

Her shock.

Her pain.

The tears had come once more, then they'd stopped and then they'd come again. She must have cried herself to sleep for she'd woken up cold and stiff at some time in the night which was when she'd dragged herself down to her bedroom and into her bed.

Going by how she felt now, Mats would put good money on the tears having sent her off to sleep a second time. She rubbed her face and noticed the last remaining traces of the heavy make-up from the TV show had flaked off onto her hands.

She let out a groan and looked behind her to see smears of mascara and foundation all over her pillows and quilt cover.

'Damn and blast it!' She threw back the quilt and her feet were fumbling their way into her slippers when she became aware of the noise outside. She crouched down and shuffled over to the window to peer through the thick, half-length, net curtains. Overnight, the two journalists had multiplied and there was now a throng of men and women swarming around on the pavement outside her house. There was even a television media van parked on the opposite side of the road.

'Shit! Shit, shit, shit, shit, shit!' She sat down on the floor with her knees pulled up to her chest and rested her forehead on them. She was supposed to be in the office today but there was no way she'd be able to get past the blood-sucking parasites. She looked at the bedside table for her mobile phone but it wasn't there and Mats realised it was still downstairs in her handbag. She was about to stand up when she heard a shout from outside. Turning round, she peered out through the curtains again and saw what looked like a drone taking off from the street below.

'You fucking wankers,' she yelled, as she crawled quickly to the side and pulled the cord that closed the curtains. She then stood and rushed over to ensure there were no gaps for them to see through before running into her study and pulling the blind down in there too. She paused for a moment, wondering if she should do the same in the spare rooms even though they faced out into the back garden. Deciding to err on the side of caution, she repeated the action of closing the curtains in both rooms along with the blinds on her attic reading room window and skylight. She also closed all the doors which left the hallway in total darkness. She cautiously groped her way towards the stairs and switched on the small lamp which sat on the landing table.

Mats sat down on the top step and took a moment to gather her thoughts, while trying to ignore the pressure on her bladder. She couldn't believe she was being door-stepped and tried to think back to some of the things she'd heard her musician clients talk about when they'd become successful and suddenly everyone wanted a piece of them. What was it they'd said? Oh yes, bins! They'll go through your bins! Well, that wasn't a problem as yesterday had been bin day so they were empty. Neighbours. They talk to your neighbours! Mats thought back to the last conversation she'd had with Carol next door – she was sure it was this week and the next that she and her family were away in France. On the other side was Mrs Perle – ninety if she was a day and as deaf as a post. They'd get nothing out of her except a flea in their ear and told to piss off.

Satisfied that the journos would struggle for information in the immediacy, she decided the need to wee couldn't be put off any longer. She chose, however, to use the small downstairs toilet which didn't have a window. Even though the blind was closed in the upstairs bathroom, she didn't feel comfortable using it while knowing there was a drone about.

She'd just flushed the loo when the telephone rang and almost made her jump out of her skin! She quickly washed and dried her hands before rushing out to answer it. Her hand was on the receiver when she paused… who knew her landline number? She couldn't remember the last time she'd given it to anyone – she always gave her mobile details. More to the point, she couldn't remember the last time this phone had rung…

Tentatively, she picked it up and put it to her ear.

'Hello?' she said quietly.

'Mats, is that you?'

'Penny!' She slumped against the wall and drew in a breath.

'Of course, it's me, who else has this number?'

'Only my dad and as he always calls me on the mobile, I don't know if he can remember it anymore.'

'I've been trying to call your mobile since early this morning, I only just thought of trying this number – what's going on?'

'Have you? Hang on…' Mats placed the handset on the table and walked through to the kitchen where she'd left her bag the night before. She took her phone from the front pocket and looked at it as she walked back towards the landline.

'Oh, Pen, it's switched off. We had to turn them off before going on the air last night and I forgot to put it back on again.' She pushed the button at the side and waited for it to boot up.

'How are you, hon? I couldn't believe what I was seeing when that bitch did what she did?'

As Mats scrolled through the missed calls and texts which had arrived on her phone in the last fourteen hours, she filled Penny in on all that had happened and also the journalists camped outside her door.

'Do you want me to come round? I'll sort them out for you...'

Mats let out a small laugh. 'Penny, I have no doubt that you would but for now, it's probably best for you to keep your distance. The less people they're aware of, who are associates of mine, the better. I don't want anyone else being dragged into this shit show.'

'How's Steven, is he okay? I hope he's looking after you.'

'Steven's not here.'

Mats pulled the receiver from her ear as Penny screeched her disgust. 'Pen, calm down. I wanted to be on my own. He offered to be with me, in fact, he practically begged to be with me, but I said no. He asked me to stay at his place—'

'So, why didn't you?'

'Because I was angry! I was being a bitch. I was in shock and hurting and took it out on him. I told him it was all his fault!'

'How the hell did you work that one out?'

'If he hadn't sent the email to the radio station, none of this would have happened.'

'Well, you can just back it up there, girlfriend, because if *I* hadn't contacted the radio station, this wouldn't have happened to you! If you're intending to blame anyone, you can start with me. Steven is as much of a victim as you are.'

Mats slid down the wall till her bottom was on the floor and pulled her knees up to her chest. Aware that this was the second time she'd been in this position since she got out of bed, she realised that even as a kid, this was the stance she always took when something upset her. She placed her forehead on her knees again and listened to Penny talking.

'Mats, are you still there?'

'Yes, Pen, I am and you're right, it's not his fault. I lashed out and he got the brunt of it. It's not anyone's fault. I just need to get to the bottom of everything and find out the truth of my mother's death.'

'Have you spoken to your dad?'

'Not yet.'

'Well, he's the first person you should be speaking to.'

'I know but… not today. I'm tired and washed out. I need to get my head right first.'

'What are you going to do then?'

'For now, eat something, take a sleeping tablet and go back to bed. Hopefully, I will feel more human tomorrow, the scumbags outside will have disappeared and I can get on with sorting this out.'

'Okay, sweetie. That sounds like a plan. If you need anything, let me know and I'll give you a call later to see how you're doing.'

'Thanks, Penny. Oh… I would also suggest you call me on this number for now, if that's okay? We've both heard about folks having their mobiles hacked and I'm not taking any chances.'

'I hear ya! Landlines all the way. Not a problem. Now go and get some rest. Laters, taters! Mwah!'

'Laters to you too! Mwah back!'

Mats replaced the receiver and sat curled up on the floor until her bottom became cold and numb. When she finally stood, her legs had cramped and she hobbled into the kitchen. She made herself some tea and toast, picked up the packet of sleep remedy which she occasionally used and putting them on a tray, made her way back to bed.

An hour later, she was sound asleep, curled up tightly under her duvet with her forehead on her knees.

FORTY-SIX

'Oh, for the love of all that's holy…' Mats dropped the corner of the bedroom curtain and aimed a kick at the skirting board. 'Five bloody days now! Are they EVER going to leave?' she yelled into the empty room.

She gathered up her clothes for the day and took them into the hallway to get dressed, checking that all the other bedroom doors were closed first. Even though she was positive there were no chinks in the blinds or curtains around the house, she was still taking no chances. Her daily showers had been moved to before bedtime and were being taken in the dark because she now felt so vulnerable.

She took her pyjamas downstairs and had just put them in the washer when the landline rang. Mats noted the time and knew it was Penny. She had taken to calling dead on nine in the morning and seven in the evening so Mats would know when it was safe to answer the phone.

'Hey, beautiful lady, how are you faring in your ivory tower this morning?'

'Ha ha, Penny, very funny… NOT! I'm fine, thank you, how are you?'

'Nothing new to report here but then, I don't have piles of dirty, unwashed, paparazzi clogging up my street. Are they still there?'

'Yup! And the numbers don't seem to be diminishing either. I wish some other news story would break – that would get them off my back.'

'I can always go and have a sordid, kinky affair with a Member of Parliament if that would help...'

'It would help immensely but the two problems with that suggestion are, one – it would take far too long for the story to hit the headlines and two – I don't think Sparks would be very happy about it.'

'I see! I'm not too sure I'm happy about the lack of the third option – that it would be frightfully demeaning for me to have to be sordid and kinky!'

'Oh, we both know that's second nature to you, Pen. I didn't think it needed discussing!'

Amidst their laughter, Mats heard Penny agreeing.

'Anyway, apart from justifying why I bother to keep you as a friend, given your so-very-low opinion of me, is there anything I can do for you, or help you with, today? In between my job, my boyfriend and my sordid, kinky lifestyle, I'm sure I can assist you however you need.'

'Thank you, Pen, but I'm good for now.'

'Have you spoken with your dad yet?'

Mats hesitated. 'No... not yet.'

'Why not? He's the one who can answer your questions. How many times has he tried to call you?'

'It was every hour for the first couple of days but that's now dropped down to four times a day.'

'Have you listened to his messages – assuming he's left some, that is?'

'He did to begin with – just asking me to call him and saying we need to talk.'

'Which you do!'

'I know but… I don't think over the phone is the way to do it. This is a conversation which needs to be face to face.'

'Well, given your current locked-in situation, it might be a while before that's a possibility.'

'I agree. It's not ideal but it's the best I can do for now.'

'You should at least call him to let him know you're okay.'

'Again, I know but… to be honest, Penny, you're the only person I can face speaking with right now.'

'Then send him a text. Let him know that you're safe, explain how you feel and that you'll be in touch with him soon.'

'I will. I'll do it as soon as we hang up.'

'What about the police – anything further from them?'

'No. I'm really hoping they'll be in touch again soon – they did say they didn't expect their enquiries to take too long.'

'Hmmm! And finally, before I hang up, have you heard from, or spoken to, Steven?'

Mats closed her eyes and rubbed them. 'He's been sending texts and calling but I haven't replied apart from one text apologising for the way I behaved towards him and saying I'll call when this has all settled down but he hasn't taken any notice of that. I just… I just can't speak with him either right now.'

'Sod the calls and texts! Personally, I think he should be there, banging on your front door and demanding to be let in.'

'Yeah, cos that would look really good on the front of tomorrow's newspapers! It's better that he stays away – I wouldn't wish this kind of scrutiny on anyone.'

'I disagree but I see the point you're making although you should know he's not getting off scot-free either. He's had his fair share of the headlines but it seems to be mostly about the rift between him and his brother. I think they're clutching at straws – trying to keep the story alive in the hope of eventually getting something more on you.'

Mats listened to Penny's words but didn't reply.

'Righto, time for me to lick some bridezillas into shape. I'll speak to you this evening. Laters, taters!'

'Laters!'

Mats put the phone down and let her fingers linger on it for a moment. Up till now, this had been her only link with the outside world. However, if things had gone according to plan, Peter in the IT department should have performed some magical, jiggery-pokery which would enable her to work as efficiently from home as if she was in the office. Through Penny, she'd passed a message to Tinks telling him to call her. They'd discussed the situation and he'd brought Peter in on the call who had gone on to say it would be easy enough to put a few programs on her laptop which would allow full access to all her office files. All he needed was some time.

Once she'd made some more tea and toast – her current diet thanks to the loaves she had in the freezer – she went upstairs to her study to see if Peter had been successful. She opened the door, placed her mug on the desk and switched on the desk light. Last night, she'd dug out some old black-out curtains and had draped them on the curtain rail which till now, had been merely decorative with some voile wrapped artfully around it. The curtains were hideous old things and far too big for the size of the window but Mats was happy with that. Between them and the blind, she should be able to work without fear of being spied on.

A few hours later, she sat back and stretched her arms above her head before dropping her hands onto her shoulders to rub out the tension in her muscles. She'd been hunched up over the laptop since she'd sat down and hadn't noticed the time passing. Peter had been as good as his word and had even put on some program which had enabled her to have a virtual face-to-face meeting with Tinks and Malcolm, the night manager who'd been covering her days while she was stuck at home.

It had been a productive meeting and after assuring Tinks she was using an ethernet cable and wasn't on Wi-Fi therefore the connection was secure, they'd restructured her role to accommodate her absence from the office. She would continue to do the bulk of her tasks but Malcolm would remain working days to do the meet & greet when the new appointments arrived and perform the on-site studio checks at the beginning and end of each session. His brother-in-law would cover his night role for the foreseeable future.

Tinks had also made the suggestion of her using the time to take a long-overdue break away from the studio. When he'd asked her to tell him when she'd last had a proper holiday, not just a long weekend, she'd been unable to answer for they both knew that since the new studios had opened, she hadn't been able to take a step back and have a breather. Or, as Tinks has said far more bluntly than she'd felt was necessary, she hadn't trusted anyone else to look after her baby even though her baby was not far off being a teenager and able to stand on its own two feet for a while if she wasn't around.

Mats let out a sigh – knowing he was right was not helping her. She stood up for another stretch then picked up her used crockery and headed back down to the kitchen for a refill.

She was waiting for the kettle to boil and while getting the milk from the fridge, her eye was caught by the picture postcard of Broatiescombe Bay, the small village in Devon where her father now lived. He'd sent it to her not long after he'd moved and it had been pinned to the fridge door with a magnet for almost three years. She rarely noticed it anymore but today it seemed to jump out at her. A tiny winkle of an idea began to form. Mats took the postcard down and stared at it as the tea-bag stewed in her cup. The brightly painted houses, the sparkling blue sea and the pretty orange sunset appeared even more vibrant in her current world of shade and darkness. With every curtain in the house drawn, and every blind pulled down, her life had become grey and dull. Suddenly she longed to feel daylight on her face. Sunlight would be even better but hey, she wasn't in a position to be choosy. She'd take what she could get.

With the postcard in her hand, and the forgotten cup of tea still sitting on the worktop, Mats rushed up the stairs to begin putting her escape plan together. She was getting out of here – she just needed to figure out how to do it!

FORTY-SEVEN

When Penny called her that evening, Mats could barely contain her excitement.

'Good evening, do I have the pleasure of speaking to the Prisoner in Cell Block H?'

'Still with the shitty jokes… yes, you do!'

'How are you this evening?'

'Feeling great, as it happens. I'm getting out of here!'

'Fantastic! Have the gutter press disappeared back down into their sewers?'

'No, they're still here but I have a plan on how to get past them. Or, I hope I have.'

'Is there anything I can do to help?'

'Penny, I won't be able to do it without your help.'

'Then I'm all ears, doll! What do I need to do?'

'You have my spare car key, don't you?'

'Yup! It's hanging right next to your spare house keys.'

'Brill! Would you mind very much moving my car for me?'

'Of course, I don't mind but won't the paps see me?'

'As luck would have it, I had to park around the corner in the next street when I was last out so they're unlikely to make the connection that it's my car being moved.'

'That's probably the first bit of luck you've had this week! So, I'm moving your car – where to and why?'

'Could you check how much fuel is in it, top it up if needed and then park it outside Beryl's house for me?'

'I can do that. When?'

'By tomorrow night.'

'Consider it done. How do you intend to get to it and where are you going?'

'I'm going down to Devon. The police called this afternoon to say they've concluded their investigation and are satisfied my mum didn't die in suspicious circumstances.'

'So how on earth could this Freddie bloke have thought otherwise?'

'That's why I'm going to Devon. It's time I spoke with my dad.'

'Good call! You also need some time out so this would be a good chance to have a break and relax for a while.'

'Oh, don't you start! I've already had Tinks nagging me on the very same thing this morning! I'm only going down for a few days. Just long enough for the police to make their statement to the press and for all this to blow over once the media realise there's no story to be had.'

'How are you going to get past them? You said they were even camping out overnight.'

'They still are but most of them leave about ten o'clock. There's only a handful through the night. But what I'm hoping, and pinning all this on, is that they haven't worked out there's an old alleyway behind these houses. It's more-or-less disused now, has been for several years, and it's pretty overgrown. The alley goes round to the main road and brings me out just up from the pub. The back gate out of the garden takes me into it so I reckon I should be able to sneak out under the cover of darkness, in the early hours of the morning, without being spotted and be on my way to Devon while the pests think I'm still holed up in the house. What do you think?'

'I think that sounds well considered and thought out. Fingers crossed for you that they haven't sussed its presence. I'll try to have a discreet look when I come for your car and let you know if it looks like any weeds, grass, whatever, have been disturbed. Now, do you want me to pack anything for you? A few Red Cross parcels in the boot?'

'No, I… actually, Pen… if you *could* lend me some tops, cardigans and sweatshirts, then I'll only need to pack undies, jeans and toiletries. I'll be less obvious walking along the main road with a rucksack than I would be with a suitcase.'

'Tops, cardigans, sweatshirts etc… Got it! Anything else?'

'Yes, there's one last thing. I need you to send Steven an email once I've gone…'

Mats lifted the corner of the front bedroom curtain. It was one in the morning and she could see three people loitering by the front gate. A small flame appeared and was soon followed by the glowing red tip of a cigarette. No one appeared to be moving about much. She picked up her backpack and tried not to groan with the weight of it. The laptop was in there and felt considerably heavier than it usually did! Well, she was blaming the laptop and not the bottles of toiletries, boots, shoes, shorts, jeans, and other assorted clothing because you just couldn't trust the British weather to deliver sunshine in the summer and rain in the winter. Having to pack for all four seasons in one day was the downside of any British staycation.

She carried it down the stairs and dropped it by the back door before looking at the list on the table and ticking off another few lines. She'd already unbolted one of the storm doors but despite searching high and low, she'd been unable to find the key for the lock so had placed a couple of bricks behind it to keep it closed but which she'd be able to push to the side when she returned home. Now she just had to undo the bolts on the front door and take off the chain. The window locks had also been checked and the annoying street light which was right outside the house, and had kept her awake so many times when she'd first moved into the front bedroom, had become her friend as the light reflected off the windows and hid her while she briefly opened the downstairs shutters.

She ran back up the stairs and peeked out of the bedroom window for the last time – three silhouettes were still hovering about. She should be safe from discovery.

Mats returned to the kitchen, picked up her keys and slipped out the back door. She locked it as quietly as she could but still cringed when the lock clicked. It sounded so loud in the quiet of the night. She'd had the foresight to turn off the security light and, staying along the line of the fence, made her way to the bottom of the garden. She took the key for the old padlock on the garden shed from her pocket and hoped it would open without too much trouble. She'd made this same little journey last night to spray lubricant generously over the padlock, bolts and hinges on the shed door while saying a prayer that her usual over-the-top attention to detail would stand her in good stead tonight. She inserted the key and held her breath as she turned it. There was a small click inside and although the lock didn't spring open as it should, a gentle tug released

263

it. Both bolts slid open without any fuss and there were no give-away creaks or groans from the hinges as she eased the door slowly open.

So far, so good.

Mats let her hand slide gently along one of the shelves until it landed on a length of rope which she picked up and tied around the handle of her rucksack. In the dim light of the night, she could just about make out the folding wooden stool which she also needed. She took a hold of it, lifting it slowly in case anything was propped against it and then placed it gently by the side of the gate. She locked the shed back up and pushed against some of the weeds in front of it so it looked as it had earlier in the day. With her back against the gate, Mats looked along the row of terraced houses and scanned the windows for any sign of lights or movement. The next few minutes were make-or-break time and the last thing she needed was some less-than-helpful neighbour to see her escaping and inform the journalists of her whereabouts.

When she was as sure as she could be that she wasn't being watched, Mats pulled up a short wooden ladder from the side of the shed and propped it against the wall, all the while cursing the garden gate that could only be securely locked from the inside although, she concurred, the undisturbed weeds on either side of it would hide the fact that she'd escaped. She quickly climbed up, lowered her rucksack down into the alley with the rope then leant down as far as she could to drop the stool which luckily landed the right way up. Satisfied there was nothing more to do, she swung herself onto the top of the wall, lay down flat along it and gave the ladder a gentle push to the side. It fell back into place along the side of the shed and she lay still for a moment or two, waiting to see if the noise had alerted anyone but she heard no windows opening or any voices calling out. Swinging her legs over to the alley side of the wall, she held on tightly as her feet floundered around beneath her, trying to find the stool. A few seconds later, her toes made contact and she stepped down onto the old, uneven cobbles. After undoing the rope and throwing it back over her garden gate, Mats lifted her backpack up onto her shoulders, picked up the stool and happy that she'd covered her tracks, set off down the alley. She stepped over to the wall where she'd seen a vast curtain of ivy from her attic window and pushed the stool underneath it. She would come back to collect it when she returned home. She found herself holding her breath in an attempt to try and calm her heart which was pounding furiously underneath her dark, hooded top as she carefully made her way down the alley. It was only once she'd turned the first corner that Mats felt comfortable enough to switch on the small torch she'd brought with her. There was no moonlight to guide her through the alley and she didn't fancy falling over any old debris which people had been known to chuck over their fences from the gardens which lined it.

She picked her way through the long grass and nettles until a few minutes later, she pushed past an old bit of fencing and came out onto the main road. Keeping in the shadows of the buildings, she quickly walked up to where Penny had parked her car. Mats looked at the pretty pink house across the street. When she'd been little, a lovely lady called Beryl had lived there and she'd always had a sweetie to give Mats whenever she saw her passing by. Beryl hadn't lived there for a long time now but it would always be Beryl's house to her. She opened the boot to put in her backpack and saw the suitcase Penny had already stashed for her. With a smile, she got in behind the wheel and found two bottles of water alongside some bags of sweets on the passenger seat and a thermos, no doubt filled with something hot, peeking out from underneath. She sent a silent "thank you" up into the night for the thoughtfulness of her best friend as she turned the key to start the engine.

It was only when Mats pulled off the slip road and onto the motorway that her racing heart finally began to slow and her breathing returned to normal. She'd done it. She had escaped. Now to find out what her father had to say. What on earth had caused all of this in the first place?

FORTY-EIGHT

Steven let out a sigh as the alarm on his phone began to buzz. He flung his arm out to switch it off before bringing the same arm back to rest across his eyes. Yet again, he'd barely slept a wink and was so tired his automatic pilot was now operating on automatic pilot. He hadn't heard from Mats apart from the text she'd sent to apologise for her outburst in the taxi and then a second to say she'd be in touch when this was over. He'd spoken with Dave and Marky but they were also receiving the silent treatment. Marky had mentioned that Penny was in touch with her every day but nothing was being relayed back to him.

Steven forced his tired, shattered body into an upright position, perched on the edge of the bed and sent another text. He now found himself with a bit of a dilemma – he wanted to let Mats know he was here for her but also didn't want to crowd or pressure her by making any requests or demands so he'd opted for sending her a text every morning to say hello and every evening to say goodnight. He told her he was waiting for her and she should take as long as she needed to deal with all she had to deal with.

Once he'd sent his daily greeting, he went downstairs into the lounge where, standing to one side of the window, he lifted the blind just enough to check out the pavement below and count how many members of the media were loitering outside his door today. He'd seen the hoard which had gathered outside Mats' home and was grateful that he hadn't attracted quite the same numbers although that hadn't stopped it being an unpleasant surprise when he'd tried to leave the house the morning following Katherine Adamson's shock revelation only to find it impossible to move through them. He'd quickly turned around and had all but head-dived back through the front door. Florrie had popped her head out of her flat door when she'd heard the main door slam and had been quite vocal in her opinion of the people standing outside.

'Bloody media wolfhounds! First, they kill that lovely Princess Di and now they're coming after you. They've got no shame! No shame at all! Well, they'd better not get in my way when I go out to do me shopping or they'll get the sharp side of my tongue, let me tell you.' She'd looked him up and down before continuing, 'I'll take my little trolley with me today so I can get you some bread and milk if you like. I'm guessing you're going to be sitting indoors for a few days… unless you're planning on running the gauntlet of that lot out there!'

'You're right on the first count, Florrie, it looks like I'm going to be holed up here for a while so if you don't mind picking up a few bits, I would be more than grateful.'

'Write me a list and bring it down. I'll go in an hour.'

Florrie had been as good as her word and she'd kept him stocked up daily with fresh produce. Steven suspected she'd purposely gone shopping each day just so she could verbally abuse the paparazzi on her way past because he was quite sure she normally only went twice a week.

He let out a sigh as he saw the people with cameras

still standing close by but felt more positive when he noticed the numbers had dropped. Maybe they were finally getting bored and would be gone in another day or two. He dropped the blind back into place, switched on his laptop as he walked by and went off to grab a shower and some breakfast.

When he returned with a bowl of cereal, he pushed the computer to one side and looked at the paperwork in front of him. His company was working on a new marketing campaign and to a degree, having to work from home had turned out quite well for he'd been able to get his head down and concentrate – something that wouldn't have been so easy in the office where there were always interruptions.

For the next few hours, he focused solely on the job in hand and it was only when he had to go online for some information, that he woke up the laptop for a second time. After he'd finished his research, Steven noticed the time and decided to take a break. He would have a coffee and check his emails.

He ran his eye down the unread items in his inbox and was weeding out the junk items when one made him stop. The email from "YourBigHappyDay" was halfway to being deleted when he suddenly remembered that Penny was a wedding planner. He couldn't recall her company name, or if Mats had ever mentioned it, but he decided to take a closer look anyway.

He opened it up, read the first line and let out a gasp. He stopped, took a large gulp of coffee, a deep breath and then began reading again.

Dear Steven,

I hope you are well. I am dictating this email to Penny and have asked her to send it onwards to you. I didn't want to risk sending it myself as I know the press will stop at nothing to get their story. By the time you read this, I will have made my escape – fingers crossed – and be out of London. I won't say where I'm going as I don't want to put anyone in an awkward situation if they are asked of my whereabouts.

Firstly, I need to apologise again for the cruel way in which I behaved last week. It was uncalled for and despite the situation, it was not an excuse for my rudeness. You could never have anticipated how this was all going to turn out and even though I knew that deep inside, I couldn't stop myself from lashing out. They say you always hurt the ones you love – I'm so deeply sorry that I hurt you.

I'm sure it won't come as a surprise when I tell you I won't be continuing with our radio dating. I've closed my social media accounts and another email will be sent to Sparks and Dave to advise them of this. The very thing I'd feared could happen, when I agreed to be a part of this venture, came to pass and now I have to deal with the fallout from it. We were naïve to think we could come out of this unscathed.

I don't for a moment, however, regret meeting you and the time we shared together. You are a wonderful man and I love you so much. You are witty, funny, handsome, and kind, and these are only a few of the things which I adore about you. However, I also love you enough to let you go. I do believe we could have had something quite amazing but the media interest has killed that. From the moment Adamson spilled her poison, we were doomed. I've spoken with the police and they are satisfied that no foul play was involved in my mother's death but I need to find out why someone out there believed otherwise. I don't know how long I'll be away – right now, the thought of leaving London and never returning is foremost in my mind. Only time will tell if I feel differently further down *the line.*

So, my darling Steven, this is my goodbye. Thank you for the good times we had and the love we shared albeit so briefly. Please keep believing in yourself as I have always believed in you and always will.

Mats
xxx

It was only when Percival licked his face, that Steven realised he was crying and the ache which had been in his heart for the last week intensified, causing him to double over as it continued to grow inside him. An ache he knew would never leave him for as long as he lived.

FORTY-NINE

Marky read the email and threw it back across the table to Dave.

'I guess that's that, then! End of "Love is on the Air". Pity, it was going so well.'

'It might be the end of Mats and Steven's participation but the noises coming down from the bodies upstairs are that they want it to continue. The suggestion is to amend the format so that instead of focusing on one couple for the long term, we only run them for a maximum of three dates and then leave them to get on with it in private.'

'Oh! I see!' Marky mulled over the information. 'Yeah, that might work. There won't be time for the press to become interested in them before they disappear back into obscurity. Do you think anyone will go for it?'

'Go for it? Marky, we're drowning in emails from more-than-willing participants! This thing could run for goodness knows how long. The question is, are you up for it?'

Marky thought it over for a few moments.

'Yeah, let's do it although I do have one condition.'

'Which is?'

'We don't start straight away. We need to allow some time for the dust to settle after what Mats has gone through.'

'I disagree!'

'You do?' Marky couldn't keep his surprise to himself. He knew Dave had been beating himself up over what had happened to Mats and Steven.

'Yes, I think the sooner we move on, the sooner people will begin to forget about Mats and Steven and they can get back to how their lives were before we came along.'

'Well, I don't think that's ever going to happen! Being told your mother was murdered on live television takes some getting over.'

'Trust me, Marky, they'll be chip paper before you know it.'

'Hmm, unless Mats or her family decide to sue The Weekday News. And there would definitely be some recompense due after that one. Has anyone heard anything from Katherine Adamson?'

'Only one tweet saying she'd been given the information by a reliable source and she was standing by it. Unfortunately, or fortunately, depending on your viewpoint, she's shown herself to be less than reliable and the rumours are that a few of her contracts have been cancelled.'

'If only someone would cancel out Swatterhouse too because it was his by-line on that page. His incessant desire to dig out people's skeletons is at the root of all this. He's the one who should be held to account.'

Dave smiled at Marky. 'Well, it's funny you should say that...'

Swatterhouse re-read the emails which had arrived in his inbox, unable to take in what he was seeing.

The day after the "Reveal" he'd been summoned to the Big Cheese's office. To say she'd been livid was an understatement – at one point he thought he might have to call an ambulance, such was the ferocity of her rage. He still didn't know which action had infuriated her more – the fact he'd gone against her specific orders not to get involved in that particular story or the fact he'd ignored all her phone calls after the story had broken, when she'd been trying to put in damage limitation measures. Whichever one it was, it had tipped her over the edge and twenty minutes after walking into her office, he'd walked back out minus a job and with Coulsen's words ringing in his ears that by the time she was finished, he'd never work in the UK again.

For the first couple of days, Swatterhouse had taken her words with a pinch of salt but when every email of enquiry he sent out to his various contacts around the capital came back within thirty minutes with a rejection attached to it, he'd begun to worry.

He then sent out similar emails but further afield. He could work the home counties if he had to – there were still small local papers who'd be lucky to have a journalist of his calibre on their books. However, when they too came back with a politely worded "no", the panic really set in.

Finally, in desperation, he threw out emails to every corner of the country and he was now sitting reading the responses, hoping that one of them would contain a job offer. A few minutes later he knew that Barbara Coulsen had been true to her word. He'd underestimated her power and also how respected she was within the industry. If she said "Don't touch him with a barge-pole" then people would listen.

With his head in his hands, Swatterhouse now knew how it felt when a nation turned against you. In his mind's eye, he could see his own headline:

Scumbag Swatterhouse Silenced!

FIFTY

Mats sat and watched the sun come up over the bay as she sipped the remaining coffee from the thermos Penny had kindly provided. She was parked in the visitor's car park just outside Broatiescombe Bay. She hadn't let her father know she was on her way in case her plans were thwarted and didn't want to just turn up on the doorstep at the crack of dawn. She knew he'd already be up, getting everything ready to feed his B&B residents, but she'd prefer to wait until the morning rush was over before she sprung her presence upon him.

She was desperate for the loo, having driven non-stop since making her escape, and was watching the time anxiously as she waited for the car park conveniences to open. She saw movement in her rear-view mirror and quickly shuffled down in her seat, trying not to be seen. Hopefully, the attendant who was now unlocking the doors to the public toilets, would think her car belonged to a keen walker who'd arrived before the break of dawn to enjoy the early morning solitude of the cliff-top paths.

She waited a few minutes for the attendant to leave

and then scurried across as fast as her almost crossed legs would allow. When she returned to her car, Mats felt considerably more refreshed. A quick hose-down with some baby wipes and a brush of the teeth had revived her so she decided to take a walk through the small coastal town. A pang of guilt hit her as she locked the car, over the fact that she'd never really given any time to exploring or learning about Broatiescombe. Her father had moved here with Sue nearly three years ago but she'd been in the middle of renovating the studios and had barely had the time to breathe, never mind help her father relocate. Since then, the handful of visits she'd made had been brief and mostly spent at the kitchen table swapping news before she left to rush back to London. Where she once couldn't wait to return to the big smoke, Mats now felt that, if she never saw London again, it would be too soon!

She pulled on a baseball cap which had been thrown on the back seat after some promotional event, pushed her sunglasses up to cover her eyes and hoped the two items would be enough to constitute some kind of disguise. It wasn't that she expected everyone to know who she was, it was just in case someone did.

She walked along the path which led from the car park and couldn't help the gasp which slipped from her lips when she turned the corner onto the main street and saw the town set out below her. Most of the buildings had been painted in all the various pastel shades of the colour palette, just like those on the postcard, and they shone vibrantly in the morning sun. Every one appeared to have some form of floral display in the shape of pots, hanging baskets or window boxes and these added to the glorious explosion of colour. Just taking in this delightful scene was enough to lift her spirits. Mats drew in a deep breath and inhaled the scent of the sea all the way down to her toes. There really wasn't much that could beat the smell of salt, sand

and seaweed. It was a combination which blew away even the hardiest of cobwebs and left you feeling refreshingly alive.

She meandered slowly down the old cobbled lane and once again berated herself for her past indifference. On her previous visits, she'd used the small private access road to park behind the B&B and hadn't bothered to venture out onto the main thoroughfare. She made up for that now by taking in everything around her. She passed a small hotel, aptly named "The Top O' The Hill", and which boasted a raised decking area where the clientele could soak up the view. A brass bell hung outside and she thought how quaint it was. The handful of shops consisted of a fishing shop, a newsagent, and a florist. They weren't yet open but Mats could see their street boards and postcard stands just inside the doors, waiting to be pulled out at opening time. A few even had brass bells just like the one outside the hotel. The cobbled road twisted gently downwards and she passed many more pastel-coloured homes and shops, again with their cute brass bells outside. She strolled by Sue's bakery which had a small queue already waiting for her to open, her father's B&B right next door to it and a second inn called "The Halfway House" – because it was halfway up, or halfway down, she guessed. A small board pointed up a side-street towards Hettie's Hairdressers and further down the hill she came across "Adam's Fresh Fish & Chips". She stopped to read the signage outside which advised bookings to eat-in had to be made twenty-four hours in advance as the fish was caught fresh each day. She made a mental note to give them a try while she was here.

Mats continued to casually meander and was so busy looking at everything around her that she was unaware of having come to the bottom of the hill and exclaimed for a second time when she walked out from between two buildings to see the sparkling sea of the bay directly ahead of her.

She crossed the wider than expected esplanade and came to a standstill by the railings. The waves gently glided across the sand below the wall and their close proximity suggested the tide was currently in. Mats looked around and noting there were few people about, she put her legs through the gap between the middle and upper section of the railings and sat down, letting her feet dangle down towards the beach. She folded her arms on top of the cool steel of the upper rail and rested her chin upon them.

She sat like this for some time, allowing the gentle sound of the waves lapping beneath her feet, the gulls screaming above her head and the mesmerising twinkle of the sun on the water to soothe the turmoil inside her. As the sun rose higher in the cloudless sky and the shops and cafés behind her opened their doors, she felt some of the tension leave her shoulders and the knot which had twisted her stomach for almost a week, eased a little. She closed her eyes and let the feeling of peace, which she'd so often taken for granted, make its way through her. Eventually, after the best part of an hour had passed, she stood up and tried not to groan at the cramp which had set in from perching on the metal rail for so long. As she shook out her legs and tried to discreetly rub her sleeping buttocks, her nose twitched at the smell of freshly brewed coffee. Mats looked over to the row of shops opposite and saw a small café with outdoor tables. The rumbling of her stomach was all she needed to prompt her into movement and within a short time, she was tucking into two large bacon rolls with an equally large mug of gloriously milky coffee on the side. She looked at the time and decided to allow herself another couple of hours of taking in the peaceful ambience around her before heading back up to the B&B and speaking to her dad for the first time since her life had fallen apart.

FIFTY-ONE

'Mats! How wonderful to see you?'

Sue rushed out from behind the counter of the bakery to give her a hug. Mats smiled as she leant down to hug Sue back.

'It's wonderful to see you too, Sue.'

'It's far too long since you've been for a visit, girl, it's not good enough.'

The wagging finger combined with the mile-wide smile on Sue's face told Mats that the gentle scolding was a jest rather than a reprimand. She looked at the woman who was her father's partner. She was petite – barely skimmed the five-foot mark – had delicate pixie features, short spiky hair which changed colour on a weekly basis and enough strength in her arms to lug around great big sacks of flour and pummel piles of bread dough into submission on a daily basis. Today, the hair was a vivid purple with golden tips and her pale, ethereal-green eyes were bright with joy beneath her fringe.

'You didn't let us know you were coming. Have you been in to see your father?'

'Not yet, Sue. I thought I'd check with you how things were first. You know, get the lie of the land and all that. I couldn't let you know I was on my way because I wasn't sure if I'd be successful in my prison break.'

'Oh, sweetie, was it really bad? We saw clips on the news...'

'I couldn't go out and no one could come in so, yeah, it was pretty horrendous.'

'Oh, you poor love!' Sue hugged her again and Mats was surprised by how lovely it felt. Yet another little thing she'd never given much thought to before but was now realising how important it was in her life.

'How is dad? Is he angry with me?'

'Why on earth would he be angry with you? He's bloody furious with everyone else but not with you. Never with you, Mats.'

'Would it be okay if I went to see him now?'

'Darling girl, he will be thrilled to see you. Just make sure he doesn't use your arrival as an excuse to avoid cleaning the bedrooms. We've got two new guests tonight so those rooms need to be spotless.'

'Well, I'll give him a hand – we'll get them done quicker then.'

'Walk out through the back to the garden and go in via the patio doors. They'll be open by now.' Sue pointed her towards the back door of the bakery and gave her a gentle push.

Less than a minute later, she was walking through the dining room of the B&B.

'Dad, where are you?'

There was no reply but when she reached the bottom of the stairs, Mats could hear a vacuum trying to drown out the sound of a radio playing. She walked up and found her dad busy cleaning in one of the bedrooms. She stood by the door and watched him as he wrestled with the hose and attachment, ensuring he got into every corner. She seemed to be seeing life through new eyes today for she noticed how well he was looking and that he appeared much younger now than when he'd left London. His face was lightly tanned and oozed of good health. The pale, grey pallor of city living was no longer in evidence. The dark hair which Mats had inherited was now almost totally grey but was still thick on his head although shorter than she could ever recall seeing it. Her heart twanged again in guilt at how very little of her time she'd given to him since he'd moved. Weekly telephone conversations just didn't give the same comfort that a hug or a cuddle did and right now, she wanted one of her dad's cuddles more than anything in the world.

He bent down to switch the vacuum off and in the silence that followed, Mats said, 'Hi Dad,' before quickly crossing the room and throwing herself into his arms.

'Pass your glass over, Mats.'

Sue was pouring out the wine while Alex carried the large chicken and mushroom casserole to the table. A mountain of rice had already been placed there. Mats looked at the food in front of her and couldn't refrain from asking, 'Are you expecting company?'

Her dad smiled as he threw the oven gloves over onto the worktop and sat down across from her.

'You'll be surprised at how much you'll eat, young lady. The sea air gives you one heck of an appetite, let me tell you.'

'So, how come you're not the size of a house?' she asked, as she saw how much food her dad was ladling onto his plate.

'Running up and down three flights of stairs every

day, combined with cleaning, hoovering, cooking breakfasts, serving them, clearing them and then setting up again for the following day, helps to burn off the calories. Add into that going down to the seafront and back up the hill again on an almost daily basis – let's just say there'd be nothing left of me if I didn't put plenty in the tank of a night-time!'

'Well, I have to say that this,' Mats pointed to her plate with her fork, 'looks absolutely delicious.' She scooped a mouthful up with her fork and almost moaned with pleasure. She'd had a cake and coffee with her dad at lunchtime, when they'd finished cleaning the rooms, but other than her rather early breakfast, that was all she'd eaten all day. The sea air must have been working its magic though because her stomach had been rumbling when she'd sat down at the table. Mind you, she reminded herself, she'd been eating nothing but toast for a week so any kind of real food was going to be well received. She even found herself leaning over to pick up a piece of warm pitta bread to wipe up the creamy sauce.

There was light-hearted chatter through the meal and Mats let out a small groan when Sue stood to clear the plates away.

'I am stuffed! I couldn't eat again for a week!'

'So, you won't be wanting any pudding then?'

'Absolutely not! I couldn't squeeze in another morsel.'

'What if I said it was rum and raisin ice-cream, freshly churned this morning.'

'Oh, you… absolute sod!' She looked at her father as he tempted her with her favourite ice-cream flavour. 'You know I can never resist a dollop of rum and raisin.'

'So, that'll be a yes then?' he laughed, as he made his way to the freezer.

She was half-way through her bowlful when Mats

suddenly stopped and looked at her dad. 'How did you just so happen to have a tub of rum and raisin ice-cream in the freezer? I know you prefer strawberry.'

'I phoned "The Ice-Cream Parlour" down on the seafront, when you said you were staying, and asked them to run a tub up if they had any spare. It was delivered this afternoon while you were settling into your room. Since you're stopping a while, I figured you'd be around long enough to eat it all.'

Mats took her dad's hand and gave it a squeeze.

'Are you both sure you don't mind me suddenly landing on you like this and declaring that I plan to be an uninvited guest for I don't know how long?'

Sue leaned over and placed her hand on Mats' arm.

'Mats, we genuinely couldn't be happier to have you here. Your room is yours for as long as you need it.

Tears filled Mats eyes when she heard the kind tone in Sue's words and knew she meant every word.

'Thank you, Sue.'

'Hey, no need for that. Now, how about some coffee out on the patio.'

They all sat in silence for a time on the patio, nursing their mugs of coffee and listening to the faint sound of the sea. The way the town twisted and turned down the hillside, meant the sea could be seen from the little terrace area above the bakery kitchen. The bakery had been in Sue's family for decades and her parents had been looking to retire when the B&B next door came up for sale. Alex decided to buy it as a going concern for it meant Sue could return to Broatiescombe to take over the family business. They'd knocked a door through on the first-floor level so Alex had quick access to the B&B and they lived in the two bedroomed accommodation which came with the bakery. Some money had been spent on the refurbishment of both buildings and the attic of the bakery had been turned into a third bedroom with its own en suite. This had now been designated to Mats and a little table had been placed in the corner for her laptop.

'Shall we address the elephant in the room and get it over with?'

Mats looked at Sue with gratitude. She'd been going over and over in her head how to open the conversation which needed to be had.

'Yes, I suppose we should. Mats, no doubt you have a ton of questions so please ask them and I'll answer as best as I can.'

She looked at her father for a moment and saw the sadness in his eyes. For all that he looked to be, overall, in far better health, the strain on his face couldn't be missed. The shadows under his eyes were the biggest give-away. This was clearly going to be difficult for him and she had no desire to make it any worse.

'Actually, Dad, I've really only got one – Freddie Haycock was your best friend. He was always visiting and he saw how ill she was at the end so why on earth did he think Mother had been murdered?'

Alex hesitated and looked at Sue. She took his hand and said, 'You need to tell her, Alex. The time has come for the truth to come out – all of it!'

Mats saw her father's eyes fill with tears and suddenly she began to wonder if she really wanted to hear the truth after all.

FIFTY-TWO

Alex cleared his throat, took a deep breath, paused and then cleared his throat again. He looked at Mats and she got the impression he was struggling to know how to start. Sue edged her seat closer to him, took his hand and squeezed it gently – giving him the support he needed to begin.

'I…' he coughed again. 'When I first met your mum, she was – as you know – an up-and-coming actress in the West End. I was a mere underling in the theatrical music world at the time. I was also a scrawny lanky piece of string with barely a muscle to my name. I'd managed to secure myself a place in the Broadway Theatre, where I was the assistant to Marcus Ashley. Alicia, at that time, was dating Freddie Haycock—'

'No! Mum was going out with Uncle Freddie?'

'She certainly was and they made a very handsome couple – with them both being blonde haired and blue-eyed, they turned heads wherever they went. They also had many admirers but seemed to have eyes only for each other. I was one of Alicia's admirers but knew I didn't stand a chance with someone like her so I worshipped from afar and took what little joy I could from the brief encounters I had with her.'

Mats found herself leaning forward as she listened. She'd never been told the full story of how her parents got together, only that they'd met through the theatre, and was now intrigued to finally be hearing their story.

'One afternoon, I was in the theatre getting things ready for the evening's performance – you know, checking the seating in the orchestra pit, making sure all the music stands were secure and not going to topple over half way through, ensuring all the music scores were in the correct order for all the various instruments. I thought I was alone when I suddenly heard the sound of someone crying. Well, let me tell you, I almost needed a change of underwear! As with most old buildings, there were rumours of a ghost on the premises and while I'd never paid much heed to them, it's a different kettle of fish when you're all on your own! Bravado goes out the window then, that's for damn sure!'

Alex paused to take a drink of his coffee and Mats had to fight against urging him to get on with it.

'Anyway, I followed the sound, which is not easy given the acoustics in a theatre, and found Alicia hiding behind some old scenery, sobbing her heart out. It turned out that Freddie hadn't been so good at keeping his admirers at arms-length after all and one of them had cornered Alicia and told her everything. Your mum had adored Freddie with every part of her being so to find out he'd been unfaithful left her devastated. I managed to calm her down, told her he wasn't good enough for a fabulous girl like her and that she was better off without him. I helped her to dry her tears and then took her for a coffee. She was on stage that night and she had to get herself together.'

'The show must go on?'

'In a nutshell, Mats. Not even a broken heart was

287

going to stop Alicia performing her part.'

'So, what happened next?'

'After the show, word came through that Freddie was waiting outside for Alicia as he would normally do but she didn't want to see him or have anything to do with him. I helped her to sneak out of a side door and I saw her home. This became our routine for the next two weeks until Freddie finally got the message and stopped coming round for her. By this time, our friendship had begun to grow and much to my astonishment, we began dating. I never expected it to last but it did and the next thing I know, I've proposed and Alicia has accepted. It was the second happiest day of my life.'

'Second?'

'Yes, darling. The day you were born takes first place.'

Mats felt a glow of warmth inside her.

'Anyway, we got married, found a little studio flat in Soho near the theatre and life was good. Both of our careers were on the up, we were feted in the press and with your mother's radiant beauty, photographers were always in the vicinity whenever we went out. Everything was rosy. That is, until your mum fell pregnant. With you. It was the twentieth century when women didn't have the rights they have now and a pregnant actress had no hope of working. Your mum, however, didn't seem to mind – she was so thrilled with the thought of you that her career was pretty much forgotten. That is until you were about a year old. By this time, the novelty of being a mum had passed and she was itching to get back to the stage. Now, don't misunderstand me,' her father put his hand on her arm and gave it a gentle rub, 'your mother still adored everything about you and she still loved you deeply but she needed more. She needed her career back.'

'I get that, I understand. Children should be a part of

you, not define you.'

'The problem was that, in the time she'd been away, other actresses had come along and filled the gaps where Alicia used to be. The role of ingénue doesn't sit so well on women who are mothers and so she found herself getting smaller, less noticeable roles but she kept plodding on, hoping that something better would come along. Of course, in time, her self-confidence began to stutter so when Freddie Haycock turned up one day out of the blue, and started piling on the flattery, your mother fell for it again, hook, line and sinker. I was oblivious to begin with, she hid it well, but when I got my promotion, I had to spend more time at the theatre and it didn't take long for me to see what was going on.'

'Oh, Dad, that must have been so horrible for you.' Mats recalled how she'd felt when Vic the Prick had cheated on her and he *wasn't* the love of her life so how must her father have felt?

'I was shattered, Mats, I'm not going to lie. I couldn't understand why she'd gone back to Freddie after the way he'd hurt her. I was also terrified I was going to lose her – and you – and for a time, it looked like I would. We'd moved in with your grandmother by this time and it was she who brought some form of compromise by suggesting we look at having a "more relaxed marriage" – these days you'd call it an open marriage.'

'Say what?' Mats didn't need a mirror to know her chin had just dropped down into her lap. 'You had an open marriage? How come I didn't notice this? And you were okay with that?'

'I was anything but okay with it however I quickly came to realise that some of your mother was better than none of your mother so I accepted the compromise. You see, your grandmother was a very astute woman and knew her daughter well. She realised it was the attention of many that Alicia needed, not the love of one. The deal was that no one could ever come to the house and you must never find out. And, if it hadn't been for that arsehole Haycock opening his mouth to the press, you never would have known.'

'So, why did he? I don't get that?'

'Freddie, like myself, adored your mum. It turned out he'd never had the affair which had broken them up, it was some girl trying to get your mother out of the way so she could take her place. And it worked! Because Alicia refused to speak to Freddie, she never got to hear his side of the story. He was then offered a role in New York, on Broadway, and by the time he returned to London, she was married to me. He spent many years trying to persuade her to leave me but she refused every time.'

'At least you know she loved you, Dad. That must have helped a bit.'

'Not me, Mats, you! It was you she loved and she vowed never to do anything to hurt you. Besides, it suited her to have Freddie dancing attendance on her and I can only assume he turned a blind eye to her other... err... suitors, shall we say.'

'Not just Freddie?'

'No, darling. Like I said, she never lost the craving for attention.'

'So, what about you in all this? Did you also have affairs?'

'No, Mats, I couldn't. You see, while I wasn't enough for your mum, she was always more than enough for me. I loved her right up till the day she died.'

Mats looked at the pain in her father's eyes. Where had he found the strength to carry on loving a woman who couldn't return that same level of faithfulness?

'This still doesn't explain why Freddie accused you of murder.'

'Freddie always hoped he would one day wear your mother down, that she would accept his offer of marriage and they'd start a new life together but she died before that could happen. I can only assume that as time has passed, his grief over her loss twisted the truth in his head. When I spoke with the police, they informed me that he'd visited her on the day she died and said she'd been in fine spirits. We both know she was pretty pucker that day because the doctor had given her an extra strong morphine injection when he'd come out in the night and it hadn't yet worn off by the time Freddie arrived.'

'Actually, it had begun to,' Mats remembered her mum's grimace of pain when she'd been brushing her hair prior to Freddie's arrival, 'she simply refused to let him see it. I suspect now, with what you've told me, that she knew it would be the last time they'd be together and so she pulled out all of her acting skills to ensure his last memories of her would be good ones. She was too proud to let him see her at anything less than her best.'

'I think there is much truth in that. Anyway, once I advised the police of the doctor's visit and they checked Alicia's medical records, they were satisfied that she died of natural causes and the matter is now closed.'

'But, what about Freddie? He can't be allowed to get away with making slanderous comments like those.'

'The police have spoken with him and I understand he was cautioned. If we want to take out a civil suit against him, that's our prerogative but any police involvement is now at an end and the matter is closed.'

'It doesn't seem fair that he has ruined our lives with his jealousy and he walks away, scot free!'

'He's only ruined our lives if we let him, Mats. Don't let him.'

'But, don't you hate him for all that he's done?'

'No, I don't. I feel sorry for him.'

'What? Why?'

'Because all he did was love your mother. I loved her, you loved her, Freddie loved her. For all her faults, she was a wonderful, caring and loving woman. She may have needed a bit *more* loving than most but that didn't make her a bad person and I don't want what I have told you to change your perception of her. You were her jewel, her life, her everything – all of this other stuff was nothing to do with you. You had a good home, two parents, stability and love. So much love. I understand that finding out your mother had another side to her is difficult and it may take some time to come to terms with it, but please, don't let it change how you feel about her.'

Mats looked at her dad for a minute before turning to Sue who had sat quietly by his side this whole time.

'Did you know about this, Sue?'

She nodded. 'Yes, your father finally shared it with me when we moved down here. Getting away from the house and London made it easier for him to open up to me.'

'And how do you feel about it?'

'It's not my place to feel anything, Mats, nor is it my place to judge. The only thing I will say is that it has shown me that when your father falls in love, he does it wholeheartedly and from where I'm sitting, that's no bad thing at all.'

Sue looked at Alex and Mats saw the love there was between them and she was happy for him. He was right, it would take some time for her to absorb all she'd learnt tonight, but knowing he was now with someone who loved him as he deserved to be loved would make it all a bit easier to deal with.

She stood up, leaned over, put her arms around her father and held him tight. When she let go, she looked him in the eye and said, 'Thank you. Thank you for telling me. I know that must have been so difficult for you but I appreciate it.'

She turned to Sue and gave her a hug too. In her ear she whispered, 'I'm so glad he has you. Thank you for loving him as you do, he deserves it.'

Sue squeezed her tightly and when she stepped back, Mats could see her eyes were also shining with unshed tears.

'Right, you two love-birds,' she smiled, 'I'm off to my bed! I've been awake for goodness only knows how long and I need to sleep. I will see you both tomorrow although the chances of it being before lunchtime are exceedingly slim'

With their goodnights ringing in her ears, Mats made her way up to her little attic room. She was expecting the conversation she'd just had with her father to whirl around her head for most of the night but as soon as her head hit the pillow, she was sound asleep and the churning anxiety she'd been living with since that night at the television studios seeped away a little more.

FIFTY-THREE

Mats sat outside the small café she'd visited that first morning and let the sun fall upon her face. With her head tilted back and her eyes closed, she lapped up its warmth while the sea breeze gently lifted the tendrils of hair around her face. A week had passed since she'd arrived in Broatiescombe and she couldn't recall the last time she'd felt this peaceful. For all that she had set up her little workstation in her bedroom, she'd yet to switch on her laptop. A quick phone call had been made to Penny from the B&B's landline, to let her know she'd arrived safely, and that had been it. There had been no further contact with the world outside of Broatie and her mobile remained switched off as she took this time to recover, just as Tinks had ordered. It's funny, she thought to herself, that you don't realise just how manic life has become until you step off the hamster wheel and make yourself stop to draw a breath.

As she sat musing, a shadow fell across her and a deep rumble of a voice asked, 'Sorry to disturb you but do you mind if I sit here? All the other tables are full.'

She opened her eyes to find a giant of a man standing in front of her. Trying not to sound too flustered, she quickly assented and moved her bag off the spare seat.

'I'm very sorry,' she said, 'I must have been day-dreaming for longer than I realised. Half the tables were empty when I sat down.'

'Oh, I'm sure you weren't. It fills up pretty quickly down here at this time of the day.'

Mats smiled at the stranger's diplomacy which had been delivered in the soft rolling Devonshire burr.

'I'm Adam.' A large hand came across the table towards her and as she placed her hand within it, she was reminded of the scene from Harry Potter when Harry first met the giant, Hagrid, and his tiny hand had all but disappeared within the big man's grasp.

'How do you do? I'm Mats.'

'Ah, you're Alex's daughter. Lovely to meet you – I've heard a lot about you.'

'You have?'

'Oh, yes! Alex talks about you all the time – his beautiful, brilliant daughter who built up her own recording studio in London and helped with the discovery of many of today's top-selling music artists. I don't know much about the music stuff but he was certainly spot on when he said you were beautiful.'

'Excuse me?'

Mats looked up from her coffee to see Adam grow a deep shade of crimson in front of her eyes.

'Oh, my goodness! I'm so sorry... I... err... I can't believe I said that out loud...'

She let out a small giggle. Given all the press coverage she'd recently experienced, there was a lot worse he could have come out with. An unwitting compliment was something she could easily live with.

'Don't worry about it, it's very kind of you to say so.'

She smiled to ensure he knew she meant what she said. 'So, Adam, since you know my dad rather well, I'm guessing you live in Broatie and are not here on holiday.'

'Ahh, yes, yes, I do. I own the fish and chip restaurant just down from your dad's B&B. He and Sue normally dine there once a week.'

'Oh, I know your place – it's where you have to book in advance to be guaranteed a table.'

'That's the one.'

'Don't you find you lose business doing that?'

'No, because the fish is caught fresh each day and I need to know my numbers to ensure nothing is wasted or that we run out. I think I would lose more business if I hadn't caught enough to feed everyone.'

'*You* hadn't caught enough? Do you catch your own fish?'

'Yes, I do. I'm a fisherman first and foremost – it's in the family – but these days, fishing is no longer enough on its own, especially if you're doing sustainable fishing.'

'That would be the "nothing is wasted" bit of your earlier comment?'

'Correct.'

'But I thought fishermen went out before sunrise yet you are here and the sun has very much risen up in the sky.'

'My brother-in-law does the early run twice a week to give me a bit of a break. He's due back in shortly. I'll help him unload his catch and then I'll head out to get mine.'

'Does that give you enough time for prepping before the restaurant opens?' Mats was genuinely interested in how the local inhabitants made their livings. It was as far removed as you could get from the easy city-living she was used to and something she'd never given much thought to before.

'The dawn catch is always for the cod which is the bulk of our sales. This run I'm about to go on is for the speciality fish-of-the-day and requires us to fish in different areas. While I do that, my sister will prepare the chips and vegetables which she'll have picked on her farm this morning, Jed, her husband, will clean the fish and everything will be almost ready for my return with the speciality fish. It's all hands-on deck to prepare it by the time we're opening up and the evening rush begins.'

'Wow! So, it's a family business run with military precision.'

'Yup! You'll see for yourself when you come to dine on Thursday night.'

'Thursday?'

'Yes, your dad has booked a table for three. He usually comes on Thursdays as that's when we serve fresh mackerel.'

'Ah yes, he does like a bit of mackerel.'

At that moment, Adam raised his arm and waved towards the harbour. He turned back to her and stood up.

'Well, Mats, daughter of Alex, it has been a pleasure meeting you.'

'Likewise, Adam, brother-in-law of Jed and owner of fish restaurant.'

A smile spread across Adam's face and with a small nod of his head, he ambled off towards his boat.

Mats ordered a fresh coffee which was placed in front of her with a loud clatter on the table. She looked up in surprise at Coral, the waitress, who was usually rather genial and friendly but before Mats could make a comment, she'd moved off to take an order from another table. Mats gave a little mental shrug and put it down to the café now being busy. She returned her attention to her new acquaintance. While Adam's tall and solid stature may have been the first thing to grab her attention, she hadn't been oblivious to his rough chiselled good looks and the warmth of his dark brown eyes. His even darker brown hair

– some might have said black – had been cut into some kind of shaggy looking style which on anyone else, would have looked messy but suited him perfectly and set off the golden tan of his skin. He'd also been clean-shaven which had surprised her as she'd expected most fishermen to have beards.

'You've been watching too many fish finger adverts, girl!' she murmured to herself.

Mats looked across to the harbour and found the boat she'd seen Adam heading towards. She was just in time to watch him expertly turn it around and head back out to sea. She gazed at it until it disappeared around the headland and its wake had melted back into the sea. Hearing the noonday chimes from the local church ringing out, Mats gathered up her belongings and gave Coral a smile as she left. The glare she got in return, however, was unexpected. Not sure what had prompted it, she put it down to having outstayed her welcome and hogging a table as the café had become busy with food ordering customers. She dismissed it as nothing important and soon forgot about it as she strolled along the harbour and stood gazing out over the vast empty sea towards the sharp horizon in the distance.

FIFTY-FOUR

'Mats, are you nearly ready?'

'Just coming, Dad!'

Mats took one last look in the mirror, drew her fingers lightly through her hair to loosen up the curls she'd spent the last twenty minutes putting in and bent down to check the curling wand had been switched off.

'Well, look at you, don't you scrub up nice!'

'Thank you, Dad! Your compliments truly are underwhelming!'

'Don't you listen to him, Mats, you look lovely.'

'Thank you, Sue. As do you. I love your dress.'

'It's my favourite one. Tonight's a special occasion – all three of us going out for a meal together – so I thought I'd make a bit of an effort.' Sue gave a little swirling motion which caused the bias-cut skirt of her pale lilac dress to flow around her legs.

'I quite agree, Sue. I'm rather fond of this one myself.'

'That shade of red is very becoming on you, dear, and I like the simplicity of the cut – it's a perfect fit on you.'

Mats smiled as she smoothed her hands down the

crimson shift-dress she was wearing, glad now that she'd had the foresight to grab something a little dressy. It had a high, straight neckline, wide shoulder straps, tapered in gently around the waist and most importantly – it travelled well! She always felt good when she wore it. She'd donned a pair of black, kitten-heeled sandals and, with her hair in loose curls which lightly touched her shoulders, she knew she looked dressy without being over the top.

She placed a kiss on her father's cheek. 'You don't look too shoddy yourself, old man.'

'Well, if you ladies were going to all this effort, it seemed only right that I should too.'

'Darn right. We don't want you showing us up in our posh clobber by coming along in those Hawaiian shirts you seem to have a predilection for!'

Mats giggled at Sue's words. She'd noticed her dad's penchant for loud, bold tops and shorts since she'd arrived but had chosen not to say anything. If it made him happy, who was she to spoil that.

'Hmph! Come on, let's get going otherwise we'll lose our table.'

It was Thursday night and the three of them were off to Adam's for dinner. Mats was looking forward to it – it had been a while since she'd enjoyed a nice plate of fish and chips.

It took all of a minute and a half to reach the restaurant and another five minutes of waiting in the queue before they were being shown to their table.

'Alex, Sue, lovely to see you. And Mats, of course. Welcome. I hope you have a lovely evening.'

'Thank you, Adam. Another busy one, I see.' Alex looked around him as he spoke.

'Yes, we've got a stag party over in the far corner and they've taken up quite a bit of our usual seating. I had to bring in extra tables.'

'Hey, don't complain about additional business, lad! It goes a long way towards making the lean months more bearable.'

'Oh, don't you worry, Alex, I'm definitely not complaining.' A low rumble of laughter accompanied his words. 'Now, Coral will be your waitress this evening as I want to keep an eye on those lads but I'll catch up with you later. Enjoy your meal.'

'I'm sure we will, Adam, we always do.'

'See you later too, Mats.'

'Err, yes, Adam. See you later.'

Mats wasn't sure why he'd felt the need to single her out and so buried her head in the menu to hide the flush she felt growing in her cheeks.

'Can I get you something to drink?'

'Thank you, Coral. What do you say, ladies, a bottle of Chardonnay?'

'Sounds perfect to me.'

'Me too, Dad.'

Coral smiled at Alex as she wrote in her pad but there was no missing the sour look she threw at Mats as she walked away towards the bar.

'Right, Mats, the main course is already ordered because Adam fishes it fresh on the day but you can choose any starter and dessert from the menu.'

As she perused the options, Mats filled her dad and Sue in on her meeting with Adam earlier in the week.

'So, I already know we're having mackerel and chips tonight, Dad.'

'Ah, you know me too well, girl. I hope you still like mackerel.'

'I do. And I think I'll start with the melon.'

'Good choice.'

When Coral returned with their wine, Alex gave her their order before he filled their glasses and made a toast to Mats.

As Mats took a sip, she happened to catch sight of Coral from the corner of her eye and, when she turned to look at her, she was shocked by the look of ugly animosity on the girl's face.

'So, how was your meal? Everything satisfactory I hope…'

'Adam, you did yourself proud! That was fabulous.'

Mats smiled as her father sat back and rubbed his stomach. She had to agree with him – every morsel had been delicious.

'Mats?'

'I think I would have to say it's the best mackerel I've ever eaten. The herb breadcrumb was exceptional.'

'That's how it tastes when it's been caught only a few hours earlier.'

'I just need to jog up and down the hill a few times to work off the calories. Chips, even healthier sweet potato chips, followed by sticky toffee pudding and custard is both wonderful and fattening.'

'I don't think you need to worry, Mats, your figure looks mighty good to me!'

'Oh! Right! Well…erm… thanks, Adam.' Mats could feel her cheeks redden at the unexpected compliment.

'I say, Mats, I'm about due to finish up here, how would you like to join me and my friends for a drink? I'm meeting them up at the Top O' the Hill bar. You'd be very welcome.'

'Oh, well…'

'On you go, lass, hang out with some kids your own age.' Her father patted her arm. 'You must be tired of us boring old farts by now.'

'Boring old farts?' Sue shrieked, 'You speak for yourself, Alex Davidson! I'll have you know I'm still in

302

the prime of life!'

'And looking gorgeous with it, my love.' Alex leaned over and kissed Sue full on the lips.

'Oh, get a room, you two!' Mats laughed at her dad's antics, delighted to see him so carefree. 'Adam, I think I'll accept your kind offer if only to give these two lovebirds some time alone.'

'Excellent. Just give me a few minutes and I'll be right back.'

He was true to his word and reappeared at the table five minutes later wearing a fresh, clean polo top and a smart pair of chinos. His hair was damp and Mats wondered if he'd actually had a shower. If he had, it was the quickest shower known to man. He pulled her chair out as she stood up and it was impossible to miss the finely shaped biceps which filled the short sleeves of his top to capacity. It also fitted neatly across his chest and no imagination was required when it came to wondering if there were muscles under the shirt to match those on his arms.

'That's what lifting, pulling and carrying on a daily basis does to you.'

'I'm sorry, what?'

'The muscles. One might say a perk of the job but they can be a right bugger when you need to buy a dress shirt and jacket.'

'Oh, I see. Yes, I hadn't thought of it like that.' Mats tried not to sound too ruffled while feeling utterly mortified that he'd caught her staring at his physique. Mind you, it was impossible not to stare because Adam was a very good-looking man. While he was tall and solidly built, he wasn't chunky and with his dark, thick, wavy hair combed into place, his cheekbones and jawline came into their own. His dark brown eyes twinkled in merriment and the full lips were turned up in a grin which made him almost look like an overgrown schoolboy. Almost…

'Come, daughter of Alex,' he held his arm out for her, 'let me take thee to thine drinking hole where we will make merry.'

'Not too merry, young Adam, or I'll see you hauled around the keel of your boat before the week is out!'

'Dad! Seriously?'

Mats tucked her hand into the crook of Adam's elbow and Sue did likewise with Alex. The four of them walked out of the restaurant leaving a trail of laughter behind them.

FIFTY-FIVE

'Still nothing from Mats, Steven?'

'Huh?' Steven looked up from the label he'd absentmindedly been peeling off his beer bottle. 'Oh, err… no, Neil! All quiet there, I'm afraid.'

'Really? I thought she would have been in touch by now. How long has it been?'

'Seven weeks since the television show, about six since she left London.'

'And there's been nothing since the email from Penny?'

'No, Ems, nothing.'

'Hmm!'

'What?' He looked at her and then at Neil who was taking his famous – in his mind anyway – meatloaf out of the oven. Over the last few weeks, he'd spent so much time at their house, it was a miracle they hadn't asked him for rent. He'd never had a problem with his own company before but since this thing with Mats had all kicked off, he couldn't bear to be alone for any length of time. He just felt so desolate and being on his own only made it worse.

Luckily, Percival was a cat who didn't mind travelling and he seemed to enjoy the fuss from the girls although Steven was sure being dressed up in baby clothes had pushed him to his limit. There had been a few extra fishy treats after that occasion as compensation and an understanding it would never happen again and would never be discussed either.

'Well... the two of you were so right together, I just can't believe she could cut you off like that. It's not as if you were the one who ratted out to the papers.' Emma pursed her lips disapprovingly.

'Perhaps not but when you're hurting, you remove everything from your life that is associated with the pain and let's be honest, I was a mighty big part of what caused that pain.'

'You're far too understanding, Steven. You should be kicking off and venting your frustration, mate. It's not good to keep it all bottled up inside.'

'And where would that get me, Neil? What would I achieve from it? It's not going to bring her back to me, is it?'

'No, but you might feel a bit better in yourself.'

Steven managed a small grin. 'It's not really my style though. I'll just deal with it quietly until it goes away. Which I'm sure it will, eventually...'

'Has she been in touch with anyone? What about Marky Sparks? You said they'd become quite friendly.'

Steven looked back at Emma as he shook his head, 'He's in the same boat as me – it's been radio silence there too, if you'll pardon the pun. The impression I got when we met up last week is that she keeps in touch with Penny, her best friend, but Penny refuses to share any news.'

'So, are things getting serious between Marky and Penny?'

'It certainly sounds that way although Marky doesn't

say too much. I suspect he doesn't want to go on about his joyful relationship given the crap I'm going through right now.'

'I'm guessing it would be too much to ask that your family have given you any comfort or support.'

'How long have you known me, Emma? They've never managed it before so there's no chance of it happening now. All I get from my mother is that I have finally stopped embarrassing them and as for Stuart... well, he has all the sympathy of a rattlesnake. He's been gloating over the fact it went wrong, that his little brother still can't sort his life out and how typical that I should end up dating the daughter of a murderer.'

'But Mats' father didn't kill her mother. The police released a statement saying so.'

'Ah, but since when has Stuart ever cared about the truth?'

'Well, young chap, you just need to take the bull by the horns, pursue the Lady Matilda and win her back.'

'I don't think so, Emma.'

'Why not? Sometimes you have to fight for love. Fight for the woman you want to spend the rest of your life with. Fight for your own happiness.'

'And sometimes, my lovely friend,' Steven leaned over the table to squeeze Emma's hand, 'you just need to respect the lady's right to say no. I've stopped texting her now. She has my number – if Mats wanted to be in touch, she would be. The fact that she's not tells me I have to find a way to move on, no matter how impossible that feels right now.'

Neil moved from the table and got more beers from the fridge. He placed one in front of Steven and put his hand on his shoulder for a few seconds before sitting back in his chair.

Steven just nodded at him. There was nothing more

for them to say.

Marky watched Penny as she walked back into the kitchen. Her landline only rang twice a week and he didn't need to guess who was calling.

'How is she?' he asked.

Penny smiled as she made her way towards him and dipped her finger into the pan of lamb curry that was bubbling away on the cooker.

'Mmmmm, tasty, although it could do with a touch more spice.'

'Penny…'

'She's well, okay! Mats is doing well.'

'Just well?'

'Mark, I've told you before, I'm not discussing her with you. Our conversations are private and she's asked me to keep it that way.'

'I get that but surely you can share a little bit. You know, like where she is in the country… Or if she is even in the country?'

Penny turned to look at him and he felt himself wilt slightly at the expression on her face. 'Sweetie, Mats is my best friend and has been for a very long time and while I adore you to the moon and back, my loyalty lies first and foremost with her. Do not put me in the position where I have to choose between you for you won't like the outcome.'

His stomach heaved at her words. Penny was all his dreams come true and he wasn't about to risk that for anything or anyone.

'I understand, Pen, honestly, I do but… it's… I miss her too. In a short space of time, she became a good friend and they're difficult to find given the business I'm in.

When I was getting myself off the sauce, she was a great support and I miss the wacky phone calls we used to have. I mean, you are amazing and wonderful and the light of my life but no one can give out an insult like Mats can.'

'Are you in love with her?'

'What? No! Absolutely not! I love her as a dear friend but no, I can assure you I'm not *in love* with her.'

'And why not?'

'Because, you beautiful, blonde goddess,' he pulled Penny into his arms, 'I'm completely *in love* with you.'

'Oh, you are, are you?'

'Yup, I sure am.'

'Well, that's good to know because, as it so happens, I'm also *in love* with you, Mark Sparks!'

As their lips touched, and their kiss deepened, Marky couldn't prevent the feeling of guilt that ran through him as he thought of Steven and how broken-up he was right now. He remembered all too well how alone and desolate he'd been after losing Eloise and he'd sure as hell never thought he'd be lucky enough to find a love so deep and so strong a second time and yet, here was Penny in his arms, whispering how much she loved him. Marky wished he could tell Steven to hang in there, the day does eventually come when you can move on and find happiness but he knew that, right now, Steven wasn't yet ready to hear it and Marky suspected it would be quite some time before he was.

FIFTY-SIX

Mats sat up on the cliff top and let the sharp breeze from the sea blow her hair across her face. She pulled her jacket closer around her to keep the cutting wind off her bones. Her father had warned her that, despite how warm it was down in the town, the wind up here took no prisoners and had insisted she take the warm, weatherproof jacket with her. She was glad she'd taken his advice.

It was now two months since she'd arrived in Broatiescombe and she was as happy as she'd ever been. She "clocked on" to work three days a week and the other two were usually spent exploring the area or hanging out with her dad and Sue, helping them in either the bakery or the B&B. It had been quite a revelation to see how things operated in a little town like this, that was perched on the edge of the sea. She recalled the day she'd first seen the sleighs coming through. Adam had called her to come and watch the spectacle of the town's deliveries coming down the hill in two large sleighs on wheels while being restrained from running amok by three of the town's strongest lads at the helm, holding onto the ropes for all they were worth.

Adam had explained that this technique, or something similar, was used by many of the small villages and towns in the area where the roadways weren't wide enough for vehicles to get down. When she'd asked why they didn't bring the deliveries in by boat, he'd sweetly explained that while some did arrive by that mode of transport, it was easier to deliver going downhill than it was to drag the full, heavy sleighs uphill. Boy, had she felt stupid when he'd pointed out this rather obvious fact.

Mats, with a heavy sigh, closed the book on her lap and placed it in her bag. She'd been reading the same page over and over but the words weren't sinking in. Her mind was far too busy elsewhere.

She drew her knees up to her chest, dropped her chin onto them and wrapped her arms around her legs, turning her gaze out across the vast expanse of ocean in front of her. If she turned her head to the right, she could see the faint outline of the Irish coast in the distance but if she looked straight ahead, there was nothing but bright blue water all the way to the horizon. It was soothing to the soul but it wasn't settling the unease within her.

Since the night Adam had invited her to the pub, they'd been spending a considerable amount of time in each other's company. He was fun to be with and his friends had been kind and welcoming. She'd found herself unwinding and reverting back to the carefree ways she'd enjoyed when she'd been a student. Upon thinking about it some more, she'd realised that was the last time she'd felt in any way free. Since the days after her graduation, she'd had to carry the weight of her mum's illness followed by her death. From that she'd gone straight into her cock-up of a marriage and the ensuing stress of getting back out of it. Barely had her divorce come through when her mum's trust fund had matured and she'd dived head first into creating and building her recording studios. This was the first time she'd come up for air in almost fourteen years. No blooming wonder she'd always felt so knackered.

The problem Mats now had, however, was where things were going with Adam. Or not going, depending how you looked at it. She was sure he was keen for their friendship to develop further but she didn't know if she felt the same way. Thus far, nothing had happened. A small goodnight peck on the cheek after they'd been to the pub was as far as it had gone. Much of their time together was spent in the company of his friends which made it difficult to get to know each other properly. They'd had one day alone together, when he'd taken her out on his boat so she could admire the ruggedness of the coastline from a different perspective, but he'd still been working and there had been no time for deep and meaningful conversation. If anything, there had been less chatter as she'd ended up helping him out and having orders barked at her. It had certainly opened her eyes to how hard he worked every day.

She let out another sigh. While Adam hadn't come right out and said he wanted their friendship to move to the next level, she'd caught him looking at her a few times in a way that clearly suggested he did. Her father had also made a few joking comments which had cemented her suspicions – after all, if he'd noticed then it must be obvious.

The question was, what did she want? She liked Adam, he was funny, kind and handsome. She certainly found him attractive but… and while she couldn't put her finger on the problem, the fact that there was a "but" was enough to make her hold back.

Was it a self-preservation thing after all that had happened to her in London? Possibly. Being brutally honest with herself, she acknowledged that Steven hadn't hurt her and had only ever been kind and supportive. In the end, he'd also been a victim of the way the media can twist people's lives out of all recognition. They'd both entered into the venture in complete naivety, never thinking they'd become such hot news. Maybe it *had* just been a quiet time for the media. Perhaps if some married politician with three cute kids and a gorgeous, home-spun wife had been caught with his trousers down and his appendage up while dressed in a wet-look, leather bondage onesie, no one would have ever noticed their little alphabet dating game.

There was also the matter of her feelings for Steven – did she love him? Had she loved him? Or had she just been caught up in all the excitement? Had the public infatuation with them led her to become infatuated with him? Her heart said no but her mind was much more cynical and created all sorts of far-fetched scenarios whenever she let her thoughts stray in that direction. She'd once been accused of overthinking things and Mats was now beginning to believe there was more than a grain of truth in that.

She didn't know how long she'd sat, lost deep inside her thoughts, but she quickly came back to reality when a large, very wet, drop of rain landed on her face. It was rapidly followed by another and then another. The pretty white, fluffy gambolling clouds which had been above her head when she'd sat down, had gambolled away and been replaced by a heavy, thick, dark and brooding shroud. The force of the wind had increased and you didn't need to be a qualified meteorologist to know a nasty storm was on its way and being high on an exposed clifftop was not the safest place to be.

Mats quickly pushed her few bits and pieces back into her bag. She shrugged the weatherproof jacket off, pulling the long leather bag-strap over her head and across her chest before yanking the jacket on again. In the few seconds it took to do this, the rain had soaked right through her sweatshirt and T-shirt underneath. She stood up and tried to fasten the zip but the swirling gusts kept catching underneath the jacket, pulling the edges from her wet, slippery fingers. She turned her back to the wind and finally managed to close the jacket together. Her hair was sodden and rivulets of water ran down her face. She wouldn't have bothered with the hood if it wasn't for the peak at the front which would help to keep some of the rain out of her eyes. Bracing herself against the strong, angry gale, she looked out towards the sea which had been shining and tranquil earlier but was now angry, vicious, and rather terrifying. She could see the vast waves rolling in and heard them crashing against the cliff edge below her. The little oasis of calm she'd been enjoying just a couple of hours before had turned into the scariest place on the planet and all she wanted was to get back to the B&B as quickly as possible.

The sky above was now so dark, Mats struggled to see where the path was. More than once, the wind almost lifted her off her feet and she forced herself to lean forward, bending her knees in an attempt to minimise the surface area for the wind to rage against.

She had no idea how long it took but she finally reached the path which cut through the cliff and gave a modicum of shelter. The lack of wind force enabled her to pick up some speed. She tried to run but her jeans had soaked up every raindrop which had hit them and they weighed a ton! When the path twisted round a bend and the lights of the town finally came into view, Mats could taste her relief. Not long now until she'd be warming herself up in a nice hot shower followed by the biggest mug of cocoa her father could make. The thought lent some speed to her feet and she covered the last half mile in record time.

FIFTY-SEVEN

'Oh, that feels better! Thank you, Dad.'

Mats was curled up on the sofa, her hair still wrapped in a towel turban from her hotter-than-usual shower. She'd pulled on a thick pair of jogging bottoms, her favourite slouchy socks and one of her dad's warm, fleecy sweatshirts. Alex had just handed her a mug of cocoa and placed a hot water bottle by her side. Her fingers still felt a bit numb on the tips and she wrapped them tightly around her hot drink.

'I can't believe how quickly that came on. One minute it was glorious sunshine, the next it looked like the gates to hell!'

'It can happen that way. All it takes is for the wind to change direction somewhere out across the ocean and the next thing you know, from nowhere, the most horrific squall is upon you.'

'Does it happen a lot?'

Sue walked into the room and answered Mats' question.

'Thankfully, not too often but it's always a worry until

it passes. The town is so exposed and all it needs is a couple of waves to be bigger than they should for all kinds of havoc to be wreaked. The last really big one was back in the nineteen eighties – I'd be quite happy not to see another like that in my lifetime.'

'How bad was it?'

'Bad enough, Mats. Three fishing boats were out when it hit – they were found several days later, battered to a pulp against the cliffs two miles from here. Of the twelve men aboard, only four were able to be laid to rest. Add to that the devastation of the town – where the sea didn't reach, the wind did…' Sue paused for a moment and Mats saw the tears in her eyes. 'It took a long time to recover from that one. We're a small community where everyone knows everybody. The lives lost weren't just fishermen, they were fathers, husbands, boyfriends, brothers, cousins or friends. They were—'

She never got to finish her sentence because from outside, a cacophony of bells peeling suddenly rent the air.

'Oh, no! Not again…' Sue got up and ran to the window.

'What is it, Sue? Why are the bells ringing?'

'They're rung when a boat doesn't come home. They're calling the town to the shore where everyone will hold a vigil until we get some news. Come, quickly. Be sure to wrap yourself up, it's still raining out there.'

When Mats stepped outside onto the cobbles with Sue and her dad, the noise of the bells was even louder. She hadn't known that first day the significance of the bells but now that she did, the beautiful shining brasses didn't seem so quaint.

They slipped in beside the other residents of the town and made their way in silence to the harbour. No one spoke and a few older ladies could be heard muttering prayers beneath their breath as they held rosary beads tightly in their hands.

When they reached the esplanade, it was clear the whole town was there. The rain stopped as they joined the crowd and as hoods on jackets were pushed down, Mats was surprised by how many of the faces she recognised. She hadn't given much thought to how well acquainted she was becoming with her father's neighbours, friends, and colleagues. She nodded to a few who nodded back. She leant in towards her father and whispered as quietly as she could, 'Do you know who is missing? Is it one boat or more?'

'I don't know but I'll see if I can find out. Stay here.'

She watched her dad pick his way towards the front of the crowd, gently easing past until he disappeared in among the swathe of bodies. Mats stood on her tiptoes to see if she could spot Adam – after all, with his height, it shouldn't be too difficult to pick him out in a crowd. That, however, was easier said than done and no matter how she twisted and turned, there was no sign of him. She didn't know if search parties went out when it was like this or if they waited until the sea had calmed; after all, they wouldn't want to risk more lives, would they? She turned to ask Sue but she had gone over to talk to a lady Mats recognised as one of the café owners from the harbour. Thinking of café's brought Coral to mind and as if by the power of thought, she saw her standing to the side, on the very edge of the crowd. It appeared to Mats that she was on her own so she pushed her way towards her. She was only a short distance away when a ripple of whispering sound swept through the crowd. It reached her ears at the same time she reached Coral.

'It's Adam Naismith...'

'It's Adam who's missing...'

'Adam hasn't come home...'

Mats touched Coral's arm. The girl spun round to face

317

her and as she heard the name being whispered around her, her mouth opened and a low, heart-wrenching moan came out followed by the word 'Noooooooooooo'.

Mats gathered her into her arms and held her tightly. Now the looks of dislike and snide remarks over the last two months made sense. Coral was head-over-heels in love with Adam and Mats, in her eyes, was taking him away from her.

The two women stood side by side, holding hands, throughout the night. The rest of the town waited with them. At some point, the bells stopped ringing and there was silence apart from the occasional whispered thank you as hot beverages were passed around. A couple of the shoreside cafés opened up to provide free drinks but Coral's wasn't one of them. She did, however, pass her keys to one of her waitresses and told her to take supplies to the others.

Every so often, her hand would tighten around Mats for a few brief seconds as though unspeakable thoughts were tormenting her mind. Eventually Mats couldn't keep her questions to herself and she turned her head to ask quietly, 'How long?'

When Coral didn't answer, Mats came to the conclusion that she wasn't going to so she diverted her gaze back towards the sea. A sea that now looked like a heaving mass of despair. With no moonlight to make it glint romantically and heavy black clouds overhead, it was easier to comprehend how ominous and unpredictable a creature the ocean really was.

'Since forever.'

Mats looked back at Coral. 'Have you ever been together?'

'No.'

'May I ask why not?'

Coral looked at Mats and in the soft glow from a nearby street lamp, she could see the pain on the woman's face as she answered, 'Because Adam has never asked me out. He's not interested.'

'Not interested? Is he off his head? What about you? Have you ever asked him out? Women are allowed to do that these days.'

'No, no, I couldn't do that. Adam doesn't think of me like that, he doesn't notice me.'

Mats took in Coral's golden blonde hair, cut short in the same style as Gwyneth Paltrow's in the film "Sliding Doors" – a style Mats had long coveted but didn't have the bone structure to carry off. Coral, on the other hand, with her high cheekbones, luminous skin and eyes which were the palest shade of hazel she'd ever seen, had it all going on and the hairstyle only served to enhance it. Her figure was to die for and had she been just a few inches taller, all the modelling agencies in the land would have been fighting to get her on their books. She also had a funny, outgoing personality which Mats had witnessed in her first few days before she'd been relegated into the category of love rival.

'Coral, you are gorgeous beyond belief, how on earth can Adam not notice you?'

'We've known each other since we were kids. You stop seeing people when you've known them that long. In his eyes, I'm still the scrawny little kid with bright yellow pigtails and braces on my teeth, yelling at the boys that I hate them because they wouldn't let me join in their games.'

'But you *see* him…'

'I fell in love with Adam two days after I started school. I fell over in the playground and scraped my knee quite badly. I was sitting there crying when this older boy came over, helped me up, placed his hankie over the bleeding cut and spoke gently to me as he carried me inside to see the nurse. The nurse sat me up on the bed and before he left, Adam gave me the biggest of smiles, said, 'You'll be okay now,' and walked out of the room, taking my little five-year-old heart with him.'

Coral turned to Mats and said with a small, wry smile, 'He's had possession of it for twenty-two years, Mats, I don't think I'll be getting it back any time soon.'

Mats had no answer to that so she gave Coral's hand a squeeze and turned her face back towards the ocean. She'd never been one for praying or for following religious beliefs but right now, she was praying with every fibre in her body that Adam came home safely.

FIFTY-EIGHT

The night passed by, the wind blew itself out and dawn was just beginning to break over the horizon when a shout went up. Three boats could be seen coming around the headland and the news quickly came to them that one of them was Adam's. A few minutes later Adam's brother-in-law, Jed, came running down through the crowd.

'Adam's alive,' he was yelling, 'he's alive. Badly injured but alive.'

The cheer of relief was loud and prolonged. The town was happy the sea hadn't claimed one of their boys this night. Mats looked at Coral and saw the tears pouring down her face. She took her in her arms and whispered words of comfort to her. Once Coral had stopped shaking, Mats stepped back and said, 'Look, the boats are almost in the harbour. Let's move closer so he'll see you when they bring him off. Maybe he'll *see* you once he realises you've waited here for him all night.'

'I… I don't think he will. It's better I stay here, part of the crowd…'

'Coral, you've been "part of the crowd" all these years

– maybe that's the problem. You need to step forward and force yourself into his eyeline. Come on.'

Without giving the girl a chance to respond, Mats grabbed her hand and dragged her to where the boats were now tying up. A Land Rover was waiting nearby, ready to whisk Adam up through the fields to the ambulance sitting at the top of the hill which would then take him to the local hospital to be treated.

They watched as Adam was carefully helped off the boats. One ankle was encased in a plastic cast and his face was a mass of bruising and cuts. He'd clearly been in the wars but that didn't stop him smiling when people were calling out his name. Mats shuffled herself and Coral forward so they were right beside the Landy when Adam was led towards it. The smile on his face increased when he saw them there although this was quickly followed by a wince. He gripped the vehicle with one hand and on his good foot, hopped closer to them.

'Mats! Oh, my goodness, you waited for me! Thank you, thank you so much.'

Before Mats could do or say anything, his large hand was on the back of her head and his lips were upon hers, holding her so tightly there was no way she could escape from the embrace.

When he finally let her go, amidst a lot of cat-calling around them, he said, 'I'll see you when I get back from the hospital. I need to talk to you.'

He was helped into the Land Rover and as it drove away, Mats couldn't bring herself to look at Coral – she couldn't bear to see the pain she knew would be on her face. With her head down, and her hands in her jacket pockets, Mats began the walk back up the hill to the B&B. She had some thinking to do.

———❧———

Two days later, the story of Adam's Adventure, as it was now being called, was doing the rounds of the town. Alex had been down to the newsagent to get in the morning papers for the B&B when he heard the tale and as soon as the breakfasts had been served, he shared the information with Mats while they tidied up the kitchen.

'So, the story is that Adam was out checking his lobster pots but the pickings had been poor in his preferred locations. He'd just arrived close to a small, out-of-the-way, cove where he keeps a few pots as back-up when the storm hit. His plan had been to check the pots and then head into the shelter of the cove until the worst of the storm had passed. He'd cut the engine and was pulling in his pots but one of them got snagged. He leant over the side of the boat to see what was going on when a large wave hit the vessel and the side of his head encountered one of the metal cleats, knocking him clean out.'

'Cleats? That's the metal bit you tie the rope to?'

'Yes, that's right.'

'Ouch!' Mats winced at the thought.

'Yeah, "ouch" indeed! However, the angle at which he fell should have seen him in the sea but his ankle got caught up on the line of the lobster pots and it was this which prevented him going overboard and being washed away. Apparently, when he was finally found, he was hanging over the side of the boat and the buffeting waves were making his head and face bounce against the hull – this is why it was so badly bruised. The lobster line which saved his life, however, had unfortunately also caused quite a bit of damage to his ankle so that's been all strapped up and when he gets out of the hospital, he's going to be on crutches for a while.'

Mats put the last of the cooking pots away in the cupboard before asking the question she really wanted the answer to, 'So, do they know when he'll be allowed home?'

'The current prognosis is about a week, give or take. He had a pretty nasty concussion when he arrived and they just want to keep an eye on him.'

'Well, it's better to be safe than sorry, I suppose.'

'You could always go and visit him, I'm sure he'd like that.' Her father gave her a cheeky grin.

'I don't think so, it wouldn't be appropriate.'

'Why not? Plenty of us saw the welcome home you gave him when he got off that boat.'

'Dad, Adam kissed me, I didn't kiss him.'

'Didn't look like that from where I was standing…'

'Well, trust me, that's how it was! And stop winking at me like that – it makes you look like a sad old letch!'

'Who's a sad old letch?'

'Hi Sue, my dad's a sad old letch! He keeps winking and making suggestive comments regarding Adam, no matter what I say.'

Sue picked up the bread tins she'd come in for, placed a kiss on Alex's cheek and said, 'Well, I happen to be rather fond of sad, old letches and, being honest, Mats, that kiss looked like a real toe-curler from where I was standing.'

She dashed back out, leaving Alex grinning and Mats' glowering.

'DON'T say a word, Dad, not one word!'

'Very well. I'm off upstairs now to clean the bedrooms… and to decide what I'll be wearing to the party.'

'Party?'

'Oh yes, my dear, a "Welcome Home" party is being arranged for Adam and I suspect it's going to be a rather interesting night.'

With those words, he gave her another wink and

managed to make his escape before the plastic scouring brush hit the back of the kitchen door.

Mats poured herself a mug of coffee and sat down at the big, solid kitchen table. She stared into the milky liquid and tried to arrange her head into a sensible state. Ever since the day of the storm, the turmoil inside her had increased and the calm equilibrium she'd been enjoying up till then was gone. Both Sue and her dad had assumed that Adam's kiss had been one of passion. Well, it might have been for him but it had been anything but for her. When his lips had landed on hers, they'd felt all wrong. What had looked like a "toe curler" to Sue had been a stomach churner for Mats. It had taken every ounce of discretion she possessed not to wipe her mouth clean in front of everyone. Adam's kiss had also pushed her into facing up to a decision she'd been putting off making – what to do next? For a time, she'd been lulled into thinking she could stay here in Broatie indefinitely but this was now beginning to look less likely. She was an outsider and if she broke Adam's heart, she would always be an outsider. The few friendships she'd begun to make were with Adam's friends and she was sure their loyalty would lie with him. There was no way forward from here.

Mats stood up, pushed her chair in and let out a sigh. The clock above the door told her it was almost time for her Zoom meeting with Tinks. She picked up her mug and with heavy steps, made her way to her little attic bedroom. Today was going to be the day she'd be telling Tinks she was coming home.

FIFTY-NINE

Mats pulled up the zip on her red culottes and as she checked them out in the mirror, remembered when she'd last worn them – the first time she'd met Steven. A smile crept across her face as memories of that night came back; the two of them smuggling booze up to the top deck of the boat, the discovery of their shared like of "Absolutely Fabulous" with their Patsy and Edina references and the sense of wanting to make Steven feel better in the face of the crap he got from his family because of his asshole twin brother. The smile soon faded though as she thought of what had followed. She'd been blocking it from her mind since she'd all but run away to her dad's but knowing she was going home in a few days had forced her to face up to all that had happened and it filled her with shame and sorrow when she thought again of how badly she'd treated Steven. He'd done absolutely nothing wrong but she'd lashed out at him, blamed him for everything and then cut him off with no care as to what he was feeling or going through. Yes, she could make the excuse that she was in a state of shock and people would forgive her but she was unable to forgive herself. She'd told Steven she loved him and yet had gone on to treat him in the most despicable manner. She hadn't even had the decency to say goodbye herself; instead, she'd asked Penny to do it for her, almost as though they were school kids in the playground rather than grown, mature adults.

The knock at the bedroom door interrupted her thoughts.

'Are you ready to go, love?'

'Yes, Dad, two minutes.'

She looked at her reflection again. Mats didn't know why she'd brought these with her when she'd packed so hastily but was pleased she had. She needed reminding of that first night when, for a short time, she'd fixed things for Steven. Now she was hoping to fix things again – this time for Adam. Maybe she should rename them her "Bob the Builder" trousers because, thus far, she seemed to always be fixing things when she wore them.

When Mats walked into the function suite of the Top O' The Hill hotel with her dad and Sue, there was a lull as everyone stopped talking to look at her before returning to their conversations a few seconds later. Mats had seen such things happen in movies but had never expected to be the subject of one herself.

She followed her dad to the bar but her eyes were scanning the room, looking for one person. She breathed a sigh of relief when she found them. Coral was standing near the DJ box looking breath-taking. Her simple midnight-blue dress showed off her perfect figure and the colour made her hair shine like polished gold.

When her dad passed her drink to her, she took a big sip, a big breath and walked over to where Coral was standing.

'Hi, how you doing?'

'Okay, I guess.'

'I'm glad you're here tonight. I was worried that after… well, you know… what happened…' Mats' voice tailed off. How on earth could she discuss this with Coral? What could she possibly say to make things better?

Coral looked straight at her and to Mats surprise, there was no animosity on her face. In fact, if she had to describe Coral's expression, she'd say it was resignation. And the woman's words confirmed that.

'Look, Mats, I can't force Adam to love me. If he's chosen to be with you, then there's not a lot I can do about it. I just need to learn to live with it. It's not your fault and it was wrong of me to be so rude to you before. You weren't to know how I feel – after all, no one who's known me all my life knows so why should you, a complete stranger, know? All that's happened has, however, made me stop and think though.'

'About?'

'About what to do next. Should I stay here in Broatie or do I spread my wings and move elsewhere? After all, everyone likes a coffee shop – I'm sure I could do just as well in the big city. How's London looking for independent coffee outlets? Is there room up there for a little one like me?'

'More than enough room, Coral, but I hope it won't come to that.'

'Hmm, we'll see.'

Just then a shushing sound ran around the room and the lights were all switched off. A minute later they came on again and the word 'SURPRISE' was yelled from every corner.

Adam stood in the doorway, perched on his crutches, and laughed in delight at this unexpected turn of events. Mats watched as he repeated her earlier action of scanning the room and felt her stomach lurch when his eyes came to rest on her and his smile went up a couple of notches. He inclined his head towards her and she returned the gesture.

'Oh, shit! I don't think I can do this. I need to go home...'

'No, Coral. Please stay.'

'Why? Is this payback for when I was dissing you – you're forcing me to stay and watch you and Adam get together?'

'No, no! It's not like that, I promise. Look... I just need you to trust me. Please...'

Mats had a plan up her sleeve but there was no guarantee it would work. She had high hopes but she couldn't risk saying anything that might end up hurting Coral even more.

Coral looked at her for a few long seconds before giving her a small nod.

'Okay, I'll trust you but please know that, right now, I just want to be at home on my own.'

'I know.' Mats rubbed the other woman's arm gently before turning away and making her way towards Adam. The sooner they spoke, the sooner everything would be sorted.

'Hey, here she is! My lovely lady.' Adam rested one of his crutches against his side and pulled Mats into an embrace. He tried to kiss her again but she was prepared this time and managed to turn her face so that his lips landed on her cheek. She placed a little kiss on his cheek and then whispered in his ear, 'Meet me out on the decking in ten minutes.'

She pulled back, gave him a little wink and strolled away. She felt bad for leading him on like this but it was the only way she could guarantee getting to speak with him alone. Had she muttered those eternal words of doom, "We need to talk" there was every chance he'd refuse and she wouldn't be able to go through with her plan.

She was already on the deck, looking over the higgledy-piggledy rooftops of the town towards the sea, when she heard the door from the function suite open and close. She didn't need to look round to know it was Adam – the soft thump of his crutches on the wood underfoot gave him away.

'Hi you,' he said, placing his crutches against the railing and trying to take her in his arms.

'Hi you, back!' Mats smiled gently as she took a step backwards and out of his reach.

'Oh, no welcome home kiss for the big guy?'

'I don't think it would be appropriate, Adam.'

'Huh? But you kissed me like there was no tomorrow down on the harbour, when I was rescued?'

'Actually… you kind of kissed me, Adam. I didn't really get much say in the matter.'

'No, I'm quite sure you kissed me, Mats. I remember it clearly.'

'Adam, you were severely concussed so I think it would be fair to say your memory is probably more than a little hazy. Please believe me when I say I didn't kiss you.'

'Oh!' He looked down at the decking before suddenly looking back up at her with eyes wide open in shock. 'OH! Oh, my goodness, did I force you to kiss me? I am SO sorry, Mats. I would never force myself on a woman. You have to believe me. In my head, I've got this picture of you kissing me…'

'Hey, it's okay, no harm was done and the circumstances were extenuating. I can forgive you, don't worry about it.'

'But… but where does that leave us now?'

'Adam,' Mats' voice was soft as she broke the news he wouldn't want to hear. 'There is no "us". You're a great bloke, a genuinely lovely guy but we're not meant to be together.'

'Is it that other bloke? The one from London you were in all the papers with?'

'You know about him?'

'Of course, I do. We might be a little town but we still get the news every night.'

'But you never mentioned it, why?'

Adam shrugged. 'It didn't seem important. I figured if you wanted to talk about it, you would. So, is it him you're passing me over for?'

'Oh, Adam, I'm not "passing you over" for anyone. I'm just being real and telling you that as lovely as you are, I don't have those sorts of feelings for you.'

'So that's me back to being alone again. It was nice to have an almost-girlfriend for a while. Thank you for that.'

'I'm sorry, what do you mean? Being alone again? You're a wonderful man, I'm sure there are several ladies in this town who'd want to spend time with you.'

'I wish! No one sees me like that. They all just see this big, good-natured lump of a man who they can rely on to help them out when help is needed. No one sees beyond that.'

'That's where you're wrong, Adam, very wrong indeed. I know of one lovely woman who more than sees you.'

'Who?'

Mats swallowed. If this went all wrong, then Coral was going to want her guts for fishing nets!

'Coral.'

The last thing Mats expected was for Adam to burst out laughing in her face.

'Why are you laughing? Is that a bad thing?'

'Coral? Coral Withers?'

'I only know one Coral but if it's the one who works in your restaurant in the evenings, then yes.'

'Coral Withers fancies me? Are you for real? Why on earth would a woman who looks like that and could have any bloke she yearned for, want to have anything to do with me?'

'Because she loves you and has done since she was five!'

'Yeah, right!'

'Do you remember the day you helped her in the playground and took her to the nurse to fix her knee?'

'Yes...'

'So does she! Very well, in fact!'

Adam looked at her long and hard before saying in a quiet voice full of disbelief, 'Coral Withers fancies me?'

'Yes, she does, so I suggest you get back in there and ask her out on a date before someone else beats you to it!'

'Mats, you're awesome. Thank you.'

He took her hand and kissed the back of it before swivelling round on his good foot and hopping across the decking as fast as he could.

Mats smiled and turned back to look over the sea once more. She only had a few days left before she was going home and she wanted to breathe in the sea as many times as possible before her lungs were once again clogged up with London fumes.

A little while later she made her way back inside and taking a look around, she saw Adam and Coral sitting at one of the tables, their heads close together in conversation. She saw Jed make his way over to them and as Adam turned to speak with him, Coral caught her eye. Her smile was luminous and could have outshone a thousand stars.

'Thank you,' she mouthed over.

Mats smiled back and gave her a thumbs up. Her plan had worked. Now it was time to go home and sort her own life out.

SIXTY

'Hey, Steven, howzit all going?'

'Hi Marky, not so bad, thanks. Yourself?'

'I can't complain.'

'You can't? Or you daren't because Penny will skin you and turn you into shoes?'

Marky burst out laughing at Steven's shrewd comment. 'I'm not saying a word, mate! You'll get me into trouble.'

'So, she's in the room with you, you hen-pecked apology for a man!'

'Oi, that's my lady you are ball-busting there and no, she's in the kitchen, working on some autumnal wedding theme for a last-minute job that came in.'

'Things still good I take it?'

Marky paused for a few seconds before replying. He still felt awkward when it came to talking to Steven about how well things were between him and Penny – the pangs of guilt popped up and he worried that Steven might feel he was gloating about his good fortune.

'Erm, yeah, still hanging in there, ya know…'

Steven's laugh came down the phone. 'Look, there's no point in trying to play it cool with me, Marky, I know you'd do anything for that lady and I suspect she'd do the same for you. It's good to know you're both so happy, you deserve it.'

'Cheers, Steven. Anyhow… I was wondering if you wanted to meet up for a pint later in the week? Does Tuesday or Wednesday work?'

'Wednesday is good. I've got a meeting near you in the afternoon – I can meet you after that.'

'Great stuff. Usual place?'

'That works for me, I'll see you there.'

'Good. Good…'

'Was there anything else, Marky?'

'Erm…' Marky cleared his throat. He was dreading the next part of the conversation. 'Well, erm… yes, there is…'

'Okay…'

'Urm, well… the thing is… Mats is back in London.'

There was silence at the other end and Marky began to wonder if Steven was still there.

'Hello?'

'Yes, I'm here. When did she get back?'

'About six weeks ago.'

'And you're only telling me now?'

'I only found out myself last night, mate. Penny was under orders not to mention it. Also, we have an understanding – I don't ask about Mats and just say to Penny to pass on my regards when they talk. If I don't ask, it doesn't put pressure on Pen to split her loyalties. So, I'm going to assume she hasn't been in touch with you then?'

'No, she hasn't.'

'I'm sorry.'

'It is what it is, Marky. She's moved on and I'm doing the same.'

'If you say so.'

'What's that supposed to mean?'

'Nothing. Nothing at all. So, I'll see you Wednesday?'

'Sure. I'll text you when I'm on my way.'

'Okay. Till then, later.'

'Yeah, later!'

Marky ended the call and stared at his phone. It seemed that talking about Mats was a no-no all around. He let out a sigh as he got up off the sofa and went to see how Penny was doing. She'd probably be ready for another cup of coffee. Or if it was a particularly fractious bridezilla, another bottle of wine!

Steven put his phone down on the table and looked back at the laptop sitting in front of him. The picture of Mats, standing beside Tinks as he brandished an award from some industry ceremony the night before, was staring back at him. The camera had caught her unawares and the smile on her face, as she looked into the eyes of her friend, was quite radiant. Steven caressed the screen with his fingers and remembered when she used to smile at him the same way. Her hair was scraped back in some kind of up-do. He wasn't sure if it suited her or not.

Six weeks!

She'd been back in London six-bloody-weeks and hadn't even had the decency to let him know or drop him a quick text just to say she was alright and ask him how he was. He'd never had Mats pegged as being selfish but he'd seen a whole new side of her after the big revelation on the television. She hadn't been the only one affected but it would appear she thought she was.

Feeling his anger bubbling up again, Steven slammed the lid down on the laptop, pushed himself out of his chair, and walked over to the window where he stood in the semi-darkness, looking out across the park. The nights were drawing in early these days, winter was on its way and many of the shops in town were already gearing up for the Christmas season.

He gazed over at the trees which had almost finished shedding their summer leaves. Soon they would be completely bare and the lit-up windows of the homes on the opposite side of the square would shortly be sporting their yearly display of gaudy, twinkling Christmas lights and dodgy bouncing snowmen on their front lawns. He realised then that somewhere deep inside, he'd almost been looking forward to Christmas this year. He'd thought that Mats would be by his side and it would actually be fun rather than the family farce he usually had to endure.

'DAMN YOU TO HELL, MATS DAVIDSON!' he shouted, picking up a nearby mug and hurling it across the room where it smashed against the wall. Percival, who had been lying on the sofa sound asleep, leapt up with a high-pitched screech and shot out of the room in fright.

Steven turned back to the window and saw his reflection looking back at him. He'd lost weight and he didn't suit it – his face looked gaunt thanks to the hollows beneath his cheekbones and there were dark shadows under his eyes. He stared at himself for a few minutes before whispering, 'Enough! It *is* time to move on. This is over. No more!'

He straightened up, pulled his shoulders back and with a determined step, went off to make peace with his distraught cat.

SIXTY-ONE

Mats stood in the kitchen and set her favourite china cup and saucer on the tray alongside the teapot and the little matching milk jug. She picked the tray up and made her way upstairs to her reading room in the attic. It was Sunday afternoon and time for some serious chilling out. She had a new book by one of her favourite authors all lined up to be read and she was indulging herself with the luxury of a proper pot of Earl Grey and some nice macrons she'd picked up the day before.

Soon she was ensconced in her large, cosy, cuddling chair – all curled up with a soft, tartan throw over her legs. She looked around the room and let out a contented sigh. This was her favourite room in the whole house. All her books were lined up on floor-to-ceiling, shabby-chic, bookshelves. A large pale cream rug covered the varnished floorboards and her chair was placed right in the middle. Some strategically placed lamps threw out soft lighting and combated the heavy, dark sky she could see through the skylights. A floor-standing lamp was just behind the chair, making sure she always had a good light to read in.

Mats picked up her book with one hand, her teacup with the other, and began to read.

Ten minutes went by before she let out an exasperated groan and put the book down. She'd been staring at the pages but the words weren't being absorbed. She'd hoped her little haven of peace would give her some respite from her troubled thoughts but they'd followed her and invaded the one place which normally soothed her soul. Since returning to London, Mats had slowly and carefully begun rebuilding her life. The first few weeks had been really difficult and taking the bus and tube to work had created anxiety like she'd never known before. She'd been waiting for the moment when someone recognised her and would either get in her face or take a photo which would be all over the internet within five minutes. The moment hadn't come though and she gradually began to relax. There had been a couple of nights out with Penny but only as far as the pub around the corner where she was known and no one would bother her. The biggest test, however, had been when Tinks had all but strong-armed her into attending a music industry awards gala. The studio had been nominated in a few categories and he was adamant she should be there for them. To say she'd been terrified was an understatement and Tinks had actually joked at one point that he'd have to learn how to ply his trade with one hand as her tight grip was cutting off the circulation in the other.

Somehow, with him by her side – as he had been for so many years – she'd made it through the night and by the end of it, had found she was almost enjoying herself. Being back in London was so different to being in Broatiescombe. Down there, there had been no memories to deal with, it was all fresh and new, but London held memories in so many places. It was only now that she'd come to realise just how much time she'd spent in Steven's company and all the places they had visited together. Returning to London should have felt like coming home but instead, she felt totally alone. Penny was busier than ever with her business and with her blossoming relationship with Sparks, Mats had barely seen her although she couldn't be happier for Penny if she tried. Penny's happiness just brought home the loneliness of her situation and the truth was, she missed Steven. She'd behaved like a total cow and was still mortified when she thought of the cruel words she'd thrown at him, the manner in which she'd accused him and the attitude she'd taken. She'd lost count of the number of times she'd picked up her phone to call him – her finger hovering over his name before she lost her bottle and threw the phone down again. She'd tried to get information from Penny, had asked her if Sparks had mentioned him at all, but Penny simply said that she and Marky had agreed it was best not to discuss either her or Steven and so she knew nothing. She did say that they continued to be friends and met up for drinks but that was all she could tell her.

With her heart in her mouth, Mats dug her phone out of her pocket and scrolled through to Steven's name. Her stomach was clenching and unclenching, churning every which way and making her feel physically sick. She knew she had to do this. She had to apologise and hope that he could forgive her. She hadn't spoken to him for almost four months – had she left it too long? There was only one way to find out. She tapped the screen and then, holding her breath, she waited...

Mats took a small sip of her wine. As she replaced the glass on the table, she noticed how badly her hands were shaking. The wine tasted foul but she swallowed it anyway

– anything to alleviate the dryness of her mouth. Her conversation with Steven had been short and to the point. His manner had been curt and when she'd asked him if they could meet, the silence had stretched on for several seconds before he'd agreed. As soon as they'd confirmed when and where, he'd cut the call. Now she was just sitting, waiting, and hoping with all her heart that she could make things better. The sound of his voice in her ear had made her realise she still loved him and wanted nothing more than to be with him.

All around her people were gathering, the after-work crowds grabbing a quick pint before catching their train and the table she'd so carefully chosen with its view of the door was soon hidden behind the City uniform of Savile Row suits and Jermyn Street shirts. She picked up her phone for the umpteenth time to check for a text to say he wasn't coming and when she looked back up, he was standing in front of her, a beer in one hand and a glass of wine in the other. Without saying a word, he placed both on the table, shrugged off his overcoat and sat down opposite.

Mats eyes gorged themselves on the sight of him. It was the only way to describe how it felt to see him again. She noticed the shorter hair-cut, the weight loss which had produced sharper cheekbones and the grim, straight-line of his lips. His eyes, however, told a different story. They still held a softness for her and this gave her a small glimmer of hope.

Eventually, she broke the silence when it became clear he was waiting for her to speak first. Even though it sounded lame and stupid, there was only one question to begin with.

'How are you?'

'Fine, thank you. Yourself? New hair-cut I see.'

She gave the heavy fringe over her eyes a light, self-conscious sweep with her fingers. 'Yeah. I thought a change of appearance might help with... well... you know.' She gave a small shrug. 'So, how are things?'

'Good.'

'Is work okay?' Good grief, she thought, could the small talk get any smaller?

'Work is very good. I got a promotion – I'm now Marketing Director.'

'Oh, Steven, that's wonderful. How did that happen? I thought you weren't keen...'

'Kenny, my boss, was headhunted. I was made up to Acting Director until they hired a replacement but I found I actually enjoyed the extra responsibility and so asked for the position on a permanent basis. They were a bit iffy to begin with until I told them if they declined, they'd be looking for two new staff members. After that, they pulled their finger out and made an acceptable offer.'

'That's fantastic and well done for sticking up for yourself like that.'

'Yes, well... I suppose something good had to come out of all this – I seem to be less of a pushover than I was before. I appear to have developed a bit of an attitude, somewhere along the line.'

'Is that a bad thing?'

'It doesn't feel like it.'

'Was that the only good thing?'

Steven leant forward and took a drink of his beer before he replied. 'I suppose not, if I'm being honest. We had fun days out and some experiences which I'd probably never have tried otherwise.'

'Like bungee jumping?'

He gave a small laugh and she revelled in the sound.

'Yes, like bungee jumping. That would *never* have happened!'

'What about us? Were we a good thing?' Mats

decided to go for broke, slipping her hands underneath her thighs in an attempt to stop her trembling. She was trying to read him but Steven was giving nothing away. Even his eyes had lost their initial softness.

'I thought so back then but with the benefit of hindsight, I suppose it was inevitable that something would develop between us given the time we were spending with each other. We got caught up in some kind of bubble and naturally gravitated together. The public attention just fed into the belief we should be a couple so that's what we became. We did what was expected of us.'

Steven's words at slashed her heart. Mats had let herself believe the same in the early days of it all going wrong but she knew differently now; she just had to hope she could convince Steven to think the same.

'I'm deeply sorry about how I spoke to you. I blamed you and I was wrong, *so* wrong, to do that. I was hurting, and shocked, and I took it out on you. I lashed out at the nearest person and you took the brunt. I should never have said the things I said. Can you forgive me?'

Mats picked up her glass to take another sip of wine and as she put it down, Steven moved his pint to place his hand on hers.

'Mats, there's nothing to forgive. I do understand why you reacted as you did. I never had a problem with the words you threw at me. What I did, and still do, have a problem with was your silence. You just cut me off. You wouldn't answer my calls, you ignored my texts and you didn't once return a single message. *That* is what hurt me. It wasn't your words; it was your actions.'

'I'm so sorry again. I couldn't think straight. I was a prisoner in my own home. The press hounds were camped outside my door, twenty-four-seven. They even had drones to try and see inside the house. I had every curtain and window blind closed in an attempt to keep their nasty little prying eyes out. On top of that, I had the police round asking questions as they had to investigate the murder allegation. I'll be honest, Steven, on the list of things to worry about at that time, you were pretty far down it.'

'But what about when you left London? Or even when you returned? Just one phone call to let me know you were okay would have done. You've been back in town, what... eight, nine weeks? And yet two days ago was the first I'd heard from you? Can you understand how that feels?'

'Again, I can only keep saying I'm sorry. I went to see my dad down in Devon and I spent that time getting my head together. He shared some stuff from his past – to do with my mother – which I had to learn to deal with. It wasn't an easy time and I'm sorry – saying it again, I know – if that sounds like a cliché but it's the truth. My dad opened up to me with full honesty even though it was difficult for him to do so and difficult for me to hear. But the brutal truth was the only way to explain why the allegation had been made. I simply wasn't in the right place to be having this kind of conversation with you then.'

'And what about when you returned to London? You must have been feeling better in yourself to have come back?'

'I wouldn't say I was feeling better, more a case of I had to somehow try to get on with my life. I did give some serious consideration to staying in Devon permanently but realised it wasn't the answer. That was simply running away and I couldn't do that. Coming back was scary though. I didn't know what to expect – would there still be paps outside my house; if people would stop to point and stare at me... I've never suffered with anxiety before but those first few weeks... well, I was like a cat on a hot tin roof. The smallest noise had me jumping a foot in the air and I was looking over my shoulder at every turn.'

'You still managed to go to that awards ceremony. I

saw the photograph of you and Tinks with your award.'

'Tinks had to drag me to that, quite literally kicking and screaming. I didn't want to go but he was adamant. It was the first time I'd been "properly" out,' she made quote marks in the air with her fingers, 'since I came home. A quick drink in my local pub with Penny doesn't really count.'

Steven let out a sigh and ran his fingers through his hair. 'One text, Mats, just one text! Was it too much to ask for?'

'I tried, Steven, I really did. I must have picked up my phone a million times but I was so embarrassed by the things I'd said, by the way I behaved, and as time passed it grew harder and harder.'

'But you finally managed it?'

Unable to look at him, Mats eyes dropped down to her hands which were now twisting in her lap. 'Yes.'

'Well, I suppose I should be grateful and thank you for that. And thank you for meeting me. It's easier to move on when you have closure. I'm not fond of Americanisms but they sure nailed it with that one.'

'Closure?' Her head snapped up at his words. 'You mean…' She couldn't bring herself to say the rest of her sentence.

'Oh, Mats! Did you really think we could go back to where we left off?'

'No, but I'd hoped we might find a way forward.'

'I'm sorry, I really am but you left it too long, you hurt me too much. I can't go there again.'

'But—'

'Mats, you once told me I had the right to say no when I didn't want to do something… This is me exercising that right.'

He downed the rest of his pint, stood up and pulled his coat on.

'I wish you all the best, Mats, I honestly do. I wish you continued success in your business and I hope you find happiness. Have a wonderful life, you deserve it.'

With his softly spoken words, he bent down, placed a gentle kiss on her cheek and squeezed her shoulder lightly. He then straightened up and with a sad little smile, turned and walked towards the door.

Mats watched him leave, unable to bring herself to call after him. Upon reaching the door, she saw him hesitate and for the tiniest second, hope flared up inside her that he'd changed his mind, only to plummet like a stone when he pushed it open and walked out without a backward glance.

Steven stepped out into the bitterly cold wind, pulled his coat together and fastened the buttons, keeping his head bent to avoid his tears being seen. He felt his stomach begin to churn and just managed to get down a nearby side street before throwing up.

'Hey, you alright there, mate?'

He wiped his mouth with a tissue and smiled wanly at the bloke who'd called out.

'Yes, fine, thank you. Just had a bad pint...'

'Oh, that's rotten luck. Take care.'

'Thanks, you too.'

He leant against the wall as he took in some deep breaths. He'd known that seeing Mats again would be hard but he'd never expected it to be like this. He felt hollow and empty inside but with a dull, heavy ache in his chest. Some may have likened the pain to having their heart gouged out with a spoon but he couldn't say that for he knew exactly where his heart was – sitting on a pub table, in front of a woman with mesmerising purple eyes.

SIXTY-TWO

Thirteen Months Later

'All done!'

Mats looked in the mirror as the stylist patted the last flower into place. Once again, she'd had a make-over by an expert and she couldn't deny that they earned their money. Her eyes were purple-popping thanks to the colours of the shadow on them and were further enhanced by the purple and lilac flowers which had been woven like a crown through her hair.

She stood and walked over to take a look at the overall effect in the full-length mirror.

'Here, you need these to complete the effect.'

Penny handed her a posy of flowers which matched those in her hair.

Together they stood, side-by-side, gazing at their reflections – one a stunning bride and the other her beautiful maid-of-honour.

'You look amazing, Mats, you really do.'

'You're not looking too shonky yourself, Pen!'

They grinned at each other in the mirror.

A light tap on the door had them turning away and after calling out a 'Come in', Penny's assistant, Denise, stuck her head into the room.

'A couple of minutes, ladies, and then this show will be hitting the road.'

The door closed behind her and the women turned to face each other.

'How are you feeling? Any last minute nerves?'

Mats stepped back. She still couldn't get her head around the fact that Penny was about to marry her long-time, childhood crush but there it was! In approximately fifteen minutes, Penny would be standing beside Marky Sparks and saying, 'I do.'

'Not a single one! I can't wait to become Mrs Mark Sparks.'

'I remember the days when you used to scribble it all over your school books and now here you are, about to scribble it for real.'

'I'm so glad I never met him back then when I was all scrawny and riddled with pimples – can you imagine?'

'Well, you look absolutely stunning now. Sparks will know he's the lucky one when he sees you walking towards him.'

'Oh, honey, he already knows – I've made sure of that.'

Mats burst out laughing along with her friend. She picked up the flutes of Champagne sitting on the dressing table, handed one to Penny and chinked it with her own.

'Here's to your eternal happiness, each and every day.'

As they sipped, Penny looked at her with a calculating eye.

'What?'

'How are you? Are you going to be okay?'

'Of course, I am! You're only getting married, not emigrating to Mars!'

'You know what I mean, Mats…'

Mats did know what she meant – Steven was Sparks best man. She hadn't seen or spoken to him since the night he'd left her in the pub and her heart tumbled at the thought. She was actually dreading being in the same room as him but she wasn't telling Penny that. It was her special day and no way was Mats giving her anything to worry about.

'I'll be fine. We're both adults. I'm sure we're capable of being civil to one another.'

Just then, there was another tap on the door and Denise popped her head round again.'

'It's time, Penny. Your dad's here, ready to take you down. Mats, do you want to take up your position at the bottom of the stairs?'

'On my way.'

She turned and took one last, long look at her best friend. The rose-gold, bias-cut dress hung simply and elegantly on Penny's slender frame, the pearl-encrusted bodice giving way to the silken swish of the full-length skirt. Her hair was swept up in a loose chignon, held in place with rosebud hair pins. A simple gold and pearl tiara sat towards the back of her head, resting upon the updo. Even on her wedding day, she'd kept everything low-key – 'In my line of work, I've met more Bridezillas than you would care to count – I refuse to be one of them,' she'd made a point of telling anyone who would listen.

"Low-key" also meant a small, intimate ceremony of only fifty guests being held at a secluded stately home. Penny had organised a few receptions there in the past and it had been her first choice when Marky had popped the question. She'd had no problem booking the venue because there were fewer weddings in the weeks running up to

Christmas.

'See you down there, soldier.'

Penny's dad was standing by the door as she walked out.

'You look beautiful, Mats.'

'Thank you, Robert, but the real stunner is in there.'

Mats made her way to the top of the sweeping staircase and caught sight of her reflection in a decorative, full-length mirror. Her bridesmaid dress was a toned-down version of the brides with little cap sleeves and a small bolero jacket. The iridescent silver had hints of lilac through it which came and went as she walked. Her hair, which she'd continued to let grow, was now a decent enough length to have been pulled up into an artfully messy bun with loose tendrils around her face and as she carefully stepped down the stairs, Mats knew she'd be facing Steven looking her best.

When she reached her spot, at the side of the vast, curved, bottom step, the view straight down to the altar meant she could see Sparks sitting in place, waiting for his bride. She tried to see Steven but there were too many other heads in the way.

Suddenly the music changed and the guests rose to their feet, turning as one to try and get their first look of the bride.

Penny came down the stairs, her hand resting on her father's arm, and as she passed Mats, she gave her a small wink of encouragement. Mats smiled back, took a deep breath and stepped into place behind her.

'You've got this, Mats Davidson,' she whispered to herself. 'You've got this!'

'Phew! Thank goodness that's over. Now we can get on to

the fun bit – the party!'

'Sparks! I don't think you're supposed to say that about your own wedding ceremony!'

'Oh Mats, you know me, not big on the ceremonial stuff. I don't need all this palaver to let the world know how much I love my wife.'

'You wanna say that again?'

'My wife! My wife!'

They both grinned and Mats followed his gaze as it settled on Penny talking to some guests across the room.

'I'm really happy for you, Sparks. I'm glad you've found someone at last.'

'Ha! I bet if I'd said to you twenty-odd months ago that one day I'd be marrying your best friend, you would never have believed it.'

'Believed it? Sparks, I would have been going ballistic. You were a drunken, arrogant arse when our worlds came together – nothing would have been more abhorrent to me at that time.'

'And yet, here we are.'

'Indeed, we are—'

Mats stopped short and her breath caught in her throat when she saw Steven walking over to the bar with a stunning red-head by his side. She couldn't make out if they were together or if the woman was just a guest who'd quickly sussed out the most eligible bachelor in the room.

'Have you spoken with him yet?'

She forced herself to look at Sparks. Steven was looking far too good in his tailored, morning suit. The pale grey of the suit, along with the lilac and purple, double-breasted waistcoat, made her feel weak whenever she caught sight of him.

'Briefly, as you were signing the register and when we walked up the aisle behind you. It was nothing deep and meaningful.'

'You should talk to him. Properly. I think you both have a lot to say to each other.'

'Why? Has he said something?'

Before Sparks could answer, Penny came over and grabbed his arm, dragging him away for yet another photograph.

Mats stood quietly on her own for a few minutes thinking over what Sparks had said. She knew, however, there was nothing to be gained from getting into a conversation with Steven. When she'd said they'd spoken briefly earlier during the ceremony, she hadn't been exaggerating. A "You look well" and "Your dress is really nice" wasn't going to go down as the deepest and most meaningful conversation in the history of the planet.

A loud cackle of a laugh floated above the crowd towards her and Mats turned to see the red-head place a proprietary hand on Steven's arm as she leaned in to whisper something in his ear.

Well, she thought, that answers that question then. She swept her gaze around the room, looking for Denise so she could find out when they would be sitting down to eat. She needed to know how many more hours of this torture she had to endure.

SIXTY-THREE

Under the table, Steven discreetly wiped the palms of his hands along his thighs. He now knew why Dave had been more than happy for him to be Best Man – the sneaky git didn't have to do the darned speech which had given him several sleepless nights. How do you hit the right note of serious yet also funny? Even now, mere minutes before he was due to stand up, he still didn't know if it was going to work. His nerves weren't being helped by Mats' presence just along the table. He'd been dreading seeing her just as much as he'd dreaded making his speech. Her cool response to him earlier had been polite but detached. He really shouldn't have hoped for anything else – the way he'd behaved last year had been cowardly and unforgivable. He could only hope that the words he was about to speak would help her to see how sorry he was.

'Ladies and gentleman, it's time for the speeches, and to begin proceedings, I give you the Best Man.'

Steven felt the expectation of the room focus itself upon him following the DJ's introduction. With one last hand wipe, he pushed back his chair, took his notes from his pocket and stood. He cast a quick glance at Mats as he smiled at Penny and Marky but she was staring straight ahead. He cleared his throat and began.

'Ladies and Gentlemen, we're here today to celebrate the love of Penny and Mark. And it's love that I'd like to talk about first.

'Love is all things good and all things bad in equal measure. When we find ourselves in love, our hearts soar, our happiness knows no bounds and we believe we can do anything. We feel invincible. Being in love, and being loved back, gives us a high that cannot be matched by any drug. Love wraps itself around us and protects us. It makes everything brighter, shinier… better! It's the most amazing feeling we can experience.'

'Yet, being in love can also be the worst emotional place to be. It can twist our thinking and make us do irrational things – Penny accepting Marky's proposal being a prime example!'

The room let out a laugh and Steven used the moment to take a couple of deep breaths.

'When love doesn't quite work how we would like, it takes away our rational thought and skews our perception. It creates a pain inside that makes us want to curl up and hide from the world. When love is one-sided, it feels like being stabbed by a thousand knives on a daily basis. Life is no longer brighter, shinier or better – it is dark, dull and depressing. When love is painful, it forces us to make choices and decisions to protect ourselves – self-preservation is the order of the day – but sometimes those choices and decisions are the wrong ones which ultimately lead us onto greater pain and loss.

'You see, for love to be truly awesome, it needs two participants to work. A tango is the dance of love but it only works with two partners. So, when I look at Penny and Marky, it thrills me to see the two sides of their love, to see them as they dance along this new path in their lives together. I wish them a love that will continue to grow, to be bright, and to become even better.'

He lifted his glass. 'To Penny and Mark…'

'To Penny and Mark.' the guests responded back.

'Now, a Best Man's speech is nothing without a few embarrassing moments for the groom so let me tell you about the time Marky was touring the country on a summer roadshow…'

Steven sat down to a loud round of applause and took a large slug from his wine glass as relief flowed through him. The worst bit was over and he could finally begin to relax. He wondered if Mats had picked up on his veiled words and if she'd realised that he was trying to explain why he'd walked away. Each time he'd glanced in her direction, her position hadn't changed – she had maintained "eyes forward" for the whole of his speech.

He listened with half an ear to the rest of the speeches, relieved when Marky delicately swerved how his friendship with Mats had begun as he thanked her for putting him into Penny's life.

Soon, all the talking was over and the catering staff began to clear the guest tables from the floor to allow the dancing to commence. Steven chose to stay seated at the top table while everyone milled around – he'd been collared by some red-head earlier while the photographs were being taken and she hadn't been backward in coming forward when it came to letting him know she was interested. Unfortunately, it was not reciprocated. He'd found her braying voice grating and her heavy perfume cloying. She'd spent most of the time talking about herself and his impression was that she'd be hard work in a relationship. Not that he was interested in a relationship with anyone right now. He still wasn't over Mats and if he was being honest, he didn't know if he ever would be.

'You alright, mate?'

'Hey, Marky, yes. I'm good. How about you? Is married life doing it for you?'

Marky laughed. 'Well, the first two hours haven't been too bad so I think I'll stick it out for a while yet!'

'I'm sure you guys are going to do just fine. You're perfect together.'

'Have you spoken to Mats?'

'Nope! Nothing further since my earlier progress report.'

'Perhaps dancing together will break the ice.'

'Hah! That's not going to happen.'

'Erm, I'm afraid it will. When Penny and I have our first dance, it's traditional for the Best Man and the Maid of Honour to join us after a few minutes.'

Steven looked at Marky in horror.

'You are kidding, right?'

'No, my friend. It's the real deal.'

'Does Mats know this?'

Marky looked to where Penny and Mats were standing.

'I think she's just finding out herself…'

Steven followed Marky's gaze and saw Mats staring at him with the same horrified expression on her face.

'Right, we're up! Good luck!'

Marky walked over to his bride, took her hand and led her to the dance floor. When Take That's "Patience" began to play, Steven actually felt himself groan. Why couldn't they have chosen something a bit livelier – didn't they know that was more popular these days?

He looked at Mats, gave a small nod which she returned and then stepped onto the dance floor. She walked towards him from the opposite side and they met in the middle. He gently took her in his arms and they began to move to the music. She held herself away from him, her back stiff and maintaining the maximum distance possible.

'How are you?' he asked quietly.

'Fine, thanks. You?'

'I've been better, truth be told.'

'Hmmm.'

'How's work?'

'Going well, thanks. You?'

'Very good. The powers that be have finally realised they made a good choice and are leaving me alone to get on with it now.'

'Glad to hear it. And it's nice to hear you say something positive about yourself.'

Her voice had lost some of its brittleness and Steven took this as a sign of encouragement. The music ended and they stepped apart to applaud the happy couple. As the intro of the next song began, Mats went to walk away but he quickly grabbed her arm.

'Mats, can we talk? Please?'

While he waited for her reply, he saw the red-head bearing down on them with a determined look on her face.

'Aw shit!'

'What's up?'

He gave her a pleading look.

'Mats, help me. Please rescue me from this woman…'

Mats looked over her shoulder, quickly assessed the situation and let out a sigh before slipping her arm through his and walking them both off the dance floor.

'Seriously, Steven? Am I going to spend my life rescuing you from awkward situations?'

'Well, that depends…'

'I'm sorry?'

'Look… come with me.'

He led her out of the room and onto the terrace

outside. The frosty, December air cut through them straight away and Steven quickly took off his jacket and dropped it onto her shoulders.

'Now you're going to freeze.'

'I'll be fine.'

He led her over to the carved, ornate balustrade and leant against it, looking down into the shadowy landscaped gardens below. Behind them, chairs had been set out for the guests to sit during the firework display.

Steven took a deep breath, turned to look into Mats eyes and said, 'I'm an idiot! I'm a fool and an idiot!'

He gently clasped her hands and gathered them up to his chest. She didn't pull away and this gave him the courage he needed to carry on.

'That day in the pub, I did the classic "cutting off my nose to spite my face" thing. I was so hurt by your silent treatment that all I could think of was to get away from you.'

'It wasn't silent treatment, it was—'

'Shhh, I know it wasn't *actual* silent treatment, I understand, I really do. I did then but my head was all screwed up and I couldn't think straight. Something inside just kept telling me that the only way to cope was to put distance between us. I was hurting so much because I loved you so much. My head kept saying you didn't feel the same otherwise you would have come to me when you were in trouble instead of pushing me away. I was selfish and could only think of what I was feeling. I gave lip-service to understanding how it must have been for you but I realise I still kept seeing everything from my perspective. Every question I was asking had "me" at the centre of it. I was all "how could she ignore *me* like this?" Or "why won't Mats answer *my* texts" or "why doesn't she care about *my* feelings?" – you'd just been told your mother had been murdered and I was unable to comprehend what that must have been like for you or even how you begin to try and deal with a blow like that.'

He looked at Mats, hoping to see a sign that there was some hope for him but while the shadows of the night made her eyes unreadable, there was no mistaking the set of her chin, the bland, impassive expression on her face and the hands which had become rigid within his.

Steven knew now that his apology was too little, too late and, while his heart shattered for a second time, he decided it was time to let her go.

'I'm so sorry. I realise it's too late for us now and it's all my fault but I wanted you to know that I was wrong, that I still love you and I will always love you, no matter what.'

He leant forward, placed a soft kiss on her forehead, and released his hold on her hands.

'Goodbye, Mats. Please be happy.'

He lifted his hand and gently stroked her cheek before turning and walking away.

SIXTY-FOUR

Mats had felt the annoyance begin to bubble up inside when Steven had shushed her as she tried to speak but now it was overflowing like molten lava. How dare he! How dare he make his speech and walk off without giving her a chance to have her say.

'How dare you! How-BLOODY-dare you! Who the *hell* do you think you are?'

Steven turned around and looked at her, surprise all over his face.

'I'm… I'm sorry… What?'

'You bring me out here into the freezing cold to talk *at* me for five minutes and then just walk off? Not so much as a by your leave or allowing me to contribute to the conversation!'

'I didn't think… I didn't…,' he let out a sigh. 'I didn't want to hear you say you no longer love me. I know you don't – I've worked that out from your demeanour today – but to actually hear you say it… that would be a step too far for me.'

'Well, you got one thing right – you are a fool!'

'Pardon?'

'You're a fool! You heard me the first time. You're a fool because you have assumed how I feel. I still love you, Steven, nothing has changed for me since I last saw you. My "demeanour" has been me trying to keep it together, trying not to throw myself into your arms and beg for us to try again. Plus, there was the small matter of a glamorous red-head hanging off your arm…'

'Look, she just latched on to me today. I've never seen her before, honest!'

'I know that now. The look of fear on your face when you begged me to rescue you told me that.'

Steven came to stand beside her again.

'Do you really still love me? Even though I walked out on what we had?'

She looked up into his eyes.

'We both did things that, with hindsight, I'm sure we'd now do differently if we could. You said it yourself in your speech, "When love is painful, it forces us to make choices and decisions to protect ourselves…" We were so busy protecting ourselves, we didn't protect each other.'

'If you give me the chance, Mats, I will protect you for the rest of my life.'

'Only if you allow me to protect you.'

'How about we agreed to protect "us"?'

The gap between them had closed until they were mere millimetres apart. Mats could feel his warm breath on her face.

'Is there an "us"?' she whispered.

'There is if you want there to be.'

'I want there to be…'

'Then there's an "us".'

Mats lifted her chin, raised herself up on her toes, and placed her lips on his. Steven let out a small moan, wrapped his arms around her and pulled her tightly to him.

The feel of his lips on hers made Mats shudder with delight. She had missed his touch and kisses so much – she was never going to let him go ever again. She splayed her hands across his chest before gripping the front of his waistcoat tightly and holding him close.

Just then, the doors across the terrace burst open and Penny and Marky came flying through with their guests hot on their heels.

'There you both are, we've been looking for you.'

'What's up, Pen?' Mats released her hold on Steven and slipped her hand down into his.

'The fireworks are about to start.'

'Are you sure they haven't already, my love?' Marky drawled as he looked at them both.

Penny glanced down and took in their entwined hands.

'Are you two… you know?'

Mats turned to look into Steven's eyes. There was no mistaking the love shining from them. She looked back at her friend.

'I think you can say we are!'

'Hah! Yes! Gotcha, Mark Sparks! That's fifty quid you owe me!'

'Excuse me? What was that?'

Penny laughed as she explained. 'We had a bet as to whether you'd sort yourselves out at the wedding. I said you would, Mark said you wouldn't. I just won!'

'But… you said you never talked about us…'

Penny grinned. 'I lied! We often discussed how we were going to make you both see sense but we also didn't want to interfere. The wedding was the best chance in my opinion.'

'It was a bit drastic, Pen, getting married just to bring us back together.' Mats laughed as she spoke.

'Sweetie, trust me, you and Steven are merely the

icing on the cake of my day. Now, grab a blanket and let's enjoy the show.'

Mats gave Steven back his jacket and took one of the warm throws being handed out by the staff. Steven slipped it over her shoulders before taking one for himself. He stepped up behind her and enveloped her inside his jacket, his arms tight across her front. The warmth from his body flowed through her and she felt the tight coil of sadness which had sat in her stomach for over a year, begin to finally unwind. Everything was going to be okay.

The first of the fireworks went up in the air and the gathered crowd exclaimed in delight. She felt Steven's breath on her ear as he whispered something to her. Unable to hear over the noise, she turned within his arms and looked up at him.

'What did you say? I couldn't hear you.'

'I said, "How do you fancy a fast sprint through a registry office?"'

Mats looked at him and tears began to swim in her eyes.

'Are you serious?'

'As I will ever be.'

Mats glanced over her shoulder towards her best friend before bringing her eyes back to rest on Steven.

'I'm sure Penny, with all her skills, will be able to find me a wedding outfit that'll match my running shoes…'

'Is that a yes?'

She grinned at him. 'It's a yes!'

Steven bent his head and as his lips came down on hers again, Mats felt her heart explode like the fireworks in the sky above. Her head swam with joy when it finally dawned on her – she may have first gone out to rescue Steven but, in the end, he had rescued her too.

ABOUT THE AUTHOR

Kiltie Jackson spent her childhood years growing up in Scotland. Most of these early years were spent in and around Glasgow although for a short period of time, she wreaked havoc at a boarding school in the Highlands.

By the age of seventeen, she had her own flat which she shared with a couple of cats for a few years while working as a waitress in a cocktail bar (she's sure there's a song in there somewhere!) and serving customers in a fashionable clothing outlet before moving down to London to chalk up a plethora of experience which is now finding its way into her writing.

Once she'd wrung the last bit of fun out of the smoky capital, she moved up to the Midlands and now lives in Staffordshire with one grumpy husband and another six feisty felines.

Her little home is known as Moggy Towers even though, despite having plenty of moggies, there are no towers! The cats kindly allow her and Mr Mogs to share their home as long as the mortgage continues to be paid.

Since the age of three, Kiltie has been an avid reader although it was many years later before she decided to put pen to paper – or fingers to keyboard – to begin giving life to the stories in her head. Her debut novel was released in September 2017 and her fourth book was a US Amazon bestseller in Time Travel Romance.

Kiltie loves to write fiery and feisty female characters and puts the blame for this firmly on the doorsteps of

Anne Shirley from Anne of Green Gables and George Kirrin from The Famous Five.

When asked what her best memories are, Kiltie will tell you:

1. Queuing up overnight outside the Glasgow Apollo to buy her Live-Aid ticket.
2. Being at Live-Aid.
3. Winning an MTV competition to meet Bon Jovi in Sweden.

(Although, if Mr Mogs is in earshot, the latter is changed to her wedding day.)

Her main motto in life used to be "Old enough to know better, young enough not to care!" but that has since been replaced with "Too many stories, not a fast enough typist!"

You can follow Kiltie on the following platforms:

www.kiltiejackson.com

www.facebook.com/kiltiejackson

www.instagram.com/kiltiejackson